Praise for th

ROMAN CRAZY

"There are books that make you laugh out loud, make you teary, make you hot and bothered, make you smile. And then there are books that make you want to crawl inside them and live within their pages. That's what *Roman Crazy* is."
—*New York Times* bestselling author of the Tangled series, Emma Chase

"I went CRAZY over *Roman Crazy*—this is simply a perfect romance!"
—*New York Times* bestselling author Jennifer Probst

"*Roman Crazy* is a laugh out loud romantic comedy about second chances, friendship, and the beauty of Rome. You won't simply read this novel, you'll devour it as Alice Clayton and Nina Bocci transport you to Italy and guide you on an unforgettable adventure."
—Sylvain Reynard, *New York Times, USA Today,* and #1 international bestselling author of *Gabriel's Inferno* and the Florentine series

"Nina Bocci and Alice Clayton wrote a grown-up romance that is heartfelt, sexy, and transportive. As a bonus, the city of Rome is as much of a character as the swoony Marcello and the relatable Avery."
—Jen Frederick, *USA Today* bestselling author

"*Roman Crazy* is a sexy, steamy slow burn. Pack your suitcase and get ready for a wild ride through the streets of Rome with a hot-as-sin leading man. I want to clone Marcello and keep him forever. A visceral reading experience that takes you from the cobbled streets of Rome to the bedroom and everywhere in between. Get your fans out! Five stars of smolder."

—Helena Hunting, *New York Times* bestselling author

"Bocci and Clayton know how to craft an amazing romance! The beautiful descriptions of Rome will make you feel like you are on vacation. This book it a spa visit and a best friend all wrapped up into a funny, sexy, life-affirming bundle. 1-Click the heck out of *Roman Crazy*."

—Debra Anastasia, author of the Poughkeepsie series

"*Roman Crazy* is a sexy, delicious tour through Italy as well as the human heart. Marcello and Avery are as impossible to resist as a double scoop of gelato. Like fine Italian food, *Roman Crazy* should be gobbled up as quickly as possible."

—Sarina Bowen, *USA Today* bestselling author of *Rookie Move*

"Nina Bocci and Alice Clayton bring Italy to life with this hilarious, sexy, and emotional book full of yummy food and even yummier men. Get ready to laugh, cry and swoon!"

—Elle Kennedy, *New York Times* bestselling author

ROMAN CRAZY

A Novel

ALICE CLAYTON *and* NINA BOCCI

G

GALLERY BOOKS

New York   London   Toronto   Sydney   New Delhi

G

Gallery Books

An Imprint of Simon & Schuster, Inc.

1230 Avenue of the Americas

New York, NY 10020

First Gallery Books trade paperback edition September 2016

GALLERY BOOKS and colophon are registered trademarks of Simon & Schuster, Inc.

For information about special discounts for bulk purchases, please contact Simon & Schuster Special Sales at 1-866-506-1949 or business@simonandschuster.com.

The Simon & Schuster Speakers Bureau can bring authors to your live event. For more information or to book an event, contact the Simon & Schuster Speakers Bureau at 1-866-248-3049 or visit our website at www.simonspeakers.com.

Interior design by Davina Mock-Maniscalco

Manufactured in the United States of America

10   9   8   7   6   5   4   3   2   1

Library of Congress Cataloging-in-Publication Data

Names: Clayton, Alice, author. | Bocci, Nina, author.
Title: Roman crazy / Alice Clayton and Nina Bocci.
Description: First Gallery Books trade paperback edition. | New York : Gallery Books, 2016.
Identifiers: LCCN 2016027563 (print) | LCCN 2016029875 (ebook) | ISBN 9781501117633 (paperback) | ISBN 9781501117640 (eBook)
Subjects: LCSH: Man-woman relationships—Fiction. | BISAC: FICTION / Romance / Contemporary. | FICTION / Contemporary Women. | GSAFD: Love stories.
Classification: LCC PS3603.L3968 R66 2016 (print) | LCC PS3603.L3968 (ebook) | DDC 813/.6—dc23
LC record available at https://lccn.loc.gov/2016027563

ISBN 978-1-5011-1763-3
ISBN 978-1-5011-1764-0 (ebook)

To everyone who reads romance. Spread the love. The world needs it.

ACKNOWLEDGMENTS

WE WOULD LIKE TO THANK the incomparable Micki Nuding for helping us on the first leg of the *Roman Crazy* journey. You saw what Marcello and Avery could be and sent us on the path to get there. Seriously Micki, we hope you're loving retirement because we miss the hell out of you. P.S. that's us knocking on the front door, we brought wine!

To the super-sassy, hilarious, and straightforward Lauren McKenna, who doesn't pull any punches. We wouldn't be here without you and we adore the hell out of you; thank you for taking us on. To the remarkably patient and fabulous Marla Daniels for not laughing at some of the emails that we've sent. These two women deserve medals and enough wine to fill a river. Thank you both for kicking our asses into making this book what it is today. Seriously, we're sending wine and cookies. That's us down at the security check-in. They won't let us in. Help.

To the incredible team at Gallery Books, good Lord you have made this a fun experience. Louise Burke, Jen Bergstrom, Theresa Dooley, Liz Psaltis, Diana Velasquez, the XOXO After Dark ladies, Abby Zidle and Kate Dresser, the audio crew,

Sarah Leiberman and Louisa Solomon for giving Avery a real voice that shines. To the production staff: John Paul Jones (best name ever), Faren Bachelis (we're so sorry about all the dangling participles), Alicia Brancato, Davina Mock-Maniscalco (those chapter ornaments are to die for)—you deserve all the cookies. All of them. And the wine. Can we send wine?

To Kristin Dwyer, the most kick-ass and most extraordinary publicist, as well as the most tolerant human being ever, for putting up with all of the batshit emails and never telling us to calm our shit. We love you more than the banana cake from Magnolia. Which is a lot.

To our Captain Hookers, Lolo and PQ. Thank you for your friendship. For the laughs and the cries and the hysterical bouts of laughter on the rides at WDW and DL. Thank you for reading and loving this. Here's to a Captain Hooker trip to Italia. We thank Stephenie every day for bringing all of us together and we couldn't love you two more. We'll meet you with some wine and cranberry juice at the Tower of Terror. We need to beat the 9-ride record.

Christina Hogrebe, our agent and Sweet Valley High soul sister. Thank you so much for everything you did for this book. You loved Marcello first! And to the team at the Jane Rotrosen Agency, cheers to you all for keeping us sane through this whole process. You guessed it, we're bringing the wine.

To the lovely and fabulous people whom we are humbled to call our friends: Sylvain Reynard, Emma Chase, Jennifer Probst, Elle Kennedy, Jen Frederick, Debra Anastasia, Helena Hunting, and Leisa Rayven. They pre-read this book in every form imaginable and some of it was scary. Missing scenes, crazy half-assed sentences, and the backward chapter we managed to send.

Plus, our dear Italian friend Marinella, for everything she did to make it accurate.

To Heather Carrier from HEA Designs, Simone Renou from In My Dreams Designs, and Gel from Tempting Illustrations for the kick-ass graphics work. Sim and Gel, we can't send wine to your countries but you better be certain that we're drinking it with Heather in honor of you ladies. RT next year, we're all getting pickled. A sweet and adorable thank-you to Stephanie from Sweets by Steph for the beautifully perfect *Roman Crazy* cookies.

The fandom from which we met will forever be a span of time that we're both eternally grateful for. Without it, we wouldn't have met each other and become the bestest of best friends or met all of you, whom we adore. Thank you, friends and readers, for following the two of us on this fun journey.

A special note from Nina: For all of my friends who tirelessly blog and review the world of romance. You have all worked with me from the beginning, and I for one can never thank you enough for everything that you do. You guys were so excited when I announced that we were writing this book together and it was the best feeling in the world to have you want to read something from *me* that wasn't a flaily email about how much I loved a book. From the worldwide messages of congrats, to the emails asking "what can I do for you?", I will forever be grateful for everything you guys do to bring the love of romance to as many readers as possible.

Keep on spreading the love. The world really needs it.

See you next time.

xoxo

Nina & Alice

CHAPTER 1

I WAS STARING AT A PENIS.

I was staring at a penis, and yet I couldn't actually comprehend what I was seeing. Which was weird, because technically that penis in question belonged to me. Not in the anatomical sense, but in the marital sense. As in, I'm familiar with that penis, I know that penis, I'm married to that penis, except . . . this penis is, in fact, doing something it really shouldn't be doing.

Which was my husband's secretary. Correction: administrative assistant. I was reminded of this fact last Christmas when I inadvertently introduced her to my mother-in-law as, "*This is Daniel's secretary.*" She took the time to tell me her preferred title, which I appreciated, since I was ever so thoughtful when I came to visit my husband in his place of business.

His place of business where he was currently putting his penis into his administrative assistant.

It's amazing how the human brain can compartmentalize when in shock. And speaking of being in shock, what they were doing couldn't be good for that Chippendale antique desk I'd spent weeks scouring the finest stores and auction houses all over the greater Boston area to acquire so that my attorney husband would be able to host potential clients in a well-appointed office. An office that conveyed just the right amount of trustworthiness, attention to detail, and values above all, with just a touch of contemporary expertise.

And while I was compartmentalizing on the Aubusson rug, my husband of eight years was fucking his administrative assistant on that very desk. With a penis that belonged to me.

And not just fucking, *creatively fucking.* As in, bent over that desk. As in, pulling her hair. As in, riding her hard. As in, finding the little man in the canoe and making sure he came. I couldn't remember the last time I'd been creatively fucked by Daniel.

A Sunday afternoon after golf *maybe* once a month was what I got. *Nothing* creative. Now I see why.

I quietly shut the door, walked across the room with as much grace as I could muster, picked up the 2013 Red Sox World Series commemorative marble-tipped bat, and . . .

"Yeeeeooowwwwww!"

CHAPTER 2

WHERE HAVE YOU BEEN?"

"Well hello to you, too. I guess you're not dead. Jesus Christ, with the nine calls, four emails, and more ASAP texts than I can count, I wasn't quite sure what to expect," my best friend huffed good-naturedly. "Nice to know you're still breathing."

"I wouldn't have called, emailed, and texted if I weren't still breathing, Daisy."

"Don't you Daisy me in that tone. Did you forget I was in Patagonia?"

"As in the clothing company?"

"As in Argentina; remember, I told you I was going for work, and then you sang songs from *Evita* for several minutes? Also, don't sing anything from *Evita*. For any amount of minutes. Anyway, Patagonia. Do you know how far away from literally everything that is? Look at the tip of the earth and move a smidge to the left. There's barely electricity there, let alone a quality cell signal." I had to hold the phone away from my ear slightly, as she was really getting worked up. "I was on a flight

back that took a thousand years, got home, fell into bed, and
am just now surfacing. I barely know what time zone I'm in."

Argentina. *Evita.* I did remember that. *Now.* I've been so
wrapped up in hastily scheduled appointments with a divorce attorney I spaced out on it.

Wow. Divorce attorney. Never thought I'd be here.

Really? You never thought it?

Thank goodness I didn't have to answer that question right
now. Daisy was still chattering in my ear about time zones and
kids not being allowed in first class on transatlantic flights. Top-
ics she was uniquely qualified to discuss.

My best friend, Daisy, was an architect, and currently living
in Rome. She specialized in the environmental side, retrofitting,
green technology, *making old buildings work in the modern world
without sacrificing the integrity of the original shell.* I spied that last
part on her business card on one of her few trips stateside. She
traveled the world, met exciting people, was fiercely loyal to her
friends, and one of my favorite people ever.

"I'm trying to kick the last of the jet lag out of my system
with a jog, so I'm finishing up a run through the Borghese gardens. It's blissfully empty of tourists at this time of day so I figured I'd call now. So, what's with blowing up my phone?"

"I'm leaving Daniel," I stated simply, dropping the bomb as I
handed off the keys to the valet and headed into the country
club to meet my mother-in-law. She had her housekeeper call
me to request a meeting. On her turf. She didn't actually say that,
but it was certainly implied.

"Wait, what? You couldn't have said what I think you said."

"You heard me. I'm leaving Daniel. Or, I should say, technically, *left.*"

Grinning wide, I passed the greeter who held the door

open. The answering smile I got back was thin at best. No doubt I was on some sort of blacklist, considering the word must already be out about the marital difficulties of one of their most prestigious members. Daniel's family had belonged to this club since its inception. Naturally, the tribe was rallying around one of their own.

The two college kids at the coat check seemed to want to come out from behind the counter. To stop me perhaps? But their manners kicked in, and I strode with purpose past them. The greeter in the pro shop, however, scurried behind the desk and got out of sight.

Chickenshits.

"Hold on, just hold on a minute," Daisy asked, sounding out of breath. "Lemme stop." I pictured her then, jogging along the cobblestoned streets with her skintight yoga pants, turning handsome Italian heads with every stride. "Oh, Avery," she sighed. She was never a big fan of Daniel, not even when we started dating back in college, but she never would wish *this* upon me.

"Yep." Glancing around the Sunset Lounge for my guest, I explained. "Well, more accurately, I tossed all of his shit into the pool."

A woman admonished me with a Waspy how-dare-you look, while her husband turned *up* his hearing aid. I took a seat at the bar in the lounge and waited.

"You didn't!" Daisy cried, still breathing hard but with a definite tone of excitement in her voice. "In the pool?"

"Oh, I did, and it was glorious."

"Okay, but what the hell happened that made you leave him?" She paused a moment. "Wow, that's weird to say."

"What, that I left Daniel?" I found that once I said it, I

wanted to repeat it. And often. I left Daniel. Good god damn, it had a nice ring to it. I sang it like Ethel Merman in my head. I rapped it like Eminem.

I knew eventually the rage would segue into sadness, but for right now, I was cruising on sheer anger. I wondered idly if others could get a contact high . . .

Speaking of high, my usual Bloody Mary appeared in a tall glass. And on the side, along with my celery, came an encouraging smile from the female bartender on the other side of a mile of polished mahogany. The first sign I'd seen since arriving at the club that someone, anyone, might be on my side in all this.

"Don't back down," she whispered, and lifted her chin toward the door.

Looking as though she had just stepped out of Fashion Week, there stood my soon-to-be ex-mother-in-law. Her chignon was low, her tits were high, and her smile was lethal. Oh, and she sparkled. Not from being a wonderful person who emitted positive energy, but because she was iced in so much jewelry. In fact, it looked like she was wearing *all* of her jewelry. At once.

Somewhere in the world, Mr. T sighed in envy.

"Bitsy is here. I'll call you back," I whispered.

"No, no! Don't you dare! I've got to hear this! Put me on mute! I'll listen in, very secret agent. Or teenagers. Or teenage secret agents! We could be—"

"Oh, would you hush," I said, rolling my eyes but muting it nonetheless. Setting the phone on the bar, I turned to meet the firing squad.

"Avery," she said, her sharp blue eyes narrowed at the bartender.

Sitting up straighter on the stool, I sipped my drink. "Can I get you something?"

She sniffed a bit, looking down her long patrician nose at the stool, but in the end decided to actually take a seat. Settling onto it with a graceful air, she turned to me and Botox grinned. She must have just had an appointment. Everything south of her hairline was stiff, smooth, and unmoving. The sun streamed in from behind me, lighting up her neck, ears, and fingers.

"Heading to the pawn shop?" I quipped, taking another sip. The bartender snorted loudly from her perch sliding wineglasses into the rack.

Another crippling "grin." "You know, I never much cared for your equivoque."

This. This right here. Equivoque. Who the hell used words like that? With that opening volley, however, I could tell it was one of *those* conversations. It reminded me of when we first met at Thanksgiving dinner my sophomore year at BU. I was so nervous. Crippled by anxiety because they were *the* Boston Remingtons and I was dating, and doing some decidedly dirty things with, their precious son. My family's no slouch, don't get me wrong, but it's like comparing Mark Cuban with Bill Gates. There's money and then there's *money*.

"Yes, I'm sure Daniel was thinking of my *equivoque* as he was giving it to his secretary," I answered back, just as haughtily.

"I always forget how funny you think you are, Avery. Daniel always was fond of your sense of humor," she said, wrapping her jewel-encrusted hand around the glass of chardonnay that appeared. Her expression told me she was singularly *un*amused by my quick wit.

With a flick of the wrist, she dismissed the bartender, getting down to business.

Displeasure tried—to no avail of course—to furrow her brow. Her brow may never move again. But it was clear she was ready to say what she came here to say. "Things happen in a marriage. In all marriages. It surprises me that you would take this to heart. To throw in the towel so quickly over something like this."

"Something like this? You mean catching him with the secretary isn't towel worthy in your world?" I asked incredulously.

She took a sip of her chardonnay, looking around the room unconcernedly. We could have been discussing soufflé recipes for all the emotion she was showing. "It's your world, too. Don't forget that Remingtons don't get divorced."

"Bitsy, I'm not sure why you've come today, but I can assure you, if it has anything to do with taking Daniel back, I'm uninterested."

"I've come to *explain* a few things." She shifted in her seat, tilting her body away from the prying eyes that were gathering.

"Do you see this?" She pointed to her replica of the Heart of the Ocean around her neck. A ten-carat or more platinum, diamond, and Burmese sapphire necklace. "I received this from Daniel's father."

"Okay?"

"You see, I received it *after* I found out that my husband's tennis instructor was working on more than his serve."

Oh.

Tucking her blond hair behind her ear, she revealed at least a three-carat diamond earring. "These were after the au pair was released from duty. Incidentally, she was sent back to London, where these were purchased." She tittered, pleased with herself.

Ticking off one ring at a time, she explained in her own way.

Every bauble was an affair. Every gemstone the equivalent of hush money.

A giant art deco Colombian emerald was thanks to an indiscretion in Las Vegas. A pavé diamond and white-gold swirl from a gaffe in Chicago. An impropriety in Paris resulted in a cushion-cut canary diamond.

"Powerful men like Daniel and his father have *needs*, Avery."

I always hated the way she said my name. Hearing it sneered while discussing her husband's womanizing was even worse.

"There are all kinds of women, Avery, all kinds. And some are more . . . *suited* . . . for these needs."

"What exactly are you saying?"

Cracking the tiniest of smiles, she drove her point home. "He's already purchased your gift. He'll be bringing it shortly. You'll learn to live with it. You're certainly not the first wife to turn a blind eye to her husband's extracurricular activities."

I had nothing to say. I did, however, drink half of my Bloody Mary in one enormous gulp. She went on. "Jewelry is always first. Then a new car. Apartments and vacation homes in faraway places are after that, perhaps Provence or Saint Moritz," she explained with a hint of excitement.

I immediately remembered her house in the south of France. Oh my goodness.

Penis gifts. They were penis gifts.

You know how there is that Hallmark list of suggested gifts for what to buy for anniversaries? I wondered if there was a ranking system for philandering.

Standing, she patted my hand with her forty pounds of priceless gems. I sincerely hoped she had a bodyguard waiting in the wings to escort her home.

"I'll see you Sunday."

She actually thought I'd attend brunch! She felt quite sure she could swoop in, explain these new rules for a happy home, and sparkle right out of here, secure in the knowledge that I'd follow suit.

In walked Daniel, wearing a freshly tailored suit in my once-favorite shade of blue. He air-kissed his mother on her cheeks and smiled. All veneers and confidence. She'd teed me up, and he now was here for the hole in one.

Scooping up the phone from the bar, I told Daisy, "Round two."

I dropped it into my lap, facedown.

"Baby," he said softly, looking both handsome and pathetic at the same time. "We need to talk this out." He sat down next to me, his hand reaching out to touch my bare arm. The second his skin touched mine, a familiar feeling spread through me.

Maybe it was comfort from being with him for so long. Spending so many years with someone, you adopted a certain sense of contentment. Looking at him, he was so handsome, so put together and the safe choice. Perfect for this life, but . . .

Where was that guy I'd loved? The one who took me for Indian food on our first date even though he was allergic to it? The one who brought me pudding when I had my wisdom teeth out sophomore year or the guy who screamed "*That's my girl!*" when I crossed the stage at graduation? Was he ever that guy? I hated that everything I thought I knew about him and our life was now in question. Untrusted and tainted.

A very small part of me considered taking him back in that instant. How easy it would be, to forgive and forget it all. To learn to live with the pattern of guilt and then a gift. Realizing in twenty-five years that I'd become Bitsy, a shell of what I was and being content with living with the knowledge that I'd never been enough. The echo of her explanation reared its bedazzled head. What had felt like comfort for years now felt like an uncomfortable sweater: itchy and tight and smothering. A knowledge that my skin was even aware of, that I didn't have a clue who my husband really was.

I remembered the secretary. The hair pulling, the sweaty, rough-and-tumble sex that he was having.

Ignoring him, I picked up the phone and pretended like he wasn't even there.

"Daisy, you still there?"

"Jesus Christ, yes I'm still here, what happened?"

"What happened?" I laughed darkly. "Hilary happened."

"Clinton?" she asked incredulously. In spite of the chaos about to rain down on my personal life, I couldn't help but laugh a little.

"Hilary, his secretary. She prefers administrative assistant, but I think once I found her and Daniel having the down-and-dirty sex, she pretty much gave up the right to a preferred name. Although I have a few preferred names running through my head right now."

Daniel's deep intake of breath put a twisted smile on my face.

"Baby, don't do this," he begged, turning the barstool so that I faced him. Baby. I'll baby him. Did he call her Baby, too? Who else was there? Or *is* there? Had I really been oblivious to it for all these years? What gift on the twisted ladder was I on? I thought back to the diamond studs he gave me on a random Tuesday a few years ago. Then the Louboutins that I came home to after a Junior League meeting.

Most recently, the Mercedes sedan that I woke up to in the driveway after his trip to Tahoe.

"Oh you slick son of a bitch," I sneered, the phone still at my ear. Daisy was across the ocean, on pins and needles, so instead of ending the conversation with *her,* I kept going, plucking the celery from my Bloody Mary and taking a big, loud bite off the end. "The secretary. Ha! Can you believe it? Cliché." Looking him dead in the eye, I took another huge bite, this time showing my teeth.

"Are you fucking kidding me? Who would cheat on you? You're the wife that men want to nail on the side!" Daisy exclaimed, loud enough that Daniel heard.

"She doesn't mean anything, Avie," he whispered. He focused on the shiny bar top, his finger absently swirling along the grain.

"Don't you dare call me that, Daniel," I snapped, stabbing him with my celery, flicks of tomato juice spotting his pristine Bespoke shirt. "You lost the right to cute nicknames when you decided to stick your dick in your secretary."

"Avery, watch your mouth," he began, but the bartender—who'd been buffing the same glass for twenty minutes—slammed it down onto the bar, startling us both. She smiled at me, motioning me to continue. Daniel seemed surprised that anyone on the other side of the bar would have an opinion. I doubted she'd work here long after this.

"Whatever it was or is with her, I know that nothing he says will make me stay," I said to Daisy, and ended the call with the promise to call her back after this dog-and-pony show to fill her in.

"You don't mean that," he said, smiling. Taking my hand, he traced my palm seductively. Or what I imagine would have been seductively, in a different time, in a different place. "This is us. We're a team, remember?"

How could I forget? Choices were made, decisions were cemented, and paths were chosen. But no one said I had to stay running on that particular hamster wheel.

"We've been through the ringer, you and I. This was just a stumbling block."

"How many?"

"Avery, don't do this. It doesn't matter."

I waited. Waited for something in my belly to flare up. To make me truly consider continuing to live this life. Bitsy's jeweled, Lexused, Provenced life. It never came.

Scooting back the stool, I stood, rolled my shoulders, and simply stated, "You'll be hearing from my lawyer."

But there wasn't anything simple about it. In those six words, I welcomed back a piece of *Old Avery*.

I was never big on marching. I gracefully glided most days. Today was not that day.

With every ounce of confidence I could muster, I strutted my high, tight, Burberry-wrapped ass right past the dinner crowd of couples that likely heard the whole argument. I was sure my next Junior League meeting would be full of whispers and side eyes.

I was out the front door and into the sunshine without a glance backward. As I slid into my penis-gifted Mercedes, however, I realized that without the strut, I didn't feel confident at all. The strut was for Bitsy, Daniel, and the rest of the country club set, and frankly, to get me out the door without making a fool of myself. But now, alone, wrapped in tan leather and walnut paneling . . .

I didn't have a clue what to do. My life was my marriage and everything that came with it. Take that away and what was left? I'd given up so much when I married Daniel Remington. If I wasn't Avery Remington, who the hell was I?

So I called Daisy back and asked her that very question.

"What am I going to do?" I asked. "Is hiring a hit man off the table?"

She sighed. "Bless your heart, but yes, it's way off the table. As much as I want to inflict pain upon Daniel, I don't know that it's the wisest move right now."

"Then I repeat. What am I going to do?" I whispered, blotting my eye with a tissue from my purse. "I met with a divorce lawyer, Daisy, a fucking divorce lawyer! What is happening?"

"Do you want to divorce him?"

"What?"

"Do you want to divorce him?"

I sat there in my car, unable to answer the question. "I mean, I kind of have to, right?" I asked.

"You don't have to do anything, Avery. I'm certainly not going to tell you whether you *have to do* anything you don't really want to do."

Even though she couldn't see me, I nodded.

"So I'll ask you again, kiddo, do you want to divorce him?" she asked quietly.

She couldn't see me, but I was still nodding. And then in the tiniest of whispers, I answered . . . "Yes." I took a breath, then said it again, stronger this time. "Yes."

"Okay then," she answered.

I saw Bitsy leaving the front door, and I scrunched down so she couldn't see me. "But I can't be here knowing that everyone's talking. I don't want the sad looks or the *poor Avery* that will come with it."

"Come here," she said, no trace of jest in her voice. "Don't think. Just come here."

There was running away from my problems, and then there was *running away*.

"Maybe a week or two would do me some good," I admitted, thinking about what I would miss if I just picked up and left the country. I peeked over the steering wheel to see Bitsy getting into her own penis gift. The lawyer *could* wait a bit. It's not like Daniel was going to file. His balls were in my court after all.

"A week or two is nothing. Listen, it's the beginning of June and I have a spare room. And plus, I'm barely ever home anyway. You'd have the place to yourself. I know you'd love this city, and the weather is to die for! Think about it. You could eat great food, see beautiful buildings, visit museums. You could sketch." From across the ocean, on another continent, I could hear my friend's excitement. "Come and spend the summer with me."

"A summer in Rome?"

"Wasn't that a movie?"

"I don't think so, but—"

"Stop stalling. No buts. No overthinking, no stressing. Just do it. Go home, pack your things, and I'll call you back with flight info. I'll see what I can get that leaves ASAP so you don't chicken out on me."

She hung up and I stared into the visor mirror. Touching the pearls at my neck, I frowned, not recognizing myself. Yes, I was put together, and yes, I *looked* the part, but I wasn't happy. Thinking about it, I couldn't remember the last time I was.

Nodding once in silent affirmation, I slammed the car into drive.

I was heading off to spend my second summer abroad.

CHAPTER 3

ROME IS A BEAUTIFUL CITY. I'm pretty sure. I hoped one day to see it. Because right now, all I could see of it were the cobblestones below my feet, and the occasional look up to check a sign or a house number. Then back to the cobblestones, which appeared uneven because:

1. They likely were uneven.
2. Navigating cobblestones while wearing one stupidly high shoe and one recently lowered shoe was unwise at best.

Why did I wear heels on the plane? Ah yes, because I wanted to appear composed, polished, assured, perhaps even a bit worldly? But the heels that were cute while boarding the plane at Logan Airport had become very pretty torture devices by the time I landed in Rome. This was caused by both the saltiness of the airline meal and the amount of booze I'd consumed, which turned my cute feet into puffy pillows with toes. And now one of the heels was missing, after I'd stumbled on the Metro and left part of my shoe behind like some kind of half-assed Cinderella leaving bits and pieces all over Rome.

How the hell far up this street was Daisy's apartment?

I stopped for a moment to roll my wrists out a bit, tired from dragging my rolling luggage. Something else not made for cobblestones. I tried to see them for what they were, small pieces of history laid down centuries ago by the ingenious Romans, determined to make their shining city on a hill a bastion of wealth and knowledge for the civilized world . . . they were not made, however, for rolly luggage.

I grabbed my bags, lowered my head, and started to rumble-roll again.

Eventually, I heard the pitter-patter of tiny feet, looked up through the pieces of greasy airplane hair that had fallen in front of my eyes, and saw the most beautiful sight I'd ever seen.

Daisy Miller, best friend and funny gal about town.

"Why the hell didn't you call me? I've been worried sick! You were supposed to call me when you landed!" she called out, her long legs hurrying expertly over the cobblestones toward me.

Show-off . . .

I barely recognized Daisy coming at me, thanks to a newly acquired shock of blond hair cut into a chic bob. She nearly bowled me over, squeezing and hugging me while laughing out loud, exclaiming how happy she was to see me and how glad she was I was finally there. I saw all of this in fuzzy black and white because behind her, in full Technicolor with a dreamy soft focus lens, were two gorgeous men. And they were scooping up my luggage?

I noticed that Daisy was instructing them on the luggage scooping, directing them back toward her apartment.

"My neighbors. I had a feeling you'd have a ton of bags," she explained as I watched in a daze.

Pack mules. She'd brought stunning, golden-skinned, raven-haired pack mules.

As I stood unevenly on the uneven cobblestones, looking at my best friend glowing like a Lite-Brite, the weight of the crazy decision and the airplane cocktails and the crowded Metro and the heel break and the jet lag all caught up with me and poured out of me in sudden tears.

"I know it doesn't look like it," I sniffed, "but I'm so glad to be here!"

"SO WHEN I HEARD all those wheels rolling across the cobblestones, I knew that had to be you."

"Oh that's nice," I said, my voice still a little quivering and whiny post-Italian-Street-Side Breakdown. "You heard the sound of a stupid American rolling her stupid countless suitcases across the city and you thought, hey, I bet that's my best friend." I blew my nose into my tissue and waited for her to disagree with me.

"Pretty much." But her grin softened her statement.

Inside her apartment, I let my head fall back against the plush cushion, her enormous couch enveloping and cocooning me in the loveliest of ways. Feet propped up on a stack of pillows and beginning to slightly depuff, I let my tired eyes roam around her apartment, taking in the beautiful oak beams soaring overhead, the terra-cotta-tiled floor, the archways that seemed to curve and beckon from every corner. Pretty tables and occasional chairs spilled across the wide living room, haphazard and unmatching, yet somehow coming together in this sweet room filled with bits and bobs of her travel-filled life. Warm sunlight poured through tall windows, one giant patch where the French doors were thrown open to the postage-stamp-size terrace with a promising view.

"Besides the cheating, the monster-in-law smackdown, and flying four thousand miles to escape Boston, anything else interesting going on?"

"That's not enough?" I asked.

She shrugged. "It's conversation. I'm trying to keep you coherent."

"I see. Well, I was almost pickpocketed on the Metro. It's right out of a guidebook for American tourists! And the guy seemed so helpful, too, I nearly let myself get played."

"So, nothing is missing?" Daisy said. "Please tell me you didn't have your passport in your pocket."

"No, that's in my tote bag, and I've got copies packed into each suitcase."

"Smart. A bit of an overkill, but smart."

"Hey, I grew up on the mean streets of Wellesley," I said, pretending to pop my collar.

"Ha! Something tells me that no one has ever called any street in Wellesley 'mean.' Be grateful you've traveled a lot and know how not to be *that* tourist."

I frowned. "Mr. Pickpocket did get my favorite lipstick, and a Starlight mint." I patted down my other pockets, assuring myself once more that he hadn't gotten anything else.

"A Starlight mint huh?" she asked, and I rolled my eyes.

"I wanted to have fresh breath when I arrived."

"I hear that," she said. "There's so many hot men in this city, sometimes you just never know when you're going to fall on one of their mouths."

I laughed, scrubbing my face with my hands and trying to will some energy into my body. "I'm not falling on anyone's mouth. What I need right now is a shower, and then a bed."

"Nope," she said, standing up and grabbing her wrap. "What you need right now is some water, something to eat, and then a good long walk to get your blood moving. Get changed and be fashionably comfortable. The only cure for jet lag is to get on Roman time as quickly as possible. Let's go!"

———

WITH FEET NOW CRADLED by comfortable shoes, a face freshly washed and moisturized, and hair swept back into a ponytail, I stepped back out onto the cobblestones with Daisy, and out into a different world.

A caramel-colored door. An awning of crimson and cream stripes. A wall the exact color of the inside of a nectarine. The teeniest balcony I've ever seen crammed full of flowers and herbs, a kelly-green potato vine spilling over a shiny azure ceramic planter and racing with blush and baby pink creeping phlox to get down to the cobblestones below.

The cobblestones. What a difference thirty minutes can make. Now that I could see them, could really see them, it was charm central. Speckled and mottled, gray and brown shot through with the tiniest of opalescent sheen every now and again, they were arranged unfailingly in tiny rows and untidy corners, ebbing and flowing as the ground had likely rolled over the years since they'd been laid down.

I hadn't noticed earlier that Daisy's street ended just outside her apartment. Around that last bend, with the narrowest of steps going up, up, up, then out of sight, the apartment shared a small courtyard with a few other doors. Countless bicycles and scooters were parked along the narrow street, and in the center were enormous stone planters filled to bursting with red geraniums, raspberry dianthus, orange coleus, and more of that greenest green trailing potato vine.

"This is beautiful," I breathed, turning 360 degrees and seeing awesome in every direction.

"You ain't seen nothing yet," she said with a grin, looping her arm through my elbow and tugging me down the charming street, away from the courtyard.

And onto another charming street, and another, and another. We twisted and turned, the street not seeming to follow any sort of pattern or grid. I saw everything I'd missed on my earlier death march, this time seeing the then-quiet streets begin to rally and liven up for the day. We passed the Metro stop and headed a few streets past. Everywhere there was action—a horn honking, a bike passing, a scooter scooting—and under it all just a buzz, an undercurrent of energy, even on a quiet Sunday. Cafés were opening up, people crowding into what looked like standing-room-only coffee shops, drinking their tiny coffees while talking loudly and using their hands more than I was used to.

My head turned constantly, swiveling back and forth, not wanting to miss a thing. The fact that I resembled an owl, and most assuredly a tourist, didn't faze me a bit. I was perking up, my feet didn't hurt so much, and now that I was out and about, I was . . .

"Famished. I am absolutely famished," I cried, not wanting to move past the window I was currently staring into. Breads, crusty rolls, thin flat pizzas, and sweet and tempting pastries all crowded onto little trays and into pyramids, begging me to walk right in, sit right down, and cram everything into my mouth.

"Only another block or so," Daisy assured me, tugging once

more on my arm to lead me in the right direction. "I know exactly what you need."

Ten minutes later I was sitting at a corner table in a café situated at the corner of Incredible and Wow. The shiny coffeemaker behind the bar was bigger than a Fiat, and actually looked more powerful. And speaking of powerful. "That's heaven," I sighed, sipping a screaming hot cappuccino, full of frothy foam. "Oh damn, that's heaven*er*," I moaned, every nerve ending I had sizzling and snapping at the wonder that was the pastry I was eating. "Please tell me again what this little croissanty thing is?"

"*Cornetto*," Daisy said, her American tongue hidden completely inside this delicious word. "Technically that one is a *cornetto alla crema*." Jesus, she even rolled her R's. "I thought you could use a hit of custard."

"I could use several hits of several somethings," I moaned again through my *cornetto alla* whatever. "How late are you keeping me up?"

"Until normal bedtime. I've already got plans for you tonight."

"Huh?" There may have been a crumb or five of *cornetto alla* spittle clinging to my lower lip; she handed me a napkin. "Seriously, plans tonight? Couldn't I officially start my vacation tomorrow?"

"Vacation nothing—this is a lifestyle, Avery. And tonight, we celebrate your first night in Rome."

"Should I even bother trying to get out of this?"

"You can try, but it won't matter. It's no big deal, really, just a little dinner with some of my friends, some people from work."

"Just dinner?"

"Just dinner. Everyone's excited you're here, they wanted to have a Welcome Avery party."

I sipped my cappuccino, humanity seeping back into my bones.

Just a dinner. A party. For me.

"If you're gonna keep me up tonight, I'm gonna need another one of these." I sighed, pointing at my cup, then at the *cornetto* crumbs on my plate. "And another of these. Make sure you roll those R's for me."

––––––––––

WITH THE SHOCK OF FOUR SHOTS of espresso giving me a much-needed boost, I trailed happily behind Daisy, soaking up Rome. The warm air licked up my bare legs, flirting at the hem of my linen shift. I remained mindful of the gaps in the ancient roads, while she glided across them without even glancing down.

In heels.

If she was Grace Kelly, I was Bambi on new legs tripping over lifted edges and thick gaps even in my gold Tieks.

I thought I knew what Rome looked like, based on the fact that I'd studied art history, held a degree in the subject, in fact. Key word there . . . *thought*.

The truth was, I couldn't have been more wrong.

Studying thin white pages filled with reproductions of its art and travel guides for reference couldn't have prepared me for the full Roman immersive experience. What was that line from *Good Will Hunting*? *I bet you can't tell me what it smells like in the Sistine Chapel.* I was the Will Hunting of Rome. There wasn't a textbook available that could put into words what this city looked like to virgin eyes.

The brilliant late-afternoon sun chased the rooftops glistening and gleaming over steam pipes and clay tiles. The city even had its own sound. You could almost hear the history with every step on the road, every scoop of gelato, each slap of the pizza, and every *buona sera* shouted from the stoops. Daisy pointed, I gaped. An explanation of what I was gawking at always came seconds before she had to practically push up my chin to stop a pigeon from roosting inside my mouth.

We sat for a much-needed rest on the edge of a fountain. I leaned back, soaking up the last of the setting sun when Daisy said she'd be right back.

Sitting beside me, she held out a bag of arancini. "Something to hold us over until dinner."

"These are ridiculously good," I moaned, biting into it with gusto. The melted mozzarella at the center was incredible.

"You're in for a treat, then, because this is just street food. This place we're headed, Avery, you'll want to marry the gnocchi. Melt in your mouth and sinful. No, no, get the arrabiata, spicy and delectable. Wait! I know, get the fresh pesto. The garlic sings in your mouth!" she rambled excitedly.

I warmed at this version of her. Even though back home Daisy came from a well-to-do family, had a top-notch education, and grew up in the same wealthy, Waspy lifestyle that Daniel and I did, things weren't that easy for her. She never quite fit in with the crowd we ran with. She was a tomboy in a sea of debutantes.

Always the first to challenge authority, especially the mothers like Bitsy who looked down their noses at an intelligent, driven, and God forbid, *opinionated* young woman, she rankled people with her independence.

Here, European Daisy was carefree, ebullient, and so full of life it was shining out of her. Anything that may have held her back at home was fostered here, not smothered. This life suited her perfectly. She embraced the culture fully and without a care in the world. She *ciao*d and *come stai*d to everyone we passed.

"And the zuppa? *Dio mio*."

"What does that mean, *dio mio*?"

She shrugged, waving to another shop owner. "Something like *oh my goodness*. I don't know, really. Everyone says it differently, too. And don't get me started on all the different dialects; the dialects alone are a completely different language."

The area of the Rome where she lived, I was discovering, was a living and breathing organism.

"It's not as touristy as, say, right up by the Vatican or the other hugely popular landmarks. Trastavere," she said perfectly and excitedly, "is a younger crowd. Working class, amazing nightlife, but very chill. It's like this little secret corner of the city that's fiery and magnetic."

"Is that why you picked this neighborhood to live?"

Nodding, she pointed to an alley coming up. "The firm helped me scout places before I moved here from Boston. This was the first place I looked at and I didn't bother checking the rest. I fell in love with my little corner."

"I can see why." It suited her with the bursts of color and energy.

We walked down a small alley that felt like we'd entered a postcard. Bicycles leaned against the roughened lemon-colored buildings. Lines of clothes were draped between them, dripping fat water droplets around us. Tables topped with white umbrellas were filling up. Singles, couples, families—everyone taking seats and greeting each other.

Daisy chirped nonstop. "The pistachio gelato here? Orgasmic. You gotta come here some afternoon; there's a guy that sells these little flowers that he'll weave into your hair for, like, a dollar; they're so cute! If you need anything, condoms, tampons, aspirin, come here."

"Condoms?" I laughed, shaking my head.

She shrugged as if it were perfectly acceptable to assume I'd need some while here.

I knew better than to argue with her, so I just smiled and nodded. We weaved in and out of the Piazza di Santa Maria's labyrinth of streets. Glittering mosaics that were baked into the masonry glinted as the fading sunlight blanketed the buildings in a golden glow. The centers of the streets were filled with terra-cotta planters, ivy, and bright red flowers pouring over the edges. In the approaching sunset, they were bathed in gorgeous golden hues.

And pedestrians. Hundreds walked about like a Roman heartbeat livening up the city as they took in dinner menus or window shopped. Some shared a gelato or a glass of wine. It was nice to see people out enjoying their city, just for the pleasure of it. No one seemed to walk simply to enjoy Boston anymore. We were always in a rush or had a faceful of technology. But you could tell that for the people who lived here, Rome was their backyard, their front yard, their living room, their dining room . . . and maybe even their bedroom.

Turning onto Via del Moro, we passed shops and cafés readying for the late dinner rush. Each building had outdoor seating, every table loud and boisterous.

I was swept up in the city's energy. It seeped into every pore, moving me along like a marionette; by the time we reached the restaurant, I had sensory overload in the best possible way. The restaurant looked to be about the same as a dozen others that we passed. Brick, old as dirt, and full of life.

"Across the river is another favorite spot of mine. Campo de' Fiori, this gorgeous outdoor market over the bridge. You'll have to see it. It's like a color explosion. Bring your sketchbook for sure."

"Mm-hmm." I nodded absently, watching the traffic patterns and trying to discern if there was indeed a pattern or just barely contained chaos.

"Do you still like charcoal when you sketch? I know for a while there you were digging colored pencils, right?"

"Hmm? Yeah, either I guess."

"You guess?" she asked, looking at me curiously.

I stopped, chewing nervously on my ponytail, and narrowly missed getting clipped by a Vespa zipping by. The driver shouted a colorful expletive and tapped his helmet. "Where exactly are we headed to next? Are we close or—"

Daisy stopped abruptly, whipping around to face me. "Did you just change the subject? I know a sidestep when I see one, Bardot," she said, using my maiden name. She was my maid-of-honor when I became Avery Remington, but she was my only friend who refused to use that name.

I shrugged, closing the distance and walking around her to head up the narrow alley that spilled into a bustling piazza. Dozens of people were chatting near a fountain. Others were pointing their cameras at the crush of pigeons dive-bombing the crust a waiter tossed outside. It was busy, frenetic, and hopefully distracting enough to—

"Hey, hey!" Daisy shouted, catching up. Nope. She wasn't going to be distracted by this. Sighing heavily, I turned to face my friend.

I'd gotten used to avoiding that conversation over the years when it was over the phone or on Facebook. "How's your sketching going; working on anything new?" or, "Finish anything incredible lately?" Facebook posts I could beg off of. Phone calls, I was able to change the subject or blame the shitty signal because she was off on some adventure where the least exciting part was spotty cell phone coverage. Those calls proved to me how fully she was living her life, which I didn't begrudge her, but that made mine seem boring and flat in comparison.

But face-to-face? She'd called my dodge in less than a day. I couldn't hide from her disbelief.

Glancing at the signs, I looked side to side but couldn't figure out which way we were supposed to head. Everything looked the same on every street.

"It's just not something I do much of anymore."

"Not much of?"

"Or at all."

"But you loved to sketch, you loved to paint. How many hours did you used to spend in the art building at BU? You practically lived in that studio."

"Yeah, well, Boston University was a long time ago; maybe I just fell out of love with it." I could hear how thin my excuses were, so thin they were nearly transparent.

Based on the way she was shaking her head, she wasn't buying it, either. "Huh-uh, no way. You don't just fall out of love with it."

"People fall out of love with things all the time, Daisy. I think me being here is a perfect example of how true that can be."

I could feel tears beginning to build. Jesus this was hard to talk about. Blinking them back, I rubbed the invisible ache in my chest.

"I'm not trying to minimize Daniel here, but I'm actually more concerned about the fact that you're not sketching anymore than I am about you divorcing your husband."

"What do you want me to tell you?" I snapped. "That somewhere, yesterday or years ago, I set aside some of my own great stuff to focus on Daniel's great stuff. Like how getting him through law school trumped me going to grad school. That being an understanding wife when he started at the firm and had to work seventy hours a week meant that there wasn't time for me to go back to the gallery. Creating a beautiful home for us took precedent. Managing every single one of the countless bullshit details that it took to keep our lives running smoothly so that he could go and be a bigshot lawyer and I could make sure that the gardener wasn't cheating us on the price of fertilizer!"

I was yelling. I was yelling at my best friend in the middle of a crowded street in Rome just because she had the audacity to ask me about something that at one point in my life was the very definition of who I was and who I would become.

"I'm sorry, I shouldn't have—"

She held up her hand. "Don't apologize." She linked her arm through mine.

"But I yelled at you," I sniffed, wiping away frustrated tears with the back of my hand.

"Yes you did." She laughed lightly. "You want to sketch while you're here, sketch. You want to just wander around and enjoy? Do that, too. Do whatever you want while you're here, Avery, I mean that. And don't worry about stuff like fertilizer anymore, *capisce*?"

"*Capisce*," I said, nodding.

"Good, that's settled," she said. "Now come on, *Fodors*, the restaurant, is this way. Unless you want to yell at me some more."

"Oh just take me to dinner," I said, squeezing her arm, grateful to be here and with someone who actually cared about me and what *I* might want for a change. And right now, I really did want dinner.

We took off again into the crowded streets, our arms still linked as we threaded through everyone else out and about on this gorgeous night.

We finally stopped when we came upon a gentleman sitting on a step in front of a café strumming a guitar. Daisy greeted him by name. It was such a quintessential European moment: random older man, guitar, café. I half expected Robert DeNiro to slide alongside of me and throw his arm over my shoulder. With a kiss on both cheeks, she said, "*Ciao*, Bruno, this is Avery, my friend from America I told you about." She waved her hand for me to join her.

The café owner was older, tufts of white wispy hair sticking out from all over his head and kind eyes that sparkled gold in the streetlamp. His gray shirt was smattered with crumbs from the bread he had just bitten into. "*Buona sera*," he said, pulling me in for a few kisses and an extralong hug.

"I bet everyone is here already," Daisy said excitedly, walking through the street seating and into the restaurant.

Begging off from the owner, I joined her breezing through the inside, past the dining guests, clanking plates, and busy servers and out the back door to a courtyard that opened up to the star-filled sky, endless and breathtaking.

Maybe it was Daisy's comments from earlier, or maybe it was that phantom limb feeling happening again, but my hand flexed and I wanted to drop into a chair and sketch right away. No landscape, hell, no *anything* had hit me with such urgency like that in years. Daisy was right, I needed to find a store for materials. I made a deal with myself then and there that I would find one and buy supplies. Even if it was just a handful of pastels and a notebook and I didn't use them. I would at least have them.

Walking to the outer wall, I slid my fingers down the rough, peachy exterior. Smudges of chalky residue dusted over my fingertips.

Oh yeah, I would totally use them.

Ivy climbed the light colored brick walls and disappeared over the edge. Thick bunches of vibrant purple bougainvillea danced over the opposite wall. But it was the stars twinkling above that mixed with the fat, clear round bulbs of fairy lights that drew my eyes to the table full of people.

They were rowdy, so electric in their chattering that they didn't even realize we approached. As a way to announce our presence, Daisy plucked a glass of red wine from someone's hand. She drained it in a few gulps and laughed.

The table roared along with her. I hung back a bit while she was enveloped in hugs and pecks on the cheek from her friends. These were people she worked with every day and yet they cheered and loved up on her as if they hadn't seen her in years. The last dinner that I went to at the club, we had air kisses and handshakes. I couldn't remember the last time I hugged a friend in Boston.

"This is Tomaso," she said, pulling me by the hand to a raven-haired man about my height, "and this is my friend Avery."

"He's a massive flirt," Daisy explained, pinching his cheek. "He'll be half in love with you by the end of dinner."

He nodded in agreement.

"This is Sandeep, Iris, and Lewa. Architect, architect, engineer. Wicked smart, all of them." I loved that her Boston accent still poked through even in the heart of Italy. "They're working on a project with me since, gosh, what, January?"

She bounced through each person at the table with a cheeky anecdote for each. *These two are horizontally involved, this one is dealing with a very long-distance relationship with an astrophysicist in Alaska.* It was a veritable United Nations, each the top of the fields from all over the world. My mind was spinning trying to remember each person, where they were from originally, how long they'd be in Rome before winging off to another job site. An image flashed through me in that instant, an image of me sitting at this table, but not as a guest. As a part of whatever fabulous global life these people were living, full of excitement and opportunity and ability to go anywhere, do anything that they'd worked their asses off to get. If my life hadn't veered off course, could I have a seat at this table? Or some other equally awesome table? Where would I be? Maybe London? Maybe Paris? Even if it was still Boston, I would have done *something*.

We circled the table and each person stood, introducing themselves and welcoming me to Rome. I listened intently, focusing on each of their names, their jobs, answering their questions as best I could about how long I'd be in town, what I planned to do while I was here. Head spinning, I let Daisy pull me toward the end of the table.

"Come on, we're down here," she said, gesturing to the empty seats near a couple at the end, wrapped around each other and totally oblivious to anything else.

I draped my purse on the back of my chair and Daisy sat next to the guy, poking him playfully in the ribs.

"Hey, mind coming up for air a sec?" She laughed, hitching a thumb at the couple.

Pulling out the chair, I began to sit when the man turned.

It was one of those slow-motion movie moments.

"Marcello," I gasped, eyes locked with his, realization dawning on his face as I sank down onto the chair.

And totally missed.

CHAPTER 4

Milestone events in your life are linked with certain emotions. Some are so strong and powerful that you're almost transported back to that particular period in time.

Glee: my first art lesson at four. Even at such a young age, I got a rush of giddy anticipation when I picked up that beautifully sharpened pencil.

Embarrassment: at my ballet recital when I was eight, I grand jeté'd right into the piano. I can't hear the "Waltz of the Snowflakes" without breaking out in hives.

Uncertainty: the moment I took that first step onto Boston College campus as a freshman, the beginning of the semiadult part of my life.

Lust, hope, elation . . . love: my senior year at BC when I studied in Barcelona, Spain, and met Marcello Bianchi, architectural master's candidate and beautiful Italian man. He was also studying abroad and I was immediately smitten. We had a very clandestine, very lust-hope-elation-filled affair that no one else ever knew about.

I hadn't seen him since I was twenty-one. There was always

the tiniest nugget of hope that maybe someday, somehow, we'd cross paths. And in my optimistic daydreams, I never imagined that our unexpected reunion included me being on my ass on the floor in the middle of a dinner party.

Twenty pairs of eyes were looking down at me.

As I gazed up into those twenty pairs of eyes, some of their owners were stifling laughter; others were wondering how to help me up.

I looked down. My dress had hiked up to midthigh and the thin strap at my shoulder slid down. I should've moved. Rolled over. Covered up with the checkered linen napkin. Anything to lessen the embarrassment that I should be feeling.

Instead of mortification, I was focused on a pair of wide, equally shocked Italian eyes peering over the table. Eyes that I'd recognize anywhere, and they were staring down at me. Forty percent stunned, 10 percent curious, and a whole lotta angry.

He had every right to be angry, considering how we left things after Barcelona.

Even though he was clearly irked, Marcello's eyes were still the clearest, richest brown. Something akin to cognac—fitting because they always made me feel love drunk. They were usually the kind that glimmered with mischief. You couldn't help but wonder what he was thinking with each twinkle. Spots of black and flecks of gold like a fawn, and his lashes were so long and black that they looked lined in coal.

I'd painted them a hundred, maybe a thousand times while we were together. Our little bubble was my go-to for happy memories over the years since we'd parted. I treated my experiences with him in Spain like a library book. We knew from the beginning that we were on borrowed time, but for those four months I was the real me. He let me fly.

What were the chances that he would be here?

Thinking about it logically, it made sense. Daisy was constantly surrounded by the top in her field. Even then, he—

"Are you okay?" Daisy finally asked, breaking through my shellshock as she threaded her arms under mine, tugging me to my feet.

I blinked, shaking my head and breaking the eye contact with Marcello. I stood, rubbing my sore rear and brushing myself off.

My heart thundered in my ears. A wave of light-headedness mixed with nausea. The entirety of the table fell out of focus, except for him. He was crystal clear. It was my mind's way of making sure what my heart already knew. That he really was here and, judging by the look on his face, furious.

Time apparently doesn't heal all wounds when it comes to proud Italian men.

One of Daisy's friends held the chair and guided me into it—without incident this time. Thanking him, I fidgeted in my seat. I couldn't look at Marcello, but I couldn't *not* look at him, either. If nothing else, I was hoping to see some sliver of the boy I knew. Loved. Not an angry man who was facing the woman who took off, never to be heard from again.

His natural olive tone had paled. He drained his wineglass, his eyes holding mine over the rim of the glass. I watched his throat as he swallowed. The unshaven Adam's apple bobbed with each gulp.

In rapid-fire Italian he shouted to the server over the chatter of our table. The waiter appeared with a new bottle of red and a glass that he placed in front of me.

"Simone?" He held up the bottle of wine.

Simone. Even her name was pretty. Her hair was wild and black, and full of windswept curls. Gorgeous green eyes peered over her empty glass, completely focused on him. They made a stunning pair.

Marcello loved his wine. I remembered that. Looking to him, I tipped my head to the side in question. Ignoring it, he turned his head back to his beautiful guest.

So it was like that. I nodded as much to myself as to him, still numb, still staring, still unable to tear my eyes away from my ghost.

Marcello gripped the wine bottle. His large hand surrounded the bottle as he lifted it to his mouth. He pulled the cork out with his teeth. Like Eastwood with a cigar, he held it between them and smirked. Just for me. The smirk and all it led to I remembered *fondly.* My skin heated as I remembered him wanting a reversal of fortune one night. I had sketched him dozens of times, but that night *he* wanted to paint *me* with a bottle of the strongest red wine I'd ever sampled. Three glasses later he had gotten his wish.

With the wine cork between his teeth, he had painted my naked skin in homemade Chianti. Dragging the slick red liquid over every inch of me, dipping into the peaks and valleys while he watched . . . burned.

"Water?" I chirped, using the napkin to blot my fevered skin. "Agua? Aqua? How the hell do you say water?" I gulped the wine instead.

"Maybe ease up on the booze there, Jet Lag," Daisy suggested, moving the glass away from me.

Marcello harrumphed and casually draped an arm over the back of the chair where his date sat. His body turned completely away from me. A brush-off is a brush-off in any country.

Someone at the other end of the table shouted to him and he smiled. While he was pulled into a conversation, I was left with a perfect view of his jaw. His profile that made my belly flip and my heart . . .

The second I didn't seem preoccupied by ghosts of my secret past, Daisy's coworkers were there to fill the void. Like Daisy warned, Tomaso was a seasoned flirt. He was handsome, sure. Boyish good looks and that accent, oh boy. I knew about accents.

Had my life not been in total disarray, maybe I'd consider him and an Italian affair, but now . . . I was faced, quite literally, with my last Italian affair. God, that sounded so Lifetime made-for-TV movie. There had to be a better way to describe it. Dalliance? Indiscretion? That summer I spent all that time on my back, side, front, sweet holy Christ, *all of it* . . .

It took everything I had left in my energy reserve to act normally. To not let on to the entire restaurant that we knew each other. *Intimately.*

With a light hand on my shoulder, the waiter slid the plate of appetizers in front of me. Everyone was preoccupied discussing different projects. Restoration work over by the Lateran church, some stabilization nightmare at a building near the Forum. With a mouthful of the freshest tomato I'd ever eaten, I listened, watched, and absorbed it all.

With ears on the conversations, my eyes darted to check out Marcello. At first I tried to ignore the pull, the deeply hidden urge to study him. The more I tried to smother it, the more I looked over. It didn't help that he was across from me looking wickedly sexy. Marcello was only in his early thirties, and had aged *very well.*

His dark brown hair was slightly longer than I remembered, curling around his ears ever so slightly, making the waves more prominent. Any lingering softness in his features had melted away, giving way to a strong, chiseled face. His nose, which had always been his best feature, had a new bump on the ridge. Another soccer injury, I wagered. The earring he once wore was gone. A chain with a small silver medal now lay on his chest, visible through the small opening of his white shirt. As he spoke, I relished the richness of his voice and how his phrases jumped from English to Italian.

With warm soup filling my nervous stomach, I studied his hands. Long tanned fingers were speckled with scars—no wedding ring, I noted. Hardworking hands that I didn't doubt were still rough, and so very strong. I choked on said soup—a lovely roasted summer asparagus—when I fantasized about those hands on my skin.

Even seated, I could tell that his already muscular strong build had changed so much. His chest was broader, more filled out. His perpetual tan made his olive skin glow in the flickering candlelight and his angular features appeared more prominent. I wanted to get closer and yet farther away to fight the temptation to lean over and smell his skin. Would he still smell the same even though so much of him had changed?

In the end, it all came back to his eyes. That youthful sparkle was still there, even though they were older, wiser, yet still unchanging. Except when he looked at me. There was a vacancy that I never saw before.

When you think of a reunion, you tend to focus on the good parts. The warm embraces, catching up, and the sheer joy of seeing someone again. Marcello was anything but happy to see me. Though, to be fair, I didn't blame him.

I couldn't help but feel like he was actively avoiding looking at me. His body was angled to face his stunning date.

When I moaned over the gnocchi, it marked the only time that he willingly glanced my way.

"Damn, those are good."

Marcello turned and studied the fork as it entered my mouth on the next bite. He was focused on my lips until the woman next to him drew his eyes away by taking his hand and bringing him into a conversation.

It was all too much. Too much wine, too much pasta, too many pretty twinkle sparkle lights overhead, too much ambience, too many gorgeous, talented thirty-somethings with their whole fun and whimsical yet carefully laid out lives in front of them, too much tension, and most certainly, too much past smacking me upside my jet-lagged and convinced-the-world-had-stopped-spinning pretty little head.

I mentioned too much wine, right?

Feeling him—him with the eyes and the hands and the lips and the mouth and the everything—with nothing but a few planks of ancient Roman wood between us was simply too much. I needed to move, walk, run, flee, or—

"Excuse me; I need to use the ladies' room. Come with me?" I asked Daisy with an eyebrow arch that said she was required to accompany me.

"Sure. *Scusi,*" she said as Marcello stood to let her pass. He stood for her, but his eyes never left mine. Burning, questioning, wondering.

I could feel my pulse racing, my heart fluttering in my chest. It was screaming to flee, flee now, before words that I wouldn't be able to control came flying out of my mouth. Words like, *Dear God, it's you,* and *You're still the most beautiful man in the world,* and *I'm so sorry for everything.*

A nervous giggle spilled out as I followed Daisy out of the room, on the verge of . . . what?

A breakdown?

Confession?

Another crazy giggle escaped my lips.

"What in the world has gotten into you?" she whisper-shouted at me as we entered the empty bathroom. "Really, Avery, what the hell?"

"Oh my God!" I shouted, pacing in a tight circle. The bathrooms in Italy were tiny. "Oh my God, Daisy! He's *here!*"

"Who exactly is *he*?

"Avery! Who the hell is *he*?" Daisy repeated.

I breathed in, then breathed out. I took one more breath, then spilled the biggest secret I'd ever kept.

"Remember when I spent that summer in Barcelona?"

"Yes."

"And I came home and said I'd had the time of my life?"

"Yes."

"And I almost stayed another few months after the semester was over?"

"Yes."

"I almost stayed another few months because I didn't want to leave."

"Okaaaay?"

"Marcello."

"Marcello who?"

"I didn't want to leave Marcello."

"Leave Marcello what?"

"Christ, Daisy, keep up! I slept with your friend Marcello in Barcelona when I was in college!"

"No!"

"Yes!"

"No!"

"Yes!"

"And you never told me?"

"Yes!"

"No!"

"I know!" I shouted, both of us flapping our hands and waving them about and pointing and *oh my God he's here*!

"But of course he's here," I continued. "It makes sense, when you think about how much time has passed and his field of study. Of course he'd be living in Rome, it's so close to his hometown! Oh my God, he's here, and he looks so good—epically better than good, and oh my God he's here, he's actually *here*, and I'm *here*, and he's totally still pissed at me and what does this mean, and—"

I spun around, catching a glimpse of myself in the mirror, and was horrified at what I saw. Travel weary, face pale in some spots, splotchy in others, makeup smudgy in that dried-out, dehydrated-plane-air way it gets for anyone not blessed with supermodel looks, and yet . . .

My eyes were sparkling.

A smile crossed my face, a smile I hadn't seen in years, racing across my cheeks and splitting it ear to ear.

"Let me get this straight," Daisy said, walking up behind me, her gaze meeting mine in the mirror. "You slept with my friend Marcello."

My grin got impossibly bigger. "Well, technically, he was *my* friend first."

She looked at me in disbelief. "You're sure it's him? Not just another knee-bucklingly superhot Italian man?"

"You don't forget a man like him," I said honestly. "I can't forget him."

Daisy sighed, but before the long-overdue explanation could begin, the door swung open and Simone, the woman who had been seated next to Marcello and seemed to know him a bit more intimately than the rest, came inside, nodding before disappearing into a stall.

I mouthed the word *later* to Daisy, who immediately mouthed back *you bet your ass.*

I took another deep cleansing breath, smoothed back my greasy hair into its still-tight bun, and went back to the table. Where the only man to ever bring me to multiple orgasms in one sitting—or standing for that matter—was waiting.

THE PARTY WAS OVER, the guests were leaving, there were only a few still on the patio now, lingering under the fairy lights and sharing a few last glasses of grappa.

And he was most certainly lingering. He remained at Simone's side, involved in their conversation, but his eyes remained solely with me, but not in a good *I'm so happy to see you* way. And as the number of party guests continued to dwindle, it became more and more difficult to avoid direct conversation, to avoid idle chatter or not so idle real-life words.

He'd step forward and excuse himself through the crowd and I'd see him heading my way and begin to chat with a person next to me. I even went as far as inserting myself into a work conversation about I beams and whether or not steel reinforcement was necessary on this particular project. With each move toward me, I was backing out of the restaurant to try and get to the street. Even though we were already out in the fresh air, I needed to get fresh*er* air. Some much-needed distance.

Ten feet away from the man against whom I'd measured all

men, including my own husband, and found them all lacking, and I couldn't bring myself to step any closer. His eyes burned into mine, asking silent questions and getting some kind of answers.

What are you doing here?

We need to talk . . .

"Ready to go?" Daisy chirped in my ear, and I could feel my head snap back on its spine. Looking down, I could see my right foot edging closer, not quite ready to take a step but certainly closer to it than I'd been.

I looked at Marcello once more. I studied him as the man he had become, not the boy I knew. In case I never saw him again, I wanted a new memory. Something lasting that wasn't filled with hurt eyes and bottomless anger. It didn't happen. If anything he looked even more agitated than before.

"Yep, let's go home."

Daisy bundled me into a cab, keeping me occupied with her inane chatter, but before the car sped away, I turned back toward the restaurant, back to where Marcello stood with the last few guests, his arm slung over Simone. The look on his face when he stared down at her spoke volumes.

"Avery Bardot, you tell me every single detail right—"

I held up my hand. "I can't. I mean I will, but gimme a second."

"Just tell me how? I mean, what? You slept with Marcello?"

I breathed out in a whoosh, letting my head fall against the seat, my body tired but tingly. "I haven't seen Marcello in nine years. I never thought I'd see him again, let alone here and now."

"And I unknowingly just delivered him on a platter to you."

"Yup." I rubbed the ache forming in my chest.

"I had no idea. I can't believe you didn't say anything to me."

"I never told anyone about us. Obviously because if I had, you'd have been the one to know." I paused, smiling when she nodded. "After I got back and things went sideways, I erased everything about Barcelona. I didn't keep anything tangible from the trip. I kept everything to myself. And *from* myself if that makes sense. I'm not sure how to say this without sounding crazy."

"You're doing a pretty good job."

"When we met, it was *something* at first sight," I said with a dreamy sigh. "It wasn't love or lust, but something we both recognized as a possibility of something. It was so pure, so uninhibited. You know the way I mean, right? Hormone-driven madness. We just threw ourselves into it. These moments that were little pockets of perfection. It was like nothing else mattered. Just us." I gazed out the window at the passing streets, the people out and about. Did they know that two universes collided tonight? Could they hear it?

"You remember my internship at BU's art gallery, yeah?"

Daisy nodded, pushing herself up in the seat.

"My professors had suggested that if the Museum of Fine Arts was where I wanted to be, then I had to study abroad— become more well rounded. They suggested Italy, France, and Spain. There really wasn't a bad choice. But there was something about Spain that stood out for me. I couldn't wait to go."

"It was all you could talk about," she chimed in, gesturing to the driver to take a left here.

"Exactly. *It was a once-in-a-lifetime opportunity,* they said. They were only selecting a handful of art majors to study with this professor and I was at the top of the list. Everything I had been working for was finally about to pay off.

"My parents were thrilled. *I* was thrilled. Daniel—well, he wasn't thrilled. We'd only been together for about a year, and me jetting off to a foreign country for months wasn't his idea of what a girlfriend did. Not his girlfriend, anyway. Looking back on it now, knowing what I know, I wish I'd handled things differently. He wasn't very happy when I left, and I left completely unsure of what I would come home to. I loved Daniel, of course I loved Daniel, but to be honest, I was kind of excited to go off on my own for a while; no boyfriend, no parents, it felt like I had permission to go off and try something new, something different. I could go wherever I wanted and do just about anything. Being independent was something that I wasn't used to and desperately wanted to be."

I paused as the cab pulled up in front of Daisy's apartment, surprised we were already here. She paid, we climbed out, and she nodded for me to continue as we made our way into the courtyard and up the stairs.

"I landed in Barcelona and it was—I was a mess. Like I was when I got here. Excited but exhausted. Eager but nervous as all hell. I was alone for the first time in my life and truly responsible for *me*."

"How'd you meet him? I mean, he's a few years older than us and he wouldn't have been in your program," she said, turning her key into the lock and letting us inside. "You want anything to drink?" I shook my head, heading straight for the couch, while she made for the comfy armchair.

"He wasn't. We met by accident. One of my classes was canceled and I had time to kill so I went exploring," I explained, remembering the dog-eared travel book and map I brought over with me. "I'd flip a coin and just venture off on my own. I'd leave the map and take off with no plan and just enough money to get me back to the apartment safely if I ended up truly lost. That only happened once, and that was the day I met him."

Daisy settled into the chair, relaxing back and resting her head on her hand as she listened intently. There was a stack of notepaper on the end table, along with a stubby pencil. I picked them both up and began to doodle a bit as I thought back to the day we met. Unbidden, my fingers began to sketch out the hillside where I first saw him.

"You've been to Barcelona; did you ever make it to Park Güell?" She nodded. "I hit the top of the Carmel Hill and I just fell in love with the city. I sat, leaning against the steps just trying to catch my breath from the climb and think about what I wanted to sketch when a few guys came around the corner."

My Spanish was a bit rusty, so a lot of their back-and-forth was lost on me, but I knew they were asking me to join them for a drink. I shook my head, thanking them. Marcello was toward the back of the group and was lingering the way a boy does when he wants to talk to a girl away from his friends.

They all spotted a group of girls and took off down the hill, leaving the two of us alone with the rest of the tourists.

"Are you busy?" he asked in Spanish, motioning to my sketchbook, but he had already sat beside me on the steps. "Can I join you? I promise not to interrupt," he tried this time in what I thought was Catalan.

He repeated everything in Italian, and finally . . .

"Yes," I responded with a smile when he said it in English.

"And . . . " Daisy said, pulling me out of my thoughts. She leaned in, arms resting on the counter. "This is playing out like a romantic movie in my head. Keep going."

I continued, telling her how he introduced himself with a handshake and so much charisma and swagger that he charmed me in an instant. We chatted for a bit. It was easy, innocent. I had these preconceived notions on how he would be. You hear about the European men and how flirty and pushy they are, but this guy—I felt a smile creep in at the memory of that day—this guy was just cute and chill and charming and somehow totally interested in this wide-eyed American.

We discovered that we were both at University of Barcelona. I told him about Boston and my hopes to get a better position at the Museum of Fine Art until I could find a job as a restorer. He was in a master's program in architecture, so we could have gone the entire semester never seeing each other if it wasn't for that canceled class.

What I didn't mention was Daniel. It didn't even occur to me to say, "Oh hey, by the way, I've sort of got this boyfriend back home . . ." I didn't expect for us to see each other again let alone become what we did.

As I spoke I shaded and contoured the sketch with different sides of the pencil.

Daisy studied me with wide eyes. "Holy shit. I've got this odd sense of pride and yet I'm sort of irked. Mostly because, hello? Best friend!"

"I didn't just keep it from you," I defended, lining the outer edges boldly so they stood out against the white paper. I swept my thumb across the clouds, the skyline, and smudged the cobblestones.

"I can't believe you never told anyone."

"I sort of did. At least I did without actually saying anything. Remember how I went dark? No emails, no texts, calls, I think maybe I sent a postcard or two."

"Wait, *he* was why no one ever heard from you? When you got home, you said the courses were tough."

"That wasn't a lie. They were tough. Because I was skipping a lot of them. My grades suffered. His weren't so hot, either." I suddenly heard myself, and laughed out loud. "I can't believe I'm sitting here, in Rome no less, I'm about to get a divorce, and I'm chatting it up with you about my grades nine years ago! What is happening?" I laughed again, and even to my own ears I sounded a bit delirious. "And now Marcello is suddenly back in the picture and—"

"Whoa, whoa, whoa, just hold on a minute here." She held up her hands. "Back in the picture? Just because you're both here doesn't mean you're going to fall back into bed with him. Does it?"

Did it? "No, of course not," I responded weakly.

CHAPTER 5

THE LAST TIME I WAS IN EUROPE, I survived on almost no sleep. It was easy, I was young and excited to be on my own for the first time. I wasn't going to miss a thing. My life back then, at least in the beginning, was all about the art, the energy of Barcelona—full immersion. Any and every medium imaginable was used to create what I thought were masterpieces—sleep just got in the way.

Of course it was different this time around. I was weary and heartbroken and more than a little bit embarrassed, which led to a lot of anger. As if those weren't enough feelings jockeying for position in my head, I just faced someone whose life I disappeared from without a trace.

Last night after Daisy fell asleep curled up on the chair, I covered her up with a throw blanket and headed back to the guest room. Exhausted, I stretched out, propped myself up on pillows, and stared at the veined plaster ceiling trying to memorize every detail from the dinner.

Marcello.

I fell asleep thinking of him, something I hadn't done in years.

————————

I WOKE UP THE NEXT MORNING to church bells pealing like crazy, telling me, and everyone else nearby, that it was time to wake up and start the day.

I'd start the day, but that didn't mean I had to get out of bed. Pulling the pillows over my head, I burrowed down into the mattress, praying for the bells to stop. They didn't. Admittedly, they sounded lovely. I just wish they weren't so damn loud.

Ding, dong, ding. I flung the pillow at the window and nearly cried when it hit the wooden slatted shades, opening them up. Sunlight poured into the room, warming it in its beautiful Italian glow.

"Damn it," I muttered to myself, hiding my head under the blankets. Checking my watch, I calculated the time difference between Rome and Boston. A pang struck deep in my belly at the thought that Daniel would be finishing up his Sunday golf game and heading home, where we would have carried on with our routine pleasantries.

Yet here I was lying in a bed that wasn't mine, in a city that I was a stranger in when my life as I knew it was carrying on without me in Boston. I felt a subtle itch to call Daniel. To ask him when he'd be home so that I made sure everything was just *so*. Straightening artwork that I didn't paint and setting the dining room table with china that wasn't mine—these were all parts of a whole.

Or, a *hole* as it were, because there was a gaping one in our marriage and it took me going to another country to accept just how far apart we had grown.

Daisy knocked and poked her arm through the open door and jiggled a bag filled with something that smelled outrageously good. And fattening. Mmm, trans fat and cholesterol.

I burrowed further into the blankets.

"No more snoring, cupcake. Time to get up and kick the rest of the jet lag in the ass. Oh, and finish filling in the blanks, please," she said, laughing and sitting on the edge of the bed. "I'd prefer not to pry it out of you." She rolled her neck and grimaced. "I have a crick in my neck from sleeping in that chair all night."

"I did cover you with a blanket," I pointed out, reaching for the bag of pastries.

"You did; it's nice to have someone tucking me in for a change. I've been swamped with this job, not sleeping too much. Still, I know better than to sleep in that damn chair; I shouldn't have gotten comfortable. Henry Cavill could've been doing a striptease for me and I'd still probably have fallen asleep."

"Oh please, there's no way in hell you would have slept through that."

"Well, that's true," she replied with a faraway look in her eye. No doubt thinking of a dancing Henry.

"What's this job, anyway?" I asked, sitting up and pulling a pillow onto my lap. I smoothed my blond hair back, feeling how knotted up the back had gotten while I slept. Plucking a tie from the side table, I pulled it up, wrapping it into a loose bun.

Sitting on the bed and chatting felt like we were back in college. Daisy looked the same, save for the hair. She was still tall and lean, probably from all the walking she did here, and her green eyes sparkled when she talked about work.

"It's this old bank we've been working on for months. It's *almost* done, but we hit a snag. One of the volunteers found out she was pregnant and she can't be in the studio or around the chemicals anymore. Even though we're environmentally friendly, it's a lot of funk when your senses are on overdrive."

"That's too bad. Is that going to mess up the schedule?"

She sighed, flipping through messages on her phone. "Yeah, it's not great. The volunteers, well you know, they make or break a job sometimes. Especially with tight funding. We moved someone else down there to pick up some of the slack, but now we're short someone to replaster some of the Romanesque vases that we found."

"I like plaster."

"You like plaster?" she repeated, confused.

I nearly bit my lip to take back what I'd said, but then I thought about it. The instinct was right, I had the training, why couldn't I help out? "I've got experience. I mean, as recently as a few years ago at least. And it's in exactly this kind of work, restoring Romanesque vases."

She was quiet for a minute, wheels turning. "You're serious. Oh my God, you're serious? This is the best!" She catapulted her lanky body and landed on me, squeezing my neck. "It's nothing major—not that you couldn't totally handle major, but it's just a vase. Well, vases, as in plural. This is kick ass; you know that, right? We can go to work together. You can . . . oh—"

"Oh what? Oh no or oh yes? Let's still focus on the yes!"

She pulled away, sitting back on her haunches with her phone clutched in her hand. "It's at my office. We've got a restoration studio there and . . ."

"And?" I said, not seeing a problem with me coming to volunteer some time in her office and . . . oh.

"Marcello," we said together.

She shook her head like crazy after thinking a minute. "You

know what? I'll talk to him tomorrow. It'll be fine. The work area is on the first floor and he's way up on five, you'd hardly even run into each other. Maybe. Probably."

I nodded, not feeling at all as hopeful and excited as I was a minute ago. Would this work? Would he be okay with this? The idea of helping out in my field, even in a small way, was an exciting prospect. Something that I hadn't felt in a long time.

Back home in Boston, whenever I thought about what I was missing out on by choosing to stay at home and not work in my field, I bottled it up. It didn't matter that I was good, really good, at what I'd studied, what I'd worked toward all those years. I'd made a choice, and when I made that choice I knew full well what I was deciding.

But still . . . the instinct lingered. I'd been in Rome twenty-four hours and I was throwing my hat into the Romanesque vase ring without a second thought because it just *felt right*. Even just to volunteer, it was something.

"Oh, I almost forgot!" Daisy scrambled off the bed and dashed back into the other room, snapping me back from my own thoughts. When she returned, she looked very proud of herself. "I brought you some coffee to go with your pastry. I wanted you good and sugared up for the rest of the story."

"The story?" I asked, taking the coffee and giving it a taste test. Mmm . . .

"The story, she asks," she said to herself, rolling her eyes. "The story! You! Marcello! The Love That Ate Barcelona! I gotta hear the rest!"

I laughed in spite of myself, glad she was getting such a kick out of my long-ago love affair. "Sure, sure, that story. Where'd I stop?"

"Park Güell. Good-looking Italian. Naive yet attractive

American. Never told a soul even though her best friend is awesome. Comes home for a job."

"That was succinct."

"Yeah, but you left out all the good stuff, all the in-between. Gimme that part." She tucked her legs underneath her and got comfortable. There was no way I was getting out of this.

But I found that in the light of day, sitting here with a great cup of a coffee and a ridiculously good pastry, I *wanted* to tell the rest of this story. Give it some air and some light and see if it was as bad as I remembered it. Well, only the ending was bad. Everything leading up to that had been . . .

"It was fucking magic. Daisy, I can barely describe it, it was just . . . God it was good."

"Now when you say *fucking magic,* I assume you mean that the *fucking* was *magic*?" She mimed a finger going very specifically into a hole conveniently created by two other fingers, then was quite surprised when a pillow hit her smack in the face. Peeking up over the edge, she blinked. "Too soon?"

"Promise me never to do that again with your fingers and I'll promise never to hit you again with a pillow. And no, not too soon. And yes"—I covered my face with my hands, knowing I must have been blushing every shade of red—"the fucking was magic."

"I knew it!" she cried, kicking up her heels. "I always knew that man had to be killer in the sack; just look at him! I mean, I'm not interested in him, we've only ever been just friends, but come on! You just know a guy that looks like that knows how to hit it!"

"Oh he hit it," I admitted, still blushing, but determined to give Marcello his due. "I mean, I'd only been with Daniel, who was always quite nice in bed, you know, but this guy. This guy was . . ." I paused, trying to put it into words.

"What, what? This guy was what? Huge? Awesome? A freak? What?"

This. This is what was missing last time. I never got to squeal and scream and laugh and giggle over Marcello with my girl-friends because as far as my girlfriends were concerned, he never existed. Somehow, getting to talk about this now even all these years later reminded me that what had happened was real, it was tangible.

But how could I describe Marcello in bed? I'd need hours to recount all the wonderfully filthy things he'd done to me, and en-couraged me to do to him. How he'd made me gasp, moan, groan, and cry . . . all in the same moment.

". . . talented," I finally finished, keeping most of it for myself and letting Daisy draw whatever conclusions she wanted from that.

"I love it, I fucking love it!" She bit into her pastry with gusto, little bits of powdered sugar blowing this way and that as she chewed. "So were you together the entire time you were there?"

I nodded. "Pretty much. We were practically inseparable, and naked a lot of the time. Don't get me wrong, we were enjoying everything that Spain had to offer, but we were also enjoying each other, too. A lot."

"Yeah, yeah, I get it. This story really makes me regret spend-ing that summer working with my dad at the accounting office. Continue," she teased, and sipped more coffee. "How did you leave things with him when you left Barcelona? Is he why you came home early?"

"Kind of. My advisor called, a call I'd been dodging since I'd been spending so much time out of the program and in bed with Marcello, but it turned out to be a great call. Here I thought I'd be in trouble for skipping classes and hurrying through assignments, when the truth was, what I'd been turning in had been some of my best work yet. Something about that time in Barcelona, even though a lot of it felt like playtime, actually focused me, made the time I spent in the studio super sharp. And somebody saw something in the work I was doing, and just like that . . . I got an offer to intern at the museum back home."

"Right, that's right, at the Gardner!" Daisy cried, her face scrunched up as she put all the pieces together. "And when you came home you were all tanned and glorious and gypsied out and you were talking about traveling for the rest of your life and wanting to get your master's at that university in Italy and boy did that piss Daniel off but then . . . wait a minute."

Her voice trailed off, still putting puzzle pieces together. I watched and waited as understanding came over her face. "Daniel."

"Yep, Daniel. Once I was home and settled in, well, that path was pretty well set."

"And Marcello—"

"Marcello was still in Barcelona. Waiting for me." I blinked, feeling my throat begin to close up a bit, a lump forming. "Daniel, not my parents, had picked me up from the airport when I flew home. Daniel, the golden boy I'd left behind when I went off to Spain. Daniel, the boyfriend I truly and deeply loved and was convinced I'd miss terribly the entire time I was abroad. Daniel, the boy I let conveniently fade into my background when a man showed up.

"Marcello happened, and then that was it for me. But when I came down the escalator at Logan Airport, and Daniel was waiting for me at the bottom with balloons and flowers and a sign that said Welcome Home Baby! . . . there was a part of my heart that hadn't entirely been given to Marcello that softened once more for him.

"Make no mistake, I was still determined to follow the plan. Get home, get settled, get into a groove at the museum, and then once all my ducks were in a row, break the news to Daniel. Looking back now, I should have reversed that entire order. Because once I was home, and settled, and into my groove, my ducks became fucks. Well, one last duck, for old times' sake."

Daisy interrupted me, shaking her head. "You don't have to talk about this part, Ave."

"No, I do, though, you know? It's all part of the story." I wiped a tear with the back of my hand.

"I thought, what could it hurt, right? Daniel was a wonderful boyfriend, and we'd been together for such a long time, and being back at home stirred up some of the feelings that had been dormant the entire time I was in Spain. And that one night I spent with Daniel, with every intention of breaking things off once and for all . . .

"Things are never black and white. I'd planned on telling Daniel about Marcello, I really had. But it turned out I'm not this fly-by-the-seat of-my-pants-love-can-conquer-all kind of gal, at least not outside of that little bubble with Marcello.

"I chickened out. I panicked. I spent every waking hour at work, dodged Daniel as much as I could, and strung him along for three entire weeks. And that whole time, I avoided Marcello, too. He'd call, I'd email back. He'd reply to the message, I'd call when I knew he was asleep or in class and leave a voice mail. I was confused and scared and I had no idea what to do."

Until a little blue plus sign changed the trajectory of three lives.

I didn't have to say that part out loud.

"Well, you at least knew that part of the story."

She nodded, patting my hand, her own eyes bright with tears.

I never told anyone what had happened while I was in Spain, but when I found out I was pregnant, and I knew enough time had passed that it was Daniel's, I had to tell someone, I couldn't go through this alone. So I told my best friend, who knew even before I told Daniel.

"And then it all just happened so fast. Once Daniel knew he was going to be a father he went out and bought a ring the next day. Our families were toasting the proposal at the country club by that weekend. I flat-out panicked, one hundred percent, no question about it. And I made the biggest mistake of my life by not telling Marcello the truth. I couldn't face him. And like a coward, I stopped returning his calls.

"It wasn't a slow fade with promises of calls or emails. We detonated and it was all my doing. He was blindsided.

"But I'd made my decision that this was my path, this was what had to happen for the good of my new family."

She nodded her head. "And you never got back in touch with him?"

"It just felt impossible once everything happened. It hurt too much. And besides, I was going to have a baby! Who the hell tells their ex–Italian lover they're knocked up?"

"Yeah, speaking of that—"

"It wasn't his. I know it wasn't." I shook my head. "Believe me, I went over the math a thousand times before I told you, definitely before I told Daniel. I got my period a few weeks after I got back from Spain, and it was actually that excuse I used to get out of sleeping with Daniel when I first got home." I smiled ruefully. "How funny is that?"

And what you never told anyone, what you will never tell any-
one, is how for a split second you thought, you hoped, you prayed that
it was Marcello's . . .

"Anyway," I said, blowing my nose and running my hands
through my hair, "enough of that. You know all my secrets, one
day maybe I'll know half of yours."

"Oh honey, I wish I had secrets." Daisy chuckled, gathering
the coffee cups and pastry bags, taking my cue that the heavy
stuff was over for now.

"Listen, get showered and dressed. We'll grab an early lunch
and spend the day out and about in Rome like two crazy kids."

I nodded, letting her ruffle my hair a bit as she made her way
back into the kitchen. I was here, he was here, that part wasn't
changing. But what I could change was the way I smelled. I
needed a shower.

I padded into a surprisingly modern, stark white bathroom.
It was floor-to-ceiling tile that glowed from the sunlight pouring
in from all directions. This was not a bathroom that you wanted
to use when you were nursing a hangover or suffering from jet
lag and emotional baggage. No, this was the "kick you in the face
with beaming Italian sunshine" until you were awake enough to
function.

"Stupid complicated European showers," I muttered to myself, cataloging the myriad of knobs and buttons. After a few
minutes of naked tinkering, I stepped into the steam/hot water/
massage jet combo and let the water wash away the exhaustion
in my bones. But for all the jet lag and late nights and emotive
outpourings, I felt oddly . . . refreshed?

It was good to talk about this, exorcise the demons a bit as it
were. Next time I saw Marcello, I'd be ready for it.

Daisy was chatting on the phone when I stepped into the

kitchen, my hair air drying for the first time in ages. I pulled up a seat at the counter, picking up the notepad from the night before and looking at the sketch I'd done.

Not bad. Not too bad at all, actually.

I was just turning the page and settling in to start a second sketch when a loud knock sounded on the front door.

Daisy hung up the phone as she sprinted silently down the hall toward the front door, and tiptoed back wide-eyed. "It's Marcello!" she whispered.

Another knock came, this one harder, angrier. "I know you are home. I saw you at the peeking hole."

Only Marcello could make a phrase like "peeking hole" work for him. I could literally feel his voice through five inches of ancient wood and not-so-ancient steel, could feel it slip across me like brandy. But this wasn't going to be smooth. It wouldn't be the reunion I imagined.

"I came to talk to Avery."

Averrry. How did I ever think I would get over the way he pronounced my name.

Daisy's head whipped back and forth between the door and me as I considered.

"Let him in," I said, heart racing. I'd had nine years to think about what I would say to him. How to apologize, explain. In hindsight I should have written it all down because now, faced with the opportunity to make peace, I couldn't focus on it.

"Tell him I'll be ready in ten minutes."

———

I PULLED MY DAMP HAIR into a high ponytail, slicking everything back with a little bit of pomade to keep the curls from getting *too* curly. I dressed quickly, choosing a smooth white button-down shirt and a red-and-pink-striped skirt, not too tight but not matronly, either.

I could feel heat blooming in my cheeks, and when I took a quick glance in the mirror, I could see bright eyes and rosy lips struggling to contain little nerve-filled breaths. *Get it together, Avery.*

I was getting coffee with Marcello and I needed to calm way the hell down. But my heart was bursting from my chest and running wild.

Stop. Full stop.

My heart joined back up with my chest as I stood in front of the nightstand, where I'd taken off my jewelry last night. My ring, and all it represented, sat tucked in a velvet-lined box waiting for me to put it back on. But why? Why would I still be wearing my wedding ring?

Because you're still married.

My heart did a little flip. A small tremor for what Daniel and I had. The truth was that my heart never busted out and raced wild for him.

Not when I fell in love with him—and I had—and not when I fell out of love with him, which I was still processing.

I sank to the edge of the bed and gazed at it catching the light from the stained-glass window in my bedroom. There was a time when I wouldn't have left the house without it. I felt naked even though there was a permanent faint ring on my skin reminding me. It was an extension of my relationship with Daniel, and I wondered how long it would take for the line to fade.

I picked it up. It slid easily onto my finger, where it had lived for so many years.

It surprised me how easily it slid off again. Holding it between my fingers, I studied its flawlessness. If only the marriage was that perfect.

The rings were supposed to symbolize the marriage. Thinking of Daniel and the secretary, I forced myself to replay the scene. He was gripping the desk, knuckles white, and sure enough—the ring was on.

I wondered what was worse, that he had left it on, or if he had been one of those men who took it off and kept it in the glove compartment or desk drawer when they met their lovers.

Heart heavy and weary, I slid the ring back into its box with a snap. Then into the darkest corner of the furthest edge of my suitcase, which I then tucked behind the bed and out of sight.

Out of sight was one thing. Out of mind was another story.

When I left the relative safety of my bedroom, I walked into a zone where nothing was safe or relative.

It should be against the law for someone who looked like Marcello to be allowed to run free in a city as sexually charged as Rome. He was so very tall, towering in the small entryway. His body filled my entire vision: long, lean lines; sharp, see-everything eyes that were only beginning to show the tiniest hint of time; sinful-looking lips carved into an even line.

"*Buongiorno.*"

That was the first word he'd spoken directly to me in nine years.

"Marcello," I replied, and the fist around my heart squeezed a little tighter.

Our eyes locked and a thousand apologies were on my lips. Yet none of them came out. "You look well."

He huffed and shook his head a little. Taking a step back onto the porch, he said, "I know a place we can talk"—he glanced to Daisy—"privately."

I nodded, girding myself for, well I didn't know for what. Marcello was passion personified and the conversation was likely going to be fueled by hurt and anger.

"There is *such* a big part of me that wants to tag along on this, but I'll just stay home and organize my sock drawer. Avery, you've got my address written down somewhere, right?"

"Address?" I asked, my voice sounding dreamy and stupid even to my own ears. Shaking my head to clear it, I looked away from the Roman in the shrinking hallway and focused my attention on Daisy. "Yes, I have your address. I'll be fine."

"If you get lost, just find a cab. You've got money, right?" she asked, threading her arm through mine and tugging me away from the gravitational pull that was Marcello.

He turned to her, and with a kindness clearly reserved for anyone *but* me, he calmed her down. "Daisy, *cara,* you've known me how long? We are just going to talk."

"I've known you for years, Marcello, and through all of those years I've adored you as a dear friend. But this is my girl, and for me, she comes first."

This little Western-style standoff needed no more oxygen, so I waded in to set everyone straight on what exactly was happening here. "This is long overdue," I whispered, stepping between them.

"I've got your address, I've got money, and I'll be home before dinner."

"Okay, but just make sure that—"

"I love you; good-bye," I said, giving her a quick hug and joining Marcello by the door.

Sidestepping him, I stood against the railing until he closed the door behind us.

"Well, this is unexpected." I sighed, rolling my shoulders a bit. And I became aware of my hand on his arm. I didn't remember putting it there, but there it was. His skin felt warm, and he felt strong. And my hand looked dainty and ladylike resting there. My left hand, which felt lighter than it had in years.

I wanted to stay there all day, admiring how fantastic my hand looked on his skin once more, but instead I wisely started walking down the winding staircase to the front door that opened up to the street, knowing he'd follow. As I reached for the knob, he moved next to me to hold the door open. My shoulder brushed his chest as I walked past him, his scent filling my nose and making me tense up. I held my breath, keeping the air in my lungs until it burned.

We headed down the few front stairs in silence, but not an empty silence. No sir, this silence was filled with unspoken words. It was charged, heavy, a living, breathing thing. The world only heard the sound of our footsteps, one before the other. But what I heard was *Is this real, is this happening, am I actually here in Rome, walking casually down the stairs and now the street with Marcello, my Marcello? My Marcello who could make me laugh and cry and gasp and sigh and feel all of the feelings that remind me that I'm a part of this planet and experiencing good wonderful things as I was meant to? But, as quickly as I remembered all the good things, I remembered everything else.*

As we walked down the street, our eyes would meet in fleeting glances and I had the chance to admire him once more. To take in the strong hand running nervously through his thick dark curls. To remember what it was like to run my hands through those curls, not because I was nervous but because I desperately needed the anchor.

To watch those eyes light up at the simple sight of a fat yellow cat perched on a windowsill, enjoying a bath in the sun. I'd seen those eyes light up while I performed an impromptu strip-tease while shopping for bikinis on a lazy Spanish afternoon, caught half in and half out of a dressing room while his hands roamed across my body and his mouth alternated between laughing and kissing.

There was always that little nugget of hope that somehow, someway our paths might cross again and I'd be granted the privilege of seeing this man once more, to remember what I knew so well, what I loved so deeply. It was a hope I could only entertain in fleeting moments and passing thoughts, or they'd make it impossible to stay in my well-crafted life where passion was something I was no longer acquainted with.

But here I was gliding down the cobblestones of Rome only inches away from the man who could have been the love of my entire life, and it was a lesson in pure torture. With a green T-shirt snug across his chest and khaki shorts, he looked every bit the young man I fell in love with. Even knowing that the conversation would be painful, I was still happy to see him again.

"I know my timing isn't right, but I wanted to say something."

He stopped, turning to me with a blank expression.

"Is it terrible of me to say I'm actually really glad to see you?"

He looked up at the sky, then back to me, allowing a small smile. "It is not terrible."

HE TOOK ME TO A TINY CAFÉ off via Francesco a Ripa, something I made him repeat so that I could find it again. I also made him repeat it several times, because good god damn, I'd forgotten the lilt of his voice, the impossibly attractive rolling of the R's. I'd once thought it was something he played up to seduce me, but over time, I'd realized it was simply the way his mouth was made to speak English—and what a blessing it was.

We sat, a single espresso in front of him and a whipped cream coffee extravaganza in front of me. While I'd been scrutinizing the coffee menu to decipher which would be the closest to my regular order, Marcello had ordered for both of us.

"You remembered," I said, dipping in my spoon for some whipped cream.

Watching me raise the spoon to my lips, he just gave me a slightly smug smirk.

"I'm sure you have questions."

"Only one," he said. "Why you are here?"

Fair enough. He was angry and I could appreciate that, but I wasn't about to be a punching bag, either.

"My life fell apart." It was honest, direct. "Daisy offered to help me put it back together."

His features softened a bit but his tone remained cool. "She is a good friend of yours then?"

I smiled. "The best."

"And that is why you came to Italia?"

I nodded, hating that we were reduced to such a humdrum conversation. "I know that my being here is an unwelcome surprise, but seeing you last night, you've got to understand that it was a shock to me, too. I didn't know you and Daisy knew each other, and to be clear, she didn't know anything about you or *us*."

He was quiet for a minute. Processing. His brow remained furrowed, posture stiff, and he still wouldn't look directly at me, which bothered me more than I cared to admit.

Finally, after what felt like forever, he cleared his throat. "What happened?"

"With my life falling apart?" I took a deep breath. "Well, back home I—"

"No." He shook his head. "You misunderstand."

I could feel a chill starting at the base of my spine and working its way upward. So this is what it felt like, seconds before you were held accountable for your actions.

He finally looked me in the eye. "Tell me what happened nine years ago when you left to go back home and forgot all about Barcelona. And me."

CHAPTER 6

YOU HAVE TO KNOW THAT I'm so sorry for how I ended things with us. I—"

He held up a finger when the server came over with a plate of biscotti. Through the large glass window, I watched the red scalloped awning flapping in the afternoon breeze, patiently waiting for her to walk away, letting this play out on his terms. I owed him that.

Once she left, he folded his hands together and dropped them in his lap. "You lie."

My head snapped to him. "Excuse me?"

"You lie," he repeated slowly, finally looking up at me. Any crack in the angry facade was sealed up tight. The romantic side of me was thinking he would be happy to see me after all this time.

He leaned over the table and repeated himself a third time before sitting back and crossing his arms over his chest, looking smug and satisfied. Whereas I couldn't remember a quarter of the apologies I wanted to tell him, he seemed to have no problem getting anything off his chest.

"If you aren't going to let me explain, then there's no reason for us to do this." I grabbed my purse from the back of the chair and moved to stand. "For what it's worth, it was wonderful to see you. And I *am* sorry."

He stood quickly, his chair falling behind him with a crash. "You didn't end it," he growled. "An ending has a finale. *Come si dice*, a resolution," he scoffed, standing directly in front of me. "You disappeared."

As I looked up at him, I could see he was furious, but under it all, I saw the hurt. Knowing that I was the cause of it, I was itching to comfort him and not defend myself. That was something I fell into with Daniel during arguments. Sometimes it was just easier to give in, roll over. Slowly I began hating myself for it. I wouldn't do it again.

"You're right. I did disappear but I had reasons, Marcello. Work reasons, personal reasons, just . . . reasons. I was also twenty-one, and people do stupid stuff when they're twenty-one, you know? I should've gotten in touch with you, I wanted to, but life back home was crazy when I got back and then . . . All I can tell you is that I'm sorry. What I did was terrible, and I will always regret how I ended things with you. How I didn't end things with you. I know words don't always mean much, but I can tell you that I am truly, truly sorry."

His eyes moved over my face before settling on my eyes. Maybe he was cataloguing how I changed, the way I did to him last night over dinner. It could have been that he was trying to read me to see if I was sorry or if it was a lie like he assumed. I didn't ask, and he didn't tell.

Finally, he nodded and turned to set his seat upright. Sinking into it, he sat quietly and stared out of the window at the bustling traffic zipping by. I glanced around at the other customers; everyone had turned away from us.

With my hand on the chair, I waited. For what, I wasn't sure, but I hoped there would be some sort of acknowledgment that he understood. Maybe forgiveness wasn't in the cards for us, but I hoped that he could, at the very least, accept that I meant what I said.

Finally, he nodded at the chair, indicating that I could, and should, sit back down. Knowing him, and his temper, I knew it was all I was going to get.

Rolling my eyes, I slid into the chair. And waited. I eyed the coffee cup, watching the foam dissolve and waiting for him to say something. *Anything.* It didn't go unnoticed that we were together less than thirty minutes and had already fought more than Daniel and I had in years.

"I don't want to argue," I finally admitted, the silence driving me crazy. "We probably should, but I really don't want to. I just had to apologize."

He nodded, focusing on my wringing hands on the table. Could he see the white line from my wedding band? To me, it glared like a beacon screaming to all that saw it *look here*!

Married woman running around Rome with her wedding band off!

If he noticed, he didn't comment.

"I don't *want* it. I *needed* it then, but—"

"*I* need it," I said, making sure there was no way he missed this. "You deserve it. Then and now. I shouldn't have left how I did. I should have explained and not just . . . Jesus, not just panicked. When I got home I thought everything would go as we planned and, well, unplanned things happened and changes were made and—"

"I don't understand," he said, reaching out his hand but pulling back quickly.

And you can't understand because I'm afraid to tell you.

Then his phone pinged, and now he was the one rolling his eyes. "Daisy is wondering where we are and she . . . *oh*. . . she wants to know what I am planning to do with you."

I waited a beat or two, willing my heart to stop racing. Would he say nice to see you again, have a good life? Would he enfold me in his enormously powerful arms and crush me to his chest and whisper the words I was longing to hear, that he was sorry and that he had missed me and that thank God I was back?

"One more coffee?" he suggested.

Best line ever! It was innocent enough for anyone else, but for us—with the complicated history that we had—it spoke volumes. Neither one of us looked away. For the briefest moment he seemed sad, so very sad, but then the tiniest of smiles crept back in when he texted her back.

I wanted to ask what he said.

But for now, I was just grateful to have another few moments with Marcello, sitting for another coffee and getting to ask a few of my own questions, if he'd let me.

"So how long have you been working with Daisy?"

He seemed taken aback by the switch in topic. "It is, let's see . . . four years now. We have worked on several projects together since she joined the firm, and we are just finishing one up."

"Yes, she told me about that. An old bank. Lots of frescoes, mosaics, right?"

His face lit up with excitement. Marcello had always been passionate about his career.

"Yes, it's been a bank for almost 150 years, but it had been a monastery since the fourteenth century. The bank modernized it in the 1870s, and then again in the 1950s—they made some terrible changes then. We worked with them to develop several new spaces this time, strengthening the integrity of the original shell."

When Marcello spoke about work his accent became a bit more generalized, more *of the world* rather than *of a small town in Tuscany*. I could easily see him presenting his plans in a board-room, in some beautifully restored space filled with like-minded professionals. This was Grown-Up Marcello . . . and it was something to see.

"Sounds amazing. Maybe I'll get to see it while I'm here," I murmured. I knew I'd see the vase at the office, but the bank itself, that may be too much for either of us to handle.

"And how long is that?" he asked quietly.

I exhaled on a long sigh. "That's the million-dollar question."

"What does a million dollars have to do with you staying in Italia?" He looked puzzled.

"It's just an expression. I have no idea how long I'm staying. Could be a couple of weeks, could be a month, could be . . ." I let my voice trail off, not wanting reason and logic to get ahold here just yet.

His phone pinged again. Looking at it, he drew in a breath and held it, lips sealing together in a flat line. His eyes moved over the text a few more times before he looked at me. "Sorry, work." He seemed distracted.

"Oh, do you need to go?"

Why did you give him an out? Keep him talking!

"No, it's Daisy, something about she found the perfect volunteer."

Keep him talking about anything but that!

"It's just some vases," I blurted.

Brilliant work, Avery.

"What is?" he asked, setting the phone down next to his cup.

When the waitress stopped back to see if we wanted something besides coffee, I was grateful for the distraction. It gave me time to think about how to tell him that we may or may not be working in the office together. It was a distraction until she left two dinner menus on the edge of the table.

Depending on how this conversation went, I wondered if we would be making it through the coffee, let alone dinner.

"What Daisy has to talk to you about is the vases."

"I don't understand."

I nodded, draining my coffee. "You lost a volunteer. The bank job you guys are working on?"

"Yes." He nodded slowly, confused. "Anna. She is pregnant."

"So you need someone to pick up where she left off. With the Romanesque vases."

"Yes."

"I know how to do it."

"So."

"You need a volunteer."

"And . . . ?"

"I told Daisy that I would do it."

He opened his mouth, then closed it quickly with a snap. By the third time he did it, a small sound came out, but nothing more.

"They're just vases, Marcello."

"They are not just vases, Avery. You know it is not."

"It is what we decide it is. Nobody has to define it. Vases, just vases."

"What if they take you a week, a month?"

"Then they take a week or a month."

"And there is no one waiting for you at home?" he asked, his voice sounding casual, but his eyes told me otherwise.

"That's complicated."

And it was. It certainly wasn't a lie.

A lie by omission is still a lie, Daniel would say. Ironic. I wondered how many *omissions* he omitted telling me about.

"I see." His eyes narrowed. "Home is still Boston, yes?"

Huh. He was on a fact-finding mission. I nodded. "Yes. And Rome is home for you now? How far are we from where your family grew up? I know you grew up fairly close to here."

I could fact find, too.

"You remembered," he replied, allowing a small smile to escape before putting his business face back on.

Of course I'd remembered. I remembered everything.

And just like that I was thrown back to Barcelona, to him, to the lazy days and frenzied nights. To the carefree and the unhurried, when not one thing was tedious or monotonous.

For years I'd kept myself from thinking about him, hating myself for what I did. For what I didn't say. Mainly for how I let things unravel. Because if I had thought about or contacted him after months or years of silence, there'd be no way I could get through my monotonous, routine life. And now here he was, and the floodgates were open, and I was experiencing everything again like it was the first time.

These were dangerous waters.

"Your hair, it is different, no?" he said, changing the subject once again.

"Not really. It's the same curly mess it always was," I said, smoothing it back.

"Why do you tuck it away?"

"My hair plus this humidity? Nightmare."

"Hmm," he replied, but didn't elaborate. "So, you are still in Boston, where someone may or may not wait for you—"

"Yes."

"—and you are here in Rome. For a while. We don't know how long." He studied me for a moment. "And the museum is okay with this?"

"Museum?"

"Or gallery—I assume you're working for one or the other. Or perhaps you are teaching? I always thought you would make an excellent teacher."

Pay dirt. He'd unraveled me in less than five minutes. Suddenly I didn't want to play this game anymore.

"I'm not teaching. Or working, for that matter."

"So you are . . ."

"So I am. There's not much to it," I said, frustrated that I had nothing to show for my life so far. It was the same feeling I got when Daisy asked about sketching.

"And now you are in Rome," he said, glancing up at me, waiting. "And my newest volunteer."

"Am I?" I tried to keep the giddiness out of my voice, the smile off my face, and the twinkle out of my eye, but it just wasn't possible. "You're okay with it?"

Nodding once, he stood and motioned for the check. "Like you said, they're just vases."

———

WALKING ME BACK TO DAISY'S, he weaved us in and out of side streets that we hadn't taken the first time. This path had far less tourist signage to help me along the way. Usually, every corner building had a street sign on it and a stack of signs shaped like arrows pointing every which way to send you toward the landmarks.

This was more of a tour through pocket-sized neighborhoods that seemed to exist on the outskirts of the larger section of Trastevere.

Throughout the entire walk, it was agonizingly quiet. Not a cold quiet like it was on the way to the coffee shop, but a thoughtful quiet. His hands were tucked into his khaki shorts and his long legs ate up the sidewalk with purpose.

"Do you know where you're going?" I asked, unable to take the silence anymore.

He harrumphed. "Of course. It is only your second day, yes? I take you a different way so you see more."

"Oh," I whispered, taken aback by the thoughtfulness of it. "Thank you."

We had just turned a corner that I recognized as near the Metro stop I arrived at my first day. Had I been paying attention that day, I would have seen the enormous Poggi art store across the street. I stopped, but Marcello carried on not realizing that I wasn't behind him. The iron gates were down but the interior lights were lit enough that I could see that the store looked well stocked.

"What it is?" Marcello asked, coming to stand beside me.

Our shoulders brushed lightly, but it was enough that we both noticed and stepped away from the other.

"It's nothing. I was just going to snap a picture so I remembered where this was." If I was correct, this was just about two blocks away from Daisy's. And this was definitely a place I wanted to come back to.

He crossed the street and looked in the glass door before bending down to read the sign.

"Chiuso la Lunedi eh, they are closed Mondays," he explained. "Tomorrow they open at nine." He handed me a business card he'd picked up from a holder on the door.

I smiled in thanks and tucked it into my purse.

By the time we reached Daisy's, it had started to drizzle. I looked up at the late-afternoon sky, blinking through the drops and loving the coolness it brought to my skin. Even though today was mentally exhausting, I felt like I came out of it stronger, wiser even, and most certainly in a better place with someone who was once so important to me. We could even end up as friends at the end of this . . . *whatever this was.*

When I looked back to Marcello, he was watching me intently, and his features had softened the tiniest bit.

"Did you want to come in?" I choked, and quickly explained, "I meant out of the rain."

"I'll be fine. Go inside, Avery."

Climbing the stairs, I turned to where he waited. "Bye, Marcello. And thanks for today."

"*Ciao,*" he called, waving once before returning his hand to his pocket. "I guess I will be seeing you soon."

It wasn't until he disappeared around the corner that I let myself in the front door. Leaning against it, my head thudded against the wood and I counted to ten. Then to fifty, and finally, when I reached seventy-five, I felt solid enough to walk up the stairs to the apartment.

CHAPTER 7

I WOKE TO BUSTLING NOISES in the kitchen that seemed much louder than usual. Clatter. Clatter clatter. Coffee beans grinding. Clatter clatter. Grind grind grind. I'm all for a good cuppa joe, but this was ridiculous. Finally, silence reigned and I scrunched up the pillow, trying to nestle back in. Closing my eyes I tried to drift back to sleep, a sleep enhanced by the dream I'd been having about two giant men named Romulus and Remus kicking Daniel square in the—

Two more clatters, then a pronounced banging that sounded like someone repeatedly opening and closing the fridge. Giving up, I shrugged into a robe and padded out to the kitchen.

"Oh! Sorry, did I wake you?" Daisy asked, blinking at me as innocent as a kitten.

"I'm sure that someday, someone somewhere will fall for your bullshit." I yawned and grabbed a mug from the cupboard. "But today is not that day."

"I'm sure I don't know what you mean." She grinned, knowing full well she'd been caught and not giving the tiniest of a damn. "But now that you're up . . ."

"I'll tell you all about yesterday? Which I could have told you about last night. Where were you? I finally went to bed at eleven."

"Sorry about that. You got my note, right? I'm telling you this bank job is a killer. I'll be glad when it's done. Then it's on to the next one. But not right now; right now I require Marcello details. As soon as the coffee's done—I feel like this is going to be the kind of story that's told over coffee." She headed over to the Signor coffee machine, I joined her, and the two of us watched it drip.

"Didn't we do this twenty-four hours ago?" I asked.

"We did. What does that tell you?"

"That you need a new television show to obsess over?"

"Bite me, Bardot. Tell me what the hell happened—"

I grinned in a way that made her sigh with delight. "Yes!" she exclaimed.

"No, no. Don't get too excited. We just had coffee," I confirmed. "And we talked. And I apologized. And he growled a bit, in that Marcello stubborny way he has; you must have seen it before."

"He has a bit of a temper, it's true," she agreed.

"But to be fair, rightfully so. Although frankly if it hadn't been directed *at* me, it would have been something to see him hot and angry. But it *was* at me, and while things aren't great, they're not awful, either."

"Not awful is good, Avery. Great, even. It's a start," she said, emptying the dishwasher.

"Then I came home."

"And then you came home," she repeated, looking at me incredulously. "And that's it?"

"Yes?"

She stopped with the dishwasher and started pacing around the kitchen, looking in drawers.

"What are you looking for?" I asked.

"Pliers, to pry more than two words from your lips before I'm late for work."

"There's no dirt to dish—honestly. We just had coffee, I apologized for how I left things, we walked home, and then he . . ." I didn't need a mirror to know that my eyes went starry.

"He . . . he what?"

"Nothing, he did nothing, really it was just a look, and I'm not going to be that girl who reads into it," I insisted, but kept the vision of him staring up at me in the rain in my mind. "It's all very confusing, and I really don't have much to tell you." All of that was the truth. "It's just . . . I don't know. It's a lot to try and compartmentalize."

Where to put Marcello into my already-overflowing box of feelings was the question of the day for sure.

"Maybe you shouldn't? Compartmentalize it, I mean. You've got to stop bottling everything up, sister. Let yourself feel bad for hurting him. Or confused for whatever is happening. You can't keep ignoring your feelings."

"I can't?" I asked, pulling at a string on my sleep shirt. I already knew the answer, but I tended to stuff things away, forget about them, deal with them tomorrow.

She sighed and pulled a stool up in front of me. "I'm not going to sit here and tell you what *I* think you should do. Because I'd probably be halfway to his house already, naked under a trench coat and ready for Avery and Marcello 2.0, the Italian Adventure."

"Wow." I gave her the biggest pie eyes I could.

"Which is why I'm not telling you what to do," she said with a snort. "I'll just say this—"

"I don't even own a trench coat."

She ignored my comment. "Put yourself first. Do what you want."

"And that's it?"

"Honey, that's enough. Trust me, I'm a master at putting myself first," she said, lightly slapping my leg. "Now, anything else happen? Any other little tidbits you want to tell me about?"

"He walked me home, a different way than he took me *to* coffee." A faint smile crossed my lips when I remembered why. "Marcello wanted me to see more of the neighborhood."

Daisy nodded knowingly.

"Oh, and I found an art shop! They were closed but Marcello got a card for me with their hours on it. I'm going to drop in today."

My excitement was not lost on Miss Daisy, who was driving herself crazy. "*Marcello* walked you home. *Marcello* showed you the neighborhood. *Marcello* made sure you knew when the art shop was open next. Hmmm. Sounds like a great day to me."

I blushed, sipping at my coffee as an excuse not to say any more. It *had* been a great day.

"But are you seeing him again? You must be seeing him again, right?"

"Oh, I'm sure I'll see him again. Like at the office." I paused for effect.

Her eyes went wide and she hopped from foot to foot. "I was hoping you'd tell him. Hence my perfectly timed text message. How'd that go?"

"Yeah, thanks for that. A little warning might've been good. I thought *you* were going to talk to him."

"I did. I texted! Sounds like you did the rest. How'd it go?

What did you say? What did *he* say? Is he going to be okay with you working in the office?"

"Hard to say; we spoke a lot in metaphors."

She looked confused. "Metaphors?"

I nodded, pulling out a fruit salad from the fridge and scooping us each a bowl. "He said a vase is not just a vase. And I agree, but damn, I think I just want it to be a vase."

"You do?" She looked surprised, and bit into a giant strawberry.

"Weren't you just telling me to put myself first?"

"Yeah, but I thought you doing *that* would mean doing *him*." She munched on a banana slice. "Okay, so. A vase is just a vase. A sigh is just a sigh. You're sure about this?"

I thought about second chances. I guess looking at it it'd seem that the second chance here was clearly a second chance at love, with Marcello. But maybe it was getting a second chance at life, with myself, for myself, doing something that *I* loved.

Put. Yourself. First.

"Yes," I mumbled, but then I repeated it louder. "Yes, I'm sure. I just— I have to get my head on straight. Everything with Daniel has really put things into perspective. What I gave up, how really unhappy we were—or at least how unhappy *I* was. How I'm now realizing that there was an emptiness to my life in Boston. So actually, when you think about it, maybe the vase *isn't* just a vase."

Daisy nodded sagely, biting into a blueberry, watching me work my way around all of this.

"Marcello suddenly being back in my life, maybe, possibly complicates things. But the vase, this project and what it means—that's for me. I know it's not much but it's mine. Just because it involves Marcello doesn't mean that something is going to happen again there. I'd like to focus on me for a change."

"Then there's your answer. Just make it your goddamn vase," she said, setting her bowl into the sink.

TEN MINUTES LATER I'd finished my breakfast, said good-bye to Daisy, who was in fact late for work, and was working on my second cup of coffee.

What would I do today?

It was Tuesday. Back home that meant garden club at ten thirty, lunch with my mother after *her* garden club, then over to Acquitaine Boston for my Art of French Cooking class. With just enough time to zip home, drink a couple of glasses of chardonnay while staring at the television until six thirty, then throw together a salad to go with whatever fabulousness I'd made in class that day.

Sleep?

Great idea. I could sleep all day if I wanted to. After all, isn't that what you're supposed to do on vacation? I mean, going through a divorce? Relax. Cocoon.

Hide?

Shhh.

I climbed back into bed and pulled the covers over my head, like they did in every rom-com when the woman is going through something depressing. The longer I lay there, the antsier I got. I didn't want to sleep anymore, or sulk, or dwell on what was happening at home. Then I remembered what was in my purse. I hopped out of bed and rummaged around until I pulled out the card.

Poggi Art Store was open and only a few blocks away. And thanks to Marcello, I knew exactly how to get there.

And thanks to Daniel, I had an Amex that hadn't been canceled yet.

Looks like someone was replenishing her art supplies . . .

———

I GRABBED MY LEATHER BACKPACK and threw in a few snacks, a bottle of water, my wallet, and I was ready to go for a day out and about in Rome.

A guidebook with a map was the last thing I tossed inside the pack before pulling it onto my back and heading out to the art store. Would I get charcoals or pencils? Pastels? Or maybe I'd try my hand at painting again. It didn't matter. I could have picked up finger paints from a kids' store and I still would've been blissfully happy.

The walk there wasn't quite the same as it was last night. Not just the obvious fact of Marcello not being there, but because my mood had changed, lightened. Entering Poggi, I had a spring in my step.

When was the last time I'd walked into an art store? I couldn't remember. But this store was like entering Mecca. Every kind of medium you could dream of was there. And the sketch pads alone made me ache to take them all home.

There's something really special about an art store. Here you have colors and blank paper of every size and every color, every saturation and every combination at your fingertips. Everyone walks out of the store with essentially the same thing. But it's what happens after it all leaves the store . . . the possibilities are endless. I couldn't possibly count the amount of times that just being in an art store had inspired a new piece, or changed my direction on a current project.

I honest-to-God breathed a sigh of relief just *being* in this store. How in the world had I ever been gone from this world for so long?

Does anyone truly know the beauty of a brand-new box of perfectly sharpened, never-been-used colored pencils? Can anyone ever really appreciate the curve of a brand-new sable paintbrush, edge never before dipped into a vibrant cerulean acrylic and swirled across a virgin canvas?

Simply put, it's something I'd never take for granted again.

The stores, no matter the country, were set up mostly the same. Different media grouped together to make it easier for you to browse. And browse I did. With a basket and a smile, I carried myself through the store, carefully selecting a small set of pastels, a handful of pencils, and a large spiral sketch pad. I could have gone crazy in there, but I had other plans for the day, and lugging a giant bag with me wasn't practical.

After I paid, I left and decided to walk until I hit water, no matter where it took me. I rummaged through my knapsack for a euro and held it in the palm of my hand. When I had free time in Barcelona, if I wasn't with Marcello, I would flip a coin to see which direction I'd go.

It was my first full day alone in Rome and I had an idea of what I wanted to do, but I was letting fate decide. I closed my eyes and flipped the coin. It came up heads. Heads was west. I pulled out the map to see what I might run into going west as the universe had dictated.

Ooh, Campo de' Fiori. It sounded familiar. Daisy had mentioned it, hadn't she?

I quickly consulted my guidebook.

Ooh, an outdoor market.

I bounded down to the corner and headed west.

————

THE WALK TO THE CAMPO DE' FIORI took a bit longer than I'd intended. The street signs were plentiful, but so was the graffiti sprayed across them to throw you off.

But with some patience, a few surreptitious peeks at my map, and a little luck, I made it! When I entered the Campo de' Fiori square, all the air left my lungs, rendering me light-headed and in awe.

It was bustling, alive, colorfully explosive, magnetic, and I felt charged just walking through it. It was like the farmers' markets at home but so much more. These vegetable stands boasted tomatoes the size of a dinner plate. Royal purple eggplants, luscious green zucchini, and plump, hearty mushrooms. They were being gently placed into baskets across the front of one of the tables. Another stand had fruit just as colorful and lush. Cheese in wheels, some was shredded, while others were ground into a Parmesan pillow.

And pasta—lord have mercy. Maybe it was the years of carb watching, but I nearly burst into happy tears at the sight of bags and bags of pasta just waiting for me to buy them.

Maybe I could cook dinner for him? I meant Daisy. Yes, Daisy.

As if on cue, my stomach growled. Loudly. A young man carrying a basket of vegetables chuckled and pointed to a little pastry shop just outside of the square.

Food first, people watching later. Armed with another *cornetto alla crema* (they were quickly turning into my favorite breakfast) and a coffee, I moved through the crowd that milled about with their baskets.

I heard the water trickling before I saw the giant, ancient fountain that it was pouring from. Noticing the inscription, I tried out my Italian. "*Fa del ben e lassa dire*," I mumbled to myself.

An elderly woman was sliding over on the ledge, freeing up a seat for me to enjoy my breakfast, and clearly overheard me puzzling out the meaning. She smiled, looking for all the world like a sweet jack-o'-lantern with missing teeth and sparkling eyes.

"It mean, 'Do the good and let them talk,'" she explained, and pinched my cheek before hobbling away, leaning on her umbrella as a cane.

Huh. A strange woman had just pinched my cheek, and it didn't feel at all weird. I freakin' loved this town.

Scrambling up, I had a perfect view of the outlying city while being enveloped in the heart of the square. I rolled over the quote in my head while I ate, trying not to take it as some Italian sign about Marcello. Marcello was good. *Very* good. Was he the good I should be doing? Was this a sign to do him again? Hmmm.

An image of myself stumbling through the streets of Rome, clad only in a borrowed trench coat came to mind, and I immediately shook my head.

With a mental slap to get my mind out of the gutter, I focused on the market. To my left were white tented tables filled with everything from fresh seafood to the most vibrant flowers I'd ever seen. There were a few restaurants with outdoor seating and red-checkered cloths. If I could choose a postcard image to represent Italy, Campo de' Fiori would be it.

I sat cross-legged on the edge of the fountain and pulled out the sketchpad. It was wrapped in plastic and I was like a kid on Christmas tearing into a present. I lifted the cover and ran my fingers down the blank page. It was pristine white and I couldn't wait to get started.

Digging through the bag, I pulled out the pastels and eyed a fruit stand that had a tower of apples. Still life was never my favorite subject, but this was back to basics.

I'd scratched out a few drawings with Daisy, but I wasn't thinking about what I was drawing; I'd just been doodling. Here, I was putting so much behind it my fingers froze around the pastel. Pressure was always something that I succumbed to too easily.

Along the square's border I saw a group of people setting up easels, stools, and canvases, and my heart began racing and my fingers started twitching. They were clearly an organized class. Could I join them? Soon . . . baby steps.

Once they were arranged, they sat and began painting the landscape just beyond the square.

I was lost within moments, watching them work. My fingers gripped the pastel, and with one stroke down the page, I smiled. From there it wasn't smooth sailing, but it was a start.

Before I realized it, I had lost thirty minutes. Shaking my head, I stood, stretching my limbs and knocking off the dust that had collected on my lap.

It wasn't my finest work, but I was damn proud of it. The colors of the apples were captured, the farmer's charming, weathered face and hands were rough, but I was cutting myself some slack. This was the first effort, but definitely not the last.

Tucking everything back into the bag, I wandered over to the group and eyed each canvas. They were good, but they all looked the same: a beautiful Roman landscape. The only varying details were how many flowers they used or the steadiness of their hands on the fine line details.

Except one. An older gentleman toward the end of the line hadn't filled his landscape with the traditional reds, oranges, and yellows of Tuscany. He had painted the night sky. It was rich and haunting with the navy-gray base and stunning charcoal accents. The only swipe of brightness came from a building with a single lit window. Inside, a sultry-shaped silhouette gazed out over Rome.

I watched him finish it before he packed up his things and walked away, leaving the painting on the easel.

"Sir?" I called out after him.

One of the painters tapped me on the shoulder. "He comes every week," she explained in broken English. "He always leave them." She gently picked up the painting and held it out to me. "You take."

"Are you sure?" I asked, watching the others pack up their things.

"Yes, enjoy. You come next week, yes?" she said, pointing to the pastel chalk dust on my clothing. She smiled, pushing the canvas toward me. "Next week."

With a parting wave, she disappeared into the crowd, leaving me with the painting.

I carried it home, staring at it most of the way.

"ARE YOU SURE WE'RE NOT LATE? We're not going to be stuck eating leftovers or just dessert, right?"

"As if that would be so bad. Have you had an Italian dessert? And I don't mean those paltry knockoffs they serve in the States. Besides, I'm there once a week. Trust me." Daisy laughed, handing me a small paper bag with bright red paper poking out of the top as we hurried down the street to dinner.

"What's this?"

"Tools to make life easier," she explained, pulling the paper out to reveal a tiny book of maps and a common phrases book. "I saw the one in your backpack. It's a bit dated. This will help."

"You didn't have to do this!" I exclaimed, flipping through the translations for something good. "*Grazie.*"

"Well, I did it so that I felt better about you wandering around the city by yourself," she began, slipping her purse across her body. "Unless Marcello plans on wandering with you—"

This was a notion that sunk its teeth in and didn't let go. "I won't rule it out. Is that awful of me? I know I'll see him at your office, but . . . We could be friends."

Daisy wrapped a thin, vibrantly colored scarf around her neck. "I'd think you were insane to *not* want to see and *do* him while you're here, but friends works, too."

It was my turn to laugh. We took one last corner, then arrived at our restaurant.

Dozens of people, including families, were waiting on the sidewalk outside the strip of restaurants, chatting among themselves.

I checked my watch. "It's eight o'clock on a Tuesday, and these people are just starting dinner? What about getting ready for work and school the next day? My God, Daniel would be on the couch watching a game at this time."

I sounded like a stick in the mud waiting for her AARP card to come in the mail.

"Have you heard from him?"

"If you call him sending me a text hearing from him," I snipped, pulling out the phone to show her.

Avie, I need to know where you take my dry cleaning.

Daisy frowned and patted my hand. "Wine. We need wine."

She knew the hostess, so we were whisked away within minutes, tucked away at one of the outdoor tables lit with small tealight candles. I was beginning to realize my friend had this town wired. I'd checked out everyone else's table on the way in, looking to see what people were eating, and I may have inadvertently moaned out loud.

When the server arrived, Daisy waved off the menus and asked, "Do you mind if I order for us?"

"Go ahead." I was about three seconds away from sprinkling fresh Parmesan on the table and gnawing off a corner.

"Excellent. We'll start with the *bufala* mozzarella with the warm plum tomatoes and basil pesto, and the baccalà croquettes. Then the black ink taglerini with the shrimp and scallions, the oxtail ravioli, and after that we'll split the veal and polenta with the summer truffles. *Bene, grazie.*"

"How many people are joining us for dinner?" I laughed, breaking off a hunk of warm, crusty bread.

She laughed. "The portions aren't *that* big. Besides, everything is slowed down here. You sit, you drink, you laugh and drink some more—and above all else, you enjoy life. One night, dinner here lasted four and a half hours."

I gave her a searching look, and she added, "There was a lot of wine."

"While that sounds incredibly relaxing, I've got a phone call with my lawyer in the morning. I need to be sharp."

"I think you *need* something sharp. Pointed at his balls."

I shook my head, annoyed. "I just can't believe that the only contact I've had from him since I've been here has been about his shirts."

"He's probably still laying into the secretary." When I winced, she apologized. "Too soon? Sorry."

"No, you're probably right. That's not even what's bothering me. Which seems insane, I know, but I think what I really hate about all of this is the lying. And if he was lying about this, who knows what else he was lying about. How many women? How many years has this been going on?"

She nodded, handing me another piece of bread.

I talked as I chewed. "And it's like, here's this guy, this guy you've known since you were nineteen, this guy you thought you knew better than anyone on the planet, and then poof. One day you find out he's got a secret life."

"Well, his penis had a secret life." Daisy groaned, and I laughed in spite of myself. I dabbed my eyes with the napkin, wondering if I could pass off my tears as ones of laughter. "I'm sorry I brought it up," Daisy said, reaching across the table and patting my hand, not at all fooled.

I gave a watery sigh, then dabbed my eyes a final time. "I don't want to waste a beautiful Italian night or an incredible dinner with thoughts of him. Not now at least. After I talk to the lawyer, I'll need that wine."

"Want to know what *is* exciting to talk about on a beautiful Italian night over an incredible dinner?"

"What?"

"Your first day of work!" She smiled big and goofy. "We finally moved all the vases to the studio. Are you excited?"

"I am. I so, so am. Tomorrow, after the lawyer wine, we're having celebratory vase wine."

"Deal. Now tell me about that portrait you brought home."

"Home?"

She shrugged. "It's where the art is."

I explained the line of novice artists at the market; how they were all similar save for the one. "I just couldn't leave it to end up in the trash. When she said for me to take it, I just did. I don't even really know why."

Daisy examined me, the candlelight reflecting in her green eyes. "You have a new map now, and we'll get your phone set up with an international plan. Your next order of business is an art shop." She held up her hand when I started to interrupt. "No excuses, Avery. If I knew what you needed I'd buy it myself, but I know how particular you are."

"I'm not *that* particular," I protested, smothering a smile. "Besides, I was trying to tell you that I went shopping today. You should have seen me when I got home, covered in pastel chalk, but I digress."

She beamed, holding up her water glass. "I'm so proud of you."

"Me, too. I have you to thank for the idea to come here."

"To us," we said, and clinked.

The server brought the first wave of food, along with a bottle of wine, compliments of the owner. Daisy was clearly a regular.

My eyes closed and I sighed dreamily when the mozzarella melted against my tongue; when the basil pesto hit my taste buds, I heard angels singing. "Jesu—Jesuit Christmas," I choked, correcting myself when a woman at the next table raised her eyebrow in my direction. Right. Catholic town.

"Right? It's impossible to have a bad meal here. And you walk so much, you don't gain weight. It's like Disney World for foodies."

By the time dessert was ordered, it was nearly ten o'clock and I had to unbutton my pants.

"You've had American-made tiramisu, right?" I nodded. "Order it here. You'll never look at it the same way again. Sinful doesn't even cut it."

I ordered for us when she got a text and smiled broadly. I'd been so focused on Daniel, me, and seeing Marcello, that I hadn't asked Daisy about *her* life.

"Someone special?"

"Huh? Uh, no, this is work." She was unconvincing.

The waiter returned with heaven on a plate. A shareable portion of tiramisu that he garnished with freshly shaved chocolate. "Doesn't seem like work," I countered, dipping my fingertip into the creamy topping of the tiramisu.

She tried to hide her secretive smile, and failed miserably at it. "Oh it is. All work. All the time with him."

"Details, please."

She laughed, tossing her phone back into her purse. "Later. Right now, I need this chocolate to help me forget about spreadsheets and budgets."

CHAPTER 8

I DIDN'T KNOW WHO WAS MORE EXCITED, me or Daisy, when I strolled out of the bedroom ready for my first day at work. I knew she was excited, because she had a healthy breakfast and not-so-healthy cappuccino ready for me, and immediately started chirping. "I know you have to talk to the lawyer this morning so I'm sending a car when you're ready. Hopefully tomorrow we can go in on the bus together, but today, you're on your own."

"I'll be fine," I told her as she sailed out the front door. "Thanks, Mom!"

Her response was to fire some weird Italian gesture back at me that I'm pretty sure didn't mean *you're welcome* . . .

The phone call with my attorney didn't exactly go as I had hoped. I *had* hoped, pie in the sky perhaps, but hoped nonetheless that once Daniel had some time to think about what had happened, what he had done, he would have come to the same decision I had, and agree that ending the marriage was the smartest thing we could do. In fact, I also thought once he had time to get used to the idea that he'd actually relish the idea of no longer being tied down, no longer having anyone to answer to, and he could troll through Boston with his pants down.

He'd committed adultery, not me. Theoretically, it seemed clear that he'd be thrilled to be out of this marriage and back onto the scene, free and clear, single and ready to mingle. But in reality, he wanted to make this difficult.

It was clear cut for me. It hadn't been an easy decision and I still had so many conflicting feelings I felt like a yo-yo half the time, but I had to admit that once I stepped off that plane and arrived in Rome, I was seeing things much clearer. So I was letting my attorney fight the battle back home while I got to know Rome.

And frankly, I was enjoying the hell out of the freedom of owing nothing to anyone. I went where I wanted, I ate what I wanted, I drank what I wanted, and no one cared! I'd put on five pounds already, and no one had made any snarky comments! So if Daniel wanted to drag this out, so be it. I wasn't in a rush to return to Boston.

Plus, and this was the part I had never expected, I had a job to start and vases to repair and a . . . life to live?

After I hung up with the lawyer, I took my time getting dressed. Nothing too fancy because, hello, old vases and plaster, but I didn't want to look like a schlump, either.

Why are you so concerned about looking like a schlump?

Officially, it was because I was volunteering at my best friend's workplace for a job that she had helped me get and I didn't want to reflect badly on her.

Unofficially, oh please. There was one very particular reason to look good today. And he stood about six feet tall and rolled his eyes *and* his R's when he was pissed at me. A pretty dress couldn't hurt, could it?

Before I knew it the driver was knocking on my door and

the flutter in my belly was on overdrive. I checked and rechecked my purse, tote, and my little lunch bag that Daisy had prepared and was out the door and into the Roman sunshine for my first day on the job.

The architectural firm that Daisy and Marcello worked for was in the San Lorenzo district. A mix of residential and commercial buildings, the neighborhood was grittier than some of the others I'd been in. Fewer fountains and more graffiti, but there was kind of a pulse, a creative buzz in the air. Being that it was near the university, fliers were stapled to every surface imaginable, announcing exhibits and gallery shows, concerts and readings, free classes for those wanting to bone up on their Chinese, and a get-together next week of the Transcendentalism through Pasta Society, where they'd be focusing on changing the political climate while mastering the art of ravioli.

It was a vibrant part of town, young and hip, and felt very *of the moment*. I could instantly see why an architectural firm that focused on green energy and restoration would have its offices here. Making my way to Daisy's building on the corner, I headed inside and gave my name to the woman behind the reception desk. While I waited for Daisy to come down, I checked out the directory on the wall, astonished at how many people the firm employed. Daisy's name was listed along with the other architects, and it thrilled me to see her name there. She had made her own way in this field, and risen to the top with extreme dedication and hard work.

Of course, I also felt a little thrill to see Marcello's name. I marveled over how this enormous world had somehow become quite small, both of them working together across the ocean from me in Boston, not knowing these very important people knew each other, but had no idea I knew them both.

"There's my girl!" Daisy was coming down the stairs, fresh as a . . . well. "Have you been waiting long?"

"Nope, just got here." I spun around, taking in the spacious feel, the modern furnishings, the whole island of glam in a sea of semiseedy. "Very cool."

"Come on, I'll give you the five-cent tour before I show you the vase." She walked me up to her office, passing aisles of cubicles artfully arranged into pods rather than long, boring rows. There were plants everywhere, a yoga studio in one corner, a guy on a balance ball in the other, and I spied at least four dogs hanging out with their owners while they worked at their desks.

It was what I imagined Google looked like. A smaller, Italian Google.

After making our way past some of the enclosed offices and conference rooms, she led me into her office.

"Corner?"

"Hell yes." She preened, grabbing a bottle of sparkling water out of her little fridge and pouring us each a glass. "I'd say I'm doing okay."

"Okay? This looks more like killing it." Sinking into one of the plush leather chairs opposite her desk, I grinned. "Can I say something without sounding cheesy?"

"You can sure try." Her eyes twinkled.

"I'm really proud of you."

She looked surprised, but pleased. "Is this the part where I say aw shucks?"

"You can sure try." I winked.

We avoided the fifth floor altogether. I didn't know if Daisy was doing that for my benefit, Marcello's, or both. Knowing her as well as I did, I decided it was for both.

Tour over, we headed back downstairs. The studio was back on the first floor, just around the corner from reception, taking up the entire rest of the floor. A spacious, open-concept room that appeared to have every conservationist tool imaginable. Solvents, clamps, sprayers, the specialized lightbulbs to ensure that the artificial light didn't damage the pieces more than they already were.

There was a time in my life where I lived in a studio just like this, where I dreamed of a life after college making my living in a studio like this.

"You okay? You look like you're going to pass out."

I squeezed her arm and smiled. "I might."

Beneath a large glass dome sat the vase. It was beautifully preserved and unfortunately, the conservator was right, not in nearly as bad a shape as I hoped.

Hoped as in, I hoped it was in a terrible mess and would not only take me forever to restore it—thus giving me more time in the same building with Marcello in the hopes that I could make him not so much hate me anymore—but show off some of my restoration skills.

The reality couldn't have been further from the truth.

"Here it is!" she pronounced, uncovering a table with a single vase, in way better condition than I was expecting. It needed work, don't get me wrong, but thoughts of working endless hours, late into the night, stopping only to take a quick break to eat the tortellini that Marcello brought because he knew how hard I was working . . . yeah, no.

Men's voices carried through the glass walls, and my heart raced. My face must have shown what I was thinking, because she gave me a knowing look. "He's not here. Probably not all week. And before you think it has something to do with you, it doesn't. He had a few days already scheduled off. Something about his parents and going back to—"

"Pienza," I finished, pushing away my disappointment. "That's where he's from. And it's fine actually, it's probably best that he's not here. It might make me more nervous if both of you were watching me work."

"Honey, I'm not watching you. Maria is, she's the main conservator," she said, pointing over my shoulder. I turned to see the tiniest person with the most enormous hair I'd ever seen who was looking at me like I had absolutely no business being here. "Maria Salvatore consults with us on a lot of our restoration work. She technically works for the Montmartini Museum, but anytime we're working with a historical site—which is always, here—we bring in someone who can make sure we're doing it the right way. I'm heading back over to the site, tons of work to do to get ready for the opening this weekend. Have fun!"

"Bye," I whispered, nervous now that I was alone. With Maria. And a vase.

"So, you are Avery," she said, walking in a circle around me, something I'd only ever seen in movies or on bad CW shows.

"I am. You're Maria, right? So glad to meet you. I can't tell you how thrilled that I—"

"Have you worked on pottery from this time period before?"

I gulped. "Eighteenth century? I have. It's been awhile, but—"

"And this piece here, see how the neck has been broken? How would you repair?" She eyed me carefully. I took my time examining the vase, inspecting the entirety. It had snapped along the stem, but it looked to be a fairly clean break. The vase itself was beautiful. Wide bottom, long tapered neck, graceful and sturdy. A household piece, put to good use. It could have held water, but based on the faded but still discernable greenish-brown leaf patterns along the base, I'd guess it'd held olive oil.

"Has it been inspected yet for old glue?"

"Old glue?"

"Mmm-hmm." I nodded, gesturing to a hairline crack just below the current break. "This was mended before."

"That was also my assessment," she agreed. "The glue has been removed; what would your next step be?"

"Sand it, prepare it for cement. I'd use a two-part heavy-duty epoxy, archival clear of course, then polish and prime it. Looks like you haven't lost much in terms of color saturation, so I'd likely leave that alone, except for color matching along the seam, which will be small to minimize additional coloring."

These were words and phrases I hadn't spoken in years, and yet they were as familiar to my tongue as *unleaded, please* and *Coke with no ice*.

I held my breath as she studied me once more, no doubt weighing what I'd said with her instinct. Finally, she nodded.

"Then by all means, Ms. Bardot, let's get to work."

It wasn't until I stopped for a lunch break that I realized that I hadn't corrected her when she'd used my maiden name.

———

MY GOODNESS WAS THAT FUN. I wished desperately that there had been more to work on, more smashed bits of pottery dug up from beneath that bank they were all working so hard on, but by the end of the day I'd finished the vase. Oh sure, I'd stop by the next day to make sure the paint I'd used dried correctly, that there weren't any last little bits of sanding to finish it off, but it was done. Maria checked in many, many, many times to make sure I wasn't breaking her ancient vase, but in the end she seemed pleased with my work. I think. It was hard to say, based on the fact that she didn't smile or frown, just nodded and said *that'll do*.

And I never even saw Marcello. But no matter, I was seeing *Rome*.

Those first few days after the job was done, armed with my backpack and my trusty guidebook, I explored the little nooks and crannies of my new neighborhood and even a bit beyond, getting lost in this beautiful city. Literally and figuratively. And after Daisy came home from work she'd freshen up and we'd head out for the evening ritual, the *passeggiata*.

Between five and seven each night, Romans paraded around their neighborhoods for everyone to see. Couples, families, friends, everyone would stroll in twos and threes. They were dressed in their finest, to see and be seen as was the custom. The streets were alive after the heat of the day had passed, filled with friendly faces and chatter. People greeted each other as though they hadn't seen each other in years, catching up on the day's activities, making impromptu dinner plans, and deciding what they might do that weekend.

While people typically strolled in their own neighborhoods, Daisy used *our* nightly *passeggiata* as a way to show me more of this enchanting city. With Daisy by my side, we used the Metro to zig and zag across the city, turning it from a labyrinth of muddled streets into a walkable town.

Excuse me, a struttable town. Because on our evening strolls through the Trastavere, the Tridente, the Prati, I realized that Italians are strutters. They're proud of their city, of their neighborhoods, as they should be. Not to mention any woman who can navigate those cobblestones in four-inch Bionda Castanas has earned the lifelong right to strut.

What I loved most about these nightly walks were the *stuz-*

zichini, or snacks, that were laid out in the tiny bars and restaurants, free for the taking as long as you purchased a drink or two. We'd stroll for a bit, then pop into a bar and devour olives, pickles, little bites of fresh cheese and crispy fried vegetables, whatever was in season. We'd munch on cured salami, tiny pizzas, little rounds of pâté, even pastries and sweets. We typically had only one drink apiece before resuming our stroll; then the monumental task of deciding where to have dinner. There was no shortage of incredible restaurants and we enjoyed beautiful food every night.

And it was during these *passeggiatas* that I got to know Daisy again, as a grown-up. Though we'd been friends forever, there were things I'd missed as we'd pursued our opposite-direction lifestyles, and I was really enjoying spending time with my friend again.

The following Wednesday afternoon, I was napping on the couch. A habit I'd fallen into after traipsing across the city all day, it was my new favorite pastime. The phone woke me and I scrambled to answer it. In my sleep haze I never stopped to think whether I should be answering someone else's phone.

It was a good thing I answered it.

"Hello?" I said, rolling over to check the clock. Whoops, later than I'd thought.

"There is this man. He makes incredible pizza," a voice said. I knew that voice.

I sat straight up, bonking my head on the overhead lamp. "Okay? Ow!" I rubbed my head. Unbelievable.

"I am hungry."

"I'm sorry?" I asked, chuckling to myself. My body responded to Marcello's voice, little shockwaves at war with my determination to play this cool. I imagined him in his office, coffee in hand, and a smile on his face. "Wait, are you asking me out for pizza?"

"It is very good pizza," he replied, his tone giving away nothing.

"You know, it's awfully late in the day. You're assuming I don't already have plans," I teased. Wait, was I flirting? And yet . . .

Daisy was out tonight and I was only going to flip a coin again and see where it would lead me.

The new sense of freedom was intoxicating. Not having to constantly be running from one country club meeting to the next was a treat. It was nice not to have to pretend that I enjoyed spending my time with Junior Leaguers. All those women with the same pearls and the same cardigans, and the same knowing and sympathetic glances . . . It made me wonder how many of them knew what my husband was up to. Or if any of them were involved with him.

But as a ray of late-afternoon sunshine broke through the window and my thoughts of home, I realized that none of those women had what I had. What I might have.

An evening with Marcello. And *all* that might entail.

Decision made, I grinned. "I can be ready in twenty."

"I'm outside."

"Wait, what?" I cried, jumping off the couch and running to the front door. Peering out the side window, there he was on the stoop with the phone up to his ear.

"I see you." He waved.

"Gimme ten minutes," I huffed, hanging up and quickly stepping away from the window. I ran to the bedroom, ripped off my shirt, and tore through the dresser looking for a top that didn't need to be ironed.

I skidded through the hallway and stopped at the antique oval mirror. "Fuck," I groaned, and tried to smooth down my hair. I had showered and *then* napped, not taking the time to dry my hair.

For anyone with naturally curly hair, that's a disastrous combination. It was everywhere, wild and untamed. And of course Daisy's apartment had eaten every hair tie I'd brought. I looked around wildly for a hat. A fedora or hell, I'd even wear a knit cap in this humidity. There was a silk scarf hanging from the coat rack and I grabbed it just as he knocked at the door.

"Just a minute!" I called out, whipping the scarf around my head and trying to stuff my hair behind it.

"Can I at least come in?" he called.

"No!" I shouted, and frowned in the mirror. I'd tied it back as best I could, hiding the bulk of it underneath the scarf, sixties style. I hated not feeling pulled together. Daniel never saw me with a hair out of place. A button was never missed, a shoe was never unpolished, and lordy knows the occasional pimple never left the house uncovered.

"Hi," I said, swinging the door open when I finished tying the scarf's bow.

Once again, in the country where every male was always presentable and pretty damn good looking, he was stunning. The sun from the courtyard lit him up from behind, making him appear angelic and devilish at the same time—beautiful.

"Your shirt is outside inside," he said when I stepped onto the porch, the door closing behind me with a quiet click.

I looked down. Sure enough, it was not just inside out, but backward, too. What was it Daisy said? *Dio mio.*

"Turn around."

"*Che?*"

"Turn around so I can fix my shirt," I said seriously, starting to pull my arms through.

He chuckled softly, disbelieving, but turned. "You know I have seen you. All of you. Many times."

Oh my.

"That was college-age Avery. Before things started shifting and sinking like your Colosseum," I explained, tucking the shirt back into the front of my yellow capris. "Okay, I'm decent."

Marcello began descending the steps before he turned, smiling up at me.

"You look . . ." he began.

The scarf had come loose. One end was caught in my hair but the rest was flying behind me in the breeze. Along with my hair.

"That bad, huh?" I asked, self-consciously rubbing a hand over the wayward curls.

"No, now you look how I remember."

All I could do was grin. Silly, toothy, hopeless.

Until I got downstairs and until he swung his leg over a—"Scooter? You expect me to ride around town on that?"

He blinked back at me, confused. "Yes?"

"Have you seen how crazy people are on these, these, tootabouts?"

"What is tootabout?"

"You know: toot toot! And then you all drive into traffic like a bat out of hell, all over town! I'm not getting on that thing." I crossed my arms. I'd been involved in several near misses by some nutty Roman on a Vespa, and I didn't wish to experience the madness from behind easy-to-crumple handlebars.

Marcello got up, closing the distance between us once more. "What city are you in?"

I rolled my eyes. "Rome."

"Exactly. And what is that phrase? When in Rome . . ."

"Marcello, that's not the point. The point is dead—which is what I will be if I climb on that thing."

I stood with my weight on one hip, tapping one foot, frowning with arms crossed. Wild hair blowing in the breeze. He just started to laugh.

"What?"

"*Mannaggia,*" he sighed.

"What?"

"I say nothing changes," he repeated, but this time with a mischievous smile.

"I don't get it."

"How puffed up you get when you're afraid of something. You are like that little fish who blows up when it feels threatened. You did the same thing when we went on that tour boat."

"And I was right about that! We ended up half drowned!"

He shook his head, his eyes warming to the memory. "Half drowned is not drowned, is it? We got back in the boat and continued with our trip, yes?"

"Yes," I said. "Soaking wet, though."

He took another step. "My favorite part," he murmured, his mouth close to my ear. "I could see right through your blouse."

"Pervert." I smiled in spite of myself.

"Do you trust me?"

"Completely," I said without hesitation.

He looked over my shoulder at the Vespa. "I won't let you get hurt."

"You promise you won't go too fast?"

His eyes danced. "I promise."

For the record, never trust an Italian's version of what constitutes as *too fast*.

We zipped through Trastevere, around the Vatican—not a short distance by the way, in less than fifteen minutes. In traffic. Right before I had climbed on and wrapped my arms tightly around Marcello's body—which is an entirely different story and one I'd likely come back to when I was slipping off to dreamland later—I'd mentally calmed down by reminding myself that scooters weren't cars and therefore not capable of going very fast. More of a putt-putt than a vroom-vroom.

Couldn't be further from the effing truth. We vroomed our way around town, zipping in and out of traffic, taking off like a shot several times fast enough that I was sure my hair was going to blow off. The horn on a Vespa shouldn't be so weenie. It should be a giant foghorn, something more representative of its ferocity.

All I could do was bury my face against Marcello's back, my lips pressed tightly together to squelch the tirade of swearing, and hang on.

Oh, to hang on. My hands, which had been wrapped around his waist from the second we took off, were clenched against him. Twice, when stopped at a light, he reached down and slid his hand across mine, soothing . . . or just touching?

My face was buried against his back, and sweet merciful lord did he smell good. Sense memory, what a tricky thing. He no longer wore the cologne I'd been used to when we were together before, but he still had the same scent, that clean soapy smell that some men have. Earthy and pleasant and all Marcello.

These little things I picked up and noticed only in the nano-seconds between stops and starts. The rest of the time I squeezed my eyes tightly shut and prayed to whatever holy spirit seemed to be hanging over this city at all times to *let me off this thing.*

"Oh you sorry, sorry, son of a bitch," I wheezed, climbing

down from behind him when we finally stopped and I stood up on wobbly legs. "That was *too fast*."

"How can it be too fast? We were the same speed as everyone else—"

"Shush." Acting on instinct alone, I rose up on my tiptoes and pressed one finger to his lips, my hair flying wild all around me. "Give me pizza and I'll forgive you."

And because he was Marcello, he kissed that finger, bit that finger, then gave me a wolfish grin. "Pizza." He caught my hand, and pulled me inside the restaurant.

He caught my hand. I don't even know if he knew he was doing it, it was so instinctual. My hand in his snapped me right back to the past, where I hardly went anywhere without my hand in his. Squeezing tightly while exploring the tide pools in Cadaques, or linked lazily while he explored my tummy with his tongue, it seemed to me now that our entire time together could be summed up by a simple hand holding.

Daniel never took my hand. And to be fair, I never took his, either. It never felt natural, holding hands with my husband. And how telling was that?

So into the chaos of Pizzarium Bonci I went, holding Marcello's hand without a second thought, each finger knowing exactly where to go, comfortable and yet thrilling enough to make a stupid smile spread over my face.

Pizzarium Bonci was so small it could barely be called a restaurant. But I was beginning to learn that the tiniest spots in Rome tended to have the best food. This little pizza shop had three stools crowded around one little table, a stand-up bar on the window wall, and barely room for two people at the counter.

I'd never seen pizza like this before. Trays and trays of long, rectangular pizza, cut sideways almost like a French tartine, but thick and piled high with the most delicious-looking toppings. Traditional, with fresh mozzarella and basil and what looked like an incredible tomato sauce. Nontraditional, with figs and prosciutto and . . . was that mint? Foie gras, salsiccia, cherries, feta, cured black olives, capers, ricotta, Serrano ham, anything and everything that could be described as delicious was scattered across these beautiful pizzas in carefully paired concoctions.

But this was no quiet romantic spot; it was chaos. Cooks shouting from the kitchen, the guys behind the counter shouting to the customers in line, and the customers shouting back their orders to be heard over the din. It was loud, crazy, and wonderful.

Marcello was trying to ask me a question, but I could barely hear him.

"What did you say?" I asked, leaning closer to him with an expectant look on my face.

He laughed and tried again. "What . . . good . . . okay . . . me . . . decide?"

I shook my head with a laugh, gesturing around to indicate how hard it was to hear him.

He rolled his eyes, but leaned closer. And as he put his mouth right next to my ear, bringing us impossibly close once more, I shivered in spite of the overheated restaurant. "What looks good to you?"

Mmm, was that a loaded question, especially when accented by the puff of air from those beautiful lips on my suddenly frantic skin. I closed my eyes to ground myself.

"Or is okay for me to decide?"

Yes, you decide. You decide it all: the how, the when, the where, the how many times, and the how loud I'll scream.

Careful, Avery . . .

Not trusting my voice, I nodded, pointing to what looked

good, and he shouted it out, gesturing wildly along with the guy behind the counter. They went back and forth a few times, finally deciding on four pieces, all different kinds. He carried the slices wrapped in grease-dotted paper while I grabbed a couple of drinks from the cooler, and we headed out to the street where it was less chaotic, snagging a tiny table just outside the front door.

He handed me a piece. "Start with this, very traditional. Ricotta, zucchini flower, fresh mozzarella. You will love."

I bit into it, gooey, stringy cheese pulling back on itself while I chewed away. I moaned. "Thif eh suh goo."

Marcello nodded, taking his own monster bite. As he chewed, his eyes closed in an expression I knew very well. He was satisfied.

"What kind is that?"

"Spicy ham, fried onions, and a small bit of apple."

I was surprised. "Apple?"

He lifted his slice to my mouth. "Bite."

I did, and of course it was fabulous. I licked my lips slowly and sighed a little in appreciation. His eyes watched as my tongue darted out to catch a little spot of tomato sauce just below my bottom lip.

"*Madonna mio,*" he mumbled, leaning against the side of the building. It was nice to know I could still make him rock back on his heels.

"So, have you been in Rome since you finished up in Barcelona?" I asked, digging into another piece. Cherries, foie gras, and fresh basil. Heaven.

He chewed slowly and methodically; possibly weighing his options? He finally swallowed and said, "I stayed in Barcelona for another year."

"Working?"

He nodded, then arched an eyebrow. "Not just working."

"Oh." *Oh . . .*

Well you didn't think he just pined away for nine years, did you?

I bit into my pizza, chewing furiously now. "Where'd you go then?"

Amused by my reaction, he smiled. "I worked in Dubai for eighteen months, new construction mostly. Spent almost a year in Jerusalem, where I started getting more into the green technology, upcycling original materials when we could, then spent a few months in New York—"

He was in New York? He'd been that close to me and hadn't . . . How could he have gotten in touch with you? And better still, why *would he have gotten in touch with you?*

"—and then got a line on a job back in Rome."

All the places he'd been. All the things he must have seen. Once more I felt that little pang that reminded me of how one could live a life when they grabbed it by the balls and just went for it.

"And now you're here," I said, still amazed at everything he'd accomplished.

"And now *you're* here." His eyes met mine, searching, wondering.

There were so many questions I wanted to ask. In those nine years, who'd been alongside him on these great adventures? Was it one woman? Two women? Several? Many? Who had shared his bed and his life all these years, someone special or just someone? I wasn't sure which I was more interested in.

And just how special was this Simone he'd been all over the other night?

I could have sat there for hours and just asked him questions with my eyeballs, but the pizza place was hopping and there were people circling our table like sharks.

Finished, I got up and tossed our wrappers into the recycle bin at the street corner. I felt his eyes follow me with each step.

My phone buzzed as I was walking back to the table. It was the lawyer emailing to tell me that Daniel's attorneys (yes plural) had requested another meeting, and it wasn't looking good.

"Ah shit," I muttered, stabbing at my phone and shoving it back into my purse.

"Everything okay?" he asked, touching my elbow. I blinked up at him, the worry eating away at the happiness I was feeling from being with him again. "We can go?"

"No, everything is fine."

He seemed satisfied with my answer until he saw me rereading the email again on the way to the Vespa. The crowded street had gotten even crazier with the line of people outside of the pizza shop tripling in size.

"If you are in need of a friend to talk to, you can talk to me," he said, throwing one leg over the scooter and offering me his hand to help me on.

"Is that what we are? Friends?" I asked, taking his hand but making no move to get on behind him. Not yet.

He pondered, searching my eyes for *something*. Answers? Hesitation? Second thoughts? "I think I'd like to be."

I saw something in his expression change then. Guarded, yes, they'd likely be for a while. But something was breaking down, changing, smoothing out where it concerned me. Tonight was proof of that. I could feel an enormous weight lift right off and float away into the air, hanging somewhere over the pizza place. "Okay." I nodded. "Friends."

And with that I climbed onto the Vespa without a second

thought, happy to once again slip my hands around his waist and hang on so very tightly. I caught his eye in the side mirror, and he grinned, pleased that I was becoming more comfortable riding with him.

When we pulled up in front of Daisy's I let him help me off, wanting to keep him close. Now that I'd been wrapped around him once more, my body was reluctant to let him go.

I did let him go, but as he walked me up the stairs and to Daisy's door, I noticed that the distance between us was shrinking. In all ways. This made me happy. In all ways.

"The pizza, you liked it, Avery?"

God I loved the way he said my name. At the door, I turned back to him, dreamy eyed.

"I loved it. Thank you." I held out my hand to him.

He looked down, then at me and grinned. "What am I to do with this?"

"Shake it? Hold it? Kiss it?" It might be too soon for inside, but I could good night flirt with the best of them.

Taking my hand, and in the most excruciatingly slow way, he raised it to his lips and pressed them to my knuckles. He kept his eyes on mine the entire time, burning through me with one light kiss, then another, and finally a third. Bringing the other hand up, he repeated it, kissing my knuckles with three sweet pecks. With my hands in his, he brought his lips back to them together and held them there.

I exhaled a shaky breath. When he murmured, "*Buona sera,* Avery," his breath puffed out across my heated skin.

He tugged playfully on the end of my scarf, headed back downstairs, and sped off into the night, tossing a *ciao* back over his shoulder. I giggled a little at the sight of this powerfully sexy man riding a tiny scooter. I hated to admit it, but it was pretty fun tooling around town on the back of one of those things. Would it become a habit?

Maybe. Possibly. We could all use a little vroom-vroom in our day-to-day lives.

———

THE FOLLOWING NIGHT I was back out on the town with Daisy, our nightly *passeggiata* taking us to the Monti neighborhood. And after checking out the scene and making sure we were also *la bella figura*, or cutting a beautiful figure, we settled in for dinner at a lovely little bistro with outdoor tables set up to take in the scene, as well as view the Madonna dei Monti just as the nighttime lights were beginning to twinkle on.

I drank it all in, along with a perfectly chilled glass of prosecco.

"What's with the sigh?"

"Hmm?" I asked Daisy, tearing my gaze away from the fountain.

"You just sighed into your sparkly. What's up with that?"

"It was a happy sigh—don't worry about it."

"Girl, I finally *stopped* worrying about you the day you got off the plane from Boston." She snorted, digging into her purse for her ringing phone. "And speaking of worrying . . . *Ciao*, Marcello, what's going on?"

I smiled into my prosecco, shamelessly listening in on her conversation.

"What? No! No, they can't do that! Who would use duct tape on a fourteenth-century wall covering? What? Oh man, okay, you tell them that for every inch of duct tape I have to scrape off, we'll charge them another five hundred euros. That seems fair, right?"

She put her hand over the phone and whispered to me, "Who in the world would think it was okay to hang a Happy Birthday sign on a six-hundred-year-old tapestry?"

Then she returned to her phone. "Okay, let me know if I need to come down there. You know how much I love a good ass kicking. No, I'm in Monti—at that little place with the truffles and cheese? Yeah, she's here. Mm-hmm, I will. Sure, sure, I'll ask."

I was embarrassed to admit how fast my heart started beating when I knew he was asking about me. I might also be embarrassed to admit how hard it is to drink prosecco while grinning. I cleaned myself up with my napkin while she finished her call.

"Yes. Yes. Yes. Until he stops screaming. Okay, *ciao*." She put her phone back into her bag, crossed her legs, and sat back with her menu, casually flipping through it.

"So . . ." I said, prompting her to tell me about her phone call.

"So . . . I'm thinking about the tortellini with the artichokes and the porcini. Sounds good, doesn't it?"

"*And . . . ?*"

"Hmm, I suppose I could have the grilled shrimp with the lemon and fava beans—that sounds really good. There's this place over by the Trevi that has the best fava beans—"

"This is me, officially hating you," I said, sitting back and flipping through my own menu aggressively. "This is what it looks like."

"Oh stop, you're so fricking cute when you've got a crush. One night out for pizza and you're smitten all over again! Although, since you were involved before, is it technically a crush? Do you move past all of that when—"

"And this is me, officially getting ready to strangle you. This is what it looks like."

"I got that, yes," Daisy said with a laugh. "He asked about you, asked how you were doing. He wanted me to make sure that I told you well done on the vase."

"Really?" I squealed, then hid behind my menu when several tables looked over. Likely wondering why the obviously American girl was so bouncy. "Really?" I asked again, in a much quieter voice.

"He also asked if you'd be coming to the opening of the new bank we've been restoring."

"Oh. Really?" I tried so very hard to sound nonchalant and not at all interested. My best friend didn't buy it for a second.

She snorted. "It'll be filled with art people. Those old paintings and mosaics always bring out the art community in town, as well as someone from the antiquities ministry. They love to see all those old dusty pieces we unearthed during the renovation brought into the light and on display. But you know, you don't really seem all that interested, so I'll just tell him that it wasn't your cup of tea, and that—"

"This is me, officially plotting your demise. This is what it looks—"

"And this is what *you* look like when you realize you're going to get to spend an entire night with Marcello *and* a bunch of old frescoes and a vase that *you* had a hand in restoring." She made a show of grinning like a crazy person, all moony and swoony. "In case you were wondering."

———

"TELL ME AGAIN how you guys got this job?" I asked, tucking an arm in hers as we headed in the direction of the party at the bank.

She scrunched her face up, sidestepping a couple arguing on the sidewalk. "It was a mess. The firm we were going up against underbid us. We told them that it was a shady move and they'd be sorry because they weren't as qualified as we were with dealing with frescoes that age and deterioration."

"I'm guessing they didn't listen?"

"Nope. They took the cheaper bid and a month later they came crawling back."

We stopped in front of a crowd of people who had gathered near a man painting *Girl with a Pearl Earring* on the sidewalk in chalk. It was amazingly accurate for such rudimentary equipment and uneven concrete.

"So what did they do that was so terrible?"

"Someone gave Jesus Billy Idol blond hair." She paused, snapping a pic of the artist's work. "Frosted tips and all."

I was laughing so hard, it took me a second to catch up with her.

"I have a Polaroid of it at the house. I'll show you tonight."

Ten minutes later we arrived at the party celebration for the restoration. It was so crowded that people had spilled out onto the street with their champagne and hors d'oeuvres. Plucking a drink from a tray, I sipped, praying that my nerves would settle before seeing Marcello again.

Something happens on a cellular level to your body when you sense someone near you. It's amplified when it's someone you've been intimate with. My skin felt like a current was running over it, zips and zaps sparking me to life.

I could see him in my periphery, sliding through the crowd with ease. There was an awareness about his movements that drew your eyes to him. Casually, he chatted, shook hands with men in suits, and gave hugs to the women whose hands lingered a bit too long. It flared up some long-hidden jealousy.

"What's everyone surrounding?" I asked, standing on my tip-toes to check out a glass-covered pedestal table in the center of the room.

"That's one of the mosaics we uncovered and preserved," Daisy said, leading me over.

Marcello was explaining the piece's history when we arrived, a captive audience of eight women who had dazzled looks in their eyes.

"This, ladies, is Daisy Miller; her team is responsible for this. Daisy, would you like to say a few words?"

Never one to shy away from the spotlight, Daisy greeted Marcello with two cheek kisses before taking his spot in front of the mosaic.

Unsure whether I wanted to listen to her talk about the piece or disappear into the shadows with him, I waited.

"You know what this reminds me of," he said, sliding in behind me in the crowded space.

Spinning around slowly, I casually sipped my champagne, his eyes on the lipstick smudge on the crystal.

"Tell me."

He angled us toward a semideserted corner. "Catalunya."

It's incredible how one word can evoke so many memories when said by the right person.

Hearing Marcello whisper it took on an entirely different meaning. "The museum. That was a magnificent structure. I remember the Romanesque frescoes well. Have you been back?"

I was going for casual but it sounded overeager—but with good reason. The Museu Nacional d'Art de Catalunya held so much significance for us. It was the spot of our first *official* date in Barcelona.

He shook his head. "Someday . . ." *Let's go now,* I thought, mentally calculating the distance by train.

A waiter breezed by, bumping Marcello's shoulder and pushing us together. His hand slipped to my side, his thumb smoothing the fabric of my skirt at my hip.

His eyes swept the length of me; maybe he paid special attention to the cut of my blouse. It was fitted, but not *too* come hither.

"I wonder," he said, leaning back against the wall. What was he up to? "Would you like a tour?"

"A tour?"

He nodded. "See the work that we've done? That you've done?"

"The vase?"

"It is here," he replied.

I looked around, seeing Daisy still caught up with patrons, playing the part of lead architect and project manager. I saw dozens of people milling about, sipping champagne, tasting tiny treats, enjoying the party. I looked over his shoulder, around the corner where he was now headed, looking back at me questioningly.

There was no party in the direction he was headed. Not another soul.

"Lead the way."

"DAISY WAS THE LEAD on this," Marcello explained as he headed down the narrow hallway, our steps leading down across the ever-sloping cobblestones, deeper into what was originally a monastery. The farther we went, the more narrow the corridor, the closer we got. "It is beautiful, yes?"

"Beautiful, yes," I agreed. I was trying so very hard to look at impeccable woodwork, the pristine condition of the ancient stone walls, but all I could see were his fingers trailing along those walls and that woodwork. All I could think was what those hands would look like on my body, what they *had* looked like on my body, once upon a time. A nervous laugh bubbled up, and I pretended to cough. I couldn't get my bearings around him.

I could feel his eyes on me. Moving over my face, skimming over my body, which was already beginning to show the effects of an entirely carb-based diet. Here, that didn't matter. Here, men loved curves. I remembered how much Marcello had loved mine, my semester in Spain adding at least fifteen pounds. When I came home, Daniel had lightly suggested I start taking spin classes at the BU gym.

Marcello stepped closer, standing right in front of me. My heart beat harder.

"Do you want to see it?" He leaned in again, his body nearly flush with mine.

"What?" I sputtered, nearly choking on my champagne.

"Your vase. I will show you. *Vieni qui.* Follow me."

"Right. Sure," I mumbled, following blindly behind him, praying for a cool breeze.

We reached an ancient archway with painted vines that twisted and turned up the sides and across the plaster. Down here it was still old Rome. And now, in this space that was so ancient and so beautiful, I was finally in my element, and even the sight of Marcello couldn't take my eyes from the beauty of all this . . . antiquity. To me, even old, cracked walls were masterpieces here. Who had crafted these, how long had it taken?

What had they been thinking about when they built this hundreds of years ago, often with bare hands and limited tools? Those kinds of things had always fascinated me.

I could see how strongly Daisy's team tried to preserve the original structure and design of the building while bringing in the new features. What was incredible was how they merged the old and new together so seamlessly. I had trouble spotting which was which.

I circled the room, taking in the colors, trying to decipher the story from the wall art. The old, musty smell filled me with memories of Barcelona, where the two of us had explored museums and churches and structures like this. Since seeing Marcello again, nearly everything was bringing up a memory.

Walking hand in hand down a Barcelona street as we laughed. Sitting in countless cafés as he patiently tried to teach me Italian. On my tiny bed, curled around each other with the sun slanting across our naked bodies.

I turned, looking for Marcello, and found him leaning casually against a wall, studying me. His arms were crossed over his broad chest and the knowing smirk was back, along with that sexy, knee-buckling grin that had me immediately scouting for available horizontal surfaces.

"What are you looking at?" I asked, feeling the blood fly to my cheeks.

"Nothing," he said, pushing off the wall. "Everything." He circled me like prey in the jungle. "You," he said with an honesty so bare that my hand flew to my neck, where I knew my skin was now flushed.

I was aware of every step he took; I could feel him as he walked around me. Having seen, touched, and tasted every inch of this man, I knew what I was dealing with. His voice was dark, husky, and goddamn it washed over me in the best possible way.

Reaching out, he took my hand in his. "Come," he said roughly. He cleared his throat and led the way out of the antechamber and into another small room that was blocked off with velvet queue ropes and a sign in Italian that I assumed meant barred entry, but that Marcello ignored.

He lifted a leg and hopped over the rope. Turning, he held a hand out for me.

I gestured down at the tight green silk wrapping around my hips and thighs. Bending down and slipping underneath it would result in either flashing him (bad), or splitting it up the back since it was so damn tight (very bad). "No way."

Without a word, he reached around my waist and lifted me effortlessly over it. I slid down his body until my feet brushed the old floor. He could have let go. He *should* have let go—but he didn't.

Marcello's rough thumbs found the sliver of skin between my skirt and the tight top I was wearing. Sweeping it across, he rubbed the skin *just so*. Back and forth, searing into my skin.

His breath whooshed out, and I knew what would follow. The low rumble deep in his chest that I'd always heard just before he kissed me. My tongue slipped out, licking the last of the stickiness from my wine away. His eyes caught the movement and there it was. The deep resonant sound, the clenching of his fingers against my side as he tugged me the tiniest bit closer.

My breath caught. I was afraid to move, scared that whatever bubble we were in would pop and we'd realize we were out of our depth here.

His nose brushed mine, with his lips hovering close. He was almost there. It was so natural. I knew these lips. I knew what they felt like, how they moved over every inch of me . . . God, I wanted him! It was as if no time had passed, and the woman I am joined the girl I was then in wanting this to happen more than almost anything.

Because in that moment, there didn't seem to be anything at all wrong with letting nature take over. Wanting so badly to take that final step, I brought my hand up to his hair, twisting a curl around my finger. The arm that circled my waist pulled me even tighter to his body.

I was always a girl who loved to be kissed. Sweet little pecks that said I love you quickly or deep, searching ones that you felt through your body like a live wire over your skin. It had been a long time since I'd felt someone's lips against mine in such a needy way. It had been an even longer time since I felt a kiss that made my toes curl and that had me throwing caution to the wind.

Maybe because we were at a party filled with people he worked with and it happened to be in a building that used to be a monastery, but I was wild with desire and it was terrifying just how much I wanted this. But then I heard a tour group coming toward us and something changed, I changed. I didn't think, I reacted and pushed him away.

I exhaled shakily, then took a much-needed breath. This was exactly what I didn't plan to happen and I let it.

The twinkle in his eyes vanished and was replaced by that same hurt he had shown me that day at the café. "Marcello, I'm—"

"Sorry. I know."

"Marcello, wait," I called out, but he'd already taken off.

I searched the party for him, but much as I had that first dinner, he did everything he could to avoid me.

"What happened?" Daisy asked, pulling me over to the side.

"Things almost got out of hand. I have to apologize. Again." I ran my hand through my hair, frustrated. "I feel like all I do with him is say I'm sorry."

CHAPTER 9

"Y OU'RE KIDDING ME, RIGHT?" she asked, eyeing the envelope with skepticism and disbelief.

"Listen, I don't know where he lives. I'm not going to corner him in the office, either, so I need you to do this."

"If there are check boxes in here asking if he likes you Yes or No, I'm kicking your ass when I get back."

I didn't dignify it with a response.

An apology was necessary, so I did what any self-respecting, practically divorced woman of thirty would do. I sent a letter with my best friend, asking him to call, email, or text me. I gave him every option.

Being in the apartment all day wasn't how I planned to spend my time, but I didn't want to miss him, so I caught up on email. My in-box was flooded with curious questions from friends, more leading questions from acquaintances still determined to get the dirt, and no fewer than four emails from my mother.

She hadn't approved of me running off to Rome, even though both she and my father were 100 percent in my corner when it came to leaving Daniel. But leaving Daniel didn't have to mean leaving the country, or so my mother's first email told me.

Her second email wondered why I couldn't have simply escaped to their house; I shouldn't be alone right now. She'd make me my favorite brisket, she'd rent us some funny movies, she'd buy me chocolate ice cream (my mother's problem-solving methods were all straight out of a Julia Roberts rom-com), and she'd get me through this crisis, by God.

The third email allowed that perhaps I did need some time alone, but that if solitude was what I needed, then I could move into the Cape house and not see a soul if I didn't want to. Furthermore, if solitude was what I needed then why, for pity's sake, was I in Rome, a place crawling with summer tourists?

The fourth and final email told me that she was ready to give me my space, that she and my father would continue to support me any way that they could, but for the love of all that is holy, could I please return an email like a good daughter should?

She had a point. I had sort of cut and run when I left, and I know it didn't make much sense to her. I quickly fired off an email promising that yes, I was fine, and yes, I was settling in, and that yes, once they got their Skype up and running I'd love to have a "video phone call or whatever."

I emptied out the rest of my in-box, painted my nails a beautiful shade of Roman Red—fitting—and then proceeded to ruin my new manicure by deciding to grab my easel and head outside to the courtyard.

I'd been experimenting with different mediums, mostly colored pencils and pastels, but on a second visit to the art store I'd invested in a set of new acrylic paint and some great brushes. Not yet knowing what I was going to paint, or how good I'd be after such a long time, rather than investing in canvas I opted to go with some less-expensive cardboard. Some I'd purchased, some I'd scrounged from around the neighborhood. When you wanted to capture an idea, a concept, an anything, the bottom of a shoebox, once flattened, can be a great canvas.

I propped everything up on a cheap easel I'd also bought, tucked it into the corner of Daisy's guest bedroom, and spent time every day just painting whatever came to mind. The light on the tiny patio, the trash cans on the corner I could just make out from my window, anything and everything to get my hands comfortable holding the brushes again.

Today I needed to get out of the apartment, away from thinking about whether or not Marcello would accept my apology, so I gathered up my supplies and headed out into the courtyard, determined to capture the exact color of those potato vines cascading down the balcony planters.

By ten I had captured the color.

By noon I had successfully layered the purples for the bougainvillea planted alongside the potato vines.

By two I had painted the planter itself along with the two on either side, the bricks below, the sky above, and was starting in on another round of trash cans when I began to think he wouldn't call. Or text. *Or* email.

I brought my things inside, washed my hands, checked my phone one last time, then began to circle my laptop.

Should I? Should I not?

I had just sat down to email him when there was a knock at the front door.

Pulling off the apron, I held my breath, and my hope, in my chest. I opened the door, peeked around the corner, and let out a sigh when I saw him standing there.

"I was starting to think I wouldn't see you for another nine years," I said, stepping to the side so he could come in.

He stayed on the stoop, hands in his pockets. He looked every bit the boy I remembered, and the man I was beginning to know. Confident, handsome, and *happy* to see me?

"Am I interrupting?" he said, glancing at the colors splashed against my arms. "You have some"—he waved his hand near my cheek—"just there. Painting eh, *melanzana*?"

"What is that?" I asked, wondering what color was on my face. "Melons?"

He smiled, taking his thumb and smudging the still-wet paint from my cheek. "Viola, big, uh—purple vegetable."

Then it dawned on me. The bougainvillea was purple. "You mean eggplant."

Nodding, he rubbed his painted thumb between his hands. "Avery," he began, but I stopped him by pulling him into the house.

"Can I say some things? First? Before you say anything."

He thought a moment, then nodded.

"I'm sorry. I shouldn't have pushed you away," I explained, choosing my next words carefully. "I wanted you to kiss me. At the bank. *Below* the bank. Whatever."

I could feel the blush rising but I didn't care. I needed to get this out and make sure he knew why I stopped him, why I had to stop him. His eyes were searching, piercing; they always could level me. I studied my hands instead. If I didn't look right at him, I could say it. "I got spooked when it sounded like someone was coming. I kind of panicked, I guess."

How there was skin left on my hands I will never know, the way I was wringing them. But I went on.

"I didn't want you to kiss me, I mean I did, but not for the first time anyway, with people right around the corner. It's been a long time since . . . well . . . since anyone looked at me the way that you did. At the bank."

"*Below* the bank," I heard him say, his voice full of teasing, but warmth, too. My eyes swung up to find him smiling at me.

"I thought you were embarrassed," he said, glancing down to my lips.

"What? How could I possibly be embarrassed of *you?*"

He nodded and his mouth curled up in the tiniest of grins. "I've got an idea."

"Hmm?" Was I forgiven? Again?

"You take off the apron, wash off the eggplant, and you and I? We take a walk."

A walk. Yes. I could walk. I had a request, though. "I'll go wherever you want, but I want you to do something for me."

"What is this you ask?"

"Talk to me while we're walking. Explain everything. Where we're turning, how old something is. All of it. Left, right, north, south. Don't leave out any details."

DAISY AND MARCELLO had very different methods of showing me their city. Daisy's was an adopted sense of pride, so she prattled on incessantly as if it were a travel show. She loved Rome's beauty and history, but she explained everything in an academic way.

"*Did you know that Rome has over three hundred fountains?*" she'd said as she tossed a coin into one on the outer wall of a McDonald's. It was one of those instances where I was contemplating the fusion of old and the new. "*And something like nine hundred churches? That's a lot of holy.*"

"*Maybe you should get a part-time job as a tour guide.*" I'd been teasing her one night when we were walking past a guide with a lime-green flag and a trail of eager tourists. *"I'm sure that tour group Dark Rome would take one look at your résumé and hire you in a second."*

Everything she told me was interesting, sure, but sometimes you just wanted to wander and lose yourself.

And this was how Marcello played tour guide. We lost ourselves in the city, wandering wherever we wished, with me asking occasional questions and him answering, more often than not with a story accompanying. I took everything in, tried to take mental pictures at every turn, willing myself to remember so that I could re-create it later on. Even the roofs of the surrounding buildings were something I never wanted to forget. Slate gray, brick red, some were tile, some were shingle, nothing matched so everything matched. And the doors were something else that I found myself enamored of here. Santorini blue, vermillion, and evergreen—this world was saturated with color.

We eventually headed down toward the Tiber, where we walked along the tree-lined sidewalk and enjoyed the breeze coming off the river.

"Left, right, or straight?" he asked when we came upon a magnificent stone bridge filled with foot traffic.

I stood in front of one of the ornately carved pillars to read the marker: Ponte Vittorio Emanuele II. It was something that I was growing to adore about the city. Everything had a name and not just Blah Blah Street or Someone Circle. Beautiful, historic names that I butchered with my pronunciation, but I loved hearing him teach me what I was doing wrong.

"Say it again?" I asked, pointing up to the bridge's oxidized plaque.

"Ponte Vittorio Emanuele." He embellished the syllables for

my benefit. Either because he genuinely wanted me to learn how to say it properly, or more likely, because he knew his accent made me swoony.

"Why angels?" I pointed to the top of the great stone plinth where an angel held a shield and raised a sword proudly.

"These are for victory. They are named for Victoria, Roman goddess for triumph in battle. You will find them all over the city; jewelry, money, architecture. At one time she was worshipped on one of the Seven Hills."

In that moment, it didn't matter what he was talking about, I just wanted him to keep talking, and I told him as much.

And just as I requested, Marcello explained why each bridge was named what it was, and how the streets that intersected all had something to do with the bridge and the town. Each little nook had its own bit of history. It was fascinating and intoxicating listening to him.

We continued along the Tiber, the streets tree lined and crowded with couples, families, runners, tourists, and locals alike, out and about enjoying their city. Another strong breeze whipped through, giving me the perfect opportunity to lean into him for warmth. He casually slung his arm over my shoulders as he told me we were about to pass Circus Maximus.

"Oh, you mean like *Gladiator*? I love that movie." I sighed.

"You are teasing me?"

"No! You've seen it, right? Russell Crowe kicking ass in the Colosseum? So hot."

He harrumphed. "Historically inaccurate."

I laughed, poking his side when he scowled. "Don't be jealous. Russell has nothing on you. Show me more of your Rome."

He did just that. We continued to wander, making decisions about where to go on a whim, wherever we wanted to go.

When I mentioned feeling a bit hungry, he bought me a bag full of little fried fish tossed with lemon and salt. Delicious.

I wasn't warmed by just the beautiful weather, but by him; how could I not be? His bolder-than-life presence, the confidence that didn't fade a day in the years since we were together. When he caught me staring, his chest puffed up in such a self-satisfied way I couldn't help but smile.

All afternoon he'd been careful not to get too close to me. Only an occasional shoulder brush or maybe his hand in the small of back to steer me around something, but always a respectable arm's length. A few times I'd feel his hand accidentally brush mine, and then it would flex and get tucked into his pocket.

As the light began changing to something more akin to candle glow, it became harder and harder to ignore the powerful draw that was still between us. That string was still there tethering me, us, to the memories of Barcelona.

I felt an invisible hand at my back nudging me toward him. It was like the walls behind us were pushing us together. I wouldn't be backing away as I had last night.

"Marcello?" I asked, reaching out to touch his forearm. I loved the feeling of the muscles tensing. His hand flexed into a fist before laying across mine. This was the first time he purposely touched me, and even though it was innocent, nothing about it felt that way.

He was struggling. His eyebrows bunched and his eyes went to my hand on his arm, studying it. The right side of his mouth quirked up, and I was desperate to know what he was thinking about in that second.

He nodded, swallowed hard, and then *he* took a step back this time.

"Let us walk a bit more. I want you to see something before it gets too dark," he said, pointing in the direction of the less-crowded cross street.

"Tell me how many stamps you have in your passport," he asked suddenly as we rounded a corner.

"Stamps?"

"You had so many plans for traveling the world—you couldn't wait to fill all those blank pages up with stamps. So tell me all about the places you've been since you left Spain. I've been talking for hours now, it's your turn."

I remembered the conversation. We were in bed—where most of our deep conversations took place—and I used his torso as a map of the world. Each kiss I placed on his body was a country I planned to visit. To explore their lives, the culture. The art.

"Oh. Well . . ." I stalled to snap a photo of the sunset behind the ancient amphitheater. It'd make for a beautiful sketch later.

"Avery, you are avoiding the question, yes? Tell me."

I sighed and leaned against a bus stop. "I've traveled. A lot. An incredible amount really. Let's see . . . Hawaii, Grand Cayman, Maldives, Belize, the Seychelles." I ticked the sandy-beach vacations off my fingers. Let's not forget the dozens of golfing vacations or trips to Vegas, Miami, Los Angeles.

As I went on about the gorgeous blue waters and stunning resorts, the wind picked up. Unbidden, he slid an arm around my shoulder, tucking me into his side to shelter me from the suddenly strong breeze. Once I was done prattling on about the limbo contest I'd won in Grand Cayman, he looked down at me thoughtfully.

"May I ask you something?"

"Of course." Church bells dinged in the distance. Eight o'clock. We'd been walking for hours.

"These trips. They do not sound like you."

"What do you mean?"

"These are places that someone else chose, yes?"

"Yes," I admitted, contemplating if I should explain Daniel and truly what was going on back home. I opened my mouth at least three times, trying to get the words out, but I just couldn't figure out how to tell him. How to open that box again of what had happened, all those years ago, when I left him and went home.

He waited, patient and quiet to see if I'd elaborate, watching as I struggled and finally putting me out of my misery. "Avery, it is okay. You tell me what you can, when you can, yes?"

"Soon, we'll talk about my life in Boston."

Appeased, he kept us walking forward. "So you never went anywhere that you liked?"

"Once." I took a deep breath and looked into his eyes. "Spain was somewhere that I liked. Spending hours on a sketch of Sagrada. Swimming in the same sea as Dalí had, all those years ago. Getting lost in the Gothic Quarters." I dropped my gaze. "You."

He lifted my chin. "That sounds like the Avery I remember."

He hurried me along a pedestrian walkway, past the busy intersection filled with honks, screaming traffic, and a few near misses with Vespa drivers. We were walking and chasing the dying sunlight just over a giant dome in the distance. I began walking faster, eager to see whatever it was he was taking me to.

And I was speechless.

"Holy Christ—" I blurted, but Marcello wrapped one arm around my waist and slipped his other hand gently across my lips.

"Not that. Not here," he whispered, leaving me to wonder what he was referring to, the kiss or the cursing.

"That is incredible," I whispered, spinning three sixty to see light-colored stone wall that rose high above us.

He'd brought us to St. Peter's Square.

I was never very religious. We went to church when I was a kid, because it's what you did for the social aspect. Same reason I went with Daniel. You dressed in your best and brunched with the worst. Nothing about it had to do with the church.

Here you felt . . . I don't know . . . I won't pretend it was some sort of divine presence—or maybe it was. Whatever was happening made me feel *something*. It was the art in my bones, the history I'd studied for so long hunched over long wooden library desks in the fading light. Seeing it in person was something altogether different. Magnificent.

"Come." He nudged me, holding out his arm for me to take. Such an old-fashioned gesture, but for him, it fit. He led us to a gap in the queue rope where a flood of people were streaming through and I stopped, mouth agape, with a nearly crippling need to sketch it.

I didn't know where to look first. The tall, noble pillars that circled the wall above us. The huge majestic statues lining the top like sentries guarding their little city. We walked around the square, my phone filled with photo after photo. I spun, trying to memorize every inch of it, but there was too much. As if he knew what I was thinking, Marcello placed his hand on my back and guided me to one of the black folding chairs.

"You know the way here now, so you can come back. Bring your chalks or pencils, make it your own."

He was beaming, handsome, and my heart flipped.

"I feel like I could sit here for weeks and not capture a fraction of the beauty of this place."

"I hope to see them when you have finished. I've missed your work."

We didn't chat at all once we left St. Peter's. By the time we reached home, night had swallowed up the city in a magnificent navy hue. I was lost in thought, contemplating all the things I'd seen on our walk, and all the places I'd still yet to visit. Walking with him tonight really drove home how compact this city was. You could see a dozen landmarks in just a few miles.

On our way home, Marcello seemed to be getting text after text on his phone. He apologized several times, and I tried not to think about who might be blowing up his phone. We'd yet to talk about Simone, the woman he'd been sitting with (and kissing) the night I'd arrived in Rome. Was she still in the picture? How serious were they? Should he be out on the town with me? With my heart full of joy and my head full of questions, we climbed the stairs to the apartment.

I turned, and Marcello was right behind me. Close enough that I could feel the fabric of his shirt on my bare arms. So many of our early dates in Spain had ended this way, him looking over my shoulder at my door, wondering whether he'd be invited in. I thought about Daisy's note. He technically wasn't a boy . . . would I ask him inside?

"Today, well today was perfect," I said. "Thank you for showing me some of your Rome."

"This makes me happy, to know you liked seeing my city."

I knew he was telling the truth. He'd always liked to make me happy, to find out what I liked, and what I loved. Emboldened, I looked up at him. "I'm thinking right now of something I'd like."

His eyes changed instantly, smoldering. "Maybe a kiss?"

I held my breath, turning my lips up in silent answer.

He cupped my face and lowered his mouth to each of my cheeks.

"I was thinking somewhere else," I admitted, licking my lips when his eyes flickered to my mouth.

"I'm afraid if I kiss you the way I want to, I won't stop."

I nodded, not quite agreeing, but unable to say the words that would give him the okay, the "let's make this real again."

"Good night, Avery." Marcello held my eyes as he walked down the steps.

I thought back to each time today when he almost or I almost. When we were crushed together in the crowd outside the Colosseum. When he wrapped his arm around me as we walked along the Tiber. And the night before, when he'd picked me up as though I weighed nothing to lift me over the velvet rope and I almost let him kiss me the way I was desperate for him to.

And I hadn't let him.

"Marcello," I whispered, not loud enough that I thought he'd hear me.

Oh, but he did. And in three strides he was back up the stairs.

He was on me before I could barely take a breath, his body flattening mine into the brick wall. His mouth hot, hungry, and demanding against my neck, along my shoulder, and up to my ear, where he whispered, "Give me your lips."

I wanted nothing more than to pull him into the shadows and have my wicked way with him.

Why can't you? a voice whispered in my head. *You deserve this.*

I put my hand under his chin to stare into those beautiful eyes before I took those beautiful lips. Oh my goodness, his lips. Soft and strong, they felt the same, they tasted the same. He kissed me crazy once, then twice, then what felt like a thousand times, and still not enough.

"I didn't realize how much I missed you. Missed your mouth," he purred, frantically angling me up the stairs.

"Marcello," I sighed, my lips tangled with his. There was nothing in the world like kissing this man. And I wanted more than ever to kiss him for hours without a care in the world, reacquaint myself with every contour and plane of his exquisite mouth.

But this reunion was anything but relaxed. This was nine years, *nine years*, of going without this kind of passion.

With a thud, my back hit Daisy's front door. We fumbled against each other, laughing and still kissing, as he held both of my hands above my head in one of his. His other hand quickly untucked the hem of my shirt, slipping beneath with ease. I gasped into his mouth as his fingers danced along my rib cage. I needed this, oh, God I needed him! I needed his hands on my body more, now, in this instant. My gasp turned quickly into a groan, spurring on his movements as his fingers slid underneath the edge of my bra, smooth and rough, and I loved it.

I was pushing my body toward him while trying to loosen his grip on my hands. I wanted to touch him back. To thread my hands into his hair, to hold his face in my hands while he panted heavily against my skin, but he wouldn't ease up.

When he finally did let go, I overshot my mark and lost my balance, sending us both bumping into the wide-mouthed planters on Daisy's porch. They clattered and smashed against the wrought-iron railings before cracking against the steps.

Within seconds, Daisy popped out of the window and looked over at us, laughing.

"Oh, hey guys. What's going on? Aw, I liked that planter."

Marcello leaned heavily against me, resting his forehead in the crook of my neck, and I could feel him smiling against my skin. "Daisy, *cara*," he said, his voice muffled. "I will replace the pot. *Buona sera*."

She began to hum before disappearing into the window.

Marcello took a minute to help me straighten my clothes. I watched him smooth my blouse with painstaking care. He was quiet, thoughtful while he took care to make sure I was put back together after being wonderfully ravaged. Maybe it was a reflection of what had just happened or perhaps what we both knew would happen if he stayed.

I took his hand from the edge of my shirt and brought it to my cheek, loving the feeling of warmth against my skin.

"When can I see you again?" he asked when I leaned in to kiss him again. A light brush of my lips quickly turned into another deep, searching kiss.

"Avery, when?" he begged, kissing my lips, my cheeks, forehead. "When?"

My brain was fuzzy, kiss addled, and blank. "Soon," I said between kisses. "I promise. It needs to be soon."

With another quick peck, he said, "Soon." With a wink, he slid down the railing and disappeared around the corner, whistling the whole way.

———

WITH THE WEEKEND UPON US, I danced barefoot into the kitchen, humming a tune I'd heard at the pizzeria yesterday. I didn't know what it was, but it was going to be my new cheery go-to song.

"Good morning, best friend," I sang, clinking the cups to the beat in my head. I grabbed a wooden spoon and the coffee tamper and began my own rhythmic beat on her countertop while shaking my ass at Daisy.

She was sitting at the counter, coffee in hand, waiting.

"Someone is feeling good this morning, sorry it's technically afternoon. Singing through the pain?"

"The pain? Whatever do you mean?" I replied as the shiny espresso monster roared to life.

"You had my door knocker digging into your back last night. I figured you'd be sore. I can see that your lips got a workout." She snickered.

Last night as I passed the hall mirror on the way to bed, I studied my face. Sure enough: my lips were very pink and swollen. My head whipped around and I pretended to glare. "Just how long were you watching us?"

"I peeked outside just as he was charging back up the sidewalk. Good lord that was sexy. He swept you up and pinned you to the door in one swoop! I was fanning myself while I was pretending not to watch."

"It was pretty great," I admitted, running my fingertips across my lips just thinking about it. But something was bothering me. "I have a confession to make."

She was reading the paper and peered at me over the top. "Yes, dear child. Confess."

I made a face. "That's beyond creepy and I'm guessing sacrilegious."

With a shrug, she folded the paper and set it down. "Sit down and talk to Dr. Daisy."

"I'm serious. I feel like . . . I don't know . . . I'd feel better if I made it official."

"Made what official?"

"My sins. All of my *good lord look what I did now; tell me it's okay*. Do I pick one of the ninety-five thousand churches to confess in, or is Rome just so holy that you yell your sins outside at the sky and wait for judgment to befall you?"

Throwing her head back, she groaned. Loudly. "You're so dramatic. Loosen the clutch on those pearls, will you? What is this, Doomsday? You went out with a hot guy who you have a history with. What could you possibly have to confess? That you're enjoying your time with Marcello? That you're loving your life for the first time in ages? That you're sketching again? Please explain this to me, because I don't understand why you feel bad, when Daniel is dipping his tiny dick into all of fucking Boston."

"We don't know that he's sticking his . . . dick . . . into all of fucking Boston," I muttered. And I wasn't going to say tiny, because it wasn't, poetic justice aside. Normal sized? Yes. Boring? Yes. Tiny? Sigh. No.

"Well, we don't know that he isn't, do we? So you might as well get yours while he's getting his, because of course he's getting his and—"

Frustrated, I stood quickly, bumping the table and sloshing her coffee over the edge of the blue cup. "That's exactly my point! I don't want to be Daniel! Don't you see, if I get mine, doesn't that make me just as bad?"

"You're not cheating, Avery. You're separated—practically divorced. You're like . . . divorced adjacent. A piece of paper just needs to be signed for you to be officially free and back on the market."

"I don't know." My stomach was in knots. "Maybe it's because I feel like I shouldn't be enjoying myself right now? Shouldn't I feel worse about all of this?"

She threw her hands in the air. "Why? *He* cheated. Not you."

That was the thing, though. This little sticky sticking point. I had cheated. Years ago. So was I mad that Daniel had cheated? Yes, but was I more mad that it made us the same?

Ugh.

But when I cheated on Daniel with Marcello . . . oh my God I'd do it again in a second.

Daisy was still talking. "You're picking up the shitty cards he dealt you. So please don't put yourself in the same category as that crap weasel."

That made me chuckle. "Crap weasel? Wow, you're not kidding."

"Let me ask you this, if you went back to Boston today and he said he was sorry and he still loved you and he'd never cheat again, could you forgive him?"

There it was. Probably the single most important question about the single most important relationship in my entire life. And I knew the answer immediately.

"No," I said simply, and I knew then without any shadow of a doubt that no matter what he said or did, I'd never forgive him.

"Then you shouldn't feel guilty. A piece of paper does not a marriage make, Avery."

"You're right."

"And to be clear, I love you, but I will kick your ass down the Spanish Steps if I hear you feeling guilty again."

Then I wouldn't say it out loud again. I was grateful for her input, but I still couldn't say with all sincerity that the guilt over what I might be getting up to in Rome while my divorce was still being hashed out was over just because my best friend snapped her fingers. I did feel better for actually saying it out loud, though. Kind of.

144 ALICE CLAYTON *and* NINA BOCCI

A few hours later we were both getting ready to head out. Daisy was meeting up for dinner with some friends she made from a project she worked on months ago. "I feel like all I do here is eat, sketch, paint, sketch, eat, walk, and sometimes sleep. Is that wrong?" I asked, smoothing on my lipstick. "I was emailing my parents and it read like instructions for a retired person's handbook."

"If that's wrong, who the hell wants to be right?" Daisy answered, stepping into another pair of killer stilettos. I still don't know how she does it with all those cobblestones.

"I've got to mix it up a bit, though. More tours or more art groups."

"What about the art group from the campo? The class you saw when you first got here?"

"Way ahead of you. I actually spoke with the woman the other day. I'm going to start with them soon. I just have to buy a few more brushes."

"Excellent. I'll hang everything up that you bring home."

"You're like my mom when she used to hang up my artwork on the fridge. She did that until I graduated BU, by the way . . ."

"Speaking of, how are the parents?" she asked.

"Speaking of, they're good. Retirement suits them perfectly. I have to call soon, though; I can tell they're getting antsy. There's only so long I can dodge an actual conversation, although you should see the detail in some of my mom's emails. She said they've seen Daniel's parents at the club several times since I split, but there hasn't been an actual Daniel sighting. Which is surprising, since he practically lived there."

That was true, he was always way more into the scene than I was, even growing up and going with my family.

"I'm sure *his* mother's head exploded when *your* mother told them where you are."

"That's why she wants to talk. To find out some details to lob back at her when Bitsy starts throwing her perfectly manicured shade."

Time to change the subject. I pulled my travel guide from my tote. "Speaking of the Spanish Steps, I've decided to venture there today."

"Look at you, Lewis and Clark-ing all over Rome. I'm so proud." She wiped a fake tear from her eye. "Try the bus, it's super easy."

FAMOUS LAST WORDS.

It's super easy didn't include telling me about the metal box next to the driver that looked like a pay phone but without a receiver. Or that the driver didn't accept cash. Or that you had to buy your tickets before getting on the bus. After several near misses, however, and a delightful exchange where an old lady smelling like a rosemary bush told me exactly where to get off, and not in a nice "I'll give you actual directions" way, I finally figured it out. And after all that, it was like a five-minute ride! Ah well.

Once off the bus, however, it was surprisingly easy to find on foot. I just followed the well-placed signs that directed pedestrians to various landmarks.

I reached the Spanish Steps just as the sun was beginning to set behind them. They were filled with people eating, painting, and talking. I took a seat and pulled out my phone to take some pictures.

Then I had an idea. Turning the camera around on myself, I snapped a quick photo and sent it to Marcello before I could second-guess myself. It was a pretty good picture—the sun lit up my hair in all its wild curls, and I knew he'd love it. I looked happy and more relaxed than I'd been in ages.

His response dinged back immediately. "*Bellisima.*"

CHAPTER 10

WHEN MONDAY ROLLED AROUND, I offered to take Daisy out for lunch.

"So, where are we going for lunch? You're buying, so I'm thinking expensive. Daniel can afford it."

"And he hasn't shut off the Amex yet. Out of guilt, I'm sure," I agreed. "I saw a spot on the way over here; they had these enormous seafood towers in the window. One would be enough for both of us."

"Then we should totally get two," she pronounced, sticking her tongue out at me when I rolled my eyes.

"What's this?" I asked, picking up a sticky note that had a to-do list scribbled on it. She glanced over and smiled. "I was going to bring it up at lunch. I have to go to Amsterdam."

"Good lord, I am jealous of your life," I admitted, and jotted down, *find a sexy Dutchman to play hide the stroopwafel with.*

She snorted. "That's a pretty good idea, but they're sticky."

"Sticky isn't bad. It could be really, *really* good."

"God you're obnoxiously happy when you've got a crush."

Her phone rang and she answered, "*Ciao. Si.* Sure, sure, come on down. *A presto.*" As she hung up, she said, "Sorry, this'll just take a minute. Maria's on her way down; she's all worked up about something."

"A problem?" *Something I could help with?*

"Possibly. We're working on a villa in Grottaferrata, and the owner has already made it clear he wants no delays. Zero."

"Can't you just hire someone else?"

"You'd think, right? But since everything here is historical, everyone who's qualified to do that kind of work is always booked up."

"Everyone *is* booked up!" came a voice from the doorway. "Joe is tied up at the Lateran job, and Constance is already running back and forth between the little convent in Naples and the house in the Mont Sacro. Philippa is working at Palazzo Doria. And Franco! If I could count how many wives, mothers, and girlfriends that *sciupafemmine* has had while doing a restoration job for us, I'd run out of hairs on my head! And he's booked anyway. I've got him working on a tapestry at a monastery at Santa Lucia, so he's ready to burst!"

She suddenly realized there was someone else in the room. "Sorry, so sorry, he's a wonderful restoration artist, but honestly, he can't keep his paintbrush out of everyone's palette."

"I've got an almost-ex-husband who has the same problem." I laughed. *I laughed?* Huh.

"So, until I can track down a replacement for him, or find someone to run the department while I take on the project myself, then your villa and your frescoes will have to wait," she told Daisy. *Ask me. Ask me. Ask me.*

Daisy shook her head. "Waiting isn't really an option right now." *Ask me. Ask me. Ask me.*

"Well, it's the only option we have. I'm not using one of the interns on a project of that magnitude. Those frescoes are eigh-teenth century, very delicate and—"

"Have you stabilized the plaster yet?" I chimed in.

"Stabilized?" Maria shared a glance with Daisy, who was si-lent, listening.

"With lime. Has it already been injected?"

"No, we haven't even begun the restoration yet."

My mind was racing. "Is it water damage? Humidity change?"

"Leaking roof," she answered.

"And the colors—flaking or just dull?"

"Both. Have you worked on frescoes before?"

"Art history major, minor in conservatorship. I did my senior year in Barcelona, working in the catacombs, restoring the mu-rals in the central court." I raised an eyebrow. "Eighteenth cen-tury."

I LITERALLY DANCED DOWN the hall in the direction of Mar-cello's office. Daisy had some loose ends to tie up with Maria, so I took my bad-ass self on a mission to find Mr. Architect and tell him my good news as "Walking on Sunshine" played in my head.

A job, an actual job, helping to restore a mural in Italy! This would easily last longer than a day. I just happened to be in Dai-sy's office at the exact moment that there was a mural crisis, a crisis that would require the specific methodology that I had happened to study in college, using a protocol that I was uniquely qualified to perform. Though I was a bit rusty, formulas and techniques were already flooding my brain, my fingers al-ready itching for the tools I'd need, my hands already remember-ing what it would feel like to hold them once more.

Hey, Universe? Mad props!

I danced the last few steps to Marcello's office sporting an ear-to-ear grin, feeling the overwhelming urge to grab him and kiss him as I told him my good news. And maybe grab his tight bum a little bit.

I saw him through his glass door, seated behind a massive desk, piles of paperwork all around, and architectural models arranged on every work surface imaginable. He was on the phone, speaking quickly, eyebrows furrowed, mouth frowning when he wasn't firing back at whoever was on the other end of the line. I knew that expression, and I knew that tone of voice: frustration bordering on anger.

But when he was fired up, he was lethally sexy. There were times in Barcelona when I'd deliberately pick a fight, just to get fucked wild.

"Angry Italian words!" That's what I heard anyway. He slammed the phone down, muttering under his breath as he ran his hands through his hair.

"Bad timing?" I asked, peeking my head around the corner, along with one artfully curved leg.

There is nothing in the world better than being the reason that someone's entire face changes. His eyes lightened, then brightened. His lips bowed, and then arched upward. He leaned forward in his chair, his eyes dipping down to my ankle turned out just so in my kitten heels, drifting up along my calf, my knee, the bit of thigh peeking out of my little black dress.

"Avery." He tilted his head, curious. "What are you up to?"

"I'm visiting," I said, walking slowly toward his desk. "I have a lunch date with Daisy."

"Ah, a date."

I smirked. "Yes, we're very serious." Emboldened by the day I was having, I perched just on the edge of his desk and crossed my legs. Marcello leaned back in his chair, tugging at his tie a bit, a slow grin beginning to creep across his face. "I've got news."

"News?" he asked my knee, unable to keep his eyes from wandering.

"Mmm-hmm." I crossed my legs again.

"Let's hear this news." This was directed at the freckle three fingers above my left knee.

Ask me how I know it's three fingers.

"I got a job."

I know it's three fingers because when he used to tug me to the edge of the bed and lift my leg high over his shoulder, his strong fingers were wrapped around the back of my knee. And the span of skin between my kneecap and my freckle was exactly three fingers.

"You got a job, *here?*"

"Well, technically, I'm volunteering again. Since you know, no work visa. That villa your firm is working on in Grottaferrata. Maria needed someone to help out with a mural that needs some detail work done, and it's exactly what I used to do in—"

"—the catacombs," he finished.

Having someone be able to finish my sentences, especially with a word like *catacombs*? Priceless.

I clapped my hands, unable to contain my squeal any longer. "I got another *job!*"

Without a backward glance, I jumped off the desk and right onto his lap. His arms immediately came around me, cuddling me close, sharing this moment with me. It didn't matter that he knew very little of the particulars of my life since we'd separated, he didn't know the details of how lost I'd really been all these years. All he knew was that I was excited to work on something like this again, and he was thrilled because I was thrilled.

And he was clearly proud.

"Does this mean you will be staying longer?" he asked, running his hands up and down my back. Now that his hands were on my body, they were restless.

"Yes, I'm staying longer," I answered, shifting on his lap when I heard the voices carrying down the hallway. Glancing back toward the glass door, I began to pull back but he held firm.

"No one will disturb us," he assured me, tipping my chin up. "I like this . . . longer."

"Think you can handle it?"

He didn't answer. Because his lips were now on mine. He kissed one side of my mouth, and then the other, barely brushing my skin. I hummed into his skin, flying high from his touch now, along with my news.

He kissed me again and again, his hands sliding lower, running one down my leg where I kicked it up, pointing my toes and giggling. His lips tickled at the corner of my jaw, and just as his hand began a path back up my leg, back up to somewhere not even close to being decent in the workplace, I heard Daisy's laugh.

We quickly scrambled to put ourselves right, so that when she came sailing through the door saying, "Did you hear the good news? Avery is the new Franco!" all she saw were two people sitting with a desk between them and innocent smiles on their faces.

CHAPTER 11

I WAS NERVOUS, but my giddiness was defeating the butterflies. I had a job!

It wasn't glamorous, exciting, or paid, but it was mine. Earned by merit, education, and perhaps a wee bit of nepotism since I was best friends with the boss, but it felt *good*.

I floated home like I was starring in my own Disney movie. I held doors for strangers, bought a sandwich for a homeless man on the corner—who turned out not to be homeless but a hipster—and sang my way to Daisy's.

My home for the foreseeable future.

I needed to Skype my parents to tell them I was staying longer than I thought . . .

After two quick rings, my father's forehead greeted me.

"Dad move the laptop a bit," I instructed.

As he adjusted it, he said, "I miss the days when you just called someone on the phone; none of these bells and whistles."

My mother came in behind him, waving daintily at the screen. "Avery, how good to see you! You look outstanding," she cheered, sitting gracefully on the arm of his leather desk chair. "Italy suits you."

Dad nodded in agreement.

They both looked happy. He beamed when she rested her hand on his shoulder. She blushed when he lifted her hand to kiss it.

I thought this virtual catchup would be strained, awkward between us. At least it felt that way, given the nature of their emails since I'd arrived. Tone could be hard to decipher, especially when your mother was using absolutely zero punctuation.

"So tell me." Mom was fiddling with her diamond anniversary watch, something she did when she was anxious. "How is everything going?"

Dad chimed in, "Have you been sightseeing? Are you being safe? Is Daisy keeping an eye on you? I'd hate to have to speak with her father," he teased.

"Everything is fine, Mr. Bardot!" Daisy chirped from the kitchen. "Did you tell them yet?" she asked, squeezing into the laptop's frame. "Aren't you excited!"

"Shhh." I pushed her away playfully.

"Tell us what?" they asked together, both now leaning too far forward into the screen.

Daisy headed back into the kitchen, while I was left to face the foreheads.

I sighed. I wanted to build up to it. Ease them into the idea that I was contemplating staying here. For a while. The more I thought about what was in Boston, or what wasn't in Boston, the less thrilled I was to return. Them, I would miss. The rest, well couldn't I have that here?

Marcello aside, I needed something for me. A tether that kept me grounded. Happy.

Maybe that'd be him, or maybe this was just another flash that would burn hot. Either way, I had an opportunity that I didn't have before and I didn't know if I could let it go. If I *should* let it go.

"Things here are great," I started. "It's every bit as beautiful as I'd imagined."

"Spoken like a true artist," my father said.

"Funny you should mention that." I cleared my throat again. "You know that Daisy's an architect and she's pretty high up with her firm."

"Yes," they said in unison.

"Well, I was there visiting today, and a position for someone with my qualifications came up. It's volunteer, but it's perfect for me. Right place at the right time, and all that."

"Working in Rome?" Mom asked, fiddling with her watch again.

I nodded. "Yes."

"It must feel good, being offered it. We know you've been missing that," Dad said, patting Mom's hand.

I nodded again, elation ballooning in my chest. "I did a little bit of work for them already while I was here. It was a vase." That turned out to *not* be *just* a vase. "Something else came up, more time consuming. Difficult. Really specialized."

Then Mom said, "You're not taking it are you? What would you do? Live there? For how long?"

"Well, I was thinking that I could—"

"I'm all for finding yourself after divorcing, especially after what Daniel did to you. But, sweetie, your home is here. In Boston."

"Of course it is, Mom. That's not what I'm saying—"

"I knew this would happen if you went to Rome, I just knew

it! What's next? Traipsing all over the world like Daisy does? What kind of life is that?"

"Actually, Mom, her life is pretty great and—"

"What about meeting someone else? Getting married again someday, hmm? Something less . . . *rushed* this time. What about starting another"—her voice got weaker—"a family?"

"Whoa, hang on, Mom; I'm not even divorced yet! Getting married again is not even on my radar, and the rest, well the rest . . . I want to work as an artist. I miss the rush of adrenaline I got from finishing a sketch or creating a new piece. Remember how I would float home from class and couldn't stop smiling? And Dad used to say I was all dreamy? There's a lot of smiling and floating and dreaming here."

My parents exchanged a look.

"I need to get Avery *Bardot* back. I don't want to just be someone's wife out of obligation. And if the rest comes, well, then it comes."

Mom huffed, "What's wrong with being a wife and a mother?"

She looked hurt, her eyes sparkling with unshed tears. Damn it.

"Absolutely nothing, Mom. I just need to figure out what I want first this time and really let myself have it. And this is a great shot at that."

Dad patted her hand. "She needs this, dear. You know it and I know it. Besides, we can always visit. Right, Avery?"

I breathed a grateful sigh of relief. Of course they both wanted the best for me. "I can't wait for you to visit! I'll make a list of places for you to check out online. You'll lose your minds over the food, the landscapes, and the shopping." I dangled the final carrot for my mom to focus on.

"I just worry about you, Avery," she said, putting on a brave face. "I don't want you to get hurt."

———————

MY FIRST DAY OF WORK felt like my first day of kindergarten. *Would they like me? Would I make friends? Would I destroy the eighteenth-century frescoes and be deported?*

It was a very advanced kindergarten class . . .

I bought a bewildering array of bus maps, highlighted the best and fastest route out to Grottaferrata, and bought my weekly ticket from the tobacco shop down the street. It felt official. I was ready for work. Something I hadn't done in almost a decade.

Nine years is a long time to be away from something. To be missing that passion that you felt every day when you really loved what you did. I was ready. More than ready, and I couldn't help but feel that this was my second chance. My new start, and I sure as hell wasn't going to waste it.

With a tote filled with a sketchbook, pencils, and some other necessities, I was off and waiting at the bus stop. I even packed myself a lunch. My journey to work wasn't without a slight mix-up, of course. I was lost in my thoughts, doodling an image of Marcello's shoulders in the book on my lap, and I almost missed my stop.

Maria was there waiting for me when I arrived. "As I said, we didn't do any of the tests yet. This is a big job, Avery. I need a detailed plan from you first, your list of recommendations, and your best estimation on the time needed. We'll discuss it with the office. For today, cleaning tests are really the only thing that you have time for."

The area had already been taped up with the plastic covering, the scaffolding was still in place, and tall stands topped with work lights were spaced out around the area. I wondered what was in store for me behind the curtain. I saw from the project schedule she'd given me that we were already a few days behind with the delays over finding a restorer.

I set up shop in my little corner of the villa. Tools, brushes, long Q-tips, pails, and clean rags were spread out. My chair was puffy and padded for when I needed it, but for now, I sat on the floor and stared up at the wall.

What was under there? I wondered. Pulling out my notebook, I began my list. Overpainting dominated most of the wall. It looked like someone tried to remove it themselves, leaving some damaged areas. Taking pictures of the spots in question, I kept a record of them for reference. They'd need more time, care, and delicate touches.

With pastel, I drew a section over my testing area in five quadrants to show the levels of overpaint and damage.

I detailed my report, including the cleaning process and how it would involve swelling the top layers of paint and then lifting them away from the wall. Layer by layer in what was sure to be painstakingly time-consuming work, we would finally get to the last layer of paint that would have to be dissolved with natural solvents as to not further damage the painting beneath it.

After that, we'd varnish and touch up any spots that needed it before a final sealer was applied. Given the size of the wall and the length and width of the mural on it, we were looking at what was at least two weeks' worth of work.

———

WHEN MARCELLO CALLED AROUND MIDDAY, I was bursting with pride.

"I love everything about this job."

"I want to hear it all." It was hard to hear him; I'd forgotten he was at a construction site today. Loud Italian screaming mixed with loud Italian noise didn't make it easy for me to explain my morning. But I gave it a shot, gushing on and on about the people I'd met, the detailed frescoes I was working on, and how I'd already found three new restaurants I was dying to try in the neighborhood.

He chuckled, shouting something at a worker before what sounded like a door closing. "I'm proud of you. You are like a true Roman. Now, if I could only get you to use a Vespa."

"Nope, no way, no how. Riding on one of those is one thing, driving is something completely different."

"Just think of how much faster you'd get there," he explained, while I popped biscotti into my mouth.

"No way," I mumbled, thinking about me zipping in and out of traffic with a little red helmet on.

I looked out the arched windows onto the courtyard below and counted fifteen scooters. Clearly I was the only person here with a problem with the zippy little bastards.

"Are you busy?"

"Not now. I'm taking a break and reading up a bit on this villa. The family had documents from previous owners lying around that are fascinating."

"Like what?"

I tucked the phone closer to my mouth and whispered, "Did you know someone was murdered here? A few someones, apparently, but the bodies were never found!"

My mind went to Edgar Allan Poe's "The Casque of Amontillado," where an Italian man buries his former friend alive behind a wall in his wine cellar. I made a mental note to be extra careful with the wine cellar's frescoed wall.

"I can hear how excited you are," he purred, and all thoughts of Poe went out the window. "Tell me, what do you plan to do later?"

During the ride from my bus stop to the villa earlier this morning, I had concocted a plan. After passing an incredible market on the way in to work this morning, I also spotted a cheese shop, a wine shop, and a bakery, all within thirty steps of the bus stop.

"I was thinking of making dinner tonight."

"Dinner?"

"Mm-hmm, Daisy's flying out tonight, I'll be alone." I held my breath. "Want to come?"

"Just tell me what time," he replied.

I told him anytime after seven and hung up with a secret smile on my face.

"I MIGHT USE YOUR LUGGAGE. It's so much nicer than mine," Daisy teased, running a hand across the leather. She flicked open the lock and examined the smooth interior. "Definitely using it. Then it guarantees you'll really be here when I come back."

"Of course I'll be here." I blinked at her innocently. "I'd never leave without my Vuitton luggage."

She slapped me on the arm. "I'm serious. I travel so much, but I've never had someone waiting for me when I got back. It's kind of nice."

Daisy the globetrotter was off on a late flight to Amsterdam tonight, bidding on her next project. Who knew when she'd be back. Just last night I was raving about her nomadic lifestyle, but this put her life into a new perspective for me. Sure she had work friends here. but what's left of her family was back in Boston, and her visits back to the States had gotten less and less frequent over the years.

"Makes you want to find a nice gorgeous Italian man to settle down with, doesn't it," I said, arching my eyebrow at her.

"I think you've got the nice and gorgeous on lock. I'm in no hurry for either. Besides, I've got you. Speaking of nice and gorgeous, any plans while I'm gone? You've got a lot of nonwork hours to fill. Whatever will you do?"

I evaded, not because I didn't want to tell her, but because I didn't want to jinx anything. "Subtle. I was thinking of some day trips; Florence, Bologna, maybe Milan for a weekend." I paused, hearing the actual words I was saying. "What is this life?"

"Don't question it. You deserve every ounce of happiness that this country brings you. P.s., I hear Marcello loves Milan."

"What's another word for subtle?" I asked. "Hey, no way!" I cried as she starting pulling my matching duffel bag from my closet. "If you're taking all my fantastic luggage, I'm keeping this."

"For weekend trips—"

"For weekend trips," I said, giddy at the thoughts of planning them. I wasn't limited to Italy, either. I could revisit Spain. Pop over to Paris. Explore Greece. The sky was the limit. I just hoped that he'd be free—and interested—to join me. But what would that entail? I know what weekends away with Marcello used to mean: lots and lots of naked times. Is that still what it meant? Was I ready for that?

I was pulled out of my thoughts by Daisy, packed and ready to go.

"Don't get into any trouble while I'm in Amsterdam," Daisy teased, grabbing her purse and keys. "I worry, leaving you home all alone."

"I'll be fine, Mother."

"Whatever will you do while I'm away . . ."

When the door clicked shut, I jumped from the couch and danced to the table to find my phone to call Marcello. I danced, shimmied, and sang his name. There may have been some humming. It may have been "Let's Get It On."

"I can hear you," she shouted from the stairwell. "You can at least have the decency to wait until I leave before calling your boooooyfriend."

I swung open the door. With wide-eyed innocence, I said, "How'd you know I was calling your dad?"

She mock-gagged. "Unfair!"

"Be safe. Love you!"

When she disappeared around the corner, I closed the door, leaning against it. The phone was clutched in my hands and my nerves were climbing like vines to wrap themselves around my lungs. I had a pretty good idea of what might happen when he came over, and for the life of me I couldn't find one reason to *not to do exactly that*.

I took one more breath, then called to let him know that Daisy had left the building.

With barely one ring, he answered with an out of breath, "*Pronto.*"

"Hey, am I interrupting you?"

He cleared his throat. "Hey to you, and no, you are not interrupting me. How are you?"

"I'm good. Uh . . . Daisy just left."

"I see," he said quietly.

"Do you still want to come over? We could you know . . . hang out."

"Hang out?"

"Yeah, you know hang out. Board games, Netflix, and chill."

"Board games?" I could hear the smile in his voice.

"And dinner, you didn't forget I said I'd make dinner."

"I have not."

Everything south of my teeth clenched, tightened, and sang "Hallelujah" in anticipation. "I went shopping this afternoon. I have ingredients."

"I like ingredients."

"How's an hour? That'll give me time to get things going in the kitchen." *And reshave my legs, loofah my entire body. Slather myself in that blood orange lotion I bought at the fancy Italian soap shop. As you do.*

"That might be a problem."

My heart sank. I didn't consider there being a hiccup. "Oh, okay," I said, trying to sound unaffected. "Just come over whenever you can."

Two knocks rapped at the door.

I jumped, dropping the phone to the floor with a clatter. "No way." I gasped, picking it up and tiptoeing to the door. "Tell me this isn't you."

He let loose a low chuckle. "I would be lying."

I'd just taken my hair down from the braids I'd been wearing all day. I'd borrowed a shirt from Daisy to wear; it was a size too small, so old it was practically see-through, and happened to be covered in cartoon lobsters. To say nothing of my boxers; yes, old-man boxers that I wear around *when I am alone.*

Not exactly the seduction I had planned. And yet, I didn't care.

I tossed the phone and flung the door open. His warm brown eyes went wide when he saw me.

I didn't think or consider; I just jumped, wrapped, and held on while he pinned me to the door. He was all grasping arms and seeking fingers, and I was melting.

CHAPTER 12

IT WAS SCARY HOW MUCH I wanted this. Nine years later, and it was as if no time had passed. That feverish undercurrent was ever present, and thankfully it wasn't just me who felt it. Marcello wasn't holding back, kissing, squeezing, sliding over every inch he could reach.

"What is this you are wearing?" he asked between searing kisses, gripping the waist of my shorts.

I felt scattered, trying to remember any thought I had before he kissed me. What underwear did I have on? Does the bra even match? He kissed along my collarbone before nipping at the crook between my neck and my shoulder. *Lord*, don't kiss me there. *Fuck*, my thoughts were lost again.

"I had plans, lingerie, seduction. These are—"

"*Perfecto*," he answered, and slipped his hands beneath the shorts to cup my bottom. He just held them there, ten perfect pressure points. His arms trembled beneath me. "You don't need to seduce me. I wanted you again the moment you walked up to the table."

"Marcello," I whispered, and in response his hands squeezed *just so.*

He rocked his hips up slowly, dangerously. "Give me a minute. Don't move," he breathed against my neck.

Staying there for a moment, his chest rose and fell with shuddering breaths. My muscles were bunching, pulled so tight from being still. It was a delicious burn. I could feel him ready and impatient, and as much as I wanted to savor every moment of this reunion, I didn't want to wait.

Pulling away from my shoulder, he pressed our foreheads together, as his body tensed with each breath. "*Tesoro,*" he began, sounding nervous.

"What is it?"

Kissing me quickly, he took a deep breath and exhaled a quiet, "I want this. All of you, now. I know there are talks we need to have but I . . . if you are not ready or if there is something *else* stopping us . . . tell me. We can wait. We can wait." He finished, stumbling over the last few words.

I knew without a doubt he would have stopped then, no questions asked. He would help me get dressed and we'd carry on our night as if the past ten minutes never happened.

"I need this. You," I answered, and pulled his shirt over his head and tossed it onto a plant in the corner.

A surge lit him up from the inside out. "Thank God."

If possible, he became more eager, more harried, grasping and clutching. My legs locked around his waist, my hands twisted in his hair, and my lips touched, kissed, and tasted everywhere they could reach.

My back was against the door again with a thud, and that damn door knocker was there, biting into my skin. One of his arms held me while the other roamed, slipped, and brushed. He pulled the front of my shirt down, exposing my pink bra. He pulled back and took in the sheer fabric, muffling a curse against my chest.

"Hold on," he ordered, not giving me any time to react. He stepped over the threshold and kicked the door shut before pushing me against the window beside it. It was cool against my heated skin. *Perfect.*

Holding me with his hips, his hands snaked up between us until he gripped the top of the shirt—

"—wait, wait—"

—and tore. Tossing it off to the side to land on a lamp.

"That was Daisy's." I laughed, pulling my face away from his needy lips.

"I will buy her a new one."

I reached up and held his face in my hands. He turned his head to the side to kiss my palm once, then again, and held them there breathing deeply. It was a sweet gesture and such a strong contrast to the fevered kisses. I smoothed my hands over his shoulders, counting and remembering all the little freckles that were scattered across his bare skin. The scar on his shoulder had faded a bit since the last time I saw it, his body fuller and more muscular. My cheeks and chest were hot from staring at him. I reached down over his chest, then lower before gliding back up in a slow circuit.

My hands slid over his pecs, my thumbs rubbing just over his rib cage where he had a crop of tiny birthmarks. I realized just how much of his body I had memorized; there wasn't an inch I had forgotten. I tightened my legs at his waist while pushing at his shoulders so that I was at a slight angle.

His eyes were the darkest I'd seen them since arriving in

Italy. They were filled with a yearning that I missed. A want that I hadn't seen or felt in so long.

I wondered then what answers he was seeking.

But more than anything else, he looked like my lover from Spain. Felt like him, and made *me* feel like I was with him again. That feeling of us conquering the world was back.

"You are making me crazy," he said, moving us down the hallway.

"You're the crazy Roman who started kissing on me the second he came in the door. Or was it before you even got in?"

"I'll give you *get in*, which room?"

"I don't care." I gasped when his fingers slipped into my panties and cupped me, his thumb pushing against me *just so*. "Oh! *Dio mio.*"

He smiled against my neck, the prickles from his scruff tickling the sensitive skin there. "I can't wait," I insisted, wiggling my hips to prove my point.

He shook his head and repeated, "Which room?"

"Last door on the right."

My heart skipped as he carried me into my bedroom. He looked around the room before settling me on the tufted club chair in the corner.

Smiling down at me, he smoothed my hair off my face before reaching for his pants button.

I moved forward to stop him. "Let me."

My hands trembled, not from nerves but anticipation. Maybe he sensed my struggle, or maybe he was just as impatient as I was, but he brought his hands up and over mine to help. Together we unbuttoned his pants and slid them down before he kicked them off into the corner.

Marcello played soccer all his life and his legs showed it.

Toned, strong, and *just* the right amount of muscle. He must still play because he was just as fit as I remembered.

I toyed with the hem of his boxers, sliding my hands up and under, teasing. I loved the tightening of his muscles, the slight buck of his hips when I just barely brushed him.

"*Tesoro*, how you tease," he purred, reaching out to slide my bra strap down. He repeated it on the other side before tipping the bra cups forward so my breasts spilled out.

His fingers lightly brushed over my nipples, between my breasts, and down until he edged along the top of my panties.

"Do you remember our first time together?" he said, settling down on the hardwood to kneel between my legs. His hands rested on my knees, thumbs brushing along the sensitive skin.

I nodded, inching my body slowly down toward his. Judging by the wry smirk on his face, he was relishing my eagerness.

Marcello kissed my knee before slowly dragging his lips up my inner thigh. I was so tightly wound that it was taking everything within me not to snap. To push him down to the floor and sink down onto him.

"With the moon behind you like that? You look so much like that girl," he said between kisses against my thigh. Up, up higher with each kiss. "Wild hair, fiery eyes, and lips that would tempt any man," he whispered against me, *just there.* Just when I thought he couldn't stretch out the delicious torture anymore, he dropped one kiss against the silk covering me.

"Please," I begged, pushing forward against his lips.

With his hands under my bottom, he lifted me to his waiting mouth.

Mumbling against me, he stood quickly, picked me up, turned, and tossed me onto the bed.

I propped myself up on my elbows, quirking a finger for him to come closer. A wicked sparkle flashed in his eyes.

Leaning back along the bed, I loved the way my muscles stretched and drew his eyes, keeping him focused. He didn't care that my hair was wild or that my makeup wasn't perfect. Marcello only saw me.

"What do you want, Avery?" he asked, leaning forward to kiss one hip bone. Once, twice, three times before his lips danced across my stomach to the other. Strong fingers flexed and pressed. No thought, daydream, or fantasy compared to the feel of his callused fingers on my heated skin.

Sitting up, he smoothed my hair behind my ear and picked up a lock. Twisting a curl between his fingers, his eyes flickered to my mouth. "Tell me."

I swallowed, desperate to find the words. "You know what I want."

His chest rose and fell, fingers twirling the curl once more.

Pushing myself up, my fingers slid inside the waist of his boxers and down. His hips bucked. *Hurry.*

"I need to hear it," he said, smoothing his hands over my shoulders. Everywhere his fingers brushed, fire erupted over my skin.

"You. Just you," I said between peppering kisses over his stomach muscles. "Please."

With a tug, the panties were torn in two and tossed to the side. He laid his hand flat against my pubic bone, fingers spread wide with his thumb smoothing over me in maddening circles. Now keeping his thumb still, he dipped a finger inside me slowly, lulling me into a rhythm before thrusting in faster. One became two and his thumb just pushed and held.

He wasn't speaking. Just heavy breathing, small grunts here and there. I wanted more.

"Talk to me, Marcello," I asked, reaching up to touch his face.

"Say my name again," he whispered, kissing my fingertips.

He nibbled down my arm and across my chest and held on to me while he used his teeth along my breasts. His muscles were shaking as he kissed my belly.

"Marcello."

"Again."

Each time I repeated it, he'd ask for it again.

Until he confessed, "I missed hearing you say it when I made you come."

My head thudded back against the mattress when he hit the right tempo. Every fiber in me seized up and exploded around his fingers.

"That's my *tesoro*," he said tenderly, leaning up to kiss me again.

Tesoro. I remembered the word from our time together in Barcelona.

The moonlight slanted into the windows, the beams dancing across the bed over us. He just stared and smiled. "Avery," he said between kisses across my breasts. He placed his lips directly over my heart and spoke reverently just one word, "Tesoro."

"What does it mean?" I asked, holding his face and my breath, wondering what he would confess.

"Treasure."

To have him repeat it again, after all these years. After all the mistakes, it meant something. When he said it in Spain, there was a palpable shift in the relationship. It moved from summer fling to . . . Hope ballooned in my chest and I wondered, was history repeating itself?

Sliding off the bed, he rifled blindly through his pants and pulled out a condom.

"I want to memorize your body all over again," he said, fingers traveling over my body.

"I've missed this. You. So much," I admitted, pulling him over me.

He slid a pillow beneath my head and tucked both of our arms beneath it. With his hands holding mine and our lips just barely touching, he slid inside.

My gasp and his moan reverberated in the otherwise silent room.

With the moonlight on his face, I felt deep in my chest how much I had missed him. He wasn't slow or tender. Everything about his pace had become frenzied, powerful, and we were climbing. He was chasing our release with every thrust. Every grasp of his hands over mine made my body sing.

Marcello kissed me, bruising my lips with his intensity. A bite, then a peck, before his tongue swept into my mouth. He was reaching his end when his movements became more frantic. He pushed himself up onto his arms, muscles flexing before reaching one hand between us.

"Yes, yes," I chanted, my head shaking side to side. "That's it, Marcello."

"*Tesoro* . . ."

My hands reached up, cupping his face as I spiraled. He looked down, smiling, before dropping his lips to mine.

I was feeling the highest of highs when he collapsed next to me, just for a second before he scooted off to dispose of the condom. When he returned he flopped into bed, making sure to pull me into his side. This was familiar, too, the after. He always kept me near, making me feel so treasured. His *tesoro*.

He rolled me over to face him and brushed his lips against my neck, over my shoulder, and across my chest. Light, tender kisses that stirred a long-ignored need deep within me.

"When can we do that again?" I asked, brushing the drooping hair from his forehead. He was spent, smiling and so cute, I could barely take it.

———

IT'S FUNNY HOW YOU CAN become what you see every day. Since I'd arrived in Rome, I'd been observing couples in love, couples in lust, couples that had either just had all the sex or were on their way to having all of the sex. They were the ones draped around each other like sexy little jackets, the ones with their hands in each other's pockets and their lips on permanent meld. The couples where he seems fascinated with a lock of her hair and studies it as though it was the most incredible piece of art. The couples where she can't stop touching him, letting her fingers linger on his shoulder, his elbow, the back of his neck, that spot on his chest when she can feel his heart beating and she knows its beating faster because her hands are on his skin and isn't that the most adorable thing you've ever seen?

Well, it *was* the most adorable thing until Marcello and I hit the streets. We now held the title of Sexiest Couple in Rome.

Famished, we dragged ourselves from the apartment and walked a few blocks down to the neighborhood trattoria. We moved slowly, our steps in sync in a natural way. His arm was wrapped around my shoulder, cuddling me close to him like a blanket he didn't want to be without. My arm was around his waist, his hip bumping into mine with every step. He pushed me into a doorway to ravage my neck for one or fifteen minutes.

It was sloppy, all dreamy eyes and roving hands and quiet, contented sighs.

I'd been to this trattoria a few times with Daisy. Being here with Marcello felt totally different. The candles that seemed sweet and airy now felt sensual and dark and cozy. The tables pushed close together had seemed communal and quaint; now they were simply a reason to sit closer, skin to skin, tucked in to each other to conserve space. Everything on the menu even seemed sexier. Luscious strands of tagliatelle, looped in sensual curves around lusty tomatoes and spicy garlic.

Hungry? I was. For more Marcello.

Other than a few months in Spain with a certain neck ravager, I'd never felt comfortable sharing affection in public. But being with him again made me remember the sexier side of myself, the woman and not just the girl. I could feel every inch of my skin, my curves, every one of them this man had been intimately reacquainted with only a short while ago. My breasts pushed at my cotton shift; plumped by his kisses, nipped by his teeth, they were sensitive and just so very there. All the tiny scrapes along the inside of my thighs from his scruff, not to mention a tender spot that still throbbed with every heartbeat where he'd bitten down high on the inside of my left thigh while I cried out. Every part of my body felt alive, used in the best way possible, the way that it was meant to be used. For pleasure, mine and his.

He sighed while biting into a piece of crusty bread, mimicking the exact sigh he made when he slid into my body for the first time in years. Hearing it again made me warm all over.

"How do you feel?" he asked, pushing the strap of my dress

aside so he could drop a kiss on the exact spot where my neck met my shoulder.

Underneath the table, I placed his hand on my knee and slowly slid it up my thigh. "You tell me."

His eyes burned. His touch seared. I gasped as his fingertips ghosted higher along my skin, pressing and circling, underneath my dress now.

"You feel soft. And warm. And . . . oh, Avery," he murmured as I shifted in my chair, allowing him further access. Hidden under the tablecloth, he teased. And if it wasn't for the waiter bringing over glasses of Campari at that exact moment, I would've let him do more than tease.

"Did you ever think this would happen?"

"My hands in your panties in public? Well, almost in your panties." He grinned. So dangerous.

I leaned in, took his face in my hands, and kissed him, wet and hard, biting his lower lip, holding on to it for a second longer than I probably should. When I was done, I sat back in my chair. I could be dangerous, too. "I meant, this, us, here, together, earlier, all of it. Did you ever think it would happen?"

He fell silent, thinking. When he finally spoke, he seemed to be choosing his words carefully. "No, I did not. I never thought I would see you again." When he saw my face fall, he reached out and tenderly, so tenderly, brushed my cheek with his fingertips. "I didn't say I didn't think about you. I have, many times through the years. I wondered, where is she? Is she happy? Is she in love? Is she painting?" The faintest hint of hope flashed through his face. "Does she have children?"

I was struck with a sudden vision, walking hand in hand down the same streets we'd walked tonight. His other arm cradled a sleeping toddler, a toddler with my curly hair and Marcello's warm brown eyes. I walked beside his father, holding his hand, while the other rested on my belly, round and full. The force of this vision made me shiver, so fully formed and complete it was a wonder that my mind had never shared it with me before, keeping hidden the possibility of what my life might be like if this man, this right man for me, wandered back into it.

I hadn't let myself consider children again, not in years. What did it mean that I could envision it again, even for just a moment?

But before things could get too serious, that wolfish grin was back.

"I wondered if there was a man in your bed who could make you laugh right before he made you sigh."

"No," I answered honestly, laughing. Then sighing. To his great satisfaction. We finished our drink, asked for our meal to go, paid the man, and hurried home.

CHAPTER 13

I REMEMBER READING AN ARTICLE in a cooking magazine once about the art of the Italian meal. Everyone had their special recipes tucked away, of course, usually handed down generation to generation, but that in summertime the heat would keep many out of their kitchens. Taking advantage of the wonderful markets around every corner, people would leave the cooking to the experts when the stifling summer temperatures hovered above eighty-six degrees, and today had been no exception.

So I did what all good Romans did. I opted to let someone else cook. I cruised the market on the way home, scooping up container after container of prepared salads, roasted vegetables, a few different kinds of beautiful cheese, and a box full of decadent pastries. Schlepping everything home on the bus had been an adventure, but I'd managed it without spilling one morsel. Proud of myself for navigating the city, with packages no less, I allowed myself a little extra strut as I made my way into the courtyard of Daisy's apartment building, greeting neighbors like I'd been doing it for years.

Marcello was coming. Also, he'd be having dinner . . .

————————

THERE WAS A KNOCK at the door a few minutes past seven, just as I was slipping into a fresh linen dress, sleeveless and airy. I tucked a few flyaway hairs back up into my messy bun and padded to the door. Taking a final look at everything I'd set out, I smiled and opened the door.

"*Tesoro,* I—" he started to say, but then stopped as the door widened further and he could peek inside. "*Tesoro,*" he said again, his slow smile matching my own.

I'd lit candles, candles, and more candles. I'd practically cleaned out a stall or two at the market. Tealights, tapers, tall and fat and short and stubby—I'd set candles on every flat surface in the entire apartment and the effect was exactly as intended. I'd created a little wonderland, and who didn't look extra sexy in a wonderland lit by candlelight?

"Come in," I whispered, my pulse beginning to beat faster just for seeing him, my skin pebbling in anticipation of his touch.

"Beautiful," he told me, looking all around at the flickering light but only speaking when his gaze came to rest back on me. And what's this?

"You brought me flowers," I said as he handed me a nosegay of ruby-colored sweet peas and baby pink primrose, gathered with a bit of lace to hold them together. "You're spoiling me."

"You are meant to be spoiled," he replied, stepping into the apartment and closing the door. Reaching out, he gathered me into his arms, crushing me against his chest. "I missed you today." He bent his head, nuzzling my neck and inhaling deeply.

"You did?" Sighing, I wrapped my arms around him, twisting my hands into his hair, feeling the silky strands between my fingers.

I could feel him nodding against my skin. He dropped kisses along the column of my throat and up to my jawline, moving back along toward my ear. "I missed this face."

"This face?" I said, although to be fair it was more like a squeak. Now I could feel him smiling against my skin.

"This face," he echoed, dropping kisses on both of my cheeks. He continued kissing whatever he'd missed. "This mouth" kiss, "this neck" kiss, "this shoulder" kiss. His hands that were tight on my hips now moved down, slipping across my bottom and giving it a squeeze. "This beautiful *sedere*."

"Good God, did I miss listening to you speak Italian," I murmured in his ear, nipping at the skin just below. "You could make me come apart just with your voice."

Words, filthy words, words like *scopare* and *limonare* and *dolce figa* spoke to me in a voice that I'd dreamed of for years yet knew I'd likely never hear again outside of my own perfect memories. He kissed me stupid, pushing us, guiding us both back into the apartment and onto the couch, where my dress was promptly pulled up and my new lingerie was revealed.

"Woman, what are you wearing?"

I raised up on my elbows and looked at him innocently. "Oh, this?" I lifted my bottom and pulled the dress up and over my head, tossing it across the room so he could get the full effect.

Champagne-colored bra and panty set. Lacey. Ruffled. A little bit see-through in some places. A lot bit see-through in other places. Tasteful with a touch of cheeky. Exactly how Marcello liked me.

He licked his lips, eyes hungry. Just before he leaned down, he caught sight of the dining room table, set with plates and glasses, and the bottle of wine I had chilling in an ice bucket. He looked at me, then back at the table, then back at me again.

"*Tesoro,* you cooked, shouldn't we—"

"I didn't cook. I bought. I assembled. It can wait. Believe me, it can all wait."

"Ah yes, but . . ." At war, he continued to look back and forth until I uncrossed my legs and showed him the part that was exceptionally see-through.

"Marcello?"

His eyes never even flickered up to my face. I don't think he even tried, as a courtesy. "*Si?*"

"Wouldn't you love dessert first for a change?"

Turns out he did. And he had it three times before dinner . . .

———

"THE ARTICHOKES, they are very good."

"Right? I sampled a bit here and there, and these were too good to pass up." I passed a plate. "Try the green beans, they're fantastic."

"Mmm."

I loved hearing him make that sound. He'd made it only moments before, when he'd laid his head across my naked breasts, wrapping his arms around me tightly and sighing contentedly as I stroked his hair. All while he was still inside me. *Mmm* indeed.

After our impromptu "dessert" on the couch, we'd moved into the dining room for dinner. Wearing the button-down shirt he'd worn to work that day, I'd moved around the kitchen quickly, placing bowls and plates on the table filled with all the tidbits I'd picked up at the market. Marcello, blessedly naked from the waist up, opened a bottle of Gavi, filling our glasses and pausing only to drop a kiss on my collarbone as I passed by with a plate of vegetables. Or on my wrist as I set a wedge of pecorino down in front of him.

Or the space high on the back of my thigh just before it became my bottom when I bent over to retrieve a spoon I'd dropped.

Famished, we tucked into our assembled meal, sated . . . for now. That was the thing about Marcello and me, it was never enough. We could have sex for hours and hours, seemingly endless orgasms that stretched on an entire night and well into the morning. But when we woke? Hands were groping and hips were thrusting and it all began again. I was a different woman around this man. I *felt* more like a woman around this man, powerful and sexual and raw and wild. And as he licked a bit of lemon zest from his lower lip, crunching down on a green bean, I saw his eyes begin to darken once more. I knew this meal would be over quickly . . .

I ate with gusto, knowing I'd need the energy tonight.

IT'S AMAZING, WHEN YOU'RE IMMERSED in a new place, how quickly you begin to pick up the little things that make you a part of the scenery, rather than just observing it. When I arrived in Rome, I still craved a more American breakfast (eggs, bacon, pancakes, etc.), but now I ate my bit of pastry and drank my strong, nearly naked espresso standing up at the little bar in the window of a tiny shop with all the other Romans on their way to work.

To my relief, hearing and seeing the Italian language on a daily basis was beginning to pay off, and I found myself reading, more or less, the thousands of fliers that were posted all over town for various concerts, parties, exhibits, and countless other summertime activities.

And it was one of these fliers that I found myself reading

while waiting for the bus one afternoon after work. Advertising a concert series for the International Ensemble Chamber Music Festival at the Sant'Ivo alla Sapienza, a famous baroque church in the historic center, it appeared to be a popular evening activity for anyone who liked their music with a stunning courtyard backdrop.

I wanted to go. And I wanted to take Marcello.

"To a chamber music concert?"

I'd called him one night after work, thinking ahead to the weekend. Although originally I was hired to work only a few days a week, the frescoes were proving more difficult to restore than initially thought and I was putting in some serious overtime this week to bring the project in on time. Something that I was anxious to do, considering this was my first gig. By Friday night, the idea of relaxing under the stars and listening to some beautiful music while sitting next to a beautiful Italian man sounded like heaven.

I curled my knees under me as I sank onto the couch, exhausted after a long day but glad I could just pick up the phone and call Marcello like it wasn't a huge deal. "Sure, we used to go to concerts all the time in Barcelona. I thought it'd be fun. Looks like this Friday night it's a salute to Gershwin."

"And you are craving something extra American for some reason?" he teased, and it made me smile.

"You're not seriously picking on Gershwin, are you? And while I'm loving Roman life big time, I wouldn't say no to a Nathan's hot dog if someone put it in front of me." It was summertime, and I hadn't been to a summer society soiree at the club or the annual lobster bake and barbecue. Not complaining, but it was a different kind of summer for so many reasons. "Just say you'll go."

"Then we will go," he said, laughing. "Friday night?"

"It's a date."

———————

THAT FRIDAY I SPENT THE DAY with my frescoes. I was coming to know them so intimately.

Although from an artistic standpoint, they'd be categorized as "average," from my standpoint they were priceless. They spread across the interior as the basic wall covering. Depicting scenes from daily life in the eighteenth century, the murals were agrarian in nature: water wheels, olive trees, shepherds and their sheep.

And the colors! Rich golds, bright greens, blues the color of the Aegean—below the kitchen grease and candle smoke, the colors I was recovering were as vibrant as the day they were painted.

And here and there I'd find a flourish, not quite a signature, but a certain swirl that I was beginning to recognize as the scenes flowed one into the next. Had it been an artist, there may have been an actual signature, but back then this kind of work, beautiful and technically sound as it may be, would have been the work of a tradesman. Someone who wouldn't have been afforded the luxury of an actual commission, but certainly an artist in his own right, whoever he'd been. Hence, the flourish. I'd found it on day one while restoring a particularly festive scene of a butcher and his wares.

Some of the original paint had faded so significantly that it was only under a fine light and a pair of strongly magnified glasses that I could see the intention behind the lines, and recover it as best as I could. Between the hog being hoisted above the boiling cauldron and then the bristles being scrubbed off, there was a curious swirl of blue mixed into a scene that was composed entirely of reds and browns, yellows, and a bit of green to depict the hayfields in the background.

This swirl of blue appeared again in a scene of a gaggle of geese walking before a maid on their way to market, and once more in the corner of a field of ripe dusky olive trees. I'd begun to look for it, wondering about who it was that made his presence, however small and inconsequential it might have been, known to anyone who cared to look for it.

Who was he? What did he like? What did he love? Did he love his job, spending his days in some rich man's villa composing scenes of country peasant life? Did he dream of someday painting in a grander house, in a church, or even in the Vatican across town? Or was he simply a tradesman, happy to be working and putting food on his family's table and unable to conceive that a twenty-first-century woman dressed in denim overalls and pigtails with a device strapped to her arm linked to two tinier devices embedded near her eardrums would smile to herself as she uncovered another blue swirl as she hummed along to the tune of "Sure Shot" by the Beastie Boys.

Setting my tools down and stretching my back, I took a step back and regarded my work. Three quarters of the frescoes had been recovered and restored, and looked damn fine if I did say so myself. I was covered in drippy lime, fingers aching, skin cracked from the wet plaster drying repeatedly and taking every ounce of moisture from my hands along with it, and I couldn't remember a finer day.

"Why haven't you been doing this longer?"

Startled, I whirled around, finding Maria standing next to me and regarding my frescoes with a confused look on her face. I tugged the earbuds out, asking her to repeat what she'd said.

"I say, why haven't you been doing this longer? Or rather, all along?"

"Oh," I said, hitting pause on my music and scrunching up my nose. "Um, well, I took some time off after college and, well, got married, and I always planned to go back to work but there just never seemed to be a good time to go back and then—"

"Mmm-hmm." She nodded, stepping away from me and toward the work I'd been doing today. She scrutinized the colors, the depth, where I'd had to embellish and where I'd had to re-create almost entirely. She leaned close to the plaster, closer, so close I was afraid she'd come away with a coat of green on the tip of her nose.

It'd match the one I was sporting. I also liked to lean in.

"Mmm-hmm," she said once more, mostly to herself. I wanted to rock on my heels. I wanted to chew on my braid. But instead I stood up straight and waited for her critique.

"Very good, Avery." She nodded, casting me a sideways smile. "Very good."

I beamed! I'd come to realize that a *good* from Maria was the equivalent of an American *awesome!* A *very good*? I'd kicked some serious fresco ass today . . .

She began to walk away, but then turned just before she left. "You get married again if you want, but you don't stop doing this." She gestured to the wall. "Yes?"

"Yes," I answered, butterflies springing to life inside my belly. But right now wasn't the time to celebrate, it was time to get back to work . . .

―――――

". . . AND THEN SHE SAID, 'Very good, Avery,' in that quiet, stern way she has; you know how she can sound."

"I do. A *very good* is high praise from her," Marcello said, echoing my thoughts from earlier.

"I know!" I chattered, threading my arm through his as we walked down the street outside the concert. People were already lined up, mostly couples, but a few families here and there, and some tourists.

Tourists. I could spot them now.

"She told me I should keep on doing what I'm doing."

"And will you?"

I pondered this as he led me into the courtyard. "I don't know; I mean, I'd like to. I don't know if I can." He steered us toward the ticket line, but I patted my pocket. "Don't need to stand in line there, mister, I've got it covered."

"Covered?"

"Yep," I said, pulling the tickets out of my pocket. "I stopped by earlier this week and picked them up. I didn't want us to have to wait in line."

"You bought the tickets, yes?"

"I did," I answered, nodding toward an attendant who was tearing them and showing people to their seats. "Anyway, if the opportunity came up to do some more restoration work I would definitely be interested, but we'll have to wait and see what she says afterward. If she'd recommend me for another job." We arrived down toward the front, and I was pleased to see our seats were in the third row, pretty much right in the center. "Wow, I got us great seats, huh?"

"Great seats. Huh," Marcello echoed, pausing to brush them both off before allowing me to sit down. I knew that *huh*.

"What's the matter with the seats?" I asked him in a low voice, leaning close.

"There is nothing the matter with the seats," he replied, not taking his eyes from the stage. "I was planning on buying the tickets. I would also have gotten great seats."

"But I already bought them," I said, confused.

He *huh*'d again. "You bought the tickets."

"Why do I feel like there's something I'm missing?"

"You invited me to this concert, you should have let me buy the tickets."

"Wait, you're pissed because I paid?"

His jaw clenched. That meant I was right.

"Holy 1952, women are allowed to purchase concert tickets, they're even allowed to purchase tickets for their fella."

"You are making fun of me."

"A little bit." I placed my hand on his knee, patting it. "It's not a big deal. I bought the tickets not to supplant your masculinity, but because I didn't want to stand in that line, that line that's still as long as it was when we first got here, mind you, so look who had a great idea about buying tickets early?"

He frowned, finally looking down at me. "I would prefer to pay for things, for us, when we are out."

I shook my head. "I appreciate that, Marcello, and I'm sure that's the way things are done here, but if I want to do something nice for you, for us, even if that means shelling out a little cash here and there, I'll do it."

"But—"

I placed my finger over his lips. "I know you're used to getting your own way, and you likely still will, most of the time. But let this one go, okay? Let's just enjoy the music."

I watched his face as he listened to me, really listened to me and let my words sink in. My Italian man was old school, even more so than I realized sometimes. And I loved being taken care of by him, I'd never deny it. But I'd also been taken care of by someone for a very long time, and it was something that eventually made me feel small, weak, unable to make decisions for myself.

Did me paying for tickets to a Gershwin concert equal letting an entire marriage go by where I let my husband handle every single dollar that came into the house? No. No way. Not even close.

But it was a tiny foothold that I'd gained tonight, without even knowing it. I wasn't going to apologize for paying for something. And I'd make sure however old school Marcello was that he knew where I stood on things like this.

I'd take a tiny foothold.

The lights dimmed, the music began, and I kept my hand on his knee throughout the concert. Sometime around "They Can't Take That Away from Me," his hand covered mine, weaving his fingertips in between mine and holding tight. I grinned into the darkness.

WHAT DOES ONE WEAR to learn how to make homemade pasta? I asked my closet, rejecting dress after dress. I finally settled on an outfit, got dressed, and waited for Marcello to arrive. I sat, then stood, then sat again. Wait, was I pacing? I was pacing now, why was I pacing?

What was I feeling? It wasn't nerves exactly, but something close to nerves. Excited? Yes. Antsy? Definitely. I had the lovely thrill running through me, a thrill that ran faster whenever I thought of his face, his eyes, his lips. His laugh.

Mmm . . . I got it.

Anticipation.

What we were doing, here, now, in Rome, was something new. *We* were trying something new.

Dating.

It was something we'd skipped the first time, although not on purpose. We went from zero to naked in no time flat. Back then, we couldn't help ourselves. Our hormones were not our own, and they ran the show. But this time, on our reunion tour? Consciously or unconsciously, we both wanted to savor this, experience this together like an actual couple.

I wanted to be more of a proper girlfriend and cook dinner for us, something local and luscious, but even though I'd taken classes in the art of French cooking, I was missing something in my repertoire. An authentic Italian meal.

There were flyers all over town catering to expatriates, those studying abroad, or long-term vacationers. Italian Home Cooking was by and large the most highly recommended on TripAdvisor.

I was banking on extra points from the teacher since I was bringing my own Tuscan son. Marcello wasn't sure at first. He insisted he could teach me how to make pasta, gnocchi, and that incredible thick, crusty Italian bread I'd been served at every meal since arriving in Rome, but he'd yet to actually teach me a thing. In the kitchen that is.

A text came in from Marcello, letting me know he was late leaving the office and he'd meet me at the studio. A quick walk through Trastevere lead me to a bright, spacious building. The layout was perfect—every utensil I needed, piles of veggies that could rival the farmers' markets, and a crush of eager students all sipping wine were scattered around the room.

At the center was a long banquet table set with glasses, plates, and baskets waiting for us to complete our meal and enjoy the feast we would make together. Exactly the kind of atmosphere I'd been hoping for when I signed us up.

Photos of previous happy classes dominated one wall. Students posing with their wine, their dinners, or with the chef. He reminded me a bit of Marcello, with a genuine smile in every picture. Our menu was written on a chalkboard in the kitchen. Pasta Bolognese, chicken cacciatore, Italian broccoli, roasted potatoes, and tiramisu for dessert. My stomach growled in anticipation.

Marcello strolled in, turning heads as he moved toward me. "You want to learn to cook like an Italian, why am I not just teaching you? I am Italian, no?" he said, kissing my cheeks quickly.

"Will I end up naked before we make dinner?" I whispered, pouring him a glass of wine from the nearby table.

"I cannot guarantee that," he told me, taking a sip and winking over the glass.

I laughed and kissed him soundly, loving the sweet wine on his lips.

The instructor, looking every bit the Italian chef, came out from the back of the room and welcomed all of us to class His assistant handed out aprons along with a small instruction card, followed by a tour of the kitchens, which were pristine.

And now it was time to get to work. We were going to rotate through stations so that everyone got to have a hand in the preparation instead of one group getting to do one thing beginning to end.

To his credit, Marcello paid attention, even offering to chop parsley when the chef asked for volunteers. "Remember, you eat with your eyes first," Chef Andrea said, explaining that we needed to be careful and take pride in our work. "We don't want any ugly food. These may be rustic dishes, but you want them to look appetizing."

"*You* look appetizing," Marcello whispered, his breath smelling faintly like the wine and basil he was chewing on.

"Stop," I admonished, trying to concentrate on my very glamorous task of chopping garlic.

"Good, good. Remember, celery, carrots, and onions for the Bolognese. No garlic. No matter what anyone say, garlic is *not* in everything." Chef Andrea laughed, repeating the veggie list. "Just most things," he added, scooping up a handful of garlic and lifting it to his nose.

The groups worked quietly, sipping wine, laughing here and there, but everyone paying very close attention to detail. A videographer bounced around documenting the class for the local American college, hoping to bring in new students. He caught me dipping my finger in the tiramisu filling and feeding it to Marcello.

"Avery, good job. You two move to the pasta next," the assistant said, pointing to the stainless steel tables with an old-fashioned crank pasta machine.

We peeled potatoes, slathering them with olive oil and rosemary before lining a baking sheet with them. We pureed sauce, cut pasta, rolled gnocchi down tiny lined wooden boards, and stuffed chickens with lemons, garlic, and onions.

The class wasn't just about learning how to do each step but *about* the food. Why the garlic is good for your heart. What makes a traditional Bolognese versus a knockoff version. Why some recipes differed by region. The chef took every question and answered it as if it was the most important thing he'd ever heard.

My apron was covered in semolina and Marcello had a smudge of tomato sauce on his cheek, but we got off easy. Some students had nicks from the ultrasharp knives and sported bandages on their thumbs. Others had imbibed a bit too much wine and had to sit out and wait for dinner.

In the end, we had perfectly al dente gnocchi that we scooped from the boiling water just as they started to float, freshly shaved pecorino in bowls for sprinkling over our hearty pappardelle Bolognese. The potatoes were steaming in a ceramic bowl, the rosemary perfuming the room. Silver platters held the chicken, peppers, and cacciatore sauce.

We sat along the table, sipping wine and digging into the food eagerly. Five hours we spent together, and in many ways, we came out of it with new friends. Marcello even signed us up for another class.

We tumbled into bed that night still smelling faintly of rosemary, too stuffed with wonderful food to do anything more exciting than cuddle and whisper into the night.

CHAPTER 14

WAFFLED ABOUT ALL MORNING. There was coffee and frittata at the counter with a copy of *La Reppublica*, an Italian daily newspaper. I couldn't read a lot of it but I was working on that. I moved into the living room to continue tinkering with a sketch I'd started the day before of the Bramante Staircase. It was probably the most difficult landmark I'd worked on while in Italy, but I was hell-bent on getting the shading right. The lights hit the highlight in such a way that the spiral staircase turns into an optical illusion. Another trip to the Vatican Museum might be necessary.

But no matter where I was in the house or what I was doing, one eye was always on the clock, counting each tick until it inched close enough to eleven that I felt justified in throwing on clothes and surprising Marcello at the office.

I breezed inside, carrying two bags of pastries that would make American donuts weep with inferiority.

Of course I had a *cornetto* for me.

"*Ciao, buongiorno,*" I told the secretary, dropping the still-warm bag of goodness on her desk. "Is Marcello free?"

She waved me back before happily digging into the bag.

His office was empty. His jacket was on the back of his chair and his cell was tossed on the seat, but no Marcello. I was about to leave him a note with the bag when I felt his hands circle my waist. His lips touched the skin between my shoulder and my neck, and he bit down slightly.

"I smell *maritozzi*. Is that for me?" he said, nibbling as if I were the pastry.

"Yes." I gulped, turning around to face him. "I stopped at that little place just up the street that we love. It's all yours."

"Mmm, *grazie*. Are you staying to share it? I can feed it to you," he offered, opening the bag and inhaling deeply.

I was quickly becoming addicted to the way he savored food. You'd think living in Rome, growing up with the magnificence that is Italian cuisine, you wouldn't go full food orgasm over everything, but he did. Goddamn was I grateful for it.

"I can stay. Maria said they didn't need me today so I thought I'd visit and then go exploring," I explained, taking the small piece he offered.

"I wish I could join you. Where are you headed?" he asked, biting down, his eyes rolling back.

My mind went blank as I watched his lips close over the sweet pastry.

"Nowhere specific," I said, patting my tote. "I have free time on a gorgeous Roman day and figured I'd wander around and stop when inspiration struck."

I'd been doing it quite often when I had a spare moment. Sometimes I would hop on the Metro or the bus and just get off at a random stop. You saw so much of the city that way. Each individual neighborhood had its own vibe, eclectic restaurants, and its own stamp on history. It was a great way for me to learn the city.

Marcello got my attention with a sticky finger rubbing my bare knee. "I have some news," he said between bites. He lifted the puff pastry up to my mouth again, rubbing the powdered sugar over my lips. "I wish my office wasn't full of windows."

He leaned forward, and I felt exactly why he wished for more privacy.

"Tonight, I'm all yours. I'll buy more pastry and you can see where else that powdered sugar can go. Tell me your news."

He laughed, kissing the stickiness from my knee. "I almost forgot. You have me so distracted." I licked the sugar from my lips, earning a groan. "You don't play fair, Avery."

Shaking my head, I sat at the edge of his desk and waited while he pulled up an email on his computer.

The subject read "Como Villa?"

"There's a client we have. I did him a favor—"

"Ooh, favors. What did you do?"

"Nothing like that," he insisted, pulling up the email and the images of a gorgeous villa. Scratch that. It was a castle on the water that looked like a stone hotel in heaven. "This is the payment for the favor. A weekend. Here."

"This is Lake Como, right? *The Lake Como?*" I chirped. "Like George Clooney's Lake Como?" I was drooling over the pictures.

He gave me the side-eye. "Clooney does not actually own the lake; you know that, right?"

"Yeah, yeah sure. So, a weekend here? How big is your luggage? Will I fit? I'm flexible."

His hand moved to my thigh, rubbing small circles against it. Higher, then higher still until his fingers danced along the hem of my shorts. "Oh, I know how flexible you are."

"Now who's not playing fair, Marcello?"

"Touché."

My eyes went back to the villa photos. It was stunning: light-colored brick, climbing with ivy. Window boxes spilling over with every color flower. Your eyes were drawn to the villa's reflection in the lake. Shimmering like jewels over the water, it practically jumped off the screen.

"Are you interested?"

"Huh?" I asked, shaking my head free of thoughts of us skinny-dipping in the lake. "In what?"

"Spending the weekend there." He leaned up to give me a kiss. "With me?"

I clenched my thighs together, sealing his hand between them before I jumped off the desk and ran for the door.

"Where are you going?" he asked with a worried frown.

"Home to pack, hot stuff. We have a Lake Como villa to de-file."

"SO HIT ME. How are things in Amsterdam?"

"Things are, well, *hairy* would be the best word right now," Daisy said.

"*Hairy* is never a good word to describe anything."

"Unless it's a redheaded prince of England."

"Good point. When are you coming home?" I asked, kicking off my shoes and tucking my feet underneath me.

"I love that you're calling it home. That's a good sign." Her voice snapped me back to the present.

"You know what I meant. When *are* you coming back?"

"As soon as I convince Maarten—"

"Who's Maarten?" I asked, hearing something in her voice that caused a blip on my radar.

"Never mind that. I shouldn't be here too much longer.

About a week or so. And if you're up to no good in my apartment, please sanitize all surfaces."

"Can you hang on a second?"

"Sure."

"I have to make a note to pick up some Clorox at—"

"I knew it! I had a feeling you two would eventually get it on," Daisy said.

"We're talking minutes."

"Minutes what?"

"We only waited minutes after you left town."

"Shut your mouth!"

"I will not!" We both laughed, and it felt good. Good to be sharing this with one of my best friends. Being able to talk freely about Marcello and what was going on was new to me.

I told her some. But most I kept just for me.

Like the hunger. And sweat. And push. And pull. And don't you dare stop. And yes, exactly right there. And goddamn, that's good!

I ran my fingers across my bottom lip, thinking about how just last night Marcello had put his mouth on—

"—my box?"

"*What?*" I needed to pay more attention when I was on the phone.

"I had a box shipped from Amsterdam, so keep an eye out for it, okay? In between sessions of hide the cannoli with the Italian stallion."

"Yes. Box. Sure. Stallion. On it. Anything else?"

"Not unless you want to tell me more."

"I love it when you sound like Frenchy from *Grease*. We're actually going to Lake Como this weekend. I can't wait!"

"You two are going away together this weekend?"

"Mm-hmm, somebody he did a favor for is giving us their villa for the weekend. It's supposed to be actually right on the literal lake, how cool is that?"

"That's very cool, Avery," she agreed, but something in her voice had changed a little. "Just be careful. Don't get in too deep, too fast, so you don't get your heart broken. Or break anyone else's."

"Oh." I chewed on my lip. "I don't think—I mean, we just started—"

"Exactly," she gently interrupted. "So you might not be thinking. I'm not saying don't do this, because it's obvious there's something pretty incredible between you two. But just come up for air if you need it, okay? You went from the sorority house right into Daniel's house, and it might be good to just . . . I don't know. Marcello is great, but so are *you*. Remember that, okay?"

I smiled. "I will."

"Okay, lecture over. Now tell me about the good stuff. Is he as good as you remember? Details woman! I'm stuck in hell right now; I need to know *someone's* getting laid."

———

"WHEN WILL WE SEE the Clooney?"

"Unbelievable."

"Seriously, when will we see the Clooney?"

"What is that saying? You are like a bone with a dog?"

"Reverse it. So, Clooney. Will he be just walking free through the train station, or will it be more like we'll see him on the lake, driving his speedboat around?"

"I do not think that he—"

"A speedboat. Yeah. And maybe he's got somewhere really fancy to be, so he'll be in a tuxedo—it could happen. And what if when he gets off the boat, I happen to be right there, and he realizes he doesn't have to go to this shindig alone."

"You know that I hear you, right?"

"Yeah, it helps when I'm fantasizing to this degree to say it out loud. Dammit, I lost my train of thought." I looked up at Marcello and blinked. "Where was I?"

"Something about getting off his boat in a tuxedo?"

"Yeah, the tuxedo. And he needs me to accompany him to a fancy dinner tonight. I don't have a thing to wear, of course, but I'll figure it out. And when we get there—"

"When you get there, a tall, dark, handsome man, also wearing a tuxedo, will approach you, slap your Clooney in the face, and take you behind the bar to remind you who brought you to Lake Como in the first place."

I gasped. "You would slap Clooney?"

"It seems like more of an insult than punching him."

"Good point." I gazed out the window of the train, en route to Lake Como. "Change of plans. How about if I see Clooney, I just smile and nod like we both know something but refuse to acknowledge it. More mysterious that way."

"I think that would best," Marcello replied, nodding sagely. Slipping his arm around my shoulder, he cuddled me into his side, turning me a bit so we could both look out the window. It was a Thursday afternoon, and we were able to take off work around noon, grabbing the train from Rome to Milan. After a three-hour ride, we changed trains for the last leg to Varenna, the jumping-off point for all things Como.

And Clooney. I was mostly joking, but I'd still be scouting the lake for any signs of him.

The terrain changed several times on our way north from Rome, beginning to take on the mountainous feel being so close to the Alps. The trees were fuller, the air seemed more crisp, the sky clear blue, and what I was seeing out of the train window could only be described as something right out of a fairy tale.

And speaking of fairy tale, here I was sitting right next to my own Prince Awesome. Going away for a weekend to a luxurious villa on a romantic lake. How did I get so lucky? What is this life I was living?

I grinned, slid impossibly closer to Marcello, and watched the world go by.

———

THE TRAIN STATION IN MILAN was enormous, cavernous, glamorous, and a bit overwhelming. The train station in Varenna? Quaint. Small. Sweet. And just the right introduction to the wonder that is Lake Como. If the lake were a pair of men's trousers, then Varenna would be the belt buckle. And like a belt buckle, it was right smack dab in the center of the action. Action, in this case, being a wonderfully sleepy town dotted with grand old villas and twisty turny streets.

"Oh," I breathed as we stepped off the train and onto the platform. The air was soft, cushiony, and fragrant with just plain clean. Swinging my overnight bag easily over his shoulder, Marcello grabbed his own bag and we took off.

"It is beautiful, yes?"

"Oh my God, yes," I agreed, my head spinning like an owl to take it all in, not miss a thing. He led me through the station, pausing to consult a map on the wall and compare it to the notes he had on where the villa was located. After quickly conversing with a cabbie, Marcello ushered me into a car and away we went.

From the train, I'd caught a peek or two of the lake, little snatches of deep blue color between mountains and trees. But now, as we wound farther down toward the water's edge, the lake stretched out in all directions. To say I've never seen anything like it simply didn't do it justice. The water was calm, so calm, rippling here and there maybe behind a boat but otherwise serene. Like glass. Climbing on either side of the water were tree-covered mountains, some rolling a little, others seeming to scrape the sky with their jagged peaks. And everywhere along the lake, incredible homes built right into the hillside, perched imperiously, looking down on the water and anyone who might be approaching. Stone terraces, gardens, each one bigger and grander than the next, spread out like colorful skirts on an imposing bodice, softening the look and making everything seem a bit friendlier, more approachable.

Everything was against a backdrop of green, a green so deep and gentle it was almost blue, like an old glass bottle.

As always, I felt my fingers take on an imaginary brush, a piece of pastel, even a colored pencil, itching to sketch a landscape as pure as this was.

Vaguely I was aware of Marcello and the cabbie chatting in rapid Italian, my ear getting more attuned at picking up entire phrases now. Restaurant recommendations, which gardens to tour. I might not be able to answer back yet, but I was picking up more than I'd thought in just a short amount of time.

Driving up along a high ridge, we turned down an almost hidden driveway surrounded by wrought-iron fencing and fat palm trees. And there was the villa.

"You're kidding," I said, my jaw hanging open.

"Kidding?" Marcello asked, curious as he held my door open. I scrambled out of the cab, eyes wide as I gazed at the home that would be ours for the weekend.

"This just doesn't even seem real anymore," I muttered to

myself, my senses overwhelmed at the beauty that completely surrounded me. The home was cream colored, flanked by tall cypress trees and pure magic. Marcello paid the cabbie, took my hand, and led me through an outer door made of intricately woven copper, tarnished green with an ageless patina. While I marveled at the mosaic-tiled floor, he worried the key into a lock set into a massive mahogany door, which creaked open, affording me the first peek into old-school Italian luxury.

I saw miles and miles of travertine floor, intersected with black veined marble. I saw room after room of beautiful furniture, priceless antiques mixed with modern comfort. I saw a kitchen that any chef would have given their eyeteeth to get to cook in once, just once. But what I couldn't really take my eyes off was the water.

The house opened up onto terrace after terrace, built into the hillside and situated perfectly to highlight the main reason this region had been famous for centuries, the beautiful lake. I walked to the edge of the main terrace, just off the dining room, and headed straight for the white stone railing, warmed by the late-afternoon sun and exactly the right width for sitting. I flung both legs over the side and perched right on the edge, laughing as the wind kicked up my curls and made me 1,000 percent glad I'd decided to take Daisy up on her offer to get my ass to Rome.

"This just doesn't seem real," I repeated as Marcello's footsteps across the terrace behind me reminded me that yes, this was real and yes, this really was my life and yes, I deserved this gentle happiness that was creeping into every corner of my life.

That gentle happiness was compounded only seconds later when he wrapped his arms around me from behind, rested his chin on the top of my head, and together we watched the sun begin to set.

CHAPTER 15

HEARD THAT HE AND THE WIFE live here most of the year. Is that true?" I asked, flipping through an Italian gossip magazine that I'd made Marcello buy me when we stopped for groceries.

He laughed, pulling it from my hands and tossing it onto the counter. "I don't know. I don't care."

"Sure you do, she's hot. He's hot. They're stiflingly hot together. They could be here right now. Maybe next door. We can borrow sugar from them," I teased, stepping over to the wide kitchen window to peer outside.

The house was literally on the lake. Or LAKE, as I was calling it in my head. Everything about Lake Como was amplified. Italy by default was gorgeous, but Lake Como was Italy 5.0 and that wasn't just because we may or may not run into (become best friends with) George Clooney.

It was something magical. Something out of a fairy tale with stone villas blanketed in flowers and the shimmering water surrounding you. The crisp air ignited every sense in my body and commanded attention.

I was lost in my daydream about potential Hollywood

neighbors when Marcello came up behind me at the counter. His arms reached around mine to turn on the faucet. With his lips on my neck, he washed his hands before drying them on a tea towel on the side.

It was such a domestic thing to do. Cuddled up against each other to do something mundane, but there was nothing simple about it. It felt like more. More comfort, more openness. More like a couple.

But I was still legally a part of a couple with Daniel and the comfort melted away, allowing sadness to creep in.

"What happened just then? Your warmth, it faded," Marcello said, rubbing his hands along my arms.

I turned and rested my head to his chest. I'd wondered when this topic would come up. Frankly, I was surprised I'd avoided it as long as I did. But as patient as Marcello had been while I got my mental Daniel ducks in order, the conversation was *beyond* overdue.

"Take me out to dinner tonight, okay?" I asked, reaching up on my tiptoes to kiss his chin. My lips moved down, chin to Adam's apple, to the little hollow at the base of his throat that made him shiver.

"Then I will ravage you under the stars with the lake air as our blanket."

Now see, an Italian can get away with saying something like that . . .

———

THERE WASN'T EVER GOING TO BE a right time for this conversation, but it was time to bring it all out in the open.

And it was here, at a lovely lakeside restaurant, that I finally felt ready to share my life, such as it had been, with him. Sitting across from me, his eyes liquid chocolate in the warm glow from the candlelight, I realized that this could have been my life. Had I made other choices. Had I listened to my heart and not my head. Had I—

"You have murdered your breadstick."

"Hmm?" I asked, snapped out of my reverie by Marcello's voice. He gestured to the pile of crumbs that had once been a crispy breadstick before my nervous hands got ahold of it and reduced it to so many crackery crumbs. "Oh, whoops."

He inclined his head in question. "Tell me what is going through that gorgeous head of yours, before you make a bigger mess."

Funny he should mention a mess . . .

I took a deep breath. "You haven't asked me much about what's going on at home."

"In Rome?" he asked, and it thrilled me to no end that even for a second I could consider, that we would consider, Rome as home.

"No, *home* home. Boston home."

He swirled his wine in the glass, lifting it to his lips, his eyes on mine over the rim. Just before he sipped, he said, "You haven't wanted to tell me much. I can respect that."

"You don't want to know?"

He considered. "Of course I want to know, but I want to know what you want me to know. When you want me to know it."

I sipped my own wine. "I see."

He leaned across the table and covered my hand with his own. "Do not mistake my lack of asking as a lack of interest. I want to know what's going on in Boston, I want to know everything."

"You want to know *everything*?" I asked.

"I do, you think you can tell me something that—"

"I'm married, Marcello," I blurted out.

Remember when I said there was nothing like being the reason that someone's entire face changes? When I'd thought that, I'd just made him happy. I'd never thought about the opposite effect.

He stared at me expressionless. He was still, unmoving, like a statue. Except for his jaw, which clenched repeatedly.

Tell him the rest!

"But I'm getting divorced. I'm, well, I'm separated I guess is what you'd call it."

"Which is it?" he asked, jaw unclenching.

"Both, I suppose. I *am* separated. I *am* getting a divorce. I'm in the process now, it's complicated. Although I suppose all divorces are, aren't they?"

"I don't know, I've never been divorced," he said, his voice tinged with a touch of reproach.

I sighed. "I certainly didn't plan on getting divorced. Really, who walks down the aisle thinking, hey, I can always get out of this later on?"

"I'd never want my wife to feel that way."

"Your wife would never feel that way," I whispered, feeling my eyes spark with tears. "Who would ever want a way out if they were married to you?"

We both sat silently, eyes locked, asking each other questions without words. Finally, he spoke. "So, you are getting divorced."

"Yes." I paused to take a sip of wine.

"Why?"

"He was cheating."

He cursed quietly in Italian. "If he wasn't cheating, you would still be married? Not getting divorced?"

"I don't know. I'd like to say that I still would've left him for a host of other reasons. But the fact is, if I hadn't caught him balls deep in his secretary, then I wouldn't be here on this lovely lake, eating this lovely meal, about to go home to a lovely villa with a lovely man, and have wicked, wild, lovely sex."

He smiled at that, just a little bit, but enough that the left corner of his mouth tilted up. "What is balls deep?"

I rolled my eyes. "You'll figure it out. I had plans, promises, mistakes made that I let dictate how I lived. But I can't say with a hundred percent certainty that I would have demanded more from my life one day."

It was easy here, a world away, to convince myself that I could have more, could be more. But back home, buried in garden parties and country club dinners, it was so easy to quietly slip away from myself. A concrete cardigan as it were, sucking me down into that bored-out-of-my-mind hell.

"I had friends who'd sought refuge with the pool man. And friends whose chardonnay or two at five o'clock became three or four glasses at lunchtime. I didn't cheat, didn't drink or fill my life with another vice. Instead I became what I thought I wanted to be and gave up what I really loved.

"I so wanted to think that one day I would have woken up, packed a bag, and gone out into the world to find my own way. To sketch and paint again. To walk into a museum and not feel that sense of longing from missing it so much. It took coming here to get those things.

"The thing is, while I can't say I was happy with Daniel, I can't say I was unhappy, either. I was a whole lot of nothing. And that wasn't great."

"It sounds very not great."

Hearing my words repeated back to me in an Italian accent made me even more aware how different we were.

I smiled sadly at him. "There's more, Marcello."

"More?"

"Yes. Daniel was my boyfriend in college. We, Daniel and I, we were dating when I studied abroad. When I was in Barcelona." I looked down at my napkin. "When I was with you."

"Avery," he sighed, sitting back in his chair and looking as though the entire world was heavy on his shoulders.

"When I came to Barcelona, it was the first time I was ever alone, on my own, and I went a little crazy. I went a lot crazy with you." I thought of that first time I saw him, on that hill when I was sketching. "You were so great, and so much fun, and I thought what the hell, I'll have a little fling. I gave myself permission to have some fun, but then you turned out to be so damn great, Marcello; you weren't supposed to be so great!" I surprised us both then by laughing. "You were so amazing and wonderful and you made me fucking fall in love with you for God's sake."

His eyes burned into mine as he watched me come undone, reliving it, feeling everything again because he was feeling it, too. He knew what I went through because he felt it all right there with me.

"When I went home, Marcello, I had every intention of coming back, to you, once I had my career on track and I could apply for something near you, whatever it was, I was coming back. But things change and things happen and—" My voice cracked then, and my body gave me away because I could never talk about this, ever, without going through it all over again. "Once I was home, I slipped too easily back into my old life. And after a while, I ended up sleeping with Daniel. And then I got pregnant. And then I got married. And then we lost Hannah when she was only three months old and—" My eyes blurred, tears spilling over. "And then I got lost, too."

He was up from the table, this blurry beautiful man whom I could barely see because of my tears, and taking me into his arms and tucking me into his side and hurrying me out onto the balcony and away from prying eyes and curious looks and concerned glances. Away to a quiet corner against the railing where strong Italian arms wrapped around shaking American shoulders and words were whispered in a quiet language that couldn't possibly be understood but they were. They were because it was Marcello speaking to his Avery, to me, and he worried and fussed over me like a child, wiping my tears and kissing my forehead and telling me that it was okay, that I was okay, that *we* were okay, and when he wrapped his hands around my face and kissed me gently, so gently, I knew that this man would be the only man kissing me for the rest of my life.

We stayed that way for a moment or an hour, I'm still not entirely sure, while my tears subsided. And when I was finally under control, he leaned back to look at me with a hint of a smile.

"So," he said, breaking the silence. "Divorced?"

"Divorced," I sighed, saying it out loud as though it were already a fact. I trusted the wind coming off the lake to carry my words into the ether somewhere, making them real and true.

"Divorced," he said again, rolling around the word a bit, as though trying to decide how it felt. I shivered a bit. That word-laden wind coming off the lake was chilly.

"I like it," he finally pronounced, dropping another kiss on my forehead. "I have always wanted to have a torrid affair with an American divorcée."

"Yeah?" I asked, feeling drained but also a tiny bit hopeful. Marcello now knew all my secrets, I had nothing left to hide. And that felt pretty incredible.

"Yeah," he said, in his best American accent. "Come, let's go home. I'd thought a nice walk through the gardens would be a nice way to end the day, but . . ."

"But?" I asked.

Pressing his mouth just under my ear, he whispered, "But now all I can think about is getting you into bed. Or up against that cabinet in the entryway. I am not picky."

Goose bumps broke out across my body as he walked us back inside and over to our table. "Gardens are overrated." I shivered once more as he dropped a kiss on my neck, leaving our unfinished meal and a mess of bills behind for the waiter. There was an urgency now to get home, to be together, to feel what was here and now instead of what was over and in the past. I tugged at his hand, wanting nothing more than to be with him.

"Let me just get your sweater, *tesoro*," he said.

I looked at the heather-gray cashmere cardigan with tiny pearl buttons hanging on the back of my chair. Bitsy had bought me that cardigan, a Christmas present. It matched one that she had exactly . . .

"Leave it. I don't want it anymore." I tugged him toward me by his collar. "I'd rather you keep me warm."

He did. With his hands, his arms, his words . . . and his own sweater. Which he took off and gave to me.

———

THE REST OF THAT WEEKEND WAS, in a word, bliss. We spent hours on the lake, simply enjoying the quiet pleasure that this entire region seemed devoted to. While Marcello answered emails or went for a jog, I curled up on a chaise and sketched in the garden. Or he would row me out into the center of the lake so that I had a full view of the house to capture on the page. Sometimes it would be a single flower scribbled on the back of a napkin or billowing vases filling up my phone to get down onto paper later.

Things seemed to have changed slightly between the two of us. Something subtle had shifted, and I wondered if I was the only one who felt it.

When we went back to the villa that night, after I told him the truth about my past, and my present, he *had* taken me right up against the cabinet in the entryway, too fumbling mad with passion to get me into bed. But while the passion had been as eager as always, the hunger as impossibly growling as always, in between the scrambling hands and the frantic kisses there'd been . . . a tenderness.

The way he held my face in his hands when he pushed into me. The way he swept kisses along my spine, smoothing the skin with barely there brushes. The way I caught him staring at me as I came apart under his tongue, as though if he blinked I might've disappeared.

And the way he said my name when *he* came apart, his lips swollen from my frantic kisses, chanting like *Avery* was the only word he knew.

For the first time in a very long time, I felt treasured.

I still felt treasured as the train pulled into the station in Rome, back into the Eternal City and the eternal beautiful frenzy. I'd been reluctant to leave the countryside, but I was actually eager to get back to work the next day. I was beginning restoration work on the final section, and I'd be trying a new technique on a particularly stubborn lime deposit that had rendered the colors almost invisible in this part of the mural.

"What are you thinking about?" he asked, twisting his hands through a lock of hair that blew through the breeze as we walked through the station. So different from the last time I took the train, the first day I'd arrived in Rome.

"I'm thinking about you," I said, and he smiled, "but I'm also thinking about work." He actually smiled bigger when I completed my sentence.

"This makes me very happy," he said, his hip bumping into mine as he maneuvered us through the crowded station to the Metro line.

"It makes you happy that I'm thinking about work?" I asked, dodging a woman with a cart with a twisted wheel.

"And me, don't forget the first thing you said was you were thinking about me."

"I know, I know." I laughed, leaning up on tiptoes to kiss him, right in the hollow of his throat.

"I'm glad you're thinking about work. When you love what you do, it's hard to turn it off, yes?"

"Yes," I agreed, watching him move with such grace, such ease. To my surprise, I noticed that I was moving right along with him, following the ebb and flow of the throngs of people all around us. I was getting to know this town, know how it thought and how it moved. "I do love what I'm doing right now," I admitted, feeling my cheeks crease a little as the realization dawned. There wasn't much about my life in Rome that I didn't love.

We reached the turnoff point for the Metro line that would

take us to Daisy's apartment, where we'd been spending every night and were sure to spend this night as well. Just before heading down to the platform, he pulled me off to the side and answered his phone, motioning for me to hang on a minute. I watched the crowd as he talked, playing a game where I tried to listen in on conversations and pick up as many Italian phrases as I could understand. Phrase books and language classes had nothing on simply standing in a crowd of people speaking a foreign tongue and letting it wash over you.

That man over there was telling the woman he was walking with that if she didn't hurry up they'd miss their train to Tiburtina.

And that group of girls, maybe fourteen or fifteen years old, were talking about some kid named Mario who had apparently brought a . . . giraffe to a party? Eh, full immersion didn't always work out.

I was in the middle of deciphering a conversation between two older men about a football game when Marcello hung up the phone. "Avery, I've got to head home for a bit."

"Everything okay?"

"Yes, just something I must do. I will be done in a few hours, I will call you then, yes?"

"Oh, okay. That's fine."

He started to steer me back toward a row of waiting taxis. "Let me just get a car to take you home."

I stopped him. "Chivalrous but unnecessary. I'm fine taking the Metro."

"Are you sure?"

I looked at the map on the wall, then back at him. "I've got this."

He studied me a moment, then grinned. "You got this," he

agreed, and leaned in for a slow kiss. "I will call you when I am on my way."

"I'll be there."

"Be naked as well as there," he called out after me as he backed away into the crowd. I blushed when I saw several people look my way.

Forty minutes later I was off the Metro, a block away from the apartment, and damn proud of myself. I'd known exactly where my stop was, I'd spoken Italian to the ticket taker, and I barely had to look at the map on the train, trusting the loud squawky intercom to announce each stop.

A group of American tourists—as recognized by their sneakers, huge maps, and even huger cameras—were at the bus stop pointing at the signage, trying to figure out where they should get off to get to the Colosseum. And they asked me in Italian! *Sort of.*

With a finger on the Fodor's he asked, "*Scusame.*"

"No, Dad, it's *mi scusi*, gosh," a young boy chimed in, tapping away on his phone.

"Shh, I'm concentrating." I should have stopped him there but this was adorably fun. "*Non parlo Italeeanno. Dove aye Colosseum?*"

"*Parla Ingleeese?*" the mom chimed in when she had enough.

"Yes, I speak English."

"Oh thank God," the dad shouted, and for a second I thought the mother might hug me.

They all ended up hugging me after I sent them on their way, with a restaurant recommendation thrown in for good measure.

On very light feet I turned into Daisy's courtyard and inhaled the scent of jasmine blooming from the pots on the balco-

214 ALICE CLAYTON *and* NINA BOCCI

nies overhead. My heels (low, but still heels) expertly picked their way across like a champ. And I felt really at home in this city for the first time.

My hair had come loose from its headband, and I paused to push it back. And once I could see clearly again, I saw my soon-to-be-ex-husband, Daniel, standing on the building's front steps.

CHAPTER 16

STUNNED, I STOPPED DEAD IN MY TRACKS. As people pushed past me left and right, I stared at Daniel.

He'd always been a beautiful man. The first day I'd laid eyes on him was eerily similar to today. I'd been walking home to my dorm, distracted while thinking about a lecture I'd just attended on Pissaro, and almost didn't notice the impromptu soccer match on the lawn in front of my building. Almost to my door, I paused when I heard shouting and looked back at the group of guys playing. But what made me stare was the player off to the left, talking to a group of girls and charming the pants off anyone within a square mile.

He was literally a golden boy. Tall, with the most gorgeous honey blond hair curling slightly along his shirt collar. Dimples, twinkling blue eyes, and even though it was mid-October, enough of a tan that you just knew this kid spent his summers on a boat somewhere.

I watched him for a moment, starstruck by his looks. Even from across the quad, you could tell this guy had "it"—that quality that was going to take him wherever he wanted to go and would make sure it wasn't all that hard to get there.

And then he turned. And he looked at me. And he smiled at me. And when his blue eyes met my brown ones, I could feel in my feet that he was someone special.

Now I stood in an Italian street, watching this man who was still impossibly beautiful. Broader in the shoulders now, his body filling out as he'd grown up. His hair still that same honey blond, perhaps a little thinner on top, and perhaps the honey was graying just the tiniest bit around his temples. The hair didn't curl along the shirt collar anymore, he kept it shorter these days, but a few defiant waves perked up due to the humidity.

The dimples? Well, they were technically still there, but that's one part of his face that I don't have a clear, recent memory of. Maybe it was the pressures of his job, maybe it was the pressures of all the penis sharing, maybe it was just that he wasn't that happy to see me anymore at the end of the day—but he rarely smiled at me anymore.

I was very glad that I had that moment to study him, because when he saw me, and he smiled, I'd had time to prepare for it. And when the dimples didn't show up, even though the grin seemed wide enough to ensure dimple compliance, I saw him for who he was.

A man who desperately needed to stay married for the sake of appearances.

Taking a deep breath, I walked the rest of the block as his gaze took me in. His eyes traveled the length of my body, not in appreciation, but more like . . . cataloguing. I came to a stop in front of the stoop he was standing on.

"You changed your hair," he said in lieu of a greeting.

"A flat iron is kind of pointless in Italy." I looked at the carry-on bag sitting next to him. "You just get in?"

He nodded, shoving his hands into his pockets. "Yep, non-stop out of JFK."

"Why not Logan?" I asked, wondering why he'd gone to New York.

"Logan was fully booked. All that was left was one middle seat in the back of the plane." He smiled ruefully, shrugging shoulders. *Whaddyagonnado.* First-world problems solved by first class.

I'd been so anxious to get out of Boston I *had* sat in the back of the plane, in a middle seat. I took another step up toward him.

"I flew American—wanted the points."

I nodded. "Of course." Gotta get those points. "I made sure to use the American Airlines credit card for my purchases here." I walked up the steps, now on the landing with him. He actually took a step back. "I knew you'd want the points."

"Delta has a new program where you earn—"

"What are you doing here, Daniel?" I interrupted. "You didn't fly all the way to Rome just to compare airline loyalty programs, did you?"

"No."

"And how the hell did you know where I was? I didn't give anyone Daisy's address."

"One of the papers you sent back to my lawyer. The return address was on the envelope." His gaze dropped to the cobblestones below. "I don't think I was supposed to see it, but I did."

"So you saw a return address on an envelope containing letters about how best to resolve our divorce, and you decided to get on a plane?"

"I wanted to see you." He swallowed hard, now lifting his eyes to mine. "I had to see you."

"Daniel," I sighed, and as the breath left my body, some of the tension left, too.

"I just want to talk to you for a few minutes, explain a few things. Just hear me out, okay?" He was pleading now, in a tone that I'd never heard from him before. He was nervous, sure, but there was something else there. Panic? No, it couldn't be. But suddenly I was exhausted. The high from the weekend had dipped down into a low that I realized I didn't want to experience out here on the stoop.

I moved to lift my bag higher onto my shoulder, but he took it, sliding it gently off my shoulder and onto his own. Ever the gentleman, his kind was trained from birth to hold a door, carry a bag, and pull out a chair. Too bad he wasn't trained to keep his dick out from under other women's skirts.

I pushed past him to the front door. "Come on in," I said, seeing the relief in his eyes, knowing it would be short lived.

———————

SEEING DANIEL IN DAISY'S APARTMENT felt so . . . weird. Wrong. Total and complete upside down and inside out.

I set my bag down in my room and headed back out to where Daniel was perched awkwardly on the edge of the couch. He held the glass of water I'd offered, sipped at it, held it, sipped at it again. He *was* nervous.

Interesting.

I stifled a smile and sat down opposite him. "So what's up?"

"What's up?" he repeated. "Seriously, *what's up*?"

"What else do you want me to say? What can I do for you?

How can I help you? Are you lost? Sorry I left you hanging about the dry cleaning?"

"*What's up* is that I wanted to see you," Daniel interrupted, setting down his glass with an irritated thunk. "To talk to you, and make sure that we're doing the right thing here."

"I'm not sure that the right thing was on your mind when you were giving it to your secretary." I sat forward in my chair. "Did you really think you'd just show up unannounced, smile at me, and things would be just peachy? You slept with another woman! Several of them! I have no idea how many!"

"I realize that," he said calmly. "But if we could just—"

"If we could just nothing! I *saw* you having sex with another woman, Daniel! You think I can ever get that image out of my brain? You think that I can just sit across from you at dinner, or open a birthday present, or sing Christmas carols with our parents, and not constantly be thinking about the image burned into my brain of *you having sex with another woman*?" I crossed my leg so hard I might have sprained it. "What the hell is wrong with you? What circuit has come undone inside your mind that made you think I'd be able to get past that?"

"I'm so sorry, baby. I'm so sorry," he said, getting up to kneel in front of me, taking my hands in his. "I'm so sorry. I can't imagine what that must have been like for you."

He was in pain. He felt bad, I knew he did.

"What if you walked in on *me*? Hmm?" I volleyed, fuming that I was forced to think about it again. To rehash it all when I finally smothered the image of them together.

"Think about it, if you saw my legs over the landscaper's shoulders, how would you feel? Maybe my trainer was bending me over the free weights. No, I know, maybe I finally let your boss up my skirt. What do you think about that?"

"Avery, this isn't fair." His fists were clenched at his sides. Good. I wanted him to have the visual.

"When I walked into that office and saw what was going on, do you know the first thing that came to my mind?" I asked quietly. "It wasn't anger, or hatred, or fear. It was sadness."

"I'm so sorry."

"Sadness because I couldn't remember the last time you fucked *me* like that."

"I'm so, so . . . what?"

"Then the sadness changed to . . . static. Like white noise. I watched you plow into that girl with such passion and fire and excitement and good old-fashioned dirty, raw sex . . . and I felt nothing." I took his confused face into my hands. "Because I didn't *care*."

"But the baseball bat, you tried to—"

"Well, sure—*then* I was pissed," I replied, with a smile he looked afraid of. "Because then embarrassment kicked in, and the shame of what was to come."

"I'm really trying hard to understand what's happening here," he said, and for the first time, I actually felt a little bit sorry for the guy. The guy, my husband.

"I know you are," I said, smoothing his hair back from his forehead, then taking the time to slap him twice, lightly. "I don't love you anymore."

His face deflated, looked a little lost. "You don't love me anymore?" he echoed quietly.

"Daniel, do you love *me* anymore? And don't say what you think I want to hear right now. Really and truly think about this. Do you really, truly, love me? Are you *in* love with me?"

He thought. He opened his mouth to speak, then closed it again. Then he did that again.

"No," he said, blinking. "No, I don't." He stood up. "I really don't think I do. Of course I love you, but I'm not *in love* with you anymore. But that doesn't mean we have to divorce, does it?"

Unbelievable. I scrubbed my face with my hands, trying to figure out what I could say to make him see this, to make him understand. "Don't you want more? Don't we both deserve more?"

"I want you."

"You don't."

"I do."

"No," I finally snapped, "you don't. A man in love with his wife doesn't do what you did."

"Actually, several of my friends have, and they're still married."

I started for the door. "You should go."

"Wait, no—let's talk about this."

"There's nothing more to talk about."

He followed me through the apartment. "Do you have any idea how many of our friends are in marriage counseling, going through the same thing we are, and they're all sticking it out? Staying together. Figuring out how to make their marriage work—how can that be a bad thing?"

I whirled around. "You just said you're not in love with me anymore! How could we possibly stay married? I don't love you, you don't love me. I won't apologize for wanting that from my husband." I pushed my curls back from my face. "Don't you see, Daniel? This is *bad*. And it'd be much worse if we don't get out now."

"But I don't want to be that guy—divorced guy."

"I say this with all the love I once had for you, Daniel. I just don't care." I shook my head. "Besides, you wouldn't want me back now. I've changed over here, and you wouldn't like this Avery. I've got something pretty great going here, and I'm staying in Rome for I don't know how long, but it's exciting as shit and I love it!"

I took a deep breath and continued. "And it wouldn't be fair to you, either. You need to really think about what you want—because if you're really honest with yourself, it's not me."

I watched as the realization came over his face and the reality of what this meant, what this might mean to us, began to dawn. He looked old and young all at the same time, and actually quite vulnerable.

"I need to ask you something, Daniel. And you need to really listen."

He nodded, still looking a bit stunned at what had just transpired.

"If I hadn't gotten pregnant would you have married me?" I let my question hang in the air. *The* question, the one that had plagued me for years. The question that crept in late at night, twisting and turning into the darkest part of my mind, the part that questioned everything and always wondered what if, what would have, what could I . . . had things been different.

"I can't answer that," he said, twisting his hands in his lap.

I shook my head, unwilling to let this go unanswered for another minute of our lives, especially since *our* life was essentially over and I might never get another chance. "You have to answer, Daniel, if you ever felt anything for me, I need to know."

"I don't . . . Christ, Avery, I don't know if . . ." He looked at me with the strangest eyes. "You seemed so different *after*."

"I *was* different after, Daniel. When Hannah died, I felt lost, too, and I know you did. You can say it, Daniel. I think this is part of the problem. We never talked about her."

When I looked up at him, he was pale, ashen. He'd gone through hell, too. "But how do you talk about something like that? I couldn't, I mean, how could I talk about . . . she was my daughter."

I reeled backward, struck by the strength of these memories, memories that were so tied up and tucked away like so much of my young life had been. Fresh tears sprung to my eyes as I felt them all rushing back.

"Neither one of us dealt with it, Daniel. Not the way we should have. Not together. We have to face the fact that once Hannah was gone, there wasn't much holding us together as a couple. And whatever we did have just kind of . . . dissolved."

Taking his hand, I sandwiched it between mine. His ring was still on, the gold glinting in the lamplight. I spun it around his finger once and then covered it with my hand. "We should have focused on the memories that you and I made together before her instead of losing her. If we'd leaned on each other maybe things would have been different."

He nodded, wiping his eyes on his jacket sleeve. "I wish I could go back. Fix things."

I shook my head to clear it, to find Daniel, still sitting in front of me, still not able to answer my question. If I hadn't gotten pregnant, would he have married me?

I answered it for him. "I don't think we would have gotten married. I think if I hadn't gotten pregnant, everything would be so different. It changed *us* so much afterward that we should have realized then that this wouldn't work forever," I said, wiping a tear away. "That part of us, those incredible months we had with her, with our family, that's the most precious time of my life, but ever since then? Oh, Daniel . . . we were just a mess. A pretty, polished, looks-great-on-the-surface mess, but a mess."

I was having a Moment, and I was also Having a Moment inside of a Moment—and while that should have been really confusing, it was actually affording me perfect clarity. A moment like when I missed a chair in Rome and fell at the feet of the one who got away. I was being given a second chance.

"We deserve to be happy, Daniel," I said, wiping my nose with the back of my hand, gaining strength once more. "You just have to admit that it isn't with each other."

He gave a great sigh that sounded like it should have come from someone much older. "You really won't come home with me?"

Bless his heart. "No, Daniel. I really won't." I shook my head sadly at him.

He nodded, all the fight seeming to have drained out of him. "So there's no point in trying to get you to—"

"That's just it. There's no point in trying to get me." And with that, he got it. He finally got it. "I think at this point, it's best to let the lawyers handle it, don't you?" The tiniest sob of sadness tugged at the back of my throat, making my voice catch a bit.

He nodded once more, agreeing with me. His face looked as resigned as I felt, and he turned for the door.

As he shrugged into his jacket, I placed my hand on the middle of his back, between his shoulder blades. There was a birthmark there about the size of a dime. In the right light, it looked vaguely like a heart.

He turned back to face me with sad eyes. "You really have changed haven't you?"

"I have." *I should have a long time ago.*

"It's good," he said, and I believed him.

"Good-bye, Daniel," I said, my voice cracking. This part of my life was ending. Sure, there'd be paperwork and phone calls, emails and maybe even another face-to-face meeting when it came time to divide everything up. It might get ugly; it might get heated. But in the end, I hoped that one day I'd see him on the Boston Common, walking with his new wife, perhaps with his children. And we'd both smile.

He turned back to me and hugged me close. "Bye, Avery."

And then he left.

And I cried. Because this was one of the big decisions, the ones about responsibility and tough choices and living with them.

Part of me would always look fondly on my time with Daniel. Maybe even wonder a bit about what *could* have been had things not gone south. The years with him made me who I was, and you could only learn from that and hope not to make the same mistakes again. After all, that lesson had brought me here.

Marcello called a few hours later. He missed me. He wanted me. Could he come over?

No, not tonight. I needed to be alone, to really and truly grieve what had finally ended, and actually let myself feel it.

When I went to bed, the sliver of the moon was high, bright white, and smiling through my open window. The warm summer breeze floated in, dancing over the thin sheet like a kiss. I turned, listening to the quiet chirps from the crickets below.

I didn't know what else Italy had in store for me, but I knew this was exactly where I was supposed to be.

CHAPTER 17

REALLY GREAT WORK, AVERY," Maria commented, checking off items on her list. "The organic microemulsion solution you used was brilliant."

I beamed, rocking back and forth on my heels. "Thank you, that means a lot. But I can't take all the credit. Baglioni created it. I just adopted it to get rid of that awful polymer that someone in the sixties slapped over it."

She laughed, making a final check before moving on to speak with the supervisor about the other aspects of my working there.

While she was preoccupied with his conversation, I took one more admiring lap around the home. There were still a few laborers on the premises, but most had filed out to make room for the interior designers and the landscapers.

Fabrics were draped over the ornately carved wooden banisters, rugs were piled high on the slate floor, in an effort to find the perfect shade of basil to highlight the owner's office color.

Maria found me admiring the tumbled tile bathroom. "I must say, Avery. Finding you couldn't have come at a better time."

My cheeks pinked from the praise. "Thank you. This was a tremendous leap of faith on your part, and I can't thank you enough for the opportunity."

"Tell me something," she began, sifting through her satchel. "How long do you plan on staying in Italy?"

"It's open-ended; I haven't set any date."

"What if I told you I had another job for you?" She held up a sheet of paper. "It's strictly volunteer again, but the experience would be above and beyond any salary we could give you. I'll leave this plan with you and you can let me know on Monday. Does that sound all right?"

"Yes!" I exclaimed, quickly reading over the project info.

"Great, I'll talk to you then," she said.

"I mean yes, I'll take it! I don't need time to think."

"Wonderful! Stop by Monday and we'll figure out the paperwork."

We shook hands and after she left, I couldn't turn off the smile or figure out how to make my legs move. I sat at the edge of the tub, staring out into the city, and sighed the happiest sigh I could.

I called Marcello, but it went straight to voice mail. Same with Daisy. Leaving the villa, I said good-bye to those I wouldn't likely see on the next project and headed home, floating on air.

———

WHEN I ARRIVED AT HOME, the postman was just dropping off the mail. With a smile, he handed me a stack of tiny white envelopes that were dwarfed by the giant manila one on the bottom. Without even checking the return address label, I knew what it was.

Since his visit to Rome, Daniel had been surprisingly as anxious as I was to get the divorce handled quickly. Which I appreciated. But while I wanted it done, I wasn't going to rush through the division of assets.

I was conflicted. I had barely worked outside the home since we'd been married, but I'd worked my ass off to support his career. I didn't want tons, but I wanted my due. Enough to not have to worry for a while, and to continue taking volunteer jobs to pad my newly resurrected résumé. Enough to make sure that I could make smart choices about the way I wanted to live my life . . . and *where* I wanted to live it. His way of life could be greatly attributed to my ensuring the smooth veneer of the happiest of couples, where dinner parties went swimmingly, the wallpaper was interesting but not intrusive, and my nether regions never sported more than a half-inch-wide landing strip, all other hair banished from the kingdom.

Things had certainly changed in that area, too; Marcello liked things a bit more . . . au naturel. I couldn't help laughing out loud.

Daisy's bedroom door swung open, and there she was. "You're cackling to yourself? What the hell happened to you while I was in Amsterdam?"

"I finally lost it," I shouted.

"You lost it in college, I remember. Daniel walked around campus with an enormous grin for a week," she shot back.

"I remember. I couldn't knock that smile off his face."

"So you sat on it."

I rolled my eyes. "Heavens no, he never liked that."

Placing her hand upon her chest, she mimed a cardiac episode. "Thank God you're divorcing him."

"You just said a mouthful."

"Speaking of a mouthful, I assume Marcello is the kind of guy who likes to—"

"Can I welcome you home before you start asking me about whether or not he likes to anything?" I laughed. "If you'd shut up for thirty seconds, I could hug you."

She held open her arms. "Jesus, it's like a Disney movie. Can you feel the love?"

"Oh shush, welcome home! When did you get in?" I asked, setting my tote down and heading into the kitchen. She followed along.

"An hour or so ago. The place looks really great, though suspiciously clean." She raised her eyebrow when I turned back to smile.

"You said Clorox. I obeyed. Tell me about Amsterdam."

"Later, tell me everything that's been going on here—and don't you dare leave out a detail."

She's very bossy, my best friend. But I told her about Lake Como, Daniel's visit, how I reacted afterward—everything.

"And now there's an envelope," she said, motioning to it. "Is it bad?"

"It's just the papers from the lawyers to get the ball rolling. I won't know for a little bit yet."

And she was supportive, as always. "You're doing the right thing. You're getting a second chance here; how many people would kill for a second chance? Don't waste it."

Sound advice.

MARCELLO CALLED BACK while I was explaining to Daisy which surfaces in her home we defiled. She would never look at her kitchen island the same way again.

"You have good news?" he asked before I even had the chance to say hello.

"I do."

"Are you going to share it with me?" He laughed, and I heard it coming from just outside the apartment.

I jumped off the couch and ran to the front door, swinging it wide open. "What a nice surprise!"

He pushed the phone into his back pocket and stepped inside, eyes hungrily moving over me. Capturing my lips quickly, he pushed us up against the door, giving the pedestrians outside a bit of a show.

They hooted and hollered, but Marcello wasn't deterred. Until a bucket of ice water named Daisy breezed into the living room, dousing us thoroughly.

"Please do me a favor next time you sexually maul my best friend. Close the door so the neighborhood kids aren't scarred for life," she teased, whacking him on the rear with her clutch.

He looked just the tiniest bit embarrassed but snapped out of it quickly. Following up a quick kiss with a pat on my ass, he pulled me over to the chair, where he sat and indicated for me to drop into his lap.

"Now, tell me your news," he said, rubbing small circles on my back.

Daisy was watching us curiously. Though she knew the details about us, knowing and seeing were totally different things.

Overcome with the urge to kiss him, I held his face and laid one on him that had Daisy whistling. I couldn't help it. I was bursting with joy. Hope, love, everything in that moment, thanks to the new job offer.

And being able to stay in Italy longer. With him.

"Wow, you two, get a room. Wait until Fiona gets a load of this," she said, dropping that little nugget.

"Fiona? What about her?"

"Have you checked your phone at all?"

I pulled my phone out of my pocket and sighed. I'd disabled texting to avoid the roaming charges. "Three hundred texts? What the *hell*?"

I'd missed an entire conversation with Daisy and Fiona Bradford, our friend from Boston College who flew circles around Daisy with her crazy travel schedule. I wasn't sure if she actually had a mailing address outside her office anymore. A field producer with the Travel Channel, she explored the world in a way that I could only dream of. Time zones were a bitch for us normally, but now with Daisy and me sharing one and her God knows where, we never actually got to talk in real time all that often. "Summarize your *War and Peace*–size text conversation for me, please."

"You first. Tell us your news."

With Daisy holding my hand and Marcello's arm wrapped my middle, I had the most comforting sense of being anchored. That tether that I was looking for was present and I couldn't wait to see where this could lead.

"I'm glad that you're both here for me to tell you this. Maria unexpectedly came by the villa today. She wanted to check out my work, and praise the hell out of my mad skills, of course."

"Of course," Daisy echoed.

"She thanked me again for coming on board, and then . . . she offered me another restoration job here in Rome!"

Daisy vaulted off the couch onto my lap, making us a Daisy,

Avery, Marcello sandwich. She kissed both of my cheeks and held them, her green eyes sparkling.

"I am so fucking proud of you! Goddamn, girl, good for you! Hell, good for *us*, right, Marcello?" she joked, slapping him on the arm.

Marcello moved, making Daisy slide unceremoniously off his lap and onto the floor.

"Hey!" She laughed. "You could have just said, 'Daisy, move. I need to ravish my woman.'" She walked off into her bedroom singing, "Avery and Marcello, kissing in a tree . . ."

And kiss me he did. He dipped me, leaning me back over the arm of the chair, and kissed me like I was a nurse and he was back from war. Soundly, thoroughly, and enough to make me forget that Daisy was twenty feet away.

"I guess you're happy I'm staying a bit longer," I gasped, holding on to his hair while his lips moved to my neck.

"So much that I can barely wait to show you. For hours."

CHAPTER 18

WITH DAISY BACK IN TOWN, I didn't feel right about having Marcello stay over. I felt a little strange about just putting it right under her nose, so to speak. Not to mention, I could get a little loud when the things and the parts and the sighs and the . . . yeah, I could get a little loud. So with an overnight bag packed, Marcello and I headed out to his place.

On the Vespa. I was *so* Rome.

It felt right, zipping through the night streets behind him on the scooter, arms wrapped around him tightly, cheek pressed firmly against his back, breathing in the scents of the city and Marcello.

We headed toward Via del Corso, where the street was impossibly even more narrow, the buildings pressing in on all sides. Clothing hung on lines stretched between windows, balconies were piled high with flower pots and tiny herb gardens, and everyone was out on the street after dinner, enjoying a gelato, a grappa, a chat. We zipped quickly into a spot, Marcello taking my hand to help me down and not letting it go as he led me through the walkways thick with people. Turning down a side street, he tucked me into his side, slipping my bag over his shoulder as he cuddled me close.

"So this is your street," I said. His fingers played with my hair as we walked, twisting it around one finger then the next. "How long have you lived here?"

"Let's see . . . about four years? The last place I lived was over by the office, much smaller place. I would have been embarrassed to bring you there. It was very much a, what do you call it? A bachelor's digs?"

"Bachelor pad," I corrected, loving the feel of his fingers in my hair. It was never the big grand gestures that got me, it was the little things. That's what made me over the moon for this guy.

"Yes, bachelor pad. It was tiny. Bed in one corner, stove in the other, barely enough room to move around. If I stretched, I could be stirring something on the stove top, open the front door, and have one foot on the mattress."

I smiled to myself, thinking about his in-between years. Where he'd been, what he'd been up to in the years since Barcelona. Dubai, Jerusalem, even New York. All those years.

We arrived at his building, a four-story stone structure with a small balcony on each floor.

Pushing open a heavy oak door, we walked through a small entryway and out into a beautiful courtyard that had a fat tree with deep green leaves dotted with tiny orange fruit.

"What kind of tree is this?" I asked, leaning closer. They were oval shaped, almost the size of a thumb, and unlike anything I'd ever seen before.

"Kumquat. Have you ever tasted one?" He plucked a few fruits from the stems, holding them in his hand. "They are a little tart, a little sweet, a little citrusy—very good."

White lights strung through the tree shone down, casting a

golden glow in the night-dark courtyard. Bicycles were parked along one side, and potted tomato plants covered the opposite wall. A spiral staircase wound up to each floor, the individual apartments accessed by a shared exterior walkway, with maybe three doors on each floor. We climbed up and up, all the way to the top, where he led me to his door.

"Oh my goodness," I breathed, stunned when he opened the door. "Marcello . . ."

This apartment was the very personification of Marcello. Oaken beams soared at least fifteen feet above the room, anchored by supporting arches that crossed the wide-planked floor. Polished concrete floors next to scarred wide-plank pumpkin pine. Open kitchen. Cozy living room. Enormous fireplace.

"This is beautiful," I said, taking it all in. It was such a perfect mix of old and new, ancient and contemporary, past and present mixing and complementing each other perfectly.

"What is that expression, you have not seen nothing yet?"

"Close." I laughed, looking around. "What else am I missing?"

With a secretive smile on his lips, he led me to an old barn door at the back of his kitchen. Sliding it open, he waved a hand in front of me. "Ladies first."

A tiny staircase wound up and into darkness. With Marcello behind me, guiding me, I had no fear. At the top was an old door with a skeleton key hanging on a hook next to it. "Go ahead," he said.

I wasn't sure what I was expecting when I opened up the door. Single-guy hot tub? Playroom? Doorway to another dimension? Marcello managed to surprise me yet again.

"This is *incredible*."

When I stepped onto the roof, the first thing I noticed was the overwhelming scent of flowers. Looking up I saw a wide, rustic pergola covered in bright pink bougainvillea that had been coaxed to twist and twine around the old wood. Planters filled with lemon trees, little olive trees, and more of those kumquat trees from the courtyard below. Strung above? Hundreds of little white party lights, nestled into the corners and crisscrossing above. A little farther out toward the edge were comfortable-looking couches and chaise lounges boasting an incredible view of the city.

Turning, I found him watching me, arms crossed as he leaned against a flower-covered beam. "Incredible," I said again, stepping toward him.

"There is also a pit of fire over there," he said, pointing to the couches that I could now see were set around an outdoor fireplace.

"How private is this?" I asked, glancing around at the neighboring buildings. That was something great about this part of town—most of the structures didn't go above a few flights. Marcello's had a stunning, unobstructed view of Rome. I couldn't imagine how gorgeous this would be during sunrise.

"It is private enough," he answered, sliding his hands across my hips and up my sides, his thumbs rubbing against my nipples as he slid my shirt off slowly.

"No brassiere," he said hungrily, licking his lips.

I looked furtively left, then right, and still seeing not another soul up this high I threw caution, and the rest of my clothes, to the wind. "Nope." I hooked my fingers into my skirt and slid it down, kicking it off to the side near my top.

He inhaled quickly. "No panties, either. You rode around behind me without them? All across the city?"

In response, I threw my head back and laughed, emboldened by the feeling I had in this moment. Naked, on a rooftop in Rome.

"Naughty girl," he murmured, catching me against him and dropping kisses along my neck, my collarbone. Before he could get too far, however, I wanted to take control.

Clutching his hand, I walked him through the hanging flowers. I loved the brush of the soft petals against my skin. There was something empowering about walking naked in the hot, sticky summer air. Before Marcello, I'd never have done anything like this, but the two of us together made for an explosive combination. With this bold move, any lingering thread of Old Avery unraveled.

He kissed my fingertips as I led him across the rooftop, stopping in front of the seating area. Pulling a few pillows from the couches, I piled them onto the ground and pointed.

For a change, he did what *I* wanted, his eyes flashing as he lowered himself down, propping his arms behind his head, waiting.

"You're going to have to be quiet," I said, standing over him, cupping my breasts. I hummed, imagining that they were his hands, smoothing over me, pinching my nipples before his lips enveloped them.

"*Tesoro,* how you tease," he purred, sitting up quickly.

I lifted one foot and pushed against his chest. "No."

With his hands up in surrender, he leaned back again onto his elbows. I kneeled on either side of his hips and ruffled his hair away from his face. His eyes closed, lips parting and his tongue dipping out wetting them. "Avery," he said, kissing my cheek and the tip of my nose before capturing my lips hotly.

Reaching down, I unbuttoned his shirt first, then his jeans, undressing him slowly. His hands caressed my skin, slowly and sweetly. His lips sought me out, kissing whatever came close to his mouth as I moved over him—a shoulder, an elbow, a breast.

ALICE CLAYTON *and* NINA BOCCI

Frustrated, he circled my back with his arms, pulling me closer to his waiting mouth. "You taste so sweet. I can't get enough of you."

My mind was scrambled. My hips slid back over, over until I was right *there*. So close. He moved, searching for the best way to slip inside.

"Fuck," he swore, thrusting deep when he found it. We were sweaty, sticky from the heat, but it didn't matter.

I slid down, over and up, slowly rolling my hips. "Give me your mouth," I demanded, arching up so that my breasts were just out of reach of his lips. His tongue darted out, slipping over the taut nipple.

He pushed himself up as I rode him. Hard and fast, then slow and wicked. I held his head against my breasts, the scruff a delicious tickle against the sensitive skin.

"Faster. Please."

My hands moved across his back, fingernails scratching against the muscles as I moved faster, everything building up inside of me. I nearly spilled my thoughts, the words I was dying to say to him, finally and for the first time, *I love you*.

It was right there barreling forward along with my orgasm. Tears spilled over, splashing against our chests as I held in the confession. Soon.

CHAPTER 19

WANT TO ASK YOU SOMETHING."

"After what you just did? You can ask me anything." I smiled into his chest, breathing in the scent of satisfied Marcello. We were cuddled in one of the chaise lounges, a pillow behind him, and him behind me. I nuzzled into his skin, the little bit of hair on his chest tickling my nose.

"How about what *you* just did, *tesoro*." He groaned. "Your mouth . . ."

I kissed *his* mouth, which was just as wicked, then snuggled back into his side. "What did you want to ask me?"

He played with the ends of my hair, dragging it up and around and making little patterns on my bare back. "Do you have plans next weekend?"

"I do."

"You do?"

"Sure," I said primly. "Whatever you've got planned for me, I'm doing."

"Avery," he whispered into my hair, making each syllable count, just the way I loved. "I want you to come home with me."

"I'm here right now." I sighed, feeling dreamy and smiley and boneless.

"I mean my *home*. To Pienza."

Not so boneless. "Where you grew up?"

"Mmm-hmm."

"Where your family lives?"

"Mmm-hmm." He kissed my shoulder. "There is a festival next weekend, the Gioco del Cacio al Fuso. Everyone comes into town for it every summer. It's the one time other than Christmas that we all get together. I never miss it."

"Sounds major," I murmured, nibbling absently on my fingernail.

"Major? I do not take your meaning?"

I sat up, turning to face him. His eyes went immediately to my breasts, of course, but then tried to stay on my face.

"Come home with you, meet the family? Like, *all* the family?"

"Yes," he said simply. Did he know that in the States, the meeting of the parents was a *very* big deal?

His face was glowing, and not just from the thing I did with my mouth. He looked . . . peaceful. Hopeful. Very content. And a little bit . . . excited.

He did know what a big deal this was, and he wanted to bring me home to Mama. Was I ready for that?

"Yes."

"IT'S HUGE."

"Right? I mean, how do I? *What* do I?"

"Huge."

"Stop saying that! It's making me more nervous," I said, pacing around the bedroom, rejecting outfit after outfit. "I should just go shopping."

Daisy reclined on the bed. "Tell me exactly how he asked. The when, the where, the how."

"I'm not sure if you want *all* of those details."

"Yes. I do. I'm living vicariously through you and your magnificent life here in Rome." Daisy tossed a lacy white sundress into the fray. "That is a must-have, by the way."

I nodded, hanging it on the closet door with the others I was definitely packing. "This is a *seriously* amazing summer!" I gushed, spinning around like a teenager who'd just been asked to the prom.

"You kill it in foreign countries, girl!" She high-fived me, then sat near the window. "Okay, I'm ready. I want the details."

I prepared to dish. "We were in bed. You know, afterward."

"Uh-huh." She leaned forward. "And?"

"And he asked what I was doing next weekend, and laid it out there. There's a festival going on that all the family comes in town for every year. *All* of the family." I raised my eyebrow. "I know how these Italians are. It's not just 2.5 kids. It's kids, extra plural. Then those kids' kids, and grandkids and great grandkids and nieces and nephews and neighbors that are 'family,' and what am I going to do? I don't know what to expect. He keeps telling me not to worry, that they'll love me, but really?" I pointed a finger at myself. "Divorced, American, non-Catholic. Fornicator!" I threw myself onto the cardigans that were strewn across my bed.

When we first started scouring my closet earlier for appropriate "Meet the Family" wear, Daisy had pulled them all from my closet in a huff. She thought they should be tossed since they screamed Boston Avery.

Though Marcello did like the pearls.

With some heels.

And nothing else . . .

Regardless, the cardis and the pearls wouldn't be coming with me to Pienza—I wanted to dress to impress. *Please like me* clothing to help me prove that I was head over heels for their son, brother, nephew, whatever.

"You're crazy. This is a man who looks at you and makes you melt." She stood to rummage through my closet. "Not to mention that whenever you look at him, he beams. I've known him a long time, and he doesn't light up like that for anyone."

He *did* get that hazy, glossed-over look in his eyes whenever he stared at me. Which was often. And when he did, I got the full-blown belly flutters. Those feelings were what I needed to focus on for this event. Not the nerves.

"It's normal to be nervous about meeting the family, Avery," Daisy consoled, pulling out a few more pieces from my closet. "Besides, he's nervous, too—don't let that suave Roman thing he's got going fool you. Just remember: he's bringing you there. That means something."

Daniel's family had been wary of me from the get-go. I couldn't have been a more perfect match for their son, yet Bitsy was always standoffish. I was never able to win her over.

"I can see in your face that you're freaking out again," she said, pulling me up from my bed and setting her hands on my shoulders. "Snap out of it."

"I know, I know," I said, hugging her. "I need something else to focus on, or it's going to drive me insane."

"Let's take a quick shopping trip before we get Fiona from the airport," Daisy suggested, eyeing the white sundress again.

"What?"

"I'm thinking if we get you more of these," she said, touching the delicate lace of the bodice, "Mama, Papa, and Marcello will all be declaring their love for you next weekend."

———

"HOW THE HELL HAS IT BEEN so long since we've all been together?" I asked, looking across the table and seeing Daisy and Fiona.

"Because you've had a stick in your ass and never wanted to leave Boston?" Fiona chirped, stealing a glance at Daisy, who nodded her head vigorously.

"Oh. Right," I said, sipping my Campari and soda. "That."

"And the fact that we're never in the same place at the same time," Daisy added, waving the waiter over and ordering another round of drinks.

"There's also that," Fiona agreed, leaning across the table toward me, resting her chin in her hands. "I was kidding about the stick in your ass. Mostly."

"Your Botox looks really good, I can barely notice it." I smiled prettily at her as she cracked up.

"Good goddamn have I missed you, Bardot!" She pointed at Daisy. "Not this one, though, this one I see too often."

"You see me maybe three times a year," Daisy replied, shaking her head.

"That's too often," Fiona said, as Daisy mouthed it. The three of us had pledged the same sorority freshman year at Boston College, and became instantly joined at the hip. Fiona was a different sort of gal, and without being a legacy in the sorority (two older sisters, her mother, and her grandmother, not to mention her cousin, who was president when we were rushing), she likely would have become just a face in the crowd. Independent, free spirited, extremely political, she was brash and loud and we loved it.

There was something about the three of us that clicked, and we'd remained fast friends throughout the years. Though I was in more regular contact with Daisy, Fiona was one of those friends you didn't have to talk to very often, didn't need to check in with more than a few times a year . . . but you knew she'd drop everything and be there the second you needed anything.

"Speaking of three times a year, I heard Daniel's putting it to his secretary instead of you; what the hell is up with that?"

"Dear God," I moaned, apologizing to the people at the nearby table who'd suddenly become way more interested in our conversation than their own. "Also, Daisy? I could kill you."

"What, you think I wouldn't find out on my own? My mother told me all about it; you're the talk of the needlepoint circuit, kiddo," Fiona responded, crunching a breadstick between her teeth. "And for the record, I'm glad you dumped his sorry ass. Daniel was too pretty. You just know that guy wasn't ever going to be up for some serious fucking."

"Dear. God," I said again, this time a bit more quietly. I reached for my glass. An afternoon with Fiona was like a crash course in all things obvious. She called it like she saw it, never held anything back, and at times offered information that no one had even asked for. "For the record, he *was* up for some serious fucking. I saw him doing it, just not to me."

"Just be glad you're getting out while you've still got all those great sex years ahead," she said, nodding wisely. "You should never waste good sex years with a weenie. And no offense, but Daniel is a weenie."

"Agreed, now can we change the subject?" I begged. "Where are you off to now?"

Lately everyone I knew was coming back from or running off to a grand adventure, and Fiona was no exception. She actually got paid to go on grand adventures. A field producer for the Travel Channel, she literally went around the world and back to seek out and uncover the most interesting places in the world . . . and then make her television audience want to book a trip immediately. She spent more than nine months on the road each year, was rarely home, and gladly suffered an extreme case of wanderlust.

She was a road warrior, and she wouldn't have it any other way.

"I'm off to Ireland, a little place called Dingle, can you imagine? I can't tell you how many bad jokes I'm already writing in my head about a place called Dingle. I was just location scouting down in Sicily, so I had to stop by and see my girl here, and how great that you're here, too!"

"How long are you in town?" Daisy asked.

"Leaving tonight, can you believe it?"

"What?" I sputtered. "You just got here!"

"I know, I know, but Dingle is calling. I'll try and get back here in a few months, or will you be back in Boston by then, Miss Thing?" She looked at me expectantly, no doubt thinking I'd be back home any day now.

Daisy also looked at me, full of the same questions.

"A few months, huh?" I shrugged my shoulders. "I'll still be here."

Fiona thumped her fist on the table. "Fuck yes!"

"Dear God," I said, slinking down in my seat.

"Do you think they sing 'Dingle Bells' at Christmas?" Daisy asked.

CHAPTER 20

AFTER WE GOT FIONA OFF TO DINGLE, I spent a good portion of the night—and early morning—tucked away in my bedroom with the Italian phrase book that Daisy gave me when I first arrived.

I needed to beef up my Italian vocabulary—I was meeting Marcello's parents, for goodness' sake. People who were important to him, and I wanted to show them that I wasn't just some American floozy who was only interested in a summer fling. It was more than that. *We* were more than that.

My heart sped up as I rehearsed in front of the mirror, practicing common phrases in what I hoped was perfectly accented Italian. The harder I tried, the more ridiculous I sounded. When Daisy casually asked why I was speaking Italian with a Russian accent, I decided to call it a night and give it another go in the morning when I was more rested and relaxed . . . and decidedly less nervous.

By morning, the nerves quadrupled.

My bags were packed and waiting by the door while I sat on the couch, bouncing my legs anxiously. Then I moved to the chair. Before long I was pacing. I stared out the window before moving back to sit next to my luggage on the small iron chair that Daisy hung her purse on every day. I glanced down at my stuff and smiled.

I had consolidated everything I needed into my large duffel and oversized slouchy leather purse that I bought one afternoon at La Sella, a family-run store that I stumbled upon after taking a wrong turn on the way to work. Camel colored and buttery soft.

"Stop petting your pretty purse," Daisy said, strolling into the living room.

"I'm not petting it," I replied, absently stroking the handle.

"Where's all your stuff?"

"That *is* all my stuff," I replied, crossing my arms over my linen dress.

"You're kidding. Just one?" She picked up the large bag. "It's light, too. Are you running a fever?"

I shook my head.

"Ah, you plan on being naked most of the time?" she marveled. "If so, my hat's off to you."

I laughed, rubbing at the erratic thumping in my chest. "Not sure naked is the best first impression. You're forgetting that I'm meeting the family for the first time."

"Wait, so you think you and Marcello will go the entire weekend without trying to throw a leg around? I don't believe it, lemme see what's in here. There's no way you packed this light." She laughed, unzipping the bag to peer inside.

I shrugged. "Not having to pack all of my hair products and tools means I don't need a separate bag just for that. I brought flats, which are rolled up to save space, plus the pair I have on. Every outfit I packed is light with interchangeable separates—"

"Barring any sex or sauce accidents that you may have that'd throw a wrench in your interchangeable separates," Daisy said, interrupting.

Standing, I jabbed a finger into her arm. "If you jinxed me, I'm coming home and kicking your ass, Daisy Miller!"

My phone beeped, alerting me to an incoming text from Marcello.

I am here.

"Holy shit, he's here. I'm so nervous. How do I look? What if they hate me? What if they know I'm divorced? Well, practically divorced. Can a Catholic sense that sort of thing? Isn't that a sin? What if they know we've already had sex! Like really dirty, curl-your-toes-and-scream-about-God sex! Oh my God. Is that a sin, too? Yelling *God* during sex?"

"Oh for Christ sake, calm yourself, woman," she said, snapping her fingers to break me out of my nervous rant. "Yes, this is a big deal, but they're going to love you. Who wouldn't? You make him happy and that's what they'll care about. Not that you're American or divorced or that you play with Marcello's breadstick. But that you're obnoxiously in love with him. Just don't get caught doing the hanky-panky."

She scooped me in for a hug before pulling me out the door. I stepped onto the small landing and ran into her, dropping my duffel on my feet.

"Hey! What the hell—oh," I muttered when I saw what she was focused on.

There was Marcello, my Marcello, leaning against a sexy cherry-red convertible. The sun was hitting him *just so*, and that sight of him took my breath away. He was dressed in light-colored pants and a button-down shirt, the sleeves rolled up to his elbows, his tan arms crossed over his chest, and my heart flipped.

How could I ever have thought this was a fling? There wasn't any doubt in my mind that I was full-blown, hopelessly back in love with him. Actually, I don't think I ever fell *out* of love. As much as I wanted to believe that I got over him the first time, I hadn't.

Seeing him here, I knew that if this second chance somehow went south, I'd never get over him. "Holy—"

"—shit," Daisy finished, and I was sure she wiped a bit of drool from her chin.

He smiled and looked down in a boyish way. He pushed off from the car and stepped to the side enough to open the passenger door.

Daisy was rolling her tongue back into her mouth when she insisted, "I'm not attracted to him." She finished by giving him a very thorough once-over. "You have to know that."

"That's good."

"But, my God."

"I know," I agreed, fanning myself in the late-summer heat.

"How long is the drive?"

"About two hours."

"You're lucky if you make it in three," she said, turning me toward her. "Between that man, that car, and you in that dress? You're not going to make it out of the city without him stopping for a quickie somewhere." She laughed, swatting my butt before disappearing back into the apartment.

He was up the stairs before the front door clicked shut. Suppressing a grin, I took tiny steps back as he stalked forward on the small landing.

"Hi," I said, standing a bit taller and pushing my boobs out just enough to catch his eyes.

They flickered down and his nostrils flared at the tight bodice and squared neckline that was highlighting my sun-kissed cleavage.

"You look . . ." he began, before scooping me up into his arms to pin me against the door.

Between kisses, he murmured, "Gorgeous. Stunning. Breathtaking." He kissed me again and again, each kiss getting more frantic. "We need twenty minutes."

His hips thrust forward and Daisy's words echoed in my mind. *Quickie.*

"You're going to make us late," I panted, my head thudding back against the door while he kissed and licked a path from my neck to the strap of my dress. Slowly, he began pulling it to the side, baring my shoulder to his kisses. His fingers were hot as he nipped at my skin and I could feel the smile against my body.

"They will understand. Let us inside. I can be quick. Ten minutes."

"But we've got . . . Jesus that feels good . . . a two-hour drive ahead and—"

"I will speed."

"Daisy's home."

"She won't mind."

"Marcello," I admonished, gently pushing against him and laughing.

"*Mannaggia,*" he groaned, resting his forehead to my shoulder.

We were both breathing heavily, his hands tightening around my waist. His lips swept up for one more heated kiss before he backed away.

I looked down to see tiny red marks scattered across my chest from his beard. "I hope these fade before we get there."

"I will just make new ones," he said, swinging my bag over

his shoulder. With his free hand, he held on to mine as we walked down to the car.

"You like?" he asked, resting my duffel and purse next to his on the backseat of the sports car. "I borrowed it from a friend for the weekend."

I ran my finger along the door, down the front, and across, mindful of his heated gaze following me the entire time.

"Can I drive?"

He laughed, but I could see his mind was still on other things. His eyes burned with that heat that usually meant I'd be naked it thirty seconds.

"Five minutes," he begged.

I gulped. "We'll be late."

"This is no longer a concern of mine, *tesoro*," he murmured, beginning to push me up against the car, his hands already moving toward the straps of my dress again.

"No, no, later, I promise." I held him literally at arm's length. "If we can sneak away from your family and not get caught."

He hung his head and sighed, took a moment to collect himself, then nodded. Once we were settled in the car, he handed me a small, thin box.

"What's this?" I asked, tearing open the bow before he even answered.

He chuckled, picking up bits of flying paper and tucking them into his pocket.

Underneath a sheet of tissue paper was a large square black scarf. I pulled it out, loving the slip of the silk between my fingers.

"It's beautiful," I said, my breath catching when I got to the tiny embroidered AB in the corner. It was simple, thoughtful, and perfect. "Thank you."

"It is from that shop near the office."

"I love that shop." I'd mentioned that to Daisy once in passing. "But how did you know?"

He looked sheepish, rubbing the back of his neck. "I overheard you."

I took his hand, squeezing. "That was weeks ago."

Shrugging, he brought my hand up to his lips. "I saw it one afternoon and went in. I thought this would suit you."

"I love it." I began knotting it around my neck when he stopped me. "No, *tesoro*. Like this."

Folding it into a triangle, he rested it near my forehead and pulled it down, sweeping it beneath my hair. "Hold here," he instructed, placing my hand on top of my head. Then taking the two tails, he wrapped them loosely around my neck before tying them in a small knot at the base of my skull.

He took a deep breath and grinned. Something flickered in his eyes. "What?" I said, self-consciously touching the scarf.

"Look," he said, pointing to the small rearview mirror.

I smiled at my reflection. The scarf was covering all of my hair. Perfect for a long drive in a convertible.

"I feel like Audrey Hepburn," I said, leaning over and kissing him soundly.

Stepping away, I slid back into my seat, pulling his hand into my lap and squeezed.

"Ah, one more thing," he said, plucking a small felt bag from the dashboard.

Inside were a pair of oversized tortoiseshell sunglasses. "You shouldn't have." Slipping them on, I glanced in the mirror once more before laying another kiss on him. "I love them. Thank you." I kissed him again, then once more, my own hands now beginning to roam across his shoulders. It was nearly impossible for me to stop touching him once I got my hands on him again.

Before I knew it he'd pulled me over the gearshift, sitting me in his lap. His hands were holding my rear, kneading and keeping me right against him.

At this rate, we'd be lucky if we made it out of Rome at all.

———

"ARE YOU SURE I can't drive?"

At first I thought I'd be disappointed that I couldn't drive, especially when he explained that it was a 1967 Alfa Romeo Duetto. But once we broke free of the crush of traffic in Rome proper, it turned out that watching Marcello drive a sexy car was better than getting to drive. I leaned back against the headrest, enjoying the sun on my face as he masterfully drove through the ribbons of roads in the Italian countryside.

"You can if you like. I cannot promise I would keep my hands to myself, though," he teased, slipping his hand from the gearshift to my thigh, where he pushed my hem up, up, up.

"Seems like you can't keep your hands to yourself even while you're driving." Moving his hand back to my knee, I tried to keep my attention on the countryside outside of the car, rather than the dreamy Italian driving it. The landscape was a blur, zipping by in golds and greens. Now that we were out of the city, the air began to change, lighter and more fresh. Like any city, Rome had its own smell. It wasn't always pleasant, but you learned to live with the pockets of funk in order to bask in the incredible aromas of pasta, chocolate, and cheese. But out here, I breathed deep, filling my lungs with the earth. Freshly cut grass, wildflowers, and this inexplicable smell that I couldn't put my finger on.

"So tell me about the festival going on this weekend."

Marcello lifted our clasped hands to his mouth and gently kissed each of my knuckles while keeping his other hand firmly on the steering wheel. "I was hoping to keep it a surprise. It is nothing fancy, but it gives my family a reason to all get together and visit."

"And just how many lucky girls have come home with you at festival time?" I teased, turning in my seat to watch him as he drove. He was silent for a moment, then glanced over.

"Zero."

"Zero?"

"Zero." He nodded, kissing my hand once more. "I've never brought a girl home with me."

"Ever?"

"Never."

"But . . . why?"

He shrugged.

"But surely there have been other girls," I said.

He was quiet for a moment. "There have been other girls, this is true."

Hmm, maybe I didn't want to know this.

"But no one serious?"

"I have dated women, some longer than others. I think you could say there have been a few that were serious. But that is rarely the case."

"That seems a little lonely," I said.

"I am rarely alone," he replied, arching an eyebrow. "I work, Avery, I work *a lot*. I travel *a lot*. I meet women, I date women. But no one I would have considered bringing home."

"Never met the right girl, I guess," I mused.

"I did meet the right girl." He lifted my hand and dropped a kiss on the back of it. "Many years ago."

Stunned silent, I sat back against my seat, mulling over what he'd just said. He'd never brought a girl home. Did that mean he'd never introduced anyone to his family, either? And if not, what did it mean that he was now? With me?

I was *the* lucky girl. A grin made its way across my face, so big and wide that it made my cheeks hurt as I contemplated how truly lucky I felt. He shot me a knowing smirk, clearly pleased that he'd pleased me so.

Speaking of pleasing . . .

I brought his hand to my lips now, kissing his knuckles as he'd done to mine, then dropping his hand back down onto my knee. He squeezed it lightly and kept time with the music, tapping his left hand on the steering wheel as I slowly, ever so slowly, began to drag his other hand higher and higher along my leg. I watched the countryside speed by on my side, innocently keeping my gaze away from my leg and his hand, now disappearing under the hem of my dress.

Inch by blessed inch, our hands rose. I felt the car sway slightly, saw that we'd crept across the center lane just a bit, and Marcello swerved us back onto our side. I finally turned back to him and found him staring at me, his eyes burning as I continued to move our hands still higher.

"Avery," he warned, his voice strained. Just then, I slid his hand down along the inside of my thigh, pressing his fingers now between my legs directly over the silk of my panties.

"Do you remember that time," I purred, my voice husky, even to my own ears, "when you had me outside that restaurant in Nerja?"

The car swerved again, his hand grasping the wheel tightly. I saw his jaw clench. Emboldened, I went on.

"All those people inside, and walking by just around the corner from where we were? And you were on your knees in front of me?"

"Yes," he whispered, his right hand now moving on its own.

"And you pulled my panties aside with your teeth before your tongue—"

His eyes shot to the rearview mirror before he skidded the car to the side of the road, kicking up a plume of dust behind us. Throwing it into park next to a massive tree, he was out of the door and undoing his belt, watching me through the windshield as he stalked around the car.

"Holy shit," I choked when he ripped open the passenger door and reached in for my legs.

"I cannot wait," he said gruffly, shifting me so that my legs were out of the door, feet on the ground, and my rear was at the edge of the seat.

"Take them off," he ordered, pulling his shaft out of his pants.

He watched me slip my hands beneath my dress, slide my panties down my legs, and leave them hanging around one ankle. His hand gripped his cock, smoothing over it once, twice, before dropping to his knees and pulling out a condom from his pocket. I imagined he was hard from the second I stepped out onto the porch.

"Hurry," I pleaded, looking up the road and praying no one would drive past.

It was awkward, risky, wild, and the best fucking sex I could have asked for on the side of a deserted Italian road with the man I loved.

His knees were bleeding from the gravel, pants dirty, and my dress was rumpled where he had pulled it down to press his lips to my breasts.

But I wouldn't have changed it for the world.

Afterward, sated and reasonably collected after our roadside romp, we headed back out in the direction of Pienza. Marcello was back to happily humming along with the radio, and I tried to take in as much as I could of the beautiful country. But it was becoming so relaxing, I could feel my eyes getting heavy from the steady vibration of the car.

Checking my watch, I yawned. "Are we close?" I asked, soothed by the gentle ride.

He slowed, turning onto a tree-lined road, a sign pointing up the large hill to Pienza. "Not far now."

I nestled comfortably into the bucket seat. "Talk to me about something. Anything. I don't want to fall asleep."

Laughing, he turned off the radio and tapped his chin, thinking. "Ah yes, I will tell you about the year the festival was almost rained out and the cave holding all of the pecorino was almost flooded."

There was something about his voice. Combined with the rocking sensation of the car, the pressure of his hand on mine and the fullness of my heart made my eyes fluttered closed.

"Mmm, I love pecorino." I sighed dreamily.

A COOL BREEZE SLIPPED OVER ME. I reached for Marcello, but I was greeted with a handful of cool leather. I was curled up in the passenger seat with a fuzzy blanket over me.

Sitting up, I wrapped the blanket around my shoulders and held the ends to my nose. It smelled faintly like Marcello. There was something about waking up without him that made everything feel off.

Looking around, I saw that we were parked in a wide circular driveway beside an expansive stone farmhouse. Voices carried from behind the house.

I stretched, my back tight from falling asleep crooked. Not at all from getting plowed on the side of the road . . .

I smiled faintly to myself, rolling my shoulders as I contemplated what to do. I didn't want to wander around the grounds without Marcello, but I didn't want to just sit here, either.

The air was perfumed with something I couldn't quite identify. It was warm, earthy, and crisp. Whatever it was made my stomach rumble. There was more laughter, children playing, and soft music on the wind. The children were getting closer; I could hear them yelling back and forth.

"Zio, Zio!" they screamed, Italian for uncle, giggling as they ran over the hill toward me. Marcello was close behind them, carrying a giggling toddler on his shoulders.

A smile split my face so big it hurt my cheeks. Dark curly haired and olive-skinned children screeched to a halt when they saw me standing with the blanket around my shoulders.

When Marcello—and two goats—caught up to them, they latched on to his legs, hugging him tight.

"Oh good, you awake," he said, stepping closer to give me a kiss on top of my head. His accent was thicker, his lack of contractions more pronounced.

"You changed," I chirped, trying to smooth out my rumpled dress.

"You look perfect."

"I'm a mess," I whispered, finally noticing the enormous Marcello handprint on the bodice of my dress. I gasped. "I can't meet your family like this, I look like I've been ravaged on the side of the road!"

He winked, whispering back, "You *were* ravaged on the side of the road."

I tried to scowl, but the baby on his shoulders started laughing at the face I was making. The rest of the children giggled when he dropped down and kissed me again, holding their hands over their mouths in the sweetest way.

He pulled away, smiling and rosy cheeked himself. "These are my nieces and nephews."

"This is my . . . Avery," he said in Italian, and the little girls squealed in delight.

The boys, well they weren't very interested in me; instead they took off after the goats. Honest-to-goodness goats.

"Nice to meet you," I said to the kids in my best Italian. Practice for the big family members. They didn't laugh, so I figured I did okay. He took my hand and tucked it into the crook of his arm as we walked toward the house. "I still can't believe you didn't wake me up."

"You were sound asleep."

"So you left me in the car while you got to change?"

"And snoring," he added. He lowered the toddler from his shoulders and sent her off with the other little girls, the baby waddling unsurely across the grass.

As we watched them run off, I was able to finally step back and see the house and the grounds. We were standing atop a hill sandwiched between two larger ones, each with a deep-set lush green valley below.

Everything—from the family house behind me to all of the outer buildings that were dotted across the property—had been built to overlook the vineyard below. It stretched in pristine rows with hundreds of squatty trees filling the area. Between them, paths, nets, and large hip baskets were scattered throughout. In a word, it was breathtaking. Deep, rich greens and browns were set against a perfect cloudless sky.

I wanted to sit in the window of the barn and sketch the view. Or take a bath in the main house with a glass of wine and Marcello behind me and watch the sunset.

"Do you like it?" he asked, wrapping his arms around me. The children's laughter faded, the music was different—a strumming mandolin now filled the calm.

"I love it. It suits you," I said, leaning into his embrace.

"What does?" He kissed my cheek.

"This place. The country." *The kids.*

Marcello looked different out of the city. His top buttons were undone, his hair was mussed, probably from playing with the children, and while still gorgeous he seemed . . . relaxed.

"You look comfortable out here. Not that you don't in the city, but out here in the wide-open space, all fresh air and warm sun with no hustle and bustle and technology, surrounded by kids, you look . . . *perfect.*"

He remained quiet for a moment.

I looked around, uncertain. "What?"

"Nothing," he said, turning me slowly before dipping me, the blanket falling to the grass behind us. He dropped light kisses across my forehead and cheeks, then my lips, while whispering *tesoro* over and over.

We stopped kissing in time to see the children running over the hill toward us. They'd multiplied and I wondered just how many people were here for the weekend.

Smoothing my hair back, I tried to unrumple my dress. What was I thinking wearing linen around his roaming Roman hands? He scooped up the blanket and laid it around my shoulders.

"I am sorry for your chest." He laughed, and when I looked down, there weren't just pink scruff marks littered across my breast. A hickey was forming.

"I'm going to kill you," I said, running after him through the grass.

He let me catch him when we got to a clearing that had massive wooden steps built into the hill.

"You didn't tell me that your family made wine," I said, catching my breath and walking closer to the hill's edge to get a better look.

"Not wine, olives," he said, brushing my hair away from my shoulder to place a kiss there. He rested his chin where his lips had just been and we watched the brilliant orange sun setting behind the grove.

"Bianchis have been making it for generations. I learned how to pick them as soon as I could walk," he said, and I pictured a small Marcello weaving in and out of the field laughing like his nephews were earlier.

"I love to sleep out here. On a blanket under the moon. Maybe naked," he said, pulling me into his arms. "We'll have to try it when the house gets too noisy." He kissed my neck lightly. "Out here we could be noisy."

"I look forward to it."

"I'll show you after dinner. It's magical at night. I'll give you a tour and kiss you under the stars, but Mama wants to meet you first."

Mama.

My stomach bottomed out, body tensed, heart thundered, and my ears were ringing. My track record with moms wasn't exactly noteworthy, and she was arguably the most important that I'd ever meet.

Taking my now-sweaty hand, he led me up the hill.

Marcello's family home may have only been two stories, but it was expansive, spread out into a U shape with a large stone courtyard in the center. The home was covered in light-colored brick and each window was framed with weathered royal blue shutters.

The grounds were scattered with various colored clay pots filled to the brim and spilling over with vibrant flowers and fragrant fruit trees, similar to what he had at his house in Rome.

"Is there a side door that I can sneak into so that I could change?"

Nodding, he led us around the back of the house away from the crowd of people.

"Cello!" a woman yelled, and he squeezed my hand.

"I'm sorry, *tesoro*," he said, turning us around to see a young woman, about our age, coming toward us with a round belly.

She took one look at me, kissed stupid and wrinkled, and laughed, grimacing at him. "Why you do this to her?"

"I did nothing to her," he said, holding up his hands in surrender. "Avery, this is my oldest sister, Allegra."

"How many are there?" I asked.

"I am the youngest of five."

"Why you have to say oldest, you couldn't just say my sister?" She slapped at his shoulder, throwing a few choice curses at him. "It is nice to meet you."

"It's great to meet you, too. We'll join you in a bit," I began, but she took my hand.

"No time to change, I afraid. You look good." She grinned knowingly.

Still, she gave me the thin sweater from around her shoulders. It covered the mess a bit better than the blanket and I looked *slightly* less like a homeless person.

The three of us followed the chatter around the sprawling grounds and into the beautiful courtyard. Marcello took my hand in his and kissed my cheek.

What drew my eye away from Marcello was the endless wooden table and the cheery, boisterous family seated at it, watching us intently.

"I've never seen a table that big," I said, counting his family. It was as expansive as the table.

"My father built it when I was a teenager," he said, a reassuring hand on the small of my back. "It's a bunch of separate pieces so it can be put together or taken apart depending on how many of us are around it. When the kids started having kids—well, you can see it got bigger. Add in aunts, uncles, cousins . . ."

"*And* I'm officially nervous."

We stopped abruptly, him scrunching down so our eyes met. He took my hands in his, bringing them both to his lips, and whispered, "Don't be nervous. They will love you," against them.

"Let's skip dinner," I told him, and I was serious. Before I could whisk him away to an olive grove to have my wicked way with him, a woman carrying a pitcher called out to him.

"Are you ready?"

I squeezed his hand and said a silent prayer.

An older man sat at the head of the table, his hand wrapped around the woman's hand to his right. He was handsome, tan with a thick head of salt-and-pepper hair. I could have seen him anywhere in the world and known he was Marcello's father.

As we approached, he kissed the woman's hand and stood slowly, rubbing a spot on his hip. One of the few differences between him and his son was their height. Marcello towered over him to the point of it being almost comical.

"The height comes from my mother's side," he joked just as his father pulled him into a crushing hug.

"*Ciao, bella!*" he said, dropping a light kiss on each of my cheeks. In the most delightful broken English he introduced himself as Angelo Bianchi and he was, "*so happy that you are here.*"

He pulled me away from his son by wrapping my arm in his.

His father took the time to introduce me to his parents, then it was on to Marcello's three brothers, the in-laws, and all of twelve kids before we got to aunts and uncles, cousins, and second cousins. I'm pretty sure some of these people were random strangers they invited to dinner, because who has a family this big?

The one I was dreading was Marcello's mother. You hear stories about Italian mothers and how inherently disapproving and overprotective they are, especially to a foreigner who is sleeping with her youngest son. Suzanna Bianchi was a diminutive woman with a shock of inky black hair and a bright smile that could rival her son's. She was wearing an apron and had an honest-to-God wooden spoon tucked into one of the pockets. I watched her chase the grandchildren and give her husband a quick kiss before she came over to us.

"Sweetheart," she said, before pulling her son down to her eye level.

"Mama." He squatted down and picked her up to kiss her cheeks. "I missed you."

Setting her down, he took her hand and turned to me. "This is Avery."

I expected the sizing-up once-over. I even expected the knowing look when she saw Marcello's hand wrapped protectively around mine.

What I didn't anticipate was her pulling me into the sweetest hug this side of my own mother's arms and dropping two quick pecks on my cheeks.

Bitsy only wanted the dainty handshake or air kisses. I wasn't sure if she ever actually hugged Daniel. I'd been scared of Marcello's mother for no reason at all.

"Come, you sit by me," she insisted, pulling me along to an empty chair. "Marcello, he no bring anyone home, he tell you that?"

"Oh, Mama, no," he protested, laughing when his brothers began to tease him in Italian.

"I heard something like that, yes," I answered, sitting in the chair I was directed to.

"My son, he a romantic, *si*?"

I blushed, but nodded.

"So okay. He bring you here, you must be good girl, *si*?"

"Yes," Marcello answered, and getting the frown of the century from his mother for answering for me.

"My son bring you here, I think you a good girl. Now, you hungry, *si*?"

I watched as the biggest bowl of ravioli I'd ever seen was placed on the center of the table in front of me, waves of tomato-scented incredible wafting toward me. "Oh my yes, hungry."

And with that, everyone tucked in. Marcello's mother and two of his sister-in-laws hovered nearby, never sitting, just making sure that everyone had what they needed. Most of the people around the table spoke Italian only, but a few words of broken

English filtered through and I surprised myself when I could pick out more of the Italian than I thought I would. I mainly focused on the food . . . and Marcello.

Watching him with his family was fascinating. His mother hovered over everyone certainly, but seemed to linger a little longer behind him. A hand on the shoulder, an extra meatball or two, it was clear that the son who had left for the big city was revered when he came home.

"You okay so far?" he asked when his mother and sisters brought out another round of food. Pastas, veggies, salads, meats—it was a veritable smorgasbord.

Family dinners in Boston were quiet, reserved affairs where we spoke in low voices and never yelled across the table, let alone down the length across twenty other people.

This was boisterous, energetic, and physical at times when Marcello's sister and brothers would poke and prod him. The sense of family was so strong here, so connected, that even though I didn't understand half of what was being said I never felt like an outsider.

When dinner was over, everyone pitched in to clean up and watched the kids chase the animals through the grass.

"Was this a good day?" he said, taking my hand and leading me away from little prying eyes.

"It was the best day," I answered.

CHAPTER 21

WHEN I WOKE, the bedroom was filled with the scent of an Italian breakfast. I didn't know what treats were made, but I couldn't wait to find out. Marcello was oblivious to it, snoring softly behind me, his arm wrapped around my middle. Rolling over carefully, I smoothed my fingers over his forehead and down his arm, loving the wake of goose bumps that formed. I spent a few minutes staring at him, memorizing his face in the morning light. Suddenly, all thoughts of a hearty meal weren't as important.

I wondered if I'd ever lose that giddy feeling that I got last night when he told me he loved me. It was something that we'd never said the first go around, but we knew it. I felt it in every fiber of me then and now. Maybe it was the universe throwing us back together as part of some cosmic plot, or perhaps I was just the luckiest person alive, but I was hell-bent on not making the same mistakes I did the first time.

"What are you thinking about?" he asked sleepily. His eyes remained closed, lips fighting back a grin. Leaning forward, I kissed the tip of his nose before pressing my lips to his.

"I'm wondering if it's possible to love you more than I do right now."

His hand slid down my back, over my rear, and squeezed. "That sounds like a challenge."

"Your family is in the house," I admonished, throwing my head back when his lips traced a path down my neck.

"Then you must be very quiet, *tesoro* . . ."

———

AFTER OUR SURPRISE MORNING TANGLE, he'd tried to get me to sneak into the shower with him. I'd firmly put my foot down on that one, already feeling guilty about doing the naughty in his family's home. So while he showered, I explored the room I'd be staying in for the weekend.

I'd thought—in fact prepared myself ahead of time—that we wouldn't be sharing a bedroom while we stayed with his family. Old Italian mother, severely Catholic—it didn't take a genius to figure out that boy/girl cohabitation wasn't going to fly. But that's the thing about preconceived notions, you just never know when you're going to be surprised. Marcello's parents were very forward thinking—*hip* was the word his mother had used when she ushered us down the long central hall and into a large guest room after dinner. *"You two, you sleep together here, si?"* she'd said.

Blushing, I'd nodded, standing just behind and almost out of sight of Marcello, mortified that she knew what we'd likely be up to under her roof. Marcello laughed out loud as I stammered my good night to his mother, in my best broken Italian accent. Once she headed back down the hall, I'd yanked him inside and buried my red face in the nearest corner of the room.

When Marcello took advantage of this angle by standing directly behind me and wrapping his arms around me while placing wet, openmouthed kisses along the back of my neck, I'd quickly forgotten my embarrassment and let him pull me down into the mess of pillows.

Now, with a clearer head and Marcello and his roving hands safely half a house away in the shower, I looked around a bit. It was a beautiful room.

With a wide window overlooking the hillside below, a cozy yet comfortable bed piled high with pillows and a thick mattress, and soft plush rugs underfoot, it was heaven after a long night of eating, laughing, talking, drinking, and more eating. A heaven I'd sunk back into for a few more minutes of relaxed country snoozing when Marcello reappeared, somewhat dressed and still a bit damp from his shower.

"You should get dressed, Avery. The family leaves for the festival in thirty minutes," he said, grabbing a shirt out of the closet. "And the games begin as soon as everyone is there."

"Let me get this straight," I said, smoothing his crisp white shirt over his shoulders. "It's like the bocce game that I see the little old men play near the apartment back in Rome, but instead of balls, they play with discs of hard cheese?"

Nodding, he finished tying his black shoes. He was sitting on the edge of his bed, hair damp, and he seemed antsy, his leg bouncing nervously. He, along with one of his older brothers and some neighbors, were part of one of the six teams that would compete in the Piazza Pio in town. Dressed in black pants and the green-and-white scarf he was tying around his neck, he looked like he had stepped out of another time.

"I'm expecting some manly bouts of strength."

"You will be disappointed. I will flex my muscles for you, though," he teased, giving me a quick kiss and a swat on the behind as I scrambled out of bed, needing to get ready myself.

Twenty-five minutes later, hair swept back and body poured into a kelly-green summer dress, I was caught by a handsy Italian before we left the bedroom. Taking my hands, he pinned them over the door before sweeping me up in a kiss.

"What's gotten into you? Not that I'm complaining, but it took me twenty minutes to cover up the love bites you left me yesterday."

He rested his head in the crook of my shoulder. "Being here, at my family home with you . . . it means a lot."

"To me, too," I told him, cupping his face.

When we joined the others outside, the families were all piled into vans. We decided to take the Alfa because why the hell not. Winding Italian roads, hot Italian man, and incredible Italian car, no-brainer. Once on the road and following the others, I turned to him.

"Will you explain the festival now?"

He looked pleased that I'd asked. "It's simple, traditional. The Il Gioco del Cacio al Fuso has been around for hundreds of years.

"The architect Rossellino rebuilt my town and designed the square as a dedication to Pope Pius. In the center, there is the brick pattern, with a design created with a ring of marble. At the core there is a spindle, and rings drawn around the bricks in chalk. Each ring is worth certain points. We roll the cheese wheel to try and win."

"But why cheese?"

"Pienza is known for its pecorino. The game used to be played in yards as a pastime for peasant families, but then it became more of a town sport and celebration. Each section of the town participates. I hope you think it is fun." He loved talking about it, and I enjoyed hearing him explain it. Not just because it was interesting to hear how modern-day families kept alive the old traditions, but because he got excited like a child with a new toy discussing it.

"And this is hard?" I asked seriously. Rolling cheese didn't seem like it was anything complicated.

"Oh yes. It's more, *come si dice,* mental than physical skill. Very. My father participated for years, so did his father and his father before. It's generational. This is my first year."

"It is?" That explained why he was nervous, and it added another level of importance to me being here for him.

I wrapped my hand around his and whispered, "So you'll be using that big brain of yours today. We'll use the muscles later."

HUNDREDS OF PEOPLE MILLED ABOUT, sporting their favorite colors. All rooting for their districts—like *The Hunger Games* except without the murder. Six teams, or districts, would compete in the trials and the winner got bragging rights.

It wasn't just the game, though; it was an event for the whole weekend. I could understand now why his entire extended family gathered for this. It was a large-scale family reunion for the entire town that drew in hundreds of tourists as well. The restaurants that surrounded the main square had seating outside for people to watch the festivities during lunch and to reconnect with friends they hadn't seen since the year before.

Many stores pulled out their wares to sell on the street to the onlookers; almost all had specialized flags, shirts, and buttons for the teams. I picked up a green-and-white scarf to tie around my neck like the other women cheering on Marcello's district.

He was having a meeting with his crew when he saw me, sitting on the outskirts with his family. With a look of pure pride, he marched over and scooped me up in his arms, planting a searing kiss on me and earning a chorus of shouts from the onlookers.

"What was that for?" I fanned myself with the program a woman was handing out.

"Luck, *tesoro.*" With a wink, he took off and joined his teammates. I'd remember to buy up a few more team-centric items to bring back home.

As far as the game itself, Marcello took it very seriously. I didn't realize just how competitive he was. He was right, it wasn't just rolling a wheel, it was about accuracy and patience and strategy to try to get the wheel as close to the spindle as you could. Writing it off as a joke because it was cheese was bad form on my part. I cheered as loudly as anyone else when my man ran by, rolling a giant wheel of cheese with the biggest grin I'd ever seen plastered across his face.

I was waiting for the second round to start when his sister came over carrying gelato.

"Are you enjoying Roma?" Allegra asked.

"I am. This has been the best"—*trip, reconnection, vacation?*—"the best."

She glanced around the crowd before turning, asking barely loud enough for me to hear, "Are you staying?"

Allegra continued to eat her gelato as if this simple conversation hadn't turned serious. I was so focused on being afraid of his mother that I didn't consider the older, protective sister.

"You mean in Rome?" *Or with your brother?*

"Rome is not his home. He *lives* in Rome. He *works* in Rome. But his home? His home is here."

I waved to his mother, who was watching us curiously. "I know that."

Then with four simple words, she knocked the wind right out of me. "I know about you."

"What?" My eyes found him in the crowd, kneeling beside his father and chatting. I couldn't turn to face her, afraid of what I would see. Or what I would show her.

"When he came home from Barcelona, he told me about this American girl. A girl that he could not stop thinking about. He could not wait to hear from again."

Oh boy.

She continued. "He did not tell me at first. I had to get him to talk. He wait a long time for you, Avery. You don't do this to him again."

I turned to her. "I have no intention to."

Even though her words could be construed as threatening, they didn't feel that way. She was a woman concerned for her family and I couldn't blame her for that. With a nod, she took off into the crowd, her hand resting on her pregnant belly.

While the other teams competed, Marcello stayed with his group, giving me time to wander around the square. I wasn't avoiding his family, but I needed time to process.

Just stepping a block away from the festival quieted the streets. Seeing the architecture here, it was no wonder that Marcello fell in love with it at a young age. Plaques described the tiny village as the "City of the Renaissance," having had many famous architects visit and leave their stamps on the buildings.

Perched high atop the travertine stone buildings, flags flapped in the breeze. Following the bell, I found myself in front of the cathedral with the tolling bell tower that overlooked the square below.

Sitting out front, I tried to imagine a young Marcello coming back here after Spain. Was he really as brokenhearted as

Allegra said? Why did he keep it to himself when we went for coffee that first day?

The silence didn't answer any of my questions, but Marcello would. If we were going to give this everything we could, we had to make sure that the past was forgiven first.

I made it back to the match just in time to see his team play their last round. The crowd had thinned over the course of the afternoon, unlike my thoughts, which multiplied the longer I stood on the sidewalk watching him.

"Is everything okay?" he asked, draping his arm across my shoulders. We hung back from the rest of his family after the match and were strolling through the center of town, enjoying the last of the celebration.

When we got back to the car, he had pulled off the scarf, tucking it into his pocket. "There is a party at sunset if you want to come back," he offered, opening the car door.

"Maybe you'll win for me next year when we come back," I said, placing my hand over his on the open door.

He smiled so brightly, and looked so young in that moment, it was like seeing the past. He looked every bit the twenty-two-year-old whose heart I broke.

"*That* is a promise."

———

THAT AFTERNOON I TREATED MYSELF to a catnap in one of the chaise lounges by the pool and a walk around the gardens. Wanting to give Marcello some time alone with his family, I wandered this way and that, marveling at the colors. A path led through a winding garden with several "rooms." Whoever had designed the space did so with an exacting sense of proportion, the lines graceful but clean, the palette varying but complementary. As was becoming customary, my hand twitched as I thought of the compositions I could create here, especially now in the late-afternoon sun, the golden hour.

As the pathways took me back closer to the house, I found myself at the edge of the kitchen garden, filled to bursting with summer vegetables and herbs. Walking under an archway blanketed by flowering vines, there stood Marcello with a small spade and his mother with a keen look in her eye.

"Avery, how was your walk, good?" she asked, waving me over.

"It was good; your gardens are lovely," I answered, stepping into Marcello's outstretched arm and letting him pull me into his side. "What are you two up to?"

"Weeds," Marcello answered, rolling his eyes and earning a tug on his ear from Suzanna.

"Bah, you think you are too old to help your mother? These weeds, they choke out the tomatoes! Come."

We followed along behind his mother, who pointed out all the different herbs she'd planted and the ones she'd be using in tonight's feast. Rosemary, parsley, several varieties of oregano, and the most enormous basil plants I'd ever seen. They were bushy and three feet high if they were an inch, and she attacked them with her snippers, cutting huge handfuls for her basket.

"Cello, the yellow tomatoes, see how they are surrounded? Save them, yes?"

"Yes, Mama," Marcello answered, and stepped to wage his war on the encroaching weeds.

"Can I help?" I offered, picking up what looked like a hoe that was lying in the eggplant beds.

Marcello nodded, gesturing toward the plants opposite him and digging in.

The three of us moved about the garden for half an hour or so, Marcello and me digging while his mother puttered about, snipping here, staking there, murmuring to her plants and her son all the while. They switched between Italian and broken English as we moved down the rows, and while I couldn't understand everything, it was pleasant nonetheless to see and hear Marcello with his mother, whom he obviously adored.

At the end of my row, while digging around the last tomato plant, I struck something hard under the dirt. Loosening the soil slightly, I tugged and pulled a large piece of wood, scarred and blackened.

"What did you find?" Marcello called, peeking up over his row.

"Just an old piece of wood," I replied, turning it this way and that, examining it more closely. It appeared to have writing on one side, but it was hard to tell. "It almost looks like it was, I don't know, burned maybe?"

"Let me see," Suzanna said, setting down her basket and heading my way. Picking up the wood, she turned it over, running her fingers over the letters. "This is from the old barn; it burned many years ago."

"Before I was born, there was a barn that stood right here; you can still see the foundations, yes?" Marcello pointed, and I realized that what I thought was just a low wall around the garden was in fact an old foundation.

"It burned the year after we were married," she said, lost in thought. "Very awful, very scary. All the animals were saved, but the building? *Distrutto.*"

"That's terrible." I looked around, trying to imagine what it used to look like.

"It was terrible," she agreed. "But by the next summer,

things began to grow. First, just the weeds. But then Gabriella, Marcello's grandmother, she go and plant tomatoes. And they were *enorme*! The fire, it burned the barn, but it made the earth . . . *forte*. How do you say?"

Marcello supplied the word. "Strong."

"Ah yes, strong." She nodded, and waved her hand over the entire garden. "Bad beginning. But now?" Her eyes twinkled. "*Magnifico*."

I stared across the rows at Marcello, wondering if he was thinking the same thing I was.

"Very fertile, this family," Suzanna said. "*Scusi*, this family's land." She winked at me, then turned and headed back toward the house, calling over her shoulder, "Marcello, you finish that row, then you wash before dinner. You are *disordinato*!"

"Messy, Mama, messy!"

"Yes, you are messy, too!" came the reply.

I pushed my way through the plants, surrounded by the smell of green growing things, in a place that was once covered in blackened ruin.

"Fertile, huh?" I asked, leaning up on my tiptoes to kiss his *disordinato* face.

"We have many tomatoes."

"And you have many siblings."

Now his eyes twinkled. "Big families are good, yes?"

I kissed him then, getting his messy all over me. "I think a big family could be very good."

And with that, I went back to hoeing . . .

———

"MAMA, CAN WE HELP YOU?" Marcello asked, setting the dinner plates on the marble countertop.

"No, take a walk before the sun sets," she insisted, shooing him out of the door, me following behind.

He kissed her on top of her head and led us outside.

We followed the stone pathway to the stairs that led down to the olive groves. They were deep, old wooden planks that should have looked out of place given that they were built into the hillside. Colorful wildflowers lined the sides and the grass popped up through the cracks, making them appear more of the earth than of the men who built them.

"How long have these been here?" I asked as we descended the steep steps.

"My great-grandfather put them in to make it easier to get to the trees. Before that they went all around the property with the horses and down the lower hills."

When we got to the bottom, I inhaled deeply. I wasn't sure what the scent of an olive grove would be. Walking through oranges, strawberries, or apples was an assault on the senses. Sweet, fruity, and vibrant. This was more of a musky, earthy smell that snuck up on you and settled into your skin.

We walked the length of the center dirt path that split the property right down the middle. It was still, quiet, and with the sun beginning to set on the rise behind the house, a bit spooky.

"If I didn't know better, I'd think you were leading me out here to take advantage of me."

He hummed in response. "No one would bother us out here now."

I tamped down the flutters thinking about making love to him out here in the wide open. The car was wild, frenzied, but this could be an experience under the stars.

Taking my hand, he wove us in and out of the trees, around

the different cutting and netting stations that were spread throughout the property, but no machines. I figured with this many trees, there would be some sort of steel contraption to make it easier on his family.

"You do all of this by hand?"

"Olives and grapes don't do well with mechanization, so it is a simple, modest process."

"Where do you squish them?" I asked, looking around for *I Love Lucy*–style barrels. "Is this like grapes where you stomp?"

He laughed, rich and deep echoing in the open fields. "No, we have a mill up there," he told me, motioning to a giant stone barn at the top of another hill. "We will come back when it's harvest time. If you want."

"I want," I said without hesitation.

He was quiet as he led us to a large juniper tree. I saw why he was taking us so far out into the vineyard; the house was merely a speck on the hillside. *For the quiet.*

Set up at the base of the tree was a blanket, oil lanterns hanging from the branches flickering circles onto the ground. At the corner sat a pad and pastels.

"Marcello, what did you do?" I breathed, looking at everything he had thought to set out ahead of time.

"I know sunset is one of your favorite times to work. I thought maybe we could sit out here together while you sketch."

I broke apart from him, moving to sit in the center of the blanket. "What will you be doing while I'm hard at work?"

"Trying not to kiss you."

He pulled out a bottle of wine and two glasses from a bag at the base of the tree. After setting them down on the blanket, he grabbed get some fruit and cheese that were in a cooler.

"How'd you get all this out here?"

"Allegra helped me," he said, getting to work on the cork. "She told me she talked to you at the fair today—I'm sorry."

"Why are you sorry?" I said, reaching over to hold his hand. "She was just watching out for her brother. It makes sense." I waited, picking at the skinny olive leaves that had fallen onto the blanket. "Maybe I wasn't ready for you then, but I want you to know that I am now. I want to stay here, with you."

"It means a lot that you are here with me, *tesoro*, here with my family, in this place. It's not where I live anymore, but it's still my home. It's everything I love."

My eyes widened, tears gathering when he repeated it. "You hear me say, yes? I love you."

I nodded, smiling and burrowing my head into his chest. I squeezed my arms around his waist. "I love you, too. So much."

Happy tears spilled, but I was too busy being kissed silly to care. With his hands on my cheeks, he peppered kisses and whispered *I love you*s all over my face. "I don't think I ever stopped loving you."

Pouring two glasses, he handed me one, kissing my shoulder and taking a seat. With his back resting against the tree trunk, he watched me set up the pencils, pastels, and paper.

"Do you remember the wine?"

Like a flash fire coursing through dry brush, the memory charged back.

We were wrapped in each other's arms, a bottle of wine that we bought in town resting at the foot of the bed. I was young and knew nothing of wine. It tasted like pepper and plums.

"Y-yes," I stuttered, the green pastel scratching across the page haphazardly. I smudged it with my finger to fix it but only made it worse.

"What do you remember? Tell me, *tesoro*."

"Everything," I admitted, touching my chest with a shaky hand, my chalky fingers transferring the dust to the light-colored dress.

"You said, *'Don't mind me, I like to watch you work,'* but you weren't just watching, you were tormenting me, rubbing the wine across your lips with your finger. Sitting with your shirt off, casually leaning against the bed, you looked like heaven and hell sent to torture me."

"I felt the same about you. I couldn't keep my hands off you."

I slid the pastel across the page with a scratch. "You said you wanted to paint me."

He shifted and stretched his legs out. I settled between them, pushing back until I rested against his chest. The lanterns hanging from the trees above swayed in the breeze, making the light dance across the page.

"I saved one, you know."

I stopped, setting the chalk down on the blanket beside us. "Saved what?"

"A painting that you had left behind," he said, pulling my dress strap down.

"Marcello, I—"

"At first I kept it for you for when you returned. Then you didn't come back and I kept it for me. But you are here now." He paused, turning me in his arms so that I straddled him.

"I'm here now," I said before I hugged him, slipping my fingers through his hair. "I'm not leaving."

Laying me back onto the blanket, he covered my body with his and propped himself up on his elbows. The papers crumbled beneath us, pastels cracked against my back and under his hands.

The lantern was shining next to him, making the pain in his eyes pronounced. Palpable.

Marcello looked every bit like my greatest love and my biggest regret.

He lifted his hand, smiling at the sage-green dust on his palm and smoothed it across my forehead, brushing my hair back.

I felt a pastel near my right hand. Clutching it, I rubbed it into my palm. Bringing my hand up to his face, I cupped his cheek, leaving a slight pink imprint there.

He pulled off his shirt, tossing it to the side. Unbuttoning my dress, he opened it like a gift, laying the sides on the blanket.

"*Bellisima.*"

We took turns, each taking the broken pieces and painting the other with them. A stripe of cobalt across his stomach. A streak of yellow on the inside of my thigh. An abstract green heart over my breasts and the word *love* in purple across his chest.

"You promised me a kiss under the stars," I whispered, my hands slipping to his belt.

CHAPTER 22

I WAS BACK IN ROME after a weekend in Pienza. With my Italian. Who loves me!

And his family. Who also loves me!

I didn't have a class today, I didn't have to work today, so I was taking myself shopping.

Via Condotti. Like Bond Street in London, or Rodeo Drive in Beverly Hills, every major city had a street with all the best stores: Gucci, Ferragamo, Zegna, Bulgari, Prada of course, but also Jimmy Choo, Louis Vuitton, La Perla, the best. At the foot of the Spanish Steps, the Via Condotti could be hopelessly touristy unless you shopped early, before the crowds arrived.

Huh. Look at that. I'm avoiding tourists.

Normally I'd also have avoided the area entirely, preferring the trendier stores in the Monti district, but today I wanted to revel a little bit, I suppose. There was one store in particular that I wanted to visit. I felt like celebrating.

An email from Daniel's attorney this morning had confirmed the news I'd been waiting for. Daniel wasn't contesting the divorce, and not only that, he wasn't contesting my settlement requests. I'd had mixed feelings all along about alimony. What it represented, whether or not I agreed with the concept, but the bottom line was that I'd given up my career to make his career possible. I'd supported him 100 percent. I made the home and hearth habitable, I kept the schedules and catered the parties and bolstered the connections and played my part so that he could soar. A high-delivering lawyer in an established law firm was compensated fairly, and all I wanted was the same.

I'd waived the option of requesting to be paid until I'd married again, as if the only way I'd be okay was if I found another husband to take care of me. Five years was all I'd asked for. Half the proceeds from the house (neither of us wanted to live there again), the title to my car (especially since the brand-new BMW was probably a penis gift), and five years of a monthly stipend. I could have asked for more, and he could have fought harder to provide less, but in the end he agreed that the sooner this was over, the better.

His family was furious. My family was concerned.

He was moving on. I was blissful.

Since coming home from Pienza, the wonderful words that Marcello had said still filled my heart with puffy white clouds of happiness, and things had been truly blissful.

And I was treating myself to some bliss today. I wandered past all the stores, gazing into the window displays, stopping a bit longer outside the La Perla store and making some mental notes for another day, until I found the store I'd been looking for.

Hermès.

I'd been dying for a fix. Not normally someone who goes in for labels, I justified my Hermès scarf addition as not so much buying into fashion as it was honoring a fashionable history. Audrey Hepburn, Sophia Loren, Grace Kelly—all iconic women who wore these iconic scarves.

I sailed past the Birkin bags on display. I had very specific feelings about the Birkin. My mother-in-law had two. Daniel had tried to buy me one, had in fact purchased it from the store on Boylston Street. I kissed him, thanked him, then sent him back to return it. I felt it was ridiculous to spend fifteen thousand on something you carry your phone and tampons in.

But an Hermès scarf? Maybe it's because my mother gave me my first when I graduated from high school. Maybe it's because she wore them to church every Sunday, color coordinated with her purse and shoes. Maybe it's because my grandmother had dozens, collected over the years as she traveled the world with my grandfather, each scarf commemorating a different adventure.

I had my eye on a particularly fetching cashmere scarf, beautiful pink and red shot through with swirls of orange.

I was on an adventure, in a different country, and about to successfully divorce my husband amicably. A trifecta!

Thirty minutes later I was gazing down at the red, pink, and orange swirled around my neck, and bumped into someone coming in as I was coming out of Hermès.

"*Merde,*" a feminine voice cursed, and I fought to keep my balance.

"I'm so sorry, *mi scusa,*" I said, grabbing on to the door handle, steadying her as well. I saw beautiful jet-black hair smoothed into a fashionable ponytail, big green almond-shaped eyes, granite-sharp cheekbones, and a beautiful mouth turned down in a frown.

She looked familiar. Why did she look so familiar?

We both played "place the face" for a few seconds, realization dawning on me the same moment it did on her face.

Simone, the woman with Marcello my first night in Rome.

"Simone," I blurted, wishing I could pull the words back in, but the shock of running into her rankled me.

She stepped in front of me, blocking the path, her Dior shopping bag draped over her bent arm. There was no misjudging her anger. She would have looked like any of the other chic women moving about the fashionable district, were it not for the undiluted hatred pouring off her. I skirted around her, wanting to avoid the confrontation, but she wasn't having it and managed to side-step me again. Did she know about us? That he was with me now, that I was the girl who—

"Fucked my Italian" she growled with so much disdain.

Oh yes. She knew.

She followed, her eyes laser locked on me, the girl who—

"Fucked my Italian," she hissed.

Dammit! I had to stop setting her up in my head like that!

"If you'll excuse me," I said, taking a step back, bumping into a gaggle of tourists. The crowd moved around us like water around a couple of boulders, enjoying the beautiful day, unaware that a Wild West showdown had begun on the poshest street in town.

"I will not. We have to talk, you and I. Woman to woman," she shouted, drawing the judging eyes from the couples walking past us.

Looking for a way to placate her, I edged over to the side between two palm trees. This all felt very *Real Housewives of Rome* with the crowd of tourists getting ready to climb the Spanish Steps, or the unassuming families stopping for gelato. The last thing I wanted was unwanted attention from the peanut gallery. "Simone, this really isn't the place—"

"Don't you dare say my name after you took him away from me," she said, her accent thicker than I remembered.

French, maybe? I couldn't quite place it. Although to be fair, there wasn't much I was paying attention to other than Marcello and his beautiful face. And as a matter of fact, now that I think about it, were they even together that night? Her demeanor had seemed possessive, but who wouldn't be around someone as good looking as Marcello, especially if she'd been trying to land him? Ha! This boulder stood a bit taller.

"I don't know what you think happened, but I can assure you that—"

"You will be quiet. I have heard enough about you, from Cello. I knew something was going on that night. He acted so odd when you showed up out of nowhere, stupid American falling out of her chair—you looked ridiculous. I couldn't figure out why he wouldn't stop staring at you!"

"Marcello and I have known each other a long time. There's a lot of history there," I replied, keeping my tone even and cool, though my heart was pounding in my throat. And the fact that we shared a history made it more concrete. Real. I was his *tesoro*, his *treasure*. And this French bitch *girl* wasn't going to take that away.

"*I* had history with Marcello," she asserted, her voice beginning to crack, hurt showing through. "We were something before you—" She broke off.

A prickly cold feeling was creeping up my spine. What was she talking about?

"I didn't notice it at first. A missed dinner here, a canceled concert there. He was *always* busy, especially when he was bringing a project in, but he always made the time for me. For my needs. When he said he was too busy to bring me to the opening party for the new bank? I thought maybe . . . but he came back. He could not stay away for long."

I could feel the blood drain from my face. She must have noticed, too, because she was suddenly very pleased with herself, standing a bit taller, her chest pushed out a bit farther. She'd struck a raw nerve and she knew it.

"Wait. Just wait a minute," I said, shaking my head, trying to understand. "You and Marcello were together? Like, *together* together?"

She looked confused. "Why do you say it twice?"

"Just answer my question."

Color crept into her cheeks. "Yes, of course we were. We were together for months before you showed up. I convinced him that this was not permanent—you being here. Why end things with me in the hopes that you would stay?"

"I meant *after* I showed up. You were together? In all the ways?" I asked, knowing the answer, but not being able to stop myself from asking anyway.

"Of course in all the ways," she scoffed, but her tone shifted. She went from disdain to lethal. "Ah," she sneered, beginning to circle me. "You are wondering if we fucked? It bothers you not knowing what we did. Did you think he would drop everything for you?"

"I . . ." I wanted to say yes, that it was bothering me. Yes, I thought because we didn't discuss her that she was a nonentity, but I also didn't want to give her the satisfaction of knowing how much her words were tearing me apart.

She huffed in response, but didn't walk away.

"When was the last time you . . ."

"Oh!" She laughed. "When did he end things with me?" she asked, raising her chin a bit.

"You want to know the last time he fucked me, no?"

I nodded.

"Was it after he fucked you? Does that bother you? Wondering if he left you, not satisfied, and had to seek me out?" Her gaze was calculating, assessing. She looked at me long enough that I reflexively began to wonder if I had something on my shirt. Finally, she smiled. My heart sank. "You ask him."

I reeled back, the pavement seeming to move beneath my feet. The edges of the world went haywire and out of focus, as though the earth had tilted on its axis and I could fall off a great cliff, with nothing to hold on to.

She leaned close, murmuring, "You be sure to tell him you ran into me, no?"

Oh, I'd be sure.

WHEN I'D LEFT TO GO SHOPPING, Marcello was at home engrossed in his work. Needing quiet, he opted to skip the office craziness to do some research for a new bid he'd been putting hours and hours of work into. The job was massive in scale and would be an enormous undertaking should his team's proposal win.

When?

Oh, God.

It felt like my chest was being crushed, and I bent at the waist, trying to breathe deeply as another searing image of them together knocked the breath from my lungs.

When I finally straightened, my feet flew across the cobblestones toward his home, my disbelief becoming a chant that matched my footsteps. *Click click, click click, how long, how long?*

I needed to talk to him, to find out what really happened, and if Simone was lying. Was she a disgruntled woman who would say anything to hurt someone who left her? Or a hurt woman whose heart had been broken by the man who had given me his?

Finally reaching his apartment, I flew up the stairs, my feet pounding out my confusion and insistence that it wasn't true, that it couldn't be true.

I tried working out the timeline to see what fit. *Maybe* things fit if I were to believe her claims. That awful crawly feeling was back, making me doubt, making me wonder.

At his door I considered knocking, but he'd told me never to knock, just to enter. *Because only strangers knock,* he'd told me, then slipped a hand under my shirt to caress my belly while kissing me stupid.

Had Simone been granted the same privilege?

I opened the door, finding Marcello seated at his drafting desk, a pencil behind his ear and an enormous smile on his face when he saw me. Crossing to me with heavily lidded eyes and sinful lips he was already licking in anticipation of my kiss, he was so incredibly beautiful that only my clenched fists reminded me of what had happened earlier today.

"*Tesoro*, you're back so late?" he murmured. "I was beginning to wonder what was keeping you." He dipped his head to place a kiss along my jawline, his weekend stubble brushing my skin as I pulled away.

I looked up into those warm brown eyes. "Simone."

His hands stilled on me, his entire body stiffened, his features carved in stone. He cleared his throat.

"Simone? What about her?" he asked, crossing his arms over his chest.

His question lit something deep within me.

"She told me."

"Told you what?" When his eyes changed, I knew everything she'd implied was true.

My breath hitched. "That you were with her," I said, my voice sounding strange in my ears. High pitched, a little crazy.

"Yes, you knew that. You saw me with her at the dinner. She was someone I dated for a time. So?"

"So? She stopped me on the street today and told me how long you were together. *For a time.*"

"Yes, for a time, so?"

I went on as if he hadn't spoken. "Were you fucking us both?"

"It was never serious." He kept talking, missing what I said. Purposefully missing what I said?

I felt my heart bottom out. "She told me you were fucking us both *at the same time, Marcello.* Explain to me how that couldn't possibly be true, that she can't possibly be right about this."

"I dated Simone. Casually. Occasionally. I don't know what she told you, if she was more serious about me than I was about her, but it was not like that for me."

"It's funny that you never mentioned her to me after we started . . . after we started."

"What would I tell you? I didn't know if you were staying, or for how long. Why would I say anything when we"—he waved between us—"were not together."

"Were you with us both, Marcello?"

"What are you asking me?"

I laughed, hoarse and hollow. "It's a simple question: Did you fuck her after you fucked me?"

He reared back as if I struck him. "Now wait a minute, wait just a minute," he protested, digging his hands into my skin.

I pushed angrily at his hands, tugging free of his grasp.

He let me go, frustrated. "You and I, we weren't even together," he insisted. "And what was going on with Simone and me, it was not serious."

"Well, *she* sure thought it was!" I pushed him, hard enough that he stumbled back. If I was shocked, he was stunned. "How long after we slept together did you go to her?" My voice was barely audible over my shuddery breathing. To think that he'd been with someone else while we'd started sleeping together . . . I felt sick.

"*Tesoro*," he began, laying his hand on my shoulder.

I shook him off. "Don't call me that! Did you call *her* that, too?"

I moved as far away from him as I could in the small room.

He stood in the heart of the room looking lost.

"Just tell me the truth, Mar—" I choked on a sob. Hearing her call him Cello was another slap in the face. Even though he'd said he wasn't serious, it clearly was. They had a shorthand. She was invested.

I was invested, too.

"What does it matter?" he said, stepping back to lean against his desk. His head was in his hands while he spoke. "I don't remember. I don't care. There was no *you and I* then."

"While I was falling in love with you all over again, you were fucking someone else who loved you."

I looked up, expecting to see more of the detached response. But wait a minute—he had the nerve to look *angry*?

"Yes, and that should be very familiar to you," he said, anger thickening his accent. "In Barcelona, how long for *you*?"

My head snapped back, startled.

He was pacing now, his hands in his hair, eyes wild, hurt and filled with pain. "How many times did you call Daniel from Spain while I was in *your* bed, Avery?"

"What? What are you talking about?" I was struck cold.

"When we were in Barcelona, you would leave your bed—*our* bed, Avery—in the middle of the night to call your boyfriend back in the States. You think I did not know? You didn't say anything about him, but I knew. You didn't tell me about him; I didn't mention Simone. How is this different?"

My cheeks burned, my face flooding with anger. "It's different because we were kids! I was—" Oh, God. Everything he was saying about Barcelona, about Daniel, was all true.

"What? You were not serious with him? You never said that we were then, and you didn't say so this time," he stated, thumping his chest, enraged. His eyes were so cold it felt strange to look at him, to see that coldness directed toward me. "You could have left at any moment. I had no idea if you were going to stay in Rome, to stay with me. I'd been sure that you would stay with me in Barcelona. Or that we would figure out a way to make it work when you left. That maybe you would come with me back to Italy or that I would come to America. So yes, I was still with her. I didn't know that you wouldn't leave again."

"So, you did this to what, *hurt* me? To get back at me for what I did? Jesus Christ, Marcello, we're adults. You should have known this was different," I sputtered. "Running into you again after all of these years, how could that have happened unless we were supposed to be together—don't you see? This was our second chance!"

"I am not a mind reader!" he thundered, leaning back against the wall, scrubbing at his face with his hands. "I ended things with Simone because of you when I knew you were staying. You didn't do the same for me. You cheated on your boyfriend with me, and now you stand here and accuse me of doing the same thing?"

Oh, God. He was right. All those years ago, I'd cheated on Daniel. And I'd tried to keep him a secret from Marcello, but he'd known all along.

"But why didn't you ever say anything about it?"

"Because I assumed you would choose me," he choked out bitterly. My hand flew to my mouth.

What had I done?

Whatever it was, I'd done it twice.

Wordless, panicked, ashamed, I backed out of the apartment and headed into the streets.

CHAPTER 23

I FELT EXPOSED, RAW, AND GUTTED as I stood in the chaotic Piazza Venezia.

Cars, Vespas, and buses zipped by, narrowly missing one another around the frenzied circle. Numerous roads fed into the piazza, much like a roundabout at home, with each car jockeying for position and making it a maddening sight. People milled about taking photos of Il Vittoriano, the beautifully lit white building that loomed in front of me.

My phone buzzed again in my purse.

"I assumed you would have chosen me," he had said, and a sob ripped up from my chest, startling a few couples sitting on the wall.

"Scusi," I mumbled.

Looking back, maybe it was easier for me to compartmentalize, to rationalize my time in Spain because I knew that I was in the wrong then. Daniel and I weren't in a great place when I took off for Barcelona, but we were very much still a couple. Much as I didn't want to admit it, I was wrong. I'd willfully pursued Marcello, knowing that Daniel was at home waiting for me. I'd been unfaithful.

I stopped and dug out my phone, then ducked into an alley to call Daisy.

"Hey, I was trying to get ahold of you. Do you guys want to meet us?" she answered, and I could hear voices in the background shouting. "Hang on, I'm down the street at that little café." She paused, and it sounded like she stepped outside. "Okay, sorry. Grab your man and come have a drink. I'm out with some of our friends from work."

"Can you head home? I'll meet you there?" I checked the signs around me and calculated. "In about fifteen? I know you're out and busy but I need an ear. Probably both. I just have to flag down a cab."

"Are you okay?"

"Just meet me at home and I'll explain."

————

SHE WAS ON THE STOOP when I got there, looking a bit worse for the wear. "Are you pickled?"

She held up two fingers. "Lil' bit. I locked myself out."

When I stepped under the glare of the lamplight, she gasped at my mascara-messed face. "What the hell happened—"

"Simone," I interrupted, not wanting to say her name anymore. Digging out my key, I fumbled with the lock before letting us inside, a confused and drunk Daisy on my heels.

"Simone? Simone who? What's going on?"

"The girl. The girl with Marcello, the first night I was here?"

"The pretty one?"

"Yes! Jesus, yes, the pretty one."

"What about her?"

"He slept with her," I said, sniffling.

"What?" she howled, loud enough that I held my hands over my ears.

"Okay, we both can't be yelling."

"Avery, I'm so sorry. I can't fucking believe he'd do this. You guys seemed so solid. I'll rip his fucking balls off! Did you *see* them? Good God, tell me you didn't catch *another* man in the act, did you?"

"No, no, it's not like that." I angrily scrubbed the residual tears and makeup from my face. I carried on undeterred. I wanted her to be on my side for this. To see why I was angry. "They're not together *now*. When I got here they were."

"Well, yeah. We saw them."

"That's not the point! The point is, dammit, they definitely slept together."

"Okay. Just hold on, I'm trying to figure this out. He's been seeing you both at once? Or this wasn't since you two got back together? Or it was? I'm so confused. You knew he was with her when you got here, right? I mean you saw them at dinner. Did I drink too much tonight?"

"Yes, they were together then and for a bit once Marcello and I started to . . . well, whatever we were doing, they were still spending time together," I explained, waiting for her to get as pissed and hurt as I was.

"He was sleeping with her after he slept with you?"

"Maybe. Possibly. I don't know. I think so? I didn't really let him answer."

As I heard the words coming out of my mouth, I began to see things a little differently. The more I thought about the timeline of the relationship and when we got together, the clearer a picture I got. It didn't make the truth any less painful, but I was at least seeing his side.

And how poorly I'd reacted to it.

Daisy was silent, which was entirely unusual.

"Say it," I said.

"You're being a jackass."

"Don't sugarcoat it or anything." I sighed, sitting on the chair with my head in my hands.

"Honey, that *was* sugarcoated. The version in my head had a lot more *fucks* strewn throughout my very poignant speech, but I'm drunk, and jackass seemed quicker."

"I *am* a jackass."

"You are. I love you, but you are." She wiggled beside me on the chair, throwing her arm around my shoulder. "Lemme ask you something."

I nodded, resting my head on her shoulder.

"Is this it for you?" she asked.

"Is *what* it for me?"

"Marcello—is *he* it for you? Seriously, can you look beyond what happened with them, and likely when it happened? Or are you ready to walk away?"

She asked it without judgment, and I knew that she'd support whatever I decided.

"I love him," I said, without question or hesitation.

"Enough to overlook it? To move beyond it?"

"There's nothing to overlook. Jesus, isn't that funny?"

"What, what's funny? What did I miss?" She was drunker than I thought.

"I didn't even really consider the idea of forgiving Daniel, because I didn't want to. I didn't even want to hear his side of the story. But with Marcello . . ." I wiped away the tears that were falling. "I gotta go."

"Okay," she said, flopping back onto the chair, eyes closing.

"And, Daisy?"

"Hmm?"

"You're the best."

"Tell me something I don't know," she said with grin. She was snoring by the time I closed the front door.

———————

WHEN I GOT TO MARCELLO'S, the house was dark, save for the rooftop. There, I could see the garden lights aglow. I knocked this time, pushing the doorbell once. It wasn't that I thought he wouldn't let me back in. It was that I *wanted* him to open the door. I needed to see his face when he welcomed me in.

It took a minute, but he looked over the ledge to see me. Without a word, he disappeared, and a minute later, he opened the door. He exhaled when he saw me. A sense of relief washed over us both. Stepping forward, he scooped me up into his arms and held me tight, his face buried between my shoulder and neck.

He pulled me inside.

I let him.

———————

ONCE INSIDE, HE STEERED ME toward the couch, disappearing briefly into the kitchen, coming back with a damp towel and a bottle of water. He sat down across from me, handing me the towel. "For your face," he said.

My makeup, the tear tracks—what a mess I was. "Thanks," I said, wiping it all away.

He was wired, muscles taut, but his eyes did me in. Regret.

"Marcello, I—I overreacted." He held my hands, dropping a kiss to each when I let out a shuddery breath.

"Avery, when you showed up here, in Roma, out of nowhere, I had no idea what to do. I wanted to spend time with you, get to know you again, but—"

"You knew there'd be a chance of what happened in Spain, happening *again*," I finished, sitting up a little straighter. "I get that. I don't like it, but I understand. I realized something very important tonight. I didn't want to forgive Daniel because I didn't love him. Not anymore. And frankly, I never loved him the same way I loved, love, you. But you—oh, God, Marcello, *you*? Just one word from that woman, and I was destroyed. I felt like I was physically being torn apart. It's not whether you were with her or not once you were with me, it's that I love you that much, that it hurt that much—does that even make sense?" I pushed my hair back from my face, not wanting anything between us, not wanting to hide this at all from him, needing him to really hear me. "You're *it* for me."

And there it was. That was the question I had to ask myself and be so honest about. It came down to what were you willing to forgive, when you were forgiving The One? Seeing Daniel having sex with another woman was powerful, but the truth is, if I'd seen him just *kissing* another woman . . . it would have been enough. I couldn't have forgiven that, because I didn't want to.

But when it's The One? You cry. You scream. You overreact. And then you work it out. *Because* he's The One. And it's worth it.

He smiled, pulling me into the chair with him.

"I love you more than I can possibly say. Can you understand that?"

"I do, *tesoro*," he said, cradling me to his chest in a Marcello cocoon. "It's as much as I love you. No more secrets. No more lies. No more running away without us talking first. We cannot do that to each other."

"We need to be honest," I agreed, kissing his chin. "Just you and me."

"Just you and me."

CHAPTER 24

I HAD JUST SWIPED MY PAINTBRUSH into a shade of ripe apricot when I was overcome with a sense of melancholy. I took a deep breath, waiting for the feeling to pass. Looking up, I admired the pristine, clear blue, and cloudless sky.

In the two or so weeks since all hell broke loose, I found myself tearing up at random times throughout the day. A man helping an elderly woman across the street? I got teary.

Young kids playing stickball in the courtyard by Daisy's apartment? Tears.

Painting here with my fellow artists in Campo de' Fiori? You guessed it: teary. I didn't have any explanation other than I was crazy and crazy happy all rolled into one.

We were finishing up the final touches on the painting when my instructor stopped at my easel.

"*Bellisima*," she said, touching my shoulder. "I am glad you come back. Beautiful work, you do."

I smiled, staring at my painting with pride. My visits to this class were therapeutic and invigorating. They fueled that need for me to create.

By the time I reached the apartment, the painting was dry, and I stacked it in the hall closet with the rest of them. Checking the clock, I had just enough time to wash the paint from my face. Honestly, when would I ever *not* look like a finger-painting toddler when I was finished? I needed to be as presentable as possible, because today I was Skyping my parents to tell them my news.

A conversation that I was eager to get over with.

Earlier I had been holed up in Marcello's office, enjoying his very handsy company and trying to fill out the paperwork for my work visa.

"Stop it," I ordered, slapping away a roving finger. "My handwriting is terrible to begin with, and with your, ah . . . ah. Oh, that's nice . . . Wait!"

An email had just arrived from my mother, asking if everything was okay. Her freaky intuition and a keen knack for timing had me spelling my name wrong, and I had to fill out the damn paperwork all over again.

It was as if she and my father knew something was up. It was time to break it to them.

Pulling up the chair, I opened the laptop and waited for the beeps that they were calling me. I busied myself with opening the envelope from Maria and the board at Museo di Roma in Trastevere. I beamed, clutching it to my chest. Running my hand over the emblem embossed into the letterhead, I sighed.

When Maria had called me into her office, I was nervous. I walked in to find not only her but her boss and her boss's boss, and I panicked. I thought back to my work on the villa I'd just completed and prayed that I hadn't screwed something up.

I left barely able to contain my excitement.

When the Skype *bloop bloop* noises rang out, I gulped, gently setting the letter off to the side of the desk.

"Deep breaths, Avery," I said, clicking the green icon.

"There she is!" Dad's forehead said.

"Move it down a bit, Dad." I laughed.

"Damn it, why doesn't anyone just use phones anymore . . ." He futzed with the "thingamajig."

"That's better," I said once I could see them both.

They looked exactly the same as before. I, on the other hand, looked decidedly different. I could see them taking in the new European me.

My curly hair was left natural, pulled up on the sides. I wore no makeup save the burnt sienna paint I'd missed on my chin. My T-shirt was covered in similar splatters, and I prayed that the hickey from this afternoon hadn't yet fully formed.

My father spoke first. "I must say, sweetheart, you look—"

"Perfect," my mother finished, beaming.

"Thanks, Mom." I took a breath, then went on with the small talk. "So, how're things back in Boston?"

We chatted for a while, getting caught up on the gossip, the wrist my father had sprained playing tennis, the new flower bulbs my mother had ordered for the beds out by the pool, the usual. But while I enjoyed the conversation, they could tell something was up. I waited until I felt it was time. I took a deep breath.

"So, I've decided to—"

"Stay," my father finished, his voice gentle and knowing.

I nodded, taking another deep breath. "I am."

My mother daintily dabbed at her eyes with her embroidered handkerchief.

I picked up the letter with shaky hands and held it in front of the camera. "I don't want you to worry about me. I—"

"Research conservator?" Dad said proudly. "I'm sure it's impressive, but what is it?"

I laughed, and dropped the paper to the side. "Less field work and more office time, but that's okay. Eventually I could get back out there if I wanted, but I think I'll like this. I'll be working with a team at the museum that works closely with firms all over Rome. When they uncover antiques, either in businesses or pieces that would be sent for display in a museum, we come in and create the plan to restore and conserve them. Lots of science and math and oh my God, I'm so happy."

"We're proud of you, sweetheart," Dad said, his eyes watery.

"We thought it might happen. Daniel said you seemed very happy."

"Excuse me?"

They explained that they'd seen him—and a guest—and his parents at the club one night, and he'd stopped to talk with them. I was pleasantly surprised and grateful to Daniel for taking the high road after everything.

"He also said that he felt that there might be someone you'd been seeing in Rome . . ." My mother let her voice trail off, hoping that I might pick up that little nugget and run with it.

I smiled.

As did she. "I see. And does your staying have anything to do with him?" She nudged my father.

I sighed. "I'd be lying if I said no—"

"We're happy if you're happy," my father finished, smiling the way a father does when he knows his little girl is in love.

I felt that balloon swell up inside my chest. "His name is Marcello. He works at the same firm as Daisy. He's an architect, handsome and Italian."

My mother made a show of fanning herself.

"You'll meet him when you visit—which I hope is soon."

"Well check the calendar and send you some dates that

might work. We don't want to cut into your busy Roman life, but expect us for at least two weeks."

"Months," my mother corrected.

"Looks like it'll be months," Daddy said, with a pat on her hand. "Maybe we'll zoom around the countryside by ourselves for a few days." He gave her the smile that as a kid I'd rolled my eyes at, but secretly loved that he still looked at her that way.

Her cheeks pinked. "Four weeks," she said.

Before we signed off, I promised my mother that I'd call more often.

A FEW NIGHTS LATER I got to Marcello's a bit late, staying after a new art class I'd joined to finish up a piece I was working on. Trying to capture the rich tones of a Roman sunset over the Colosseum was difficult with colored pencils, yet it was still incredible. I zoomed up the stairs quickly, hating that I had kept him waiting when he was cooking me dinner. My God, that man could cook . . .

I opened the door and was greeted by the scent of basil, oregano, garlic, and something a little spicy. Candles glittered on the table and were scattered on the kitchen counter and above the fireplace.

Marcello, whose back was to me, was concentrating on the dinner he was preparing, and I let out a whistle of appreciation. "Looks like someone is getting seduced tonight," I teased.

He started, then turned slowly. "*Tesoro*, I did not hear you come in." His grin lit up the room, even more than all the candles. "And a seduction?" The grin changed to a cheeky smirk. "That was going to happen as soon as I asked you to dinner . . . and you said yes."

"You're feeling a bit full of yourself tonight." I chuckled, setting down my bag and shrugging out of my jacket. He caught
me up around the waist, surprising me while my arms were still
stuck in their sleeves.

"*You* will be feeling a bit full of me, too, later on, no?" He
bumped his hips into mine, in case his meaning was in anyway
unclear. I loved it when he was like this, so cocksure and
charming.

"If you play your cards right," I teased. "So what's for dinner?"

"Osso bucco, with a lobster risotto and roasted brussels
sprouts. And to start with, of course, a pasta."

"Good lord, all of that in one sitting?"

"Ah yes, we are celebrating tonight. This requires something
a little special." Before I could ask what we were celebrating, he
kissed me, slow, long, and deep.

When he released me, I struggled to catch my breath. He
flashed me a smirk and swatted me on my behind as he headed
back into the kitchen.

"What in the world has gotten into you tonight?" My legs
were a bit shaky from his kisses, and I sat down on one of the
barstools at the kitchen island. I'd learned not to get in his way
when he was cooking. I could make coffee and help with dishes,
but when it came to meal prep, the man was a machine.

I leaned over and snuck an artichoke heart from the platter
when he wasn't looking.

"You think I did not see that?" He laughed, looking over his
shoulder at me and crooking an eyebrow. "You stole my heart."

"Oh boy, you are pouring it on thick tonight. We must be
celebrating something big." There was definitely something in
the air tonight. Marcello was practically vibrating with excitement as he moved around, tossing this into a pan and that into

another pot. A handful of thick fresh pappardelle went into the pasta pot, and a pan positively shimmered with olive oil, garlic, and . . . holy cannoli, was that a white truffle?

As he shaved the tiniest of slivers into the pan, I was instantly hit with the rich, heady aroma of sizzling truffle. "Forget your news—just put that in my mouth right now."

"What is that American saying: that is what she said?"

"I literally couldn't love you more." I laughed as his ears pinked up. He tossed the pan around a bit, letting the garlic and olive oil coat the truffles.

"So, remember the proposal I was working on, for the job in Rio de Janeiro?" He expertly flipped the food into the air and caught it, not spilling even one drop.

"Sure—the new opera house built within the old one, right?"

"That is the one," he said, lifting forkfuls of the wide ribbons of pappardelle from the pot. He tossed it into the hot oil and garlic, using tongs to stir it around. He looked up at me through a haze of yummy steam. "We got the bid."

"You did! Oh that's wonderful!" I cried, clapping my hands. He beamed; this was a job he'd really wanted. "So you'll probably have to take a trip there soon, yes?"

"Yes." He nodded, gently sliding the contents of the pan onto a platter. Picking up a big wedge of Parmesan, he began to shave thin slices over the top. The aroma was divine; I couldn't wait to dig in. "I will be going down there next week, starting to put the team together."

"Wow. That works out well, actually. I'm starting work on a plan for a mosaic the power company stumbled upon over near the Borghese gardens. The Galleria has plans for it to be unveiled next year, and from what I can tell, it's going to be a bitch! I can get a bunch of it done while you're gone. You're awfully distracting, you know," I teased, giving his bottom a squeeze as he walked toward the table with the pasta. And the fish. And the veal, rice, veggies, my God. I would be rolling out of here. "I'm so proud of you."

This was a huge feather in his cap. He did amazing work, and he was being rewarded for it. "How much time do you think you'll have to spend down there?" I leaned over to smell the pasta.

"That is what I wanted to talk to you about. They want me to move to Brazil."

"This pasta looks incredi— *What* did you say?"

"The firm asked me to move to Brazil."

"To Brazil."

"Yes."

"South America."

"Yes."

"For how long?"

He shrugged. "Eighteen months, two years at the most."

Eighteen months. Two years. At the most.

I lifted enormous forkfuls of pasta onto my plate, swirling a huge bite onto my fork and spoon like an American, and stuffing it into my mouth.

Eighteen months. Two years. At the most.

"When they asked you to move to Brazil, you told them yes."

He propped his elbows on the table and leaned toward me. "This isn't really the kind of thing you say no to. It's an incredible opportunity."

I swallowed hard past a sudden lump in my throat. "I know it is." I looked down at the table, the wood grain seeming to swim before my eyes.

"It could be incredible for you, too," he said softly, and my head snapped up.

"What?"

"I want you to come with me. To Brazil."

"Come *with* you?" I repeated, stunned.

"Yes, of course. I want you to come with me." He came around the table, sat next to me, and took my hand. "I'll head down there first, find us a place to live, then come back for you. We can move there together."

"Come back for me." I sounded like a parrot. "But what about my job? That I just got. And my work visa—it hasn't even come through yet. And I just started my classes again. And I just heard about a volunteer program where Americans living in Rome give tours of local museums to tourists. I was thinking about looking into that, and—"

"We will work it all out, Avery. You'll see," he soothed, pulling me onto his lap. "That will all be waiting for you when we come back."

"In eighteen months. Two years, at the most," I said, feeling a twinge of irritation.

"Exactly!" he said, excited. He looked at the array of food on the table and chuckled. "I went a little overboard here, yes?"

"A little," I chirped. He nodded, assuming I was agreeing with him about the food and not the overall concept here. "Marcello, I need some time to think about this."

"I know, it is a lot to take in. But there is plenty of time to figure this all out. Wait until you see Rio de Janeiro—you will fall in love."

There were so many things I wanted to say, so many questions I needed to ask. But first I needed time to think, time to get my head on straight.

So I celebrated this wonderful news with him, and I let him love me like only he could. But inside?

I was unsettled.

CHAPTER 25

I STAYED AWAKE ALL NIGHT, while Marcello slept soundly. After the love, I'd tossed and turned, unable to get comfortable, unable to shut my brain off from the hurricane of thoughts.

Move to Brazil?

Leave Rome behind?

Follow Marcello?

Leave my new job behind?

Follow Marcello?

It was that last part that was giving me the most trouble.

I watched him sleeping. When he slept deeply he went full flop, one arm thrown over his head, the other out to the side, one leg thrust in my direction, the other hanging over the side of the bed.

The sheet was draped perfectly around him, low on his hips, exposing the happiest of trails . . . He looked styled for a cologne ad. Perfection.

How could I even *think* of not sleeping next to him every night?

I *couldn't* think about it—not while he was right here in all his glory. With sleep wood, which was always impressive . . .

I slipped out of the room and went up to the rooftop terrace, shrugging into a big oversized cardigan on the way. Here, where the air was clear and fresh, maybe I could think about this calmly, and rationally.

I sank into one of the big overstuffed chairs, staring up into the night sky. The city was quiet this late at night. And I needed that to help me sort out the thought that came into my brain whenever I thought about leaving Rome.

I didn't want to leave Rome.

And the part that I felt guilty about was . . . I didn't want to leave it even for Marcello.

When I graduated from Boston College, I'd more than the one offer. There was Manhattan, strictly entry level, practically no pay, but an opportunity a twenty-two-year-old rarely gets. SFMOMA in San Francisco wanted me to apprentice in their art conservator program and learn from the masters in my field how to best preserve these priceless works of art and then I was accepted into the master's program for art conservatorship at Washington University in Saint Louis—an incredibly difficult to get into program and a huge honor for me.

This was different, though. None of those paths would have included Marcello. This *had* to be different.

But could I give up who I was, again, just because he was my One?

I stayed up all night, watched the sun rise, and knew that I had to tell him the truth.

———

STILL WEARING HIS SWEATER, I was sitting in the chair on his side of the bed. I couldn't be in bed with him when I told him this.

"I can't go with you to Brazil."

As hurt filled his eyes, I said, "But before you say anything, please hear me out."

He nodded.

"I love being here. It's so busy and boisterous; there's so much energy and so many people. I never know what's going to happen next here, and I love that. I don't know where I'm going to live, I don't know how long I'm going to be able to keep a job if the work visa falls through. My life is upside down and inside out, and it's exciting and scary as hell—but I love it."

He said nothing.

I smiled at him. "And I love you. I love you so much, and I feel so lucky not only to have found you again, but to actually *be* with you."

Stand firm, Avery.

"Then you give me this incredible news about this job, which is wonderful, and I am so very proud of you. But I can't uproot my life to follow you halfway across the world. I've just started *growing* roots, Marcello. They're barely in the ground."

He sat quietly, taking it all in. When he finally spoke, he sounded confused. "Then I would think this would be the *best* time for a move like this—no?"

I sighed. "That could be true—except for one thing. After everything that happened with losing the baby, I put someone else's career, happiness, and choices ahead of my own and I buried myself. If I go with you to Brazil, I'd be doing it all over again. Even though I'd be with the man I love this time, I can't do that to myself."

He was silent. Listening. Comprehending.

I climbed out of the chair and onto his lap, wrapping my arms around him. "Marcello, I love you more than anyone on this planet. And I will wait for you here. I'll come to visit, I'll call you every day, I'll Skype you and dirty text you and send you naked pictures, and I'll do everything I can do to make this work. But I can't live someone else's life. Not again."

"You are not going with me to Brazil."

I shook my head, trying to hold back the tears that were already falling. "I love you so much," I whispered, kissing his sweet, sad face all over, eyelids, cheekbones, eyebrows, tip of his nose and all along his lips. "But I can't."

He kissed me back, but said nothing.

———

I SPENT THE NEXT FEW WEEKS second guessing, third guessing, fourth guessing, and yes, fifth guessing my decision.

Pros for Going to Brazil
The food is incredible
The beaches are supposed to be great
Carnivale
Caipirinhas
The man of my dreams asked me to move there with
    him, and who the hell says no to that . . .

Pros for Staying in Rome
Me

There were other reasons, sure. But what it all boiled down to was creating a new life for myself that would be complemented by a man, but not defined by one.

This is what I told myself the entire time Marcello was house hunting in Rio de Janeiro, Skyping with me, and showing me pictures of homes overlooking the ocean and the *Christ the Redeemer* statue in the background, blessing the city and all those lucky enough to live there.

This last part was uttered by a certain Roman.

And I had to tell myself this again when the nights came, and I was lonely and missing him in my bed. And the mornings, when I was missing him with my coffee.

But other than that, I was getting along. Classes were wonderful, work was great, I was meeting some new friends and establishing a little circle of my own.

God, I missed him saying my name, stretching it out while he stretched above me, thrusting low and deep and telling me how much he needed me, how much he loved me . . .

I considered printing up my Rome Pro list and having it laminated for exactly these moments.

For all the guilt he was giving me, which was a lot, Marcello was being as supportive as he could be with my decision to stay in Rome. He was proud of his *testa duda* (which I found out through Google meant, *a hard head*) and said we would figure everything out even if I was stubborn. That he and I were in it for the "far run" and he could see us "walking off into the horizon as the sun was setting."

Oh, God, it was torture. And the closer it got to the date he was leaving for good, the worse it got. We spent every minute we could together, saving up memories for when we wouldn't be together.

I was trying like hell to keep things light and bright and easy breezy, but it was so hard to do sometimes. But I didn't want him to leave sad.

So I decided to throw him a party.

CHAPTER 26

WHENEVER I WAS NERVOUS about a fancy party in Boston, I pregamed it with my parents in the sunset lounge of the club. A glass of wine or a shot of Jack with my dad, and things didn't seem so bleak.

But I couldn't get sloshed tonight, no matter how much I thought it would make Marcello's going-away party more bearable. I'd save the heavy liquor and tears for after his flight left to Buenos Aires.

I smoothed my dress, loving the feeling of the linen beneath my hands. He loved this dress, since I had worn it to the giant family dinner in Pienza. He lightly touched the linen cutouts before he told me that he loved me.

"Happy thoughts, happy thoughts," I chanted, trying to abate the tears. I didn't have time for *another* full face of makeup.

The firm had arranged for a private dining experience outside the Pantheon. They'd consulted there a few years ago and held a favor that they were cashing in tonight.

We had a plan. After he got settled, I'd join him for a long weekend whenever I could. He'd come to Rome whenever he could. We *would* make this work.

"Avery, it's here!" Daisy called out from the living room.

Marcello, as the guest of honor, was going to be late. Since it was about him, I didn't feel right walking in on his arm, so Daisy and I were heading over together.

What I didn't like was that I hadn't seen him all day. He'd begged off meeting for lunch because he had to go into the office for last-minute work. With the sand slipping through that damn hourglass, I wanted to get in as much time with him as possible.

"You're going to stop traffic in that outfit, honey," Daisy said as I walked out of the bedroom. She was probably sensing that I needed the extra oomph. "The lipstick? Killer with a capital K. You're getting some great good-bye sex."

I smiled and checked my hair in the hall mirror. Corkscrew curls shooting out wherever they felt like it, which Marcello loved. My makeup was light, but my lips were painted red.

"I'm counting on it," I said, grabbing a bloodred shawl from the couch, along with my clutch.

After we arrived, we snacked on some delectable appetizers, marveling at how they had transformed the stone courtyard of the Pantheon into a stunning party venue.

Ten gorgeous wooden farm tables were laid out around the fountain, benches tucked up beneath them. Above were sheer linen umbrellas spaced out just enough that they didn't block the navy-blue, star-speckled sky.

But the real gem was the Pantheon. You could see the majestic building from every angle and every table. Guests milled about talking to their coworkers—about children and what projects they were working on now—but their eyes always flitted back to the statuesque columns or the sweeping open doors, where you could see the moonlight from the oculus shining on the floor.

Then Marcello arrived, looking unstoppably fuckable. He wore the hell out of his well-tailored khaki pants and white oxford shirt. With his sleeves rolled to the elbow, he was perfect for the late Italian summer weather.

He shook hands and kissed where he had to, but his eyes never left mine. He'd move on to another person to speak with, and glance my way and wink. We circled each other in a cat-and-mouse game that nobody knew about but us.

Except for Daisy, who was bursting with excitement. "With all the sparks flying between you two and all of the flammable liquid, this part of town is going up in flames tonight. Tone it down!" Daisy teased, before making her way up to the head table.

She'd be introducing Marcello, who'd been fretting all week about what to say, saying good-bye to everyone he worked with.

For now, I reminded myself. Saying good-bye for now.

He whispered something to Daisy, and her face lit up in a broad smile. She searched the small crowd for me, then picked up a knife and clinked on her glass to get everyone's attention.

I moved to take an empty seat toward the back, in case I broke out into hysterical sobs and needed to make a quick escape to the ladies' room in one of the nearby restaurants.

"*Buona sera,* everyone," Daisy started. "I'd like to thank you all for coming here tonight to say *arrivederci* to Marcello."

I tuned her out, staring at the man she was praising. I loved hearing that he was universally respected by his peers, but I loved watching him more. He laughed at her little jokes, and feigned hurt when she hit below the belt.

But something was amiss. Though he was smiling at all the

right places and laughing where needed, his eyes were on me. He hadn't taken them off me for more than a few seconds at a time all night, but now I felt like he was trying to convey something.

When it was his turn to speak, he simply thanked everyone for coming before introducing his second in command, Federico. Who would explain everything . . . wait, what?

The confused audience started slowly clapping and whispering as Marcello stalked through the tables until he stopped at mine.

"What's going on?" I said, scooting over so he could sit beside me on the bench.

"Weren't you listening?" he asked, brushing a wayward curl from my forehead. "*Tesoro,* tell me you *heard* that."

I smiled awkwardly and shrugged. "It was hard to pay attention when you look so damn good. You need to get dressed up more often; it's killing me."

He laughed, loud enough that Federico stopped talking to shake his head, saying, "And now we know why he's staying."

Dozens of heads turned toward us, smiling and tilting to show they were happy. But why?

"Oh my God—did he say you're *staying*?" I blurted loudly, then slapped my hand over my mouth.

He gently pulled my hand away. "Please do not smudge those lips. Not until later. And yes, I am staying. *We* are staying here."

This time when the tears threatened to fall, I let them; elated tears could ruin my makeup with abandon.

"How? Why? What happened?" I pulled him into a hug so tight that I pulled him off the seat and practically into my lap.

"*Tesoro,* easy." He gasped, pulling my arms from around his neck. "*You* happened."

"But we had a plan. You were going to go and—"

"I talked to my boss today, and I told him that now is just not a good time to go. Incredible opportunity of course, and I thank him for this, but that I could not leave Italy at the moment. I'm settled here, and we need you settled here. We've got plenty of time for an adventure later on."

"But this was your big chance!" Wait, why the hell was I arguing?

"It is not as important as my second chance with you."

I promptly sat on his lap, wrapped my arms around him, then laid a red lipsticky kiss on each cheek and solidly on his mouth.

"There aren't enough words in all the world to thank you for staying here. For me."

"For us," he corrected—and kissed the rest of my lipstick away.

———

"ONCE A MONTH, I want to do something super touristy," I said, moving closer to Marcello as we strolled through town.

We'd left the party deliriously happy, hand in hand, and now he was steering us toward a part of town that I hadn't yet ventured to.

In Rome, everything was an adventure. I could live here for twenty years and never see everything. There was too much history, too much art, too much life to see. And how exciting to get to explore everything with him by my side.

We had a future to look forward to. Together, on equal footing, following our individual dreams as a team. I couldn't possibly have imagined a better life for myself.

"What are you thinking about?" he asked, kissing the top of my head gently.

"When to have dessert," I teased, slipping my hand beneath the back of his shirt. His skin was cool at first before heating up under my palm.

"*Avery,* you just had cannoli. And crème brûlée—"

"And half of your tiramisu." I laughed at his surprised face. "Hey, mister, you were leaving for Brazil! I was eating my feelings."

He stopped, tipping his head quizzically to the side. "I do not understand."

"Never mind. I don't want to talk about anyone leaving anymore—unless it's us leaving and going to see your parents, my parents, or Daisy on whatever place she's off to next."

"That's a deal."

"So about dessert," I purred, pulling him into an alley just outside an ice cream shop. "I need some sweetness here first, then inside."

"Insatiable girl," he said, leaning down to kiss me up against the bricks.

"And you love me." I sighed as he scattered little kisses along my neck, making me squeal a little. I crossed my arms around the back of his neck, watching the moonlight play along my fingertips.

"That I do, *tesoro.* That, I do."

"Mmm, you crazy Roman."

WITH A SCOOP OF PISTACHIO GELATO for me and two scoops of coffee for Marcello, we joined the crush of tourists on the street. The sea of people and their cameras were all moving toward the same area.

"Where exactly are we?" I slipped a spoonful of gelato into

my mouth. The street was absurdly crowded; people blocked the tourist signs and the ceramic plates on the buildings.

I glanced over to see him watching me intently, his eyes burning before he dipped down to kiss me again. Would we ever get enough of each other? I hoped not. I sincerely hoped that we would always be in that fevered state of love.

We drifted along with the crowd, not minding the slow pace or the constant bumping. If anything, we enjoyed being pushed closer together. When we finally reached the end of the street he turned, looking serious.

"This *is* touristy," he began, stopping just before the main line of the crowd. Whatever was around the corner was a huge attraction. "But I saw your list of places—"

"Oh my God, is it the Clooney?" I jumped up and down to see over the crowd, the motion making my pistachio gelato slop out of the cup. "Damn it!" With a big blob of green on my pretty white dress, I stood on tiptoes, trying in vain to see what was ahead.

He laughed. "You are ridiculous. Enough with that man." After tossing our cups into a recycling bin, he pulled a napkin from his pocket and cleaned my dress, dabbing the pistachio drips away from the linen. I let him; he needed to be able to take care of me from time to time. And from time to time, I wanted him to.

He threw away the napkins, then made me promise two things.

"Take what is in my hand with no questions, and close your eyes."

"Okay. . ." I said, closing my eyes and holding out my hand.

He took my hand, kissed my palm, and then my wrist. And then he lightly kissed up my arm a dozen more times before he put something in my hand and stepped away.

"You do that and then expect me to function?" I said as he pushed me gently forward.

I opened my eyes only slightly, trying to see where he was leading me. I could tell that the crowd was parting a bit to let us through.

"Once I realized that I couldn't leave you, I thought about bringing you here," he whispered into my ear. "And I see you peeking." He slipped his hand over my eyes.

"*So* not fair." I laughed, enjoying the feeling of him behind me, guiding me.

The locals and tourists who surrounded us were whispering in Italian, French, Chinese, German, and I was getting desperate to see where we were.

"You are shaking," he said, rubbing his hands over my bare arms. "Cold?"

"I'm excited."

"We're almost there."

I heard trickling water. We must be near a fountain, but which one? They were in nearly every piazza: Tritone, Navona, Barberini, the one we just left at the Pantheon. To see the icon by the light of day was impressive, but at night, it was magnificent.

Marcello stopped, lifted his hand away, but I squeezed, holding on to it and smiling at him.

We were at *the* fountain. The Trevi Fountain, possibly the most famous in all of Rome.

It was everything I thought it would be. Intricate carvings, statues, and cornice pieces adorned the iconic structure, and I couldn't pull my eyes away from it.

Until I felt him tap my hand, and I remembered he had placed something there.

I looked down, opening my hand to reveal two coins. "I love it! I used to do this at Disneyland with my parents as a kid. I toss in the coins and make a wish like Snow White?"

I plucked one from my hand and wound up, ready to hurl it into the water. He took my hand gently, shaking his head.

"Slow down, princess. This is no Disney fountain. The Trevi has history, traditions to abide by. As a man of Roma, I cannot let you mess with the tradition."

"I love it when you sound like a professor. Teach me, Dr. Bianchi," I purred, loving the sight of his nostrils flaring and his chest expanding.

Oh, it was going to be a very good night.

Doing his best to ignore my shameless flirting, he turned me so that he was behind me, pressed tightly against me, lined up *perfectly*. "With your back to the fountain, you must toss a coin with your right hand over your left shoulder," he instructed. "If one coin goes in, that means you'll return to Rome."

He waited while the group of people who were listening to him—and swooning, I might add—followed his instructions. A flurry of coins sailed into the air and landed with little plops in the water.

As I held on to my coins, they waited intently for step two.

"Two coins in, and you'll return to Roma *and* fall in love," he added, dropping a kiss on my lips.

As the group tossed their second coins in, couples embraced and kissed. Some women were scribbling on papers, trying to get Marcello's attention. He laughed, waving them off and breaking dozens of hearts.

"Now that you know the rules, it is your time." He moved away a bit to give me room.

I made a show of pocketing the coins.

His brow furrowed, confused, he asked, "Avery, you do not want to—"

I silenced him with a kiss. "I don't need a coin to bring me back to Roma. I don't plan on leaving. And the second coin?" I teared up when I saw the expectant look in his eyes. "I already fell in love in Rome—and I'm never letting go."